Heart Scarab
Taking Shield 02

ANNA BUTLER

GLASS HAT
PRESS

DEDICATION

To Sally and Claire, with love and thanks.

ACKNOWLEDGEMENTS

Editing: Val Wolfe at Wilde City
Cover Art: Adrian Nicholas

Praise for Heart Scarab

If you're a fan of sci-fi, you'll love this book. If, like me, you aren't a particular fan of sci-fi, but love a great adventure, you'll love this book. In fact, almost everyone will love this book! It's worth your time. It's worth your money. A great 5 Star read.

It's About The Book Reviews

I'm not exaggerating at all when I say this is a mainstream science fiction series that I would expect to see at the city library if I went looking for it. It is that well written. The world building is quite complex, as are the characters. I highly recommend this book, as well as its predecessor, "Gyrfalcon"… If you are as much of a sci-fi fan as I am, you will definitely enjoy this series.

Love Bytes Reviews

A fabulous sequel to Gyrfalcon. You get to see more of the emotion and relationship between everyone in this book but there's still so much going on. This book was amazing and I seriously want all of the books in the series rightnowrightnow, but at the same time I don't want the series to end.

Molly Lolly Reviews

God, what a ride this book was. As a fan of the first book, I was thrilled to read this one. It gripped me from the beginning and took me for a ride until the very end. And I cannot wait for the third book.

Novel Approach Reviews

CONTENTS

SECTION ONE:
TURNING OUT THE LIGHTS

22 Primus – 39 Secundus 7488

CHAPTER ONE

22 Primus 7488: Sais, Albion

The apartment door crashed shut so hard in Shield Captain Bennet's face, it rattled on its hinges.

Bennet took an involuntary step backwards. Shit! Another home leave ending in a fight with Joss. Another fucking fight. Hell's teeth, but this was getting old. Recently, every short leave between Bennet's missions for the Shield Regiment had been bracketed by resentful, sulky silences or screaming matches.

On the whole, Bennet preferred the silences.

"Whoa," Shield Lieutenant Rosamund said from the elevator lobby behind him. She sounded impressed. "Joss is in fine voice."

Bennet closed his eyes for a moment and let his shoulders slump. It was bad enough dealing with Joss's regular outbursts of fury at Bennet's refusal to leave the military. He didn't need a witness. Especially Rosie, his second in command.

"I'd sort of gathered things weren't still love's young dream in the Bennet-Joss household. I wasn't expecting to get proof." Rosie's glance skittered over Bennet and away again. Her face was tinged with pink and she didn't meet his eyes. "Sorry, Bennet. I didn't mean to upset Joss."

Bennet picked up his kitbag. "You didn't upset him. I did. He's been mad ever since the call came from HQ assigning us to the Telnos evacuation. It wouldn't make any difference who came to pick me up."

Joss. Joss who had been lover, partner, sort-of spouse, family, for nearly nine years. Who loved Bennet and wanted him out of the military. Joss did love Bennet. But he was also emotional and dramatic and... hell, he was damned selfish. He wouldn't hesitate to use emotion and drama to try and get his own way.

He wasn't Flynn—

Bennet chopped that thought off right there. More than a year and a half since T18, when he'd commandeered his father's ship to get him behind the lines. Infiltrating a Maess base in between battling to work out his dicey relationship with his father and shoring up his dicey relationship with Joss... child's play. Well, child's play in comparison to dealing with the distraction offered by First Lieutenant Flynn, the pilot who'd got him back from the base.

Flynn had been one hell of a distraction. No. That wasn't fair, not to either of them. He'd been much, much more than a distraction. Too much more.

He still was, damn him. Still.

Bennet's chest ached, bone deep. He rubbed at it with one hand while he and Rosie took the elevator from the penthouse he shared with Joss to street level. Rosie hadn't looked at him all the way down and what he could see of her face was still pink with embarrassment. Damn Joss! Damn him for making Rosie uncomfortable.

"It's not your fault." Bennet forced a smile. "He'll get over it. He'll be all right by the time we get back."

Rosie had parked across the narrow street. She slid behind the driving console while Bennet tossed his kitbag onto the back seat to join hers. "Still, maybe if I hadn't come to get you, it might have been easier. Joss never really took to me, you know." She edged the car into the traffic. "You know what his problem is? You're not the impressionable eighteen-year-old he seduced all those years

2

ago."

He gave her a sharp glance. She was no fool, his Rosie. "I had to grow up sometime."

"And so far as Joss is concerned, you did it to spite him?"

"Nail. Head. The. On. Hitting. The." Bennet grinned at her. "Any order you like."

She laughed. "Of course, if you're older, he can't keep fooling himself he's not, can he? If you're grown up now, what does that make him?"

"I dunno. Older than me?"

"Exactly. Years and years older than you. You're not twenty-seven yet. He's forty-five, Bennet." Rosie turned into the road cutting across the park. "And he's not making you happy."

"That's mutual. You're right. He's having a hard time adjusting to getting older, and it doesn't help he's nearly twenty years older than me. But mostly it's because I won't leave Shield." And there it was, the familiar little kick of nausea roiling in Bennet's gut whenever he thought about how difficult things were. "I'm losing patience, Rosie. There's only so much drama I can take, and Joss overdoses on it. I don't want to go home, sometimes."

Not if it meant going home to fights, histrionics and more accusations of selfishness. Joss apparently found the dramatics recreational, but they were anything but restful. Bennet got more than enough of warfare in his working day without getting it in the neck at home.

"Then think about that, too. Look, you've never told me this much before about you and Joss, but I'm not a fool. I've always known living with him can't exactly be restful. Personally, I don't think he deserves you, but it's none of my business. You've always been able to cope with him before now. What's changed? You haven't really been your old self since the T18 job." Rosie glanced at him sidelong. "You've never talked about it. At least, you've never said much about the *Gyrfalcon* and having to work with"— one hand left the controls to make some vicious air hooks—"the

Great Commander Caeden."

Bennet shook his head. The mission to T18 had thrown him and his father into closer contact than they'd had in years. They'd sorted out a lot of their differences. Reconciled, even. "No. Not that. Things are pretty good with Dad now."

"Really? I'm glad. It never made much sense to me, anyway."

"Dad was always convinced my joining Shield meant I lacked ambition. Commandeering his dreadnought put paid to that idea."

She chuckled, but it was short-lived. "Then it's just Joss? You know, you're going to have to decide what you want there and start pushing for it."

Bennet watched the city of Sais as they passed through it. The Old City first, all ancient buildings, temples and museums; the heart of Sais and the oldest settlement on the whole of Albion. Then north through the financial district and onto the great arterial road out to the distant spaceport. Rosie, bless her, left him to his silence.

They were on the outskirts of Sais before Bennet spoke again. "You've always said I was spoiled. Rich family, rich boyfriend, never wanting for anything because I always got what I wanted. Well, it doesn't always work out. There's something I want and I can't have it. I'll never be able to have it."

"Uh-huh." She gave him yet another glance, speculative this time. "All right, I'll bite. Something or someone?"

"Yes."

Rosie stared out at the road ahead. "And, rethinking what I said a minute ago about your Dad's ship and how not quite yourself you've been since, someone connected to the *Gyrfalcon*?"

Bennet grimaced at her, in lieu of an answer.

"Right." Rosie wove her way through the traffic with the speed and verve that came from piloting a fighter. Her mouth tightened. "Well, I guess this is where I'm a good and loving friend and I pat you consolingly on the arm"—she matched word to deed—"and change the subject. Telnos. We'll talk about the job on Telnos

4

instead. I don't know about you, but I can't wait to get to a planet at the backside of nowhere to evacuate hundreds of illegal colonists in the teeth of a Maess invasion. It'll be a breeze. What do you say?"

Bennet managed a laugh. "That you're the best friend a man could have. You have a knack for putting it all in perspective."

Rosie sniffed. "Well, I suppose we all need to be needed," she said, so sour that Bennet blinked.

What in hell was that about?

28 Primus 7488: Telnos

Telnos stank.

Telnos stank, both literally and metaphorically. Bennet couldn't work out which offended him the most. Sometimes it was the sheer physical awfulness of Telnos that got to him, sometimes the spiritual desolation of being at war on one of the most unprepossessing planets in the galaxy. After only a day, Telnos affected even the most equable of tempers.

When he mentioned this theory, Rosie arched one eyebrow and pasted on a sweet smile. "Self-delusion, Bennet?"

He grinned, pulling her down to sit beside him, leaning back against a tree. "I'm as bad-tempered as hell, but with this stench, who can blame me?"

Telnos was a hell-hole, so of course the Shield Regiment was in there doing the dirty work for Fleet and Infantry. Bennet's sleek scout ship was held in close orbit with half her company flying patrols in their Mosquitoes, and watching for the Maess. The rest of *Hyperion*'s crew had drawn the shortest of straws and were dealing with what had to be the worst part of the planet. Festering marshland was never his favourite terrain. The landscape was a series of shallow pools, seldom more than a few inches deep, threaded through with thin strips of what passed on Telnos for dry land. The thick, glutinous mud of the pools smelled vile.

Rosie's nose wrinkled. "It smells like something died."

"There's definitely something rotting underneath all this." Bennet waved a hand at the rampant, acid-green vegetation. "Maybe it's feeding off the decaying corpse of some long-dead leviathan buried in the mud."

"Either you've been taken with a romantic fit, which is probably hormonal, or these bloody flies have given you a fever. Either way we'd better get you off-planet before you start writing bad poetry." Rosie pulled off her helmet and scratched at the midge bites. Her nails left red grazes on her forehead. "Gods, they're even in my hair!"

Marshes the galaxy over had but one function: to be perfect breeding grounds for nasty little insects. The worst were the tiny, flying, stinging, ever-hungry gnats. There were billions of them, hanging in dark, roiling clouds under the tree cover.

"Whatever did they live on before I got here to add spice and variety to their diet?" Rosie pulled her helmet back on, settling it so far down in an attempt to keep the midges out of her vibrant red hair that Bennet, laughing, said she looked like a torpedo. She sprayed insect repellent around herself in vicious bursts, blue eyes narrowing at him.

Bennet dared to smile. "As long as they continue to prefer your spice to mine, I can live with it. No one's got sick yet."

"Yet."

Rosie had a point. Telnos was not a healthy place.

Several years earlier, small groups from an extreme religious sect, the Brethren, had crossed into the Border Zone to colonise Telnos. Putting aside the legal technicality of the Zone being closed to non-military traffic—admittedly, the illegal traders and smugglers known as Jacks treated the law as purely theoretical so why, Bennet reasoned, should it hold back religious fanatics?— Telnos was hardly the Promised Land. The Brethren established their farms where marshes were the perfect breeding ground for fever and disease. Presumably, to further mortify the flesh with gnat bites.

Bennet's Shield unit had been tasked with locating settlements and whistling up the Infantry for transports to get the colonists to the ships taking them back into Albion's space. Several of the people they'd evacuated had been sick and feverish. Colonists and rescuers alike would be spending a lot of time in decontamination when they finally got off-planet, maybe even weeks in quarantine. No one wanted to be famous for taking some deadly new infection home to Albion.

If people were stupid enough to set up illegal and unauthorised colonies on a desolate hell-hole, then the consequences were entirely down to them. Bennet's objection was the he and his people were dragged in to rescue the idiots. He said so. With conviction and bad language.

"Gives the crew someone to blame." Rosie killed another few hundred gnats with noxious chemicals. "Other than you, of course."

Bennet shrugged and wriggled to get more comfortable under the dubious shelter of the tree. It was, of course, raining. It never stopped. It might have been a blessing if the rain had brought any cool refreshment with it. But this rain was a permanent warm mist, smelling as foul as the mud. It left them damp and hot, sticky and sweaty. The Brethren had to be insane to choose to live in the marshes. Bennet could understand why the miners were twenty miles north in the mountain foothills where they could lever solactinium out of the deep mines and sell it—there was a thriving black market for it, and more than one of Albion's many colonies would turn blind eyes to a cheap source. It made economic sense, and the climate in the mountains was one helluva lot better. Choosing to live in the swampy marshland was conclusive proof religion addled the brain.

Rosie displayed her usual aptitude for mind reading. "Why did they choose to set up home here, do you think?"

Bennet slapped at an adventurous gnat or ten, settling on his neck for a snack. Rosie smirked, proffering the can, and Bennet added his mite to reducing the insect population. "Apart from escaping from the dread hand of a secular and therefore profane government, do you mean? This lot makes extreme religious fundamentalists look half-hearted. You know, my father's so religious he sweats prayers, but even he wouldn't be able to understand their mentality. I imagine this planet was perfect for them. Nowhere else in the known universe offers as much opportunity to mortify their bodies and consequently purify their souls."

"Bless you! You always came up trumps with some theory or other. I thought you'd work it out. That religious upbringing of yours, I expect."

Bennet snorted. His family of patrician Thebans, one of the foremost in the faith, did not have a great deal in common with the Brethren. There wasn't much similarity between the gold-leafed marble domes of the Theban temples back home on Albion, and the tiny wattle-and-daub chapels in the marshes.

Rosie sighed and glanced up at the sky. "How long do you reckon before the Maess get here?"

"Soon. Too soon. We'll know as soon as they drop out of hyperspace."

Rosie eased her shoulders inside her tac-vest. The damn things were heavy and uncomfortable in the heat; Bennet's own was stuck to his back with sweat. "I can't see the Maess drones staying here long. They'd rust solid in a week."

"They'll stay long enough to get the solactinium." Bennet leaned his head back against the tree and closed his eyes against the strong greenish light. "And what do the Maess care if they lose a few thousand drones in the process? All they have to do is crank up the manufacturing plant and they've covered their losses in a month."

"We should stay and fight," said someone from the shelter of a nearby tree.

Bennet twisted to see who it was. Kerr. He gave the man a quick nod of sympathy. Kerr was right. Humanity was slowly falling back from the frontier, securing an inner core of systems around Albion. It bothered Bennet. What war had ever been won from a state of defence?

"We've been talking about it in the Strategy Unit." Bennet mentioned the other job the military had him doing as well as sliding about on stinking mud. "Consolidation, they called it. I said 'suicidal ossification' came closer, and got my knuckles rapped for the use of plain language."

"If we give up too much ground now, we'll have trouble retaking it," Rosie grumbled.

"We won't be able to retake it." Bennet's voice was sharper than it should be. He reined in the irritation. "Telnos is lost. In itself, it isn't important. It doesn't sit on any of the major space routes so losing it won't threaten Albion or a settlement planet or any of the smaller colonies. I know there's some solactinium, but not enough to make this dump worth fighting for. But what it stands for, what we're giving up here…" Bennet shook his head.

He'd told the crew this in the pre-mission briefing, but he could understand their frustration at the limited job they had. They'd do it to the best of their ability. They'd get the illegal colonists and the miners off, and leave the Maess to flounder through the mud to conquer the place. They'd do it, but no one said they had to like it.

"Well, ours is not to reason why, so they tell us. We just have to get on with making sure these idiots get off-world in one piece." Rosie tried to lighten the mood. "Have you noticed every single man has a beard birds could nest in?"

Bennet snorted. "I can cope with the beards. Their never being short of a Book quotation or some prophet's raving is a lot more irritating. I just love how they can twist it to justify idiocy."

"Too close to your father's thinking, you mean? Without the beard, of course."

"No. Not really. Dad's religious, but these maniacs… no, he's hardly in their league. He's no blind fanatic." Bennet levered himself up onto his feet. Two settlements down, the gods alone knew how many left to go. "Break's over, boys and girls. Back to work. The next settlement awaits us."

Settlement! That was something of an overreach. Like the two they'd already cleared, this cluster of half a dozen small, slovenly houses on a small island in the marsh barely qualified as a campsite.

A child spotted them first. He couldn't have been more than eight, and a scrawny eight at that. The same colour as the ground he weeded, his clothes thick with dirt, he was at work in a vegetable garden. His hoe was taller than he was. When Bennet and Rosie came out of the trees into the clearing, the kid stopped and stared for a second or two. All the kids in the settlements were brought up to be distrustful. Their first instincts on seeing a stranger were to run. This one was no exception. The kid hurled the hoe aside and ran to hammer on the nearest door, yelling.

The encounters followed the same pattern in every damn settlement. Bennet walked into the hamlet with Rosie and the small company of troopers at his back. The adults straggled out to meet them, milling around the patch of ground between the huts. The women and children were waved back by the men, while the village leader faced up to Bennet. They all looked resentful, unfriendly, and suspicious.

Bennet greeted the village patriarch, getting in return dubious and half-hearted blessings from behind the most impressive and uncombed beard. Rosie was right there. Every man Jack of them had a beard Bennet could use to hide a laser cannon. Bennet's response, in the ritual Theban style ingrained in him from childhood, had so far surprised the Brethren into granting him a reluctant hearing. They didn't give Rosie any such welcome. She could have turned up in a bishop's mitre, walking on water and healing the sick, and they'd still recoil in horror. Oestrogen was an insurmountable barrier to sainthood, apparently.

The patriarchs of the first couple of settlements had been seriously rattled by Rosie's mere presence. Their women were submissive baby-making machines if the numbers of children in each settlement were anything to go by. Brethren women did not wander around dressed in combat fatigues and carrying enough armament to start a small war. Rosie's presence didn't help Bennet persuade these people to be sensible, so she'd reluctantly taken to adopting a low profile, complaining only to Bennet that she'd much prefer to ram their sexism down their throats. As soon as Bennet engaged the head man, she dropped back to send the troopers to ring the little houses to ensure the families couldn't break out. They'd learned that lesson the hard way at the first village. It had taken half a day of slipping and sliding through stinking mud to round up the adults and children who'd scattered into the marshes.

Convincing the Brethren they faced a real threat was hard work. It took more time than Bennet thought they had to spare. He was inclined to whistle up the Infantry transports and herd the colonists into them, willing or not. The armoured cars could then whisk them away to the landing site where they were shuttled up to the waiting spacecraft, Bennet and Rosie could accept the congratulations of the escort in the ironic spirit in which their Infantry liaison, Lieutenant Grant, offered them, and they could all move on to the next settlement.

The process was already taking on a dull monotony, and the gods alone knew how many settlements there were to go. At least this one hadn't taken all damn afternoon. He watched as his troopers packed the latest batch of colonists into the transports. The kid who'd first spotted them wanted to take his hoe with him.

He turned his back on them. "Hell, I hate this planet. I hate the marshes and, gods, do I hate the cockeyed religious mania that brought these people here."

"They're an independent lot." Rosie had a bad habit of patting his hand as if he was about six and in need of soothing.

The patriarch in charge stalked to the transport with slow, reluctant dignity. Bennet hadn't hesitated to use the menace of the armed troopers as the clincher in the argument. The settlers couldn't fight their guns. The man stuck out his chin until his beard bristled, mouth working, resentment making him stiff-legged.

"You handled him with less than your usual charm," Rosie

said.

"You don't normally admit I have any charm."

She gave him a pointed look.

"That's a bit harsh," he said, wounded.

"So were you. I know they're annoying, but you usually manage to control your temper with civilians."

"I don't like them." But he flushed and nodded. "I know. This is a job, like any other. Feelings shouldn't come into it. But I really hate what they've done here."

"And what's that, apart from getting free of the government to go their own way, free from interference?"

"They've been here what? Five years? They were told not to colonise this place, that it was too close to the Maess, but they took no notice. I don't care about the adults. They were able to make the decision for themselves. But how many kids have we picked up since we got here? How many kids have been dragged into danger because their parents are too blinded by religion to think straight?" Bennet turned back to look at the families. "Look at them. The kids are scrawny and undersized, they're sick half the time, and I'll bet they've had no schooling since they got here. But I'll also bet they've been working on the land since they learned to walk. It amounts to child abuse."

"Bennet," she said.

He shrugged, throwing up his hands in defeat. "But you're right. Who am I to judge?"

"You're taking this too much to heart."

He kept his gaze on the children. "I don't like to think about the kind of lives they've had here."

"You'll make a good dad, someday." Rosie paused a beat and added, "Of course, it'll have to come out of a test tube. I know."

He laughed. "Maybe I'll adopt."

"Or get adopted," she said, and grinned. "I won't tell."

"Won't tell what?"

"That there's a soft heart under your charmless exterior."

He grinned back.

She put her hand on his arm. "I'm sorry."

"You needn't be. You're right. I'll be good from now on." Bennet raised a hand to acknowledge a signal from one of the infantrymen. They were ready to roll. "You know what's really bothering me? We won't get them all, Rosie. There are too many of them and too few of us and we just don't have time. Anyone we left behind will be as good as dead. I hate that. It makes me sick. The gods help the kids when the Maess get here. We might have had the chance to get them all off if this lot weren't mindless fanatics."

"Maybe we can get more help? Another couple of units?"

"They won't send more with the Maess this close." Bennet took off his helmet and ran his hands through his hair. "They should have sent in the evacuation ships earlier, weeks ago. Now? Now we're too little and too late and we're all these fools have. The gods help us all."

CHAPTER TWO

31 Primus 7488: Telnos

They were clearing their eighth settlement when the Maess arrived.

Bennet was in the middle of yet another bitter religious dispute with a village leader whose beard rated somewhere about a nine on the scale, when Rosie got the signal. Bennet got it the same instant she did. He held up a hand to stop the farmer, ignoring the man's indignant spluttering, and turned towards her. She was already running towards him.

She paid no attention to the village leader. "They're through."

"What is it?" the Beard demanded.

"The Maess," Bennet said. "My ship signalled that a battleship and a whole slew of fighters just dropped out of hyperspace on the edge of the system. All of our ships are engaging, but they're outnumbered, even with the destroyers protecting the infantry transports. Rosie—"

"We're out of time." She put a hand on her earpiece, as another signal came through.

"Yes. And the Maess will pick up the activity at the evacuation area, if nothing else." Bennet looked at the Beard. "We've had the recall signal. We go as soon as the Infantry get here."

"Grant's just confirmed. Five minutes." Rosie glanced past him to the assembled families. "The Maess will pick us up, too."

And the Maess would. The settlements and individual homesteads themselves would be harder to spot—abandoning technology meant the Brethren weren't leaking revealing power signatures all over the place—but both the landing area and the moving transports would show up on even the most basic of scanners, like beacons in the night.

Bennet turned back to the village leader. "You have five minutes to get what you need, and only what you need. Get your people together. We go as soon as the transports arrive."

The man drew himself up, throwing back his shoulders. Maybe he thought his superior height and bulk was intimidating. "The Gods spake unto Jonas and said, Work thou, and by the labour of thine hands shalt thou glorify Us and glorious shall be the fruits thereof, and thou shalt know Paradise and drink of milk and honey—"

Bennet didn't let him finish. "I'm sure of it. No one's going to stop you labouring, friend, and if you're still here when the Maess arrive they'll make damn sure you don't stop. Until they shoot you and everyone else here, that is. There won't be a lot of glory. Not a lot of milk and honey, either."

"We are protected by the gods." The man's face flushed, the vein in his temple throbbing visibly.

"No, you're protected by me and my soldiers."

The man glared. "The gods will not allow the ungodly to harm us."

"Well, look on me as their means to that end." Bennet raised his voice to reach the group of thirty or so people grouped behind the patriarch. "We'll be leaving in four minutes."

They stared back at him, faces as expressionless as a herd of bovines. Even the children. No one moved.

"Fine," Bennet said. "Then you go as you are."

The Beard bristled. "We won't be going anywhere. The gods

led us here."

"When those transports arrive you will all get into them if I have to use force. And, believe me, I will." Bennet's voice was low and hard. Uncompromising. "Am I understood?"

The man blinked. Bennet turned away. When Rosie glanced back, the patriarch had joined the assembled families, talking rapidly, throwing out his arms and gesturing. The Beard looked up at the sky more than once. She couldn't tell if he were looking for divine assistance or evidence of the Maess.

She knew which she had her money on turning up first, and it sure as hell didn't involve religion.

Rosie took one more fast-paced jog around the clearing, checking the position of each of the troopers on guard, before returning to Bennet's side to report. "Sensors show only Grant's transports. ETA two minutes."

Bennet gave her a nod and a slight smile in return. She'd lived at close quarters with him on a small Shield ship for more than four years now and sometimes it was all too easy for her to see what Bennet was feeling. But it always impressed her when they were on some stinking planet wondering if the Maess or the infantry would get there first, how little he let it show. He might be so tense every nerve was screaming with it, but not one of the troopers or the civilians would realise it. Bennet was good at pushing self and ego away and getting on with the job. He was a damn fine soldier.

No. A damn fine Shield.

She rotated her shoulders to ease the weight of the tac-vest. Her mouth was dry. "I wish Grant would hurry it up. Definitely time for some manoeuvring. We need those transports."

"He'll be here." Bennet's mouth curved up into another slight smile. "And it's running away, not manoeuvring"

She managed to grin back. "I think the technical term is a

tactical retreat."

"Running away," Bennet repeated. He came alert as the three transports lurched through the trees, water and mud spraying up under their wide tyres. "Good. Get ready."

Infantry Lieutenant Grant dropped down from the cabin of the first transport and jogged over to join them. He didn't seem too fazed about having the Maess right on top of them. He threw Bennet a sketchy salute and winked at Rosie. "We don't have long."

"I know." Bennet nodded towards the sullen, resentful-looking families. "Herd 'em in."

"We'll be pushed to fit everyone in, including you lot," Grant said. "You'll have to ride on top."

"The view's better." Bennet went on to join the Beard, Rosie and Grant in his wake.

The colonist wasn't going to shift, arms folded over his chest, legs apart to balance his weight. "We're staying. We don't believe they're here. This is some ploy by the Ennead to get us to return."

Rosie blinked. The Ennead? The only reason the collection of self-serving rats who made up their government cared about illegal colonists on a shithole of a planet at the arse-end of the galaxy was because they always had more than half an eye on the next election. It wouldn't do to leave humans to be destroyed by Maess drones. It cost votes.

"Is he mad?" Grant asked.

Bennet shushed him with a gesture. "You've been here for five years and no one's bothered with you until now."

"They didn't want us here."

"No, because it's so close to the war zone. But they didn't make a move on you for five years. They didn't care about your colony until it became clear the Maess were on their way. If the Ennead just wanted you to move, they wouldn't have waited this long to do it."

The man stared at them.

"The Maess are here, friend." Grant glanced up at the sky. "It's not a trick."

The fighter came right that instant, as if Grant had cued it up.

The pilotless Maess fighter was another kind of cyborg drone. Capable of space and atmosphere assaults, it was a blunted arrowhead, rounded at the nose with swept back convex wings, a dark dull grey against the paler greyish-white cloud cover. The high-pitched engines screeched as it flashed overhead, shattering the normal sounds of the marsh like a hammer smashing glass, drowning the dry creaking of the invisible insects and sending flocks of wading birds flapping into the sky in panic.

It was barely past them when Bennet reacted, swinging around to face the troopers. "Run!"

The pitch of the engine noise changed as the fighter turned and banked, coming around for another pass. They'd been seen. Rosie pushed a couple of kids towards the troopers running her way. Grant caught up one little girl and ran for the transports, yelling at his people. Bennet grabbed at a woman's arm with his right hand, jerking her out of her dazed terror.

"Run!" He pushed the woman towards the transports, snatching up the small child clutching at her skirts. "They're coming back! Run, fuck it! Rosie!"

For an instant, it was stunned chaos. The Beard and the other colonists stared in blank surprise. The women were faster. Dragging at their children, they ran for it; some grim-faced, others with features slackening in terror, mouths already opening to scream. Nevertheless, they ran. The troopers moved fast, trained to a hair. Within seconds, they had the colonists surrounded, pushing and shoving until they all broke into a jog trot for the transports.

Bennet yelled orders as he ran. "Grant! Gunners!"

"We're on it!"

On every transport, a khaki-clad Infantry soldier scrambled into the gun turret, firing up the laser cannon. The big barrels

18

swung over towards the approaching fighter. Others jumped down from the transports and threw open the armoured doors at the back. Rosie ran in Bennet's wake, her hand clamped around a woman's arm, yanking her along. Bennet hurled the child bodily into the nearest transport, the mother scrambling in after her. The little girl screamed with fright. Bennet pushed the mother in hard, stuffing the next child in behind her. Rosie rushed to join him, hauling her own woman and child combination along with her.

Run!

The scream of the fighter's engines drowned out everything but the voice inside her head. Bennet spared her a glance and ran back, chivvying the panicking colonists along. Rosie jammed her laser back in its holster—stupid useless thing against a fighter!—and stumbled after him. It took her a couple of steps to get her balance.

The fighter fired as it breasted the trees, lines of laser charges from the twin guns in its blunted nose cutting the air with streaks of fire. It was using laser-guided high explosive flechettes, damn it.

Fucking hell! They were going to catch it now.

One of the little wooden houses went up first as the charges ripped through it, blasting fragments of wood and metal all over the clearing. The second round of flechettes caught at the edges of the fleeing group of pitiful, frail human bodies.

"Bring it down!" Bennet's voice was a roar over the noise.

The percussion from the nearest flechette made Rosie stagger. Everything boomed around her, the air rippling and billowing as it buffeted her, smacking up against her skin and making her ears pop. She managed to keep her feet, whooping as air was sucked from her lungs. Her forehead stung. The air tasted of fire and brimstone. Bennet was flat on his back, and her heart beat so loudly it had to have drowned out the firing.

Oh gods. Bennet.

She dragged in a harsh, stinging breath and threw herself towards him. "Bennet!"

The next barrage landed well beyond them both, nearer the

transports. The deep boom of the transport's guns answered, and the fighter was gone again. Its engines shrieked and strained against the thick air as it banked and turned and headed back towards them for another strafing run.

Bennet rolled over as Rosie reached him, pushing at the soggy ground to get himself to his knees. She grabbed his arm and hauled him up.

"Okay. I'm okay!" Bennet started running the instant he regained his footing. He ran past her, heading for the obscene, tumbled mass of people who had been caught by the explosions. How could he run like that? Rosie's legs shook and her heart hammered. She gasped for every breath, struggling to catch up with him.

The Beard, dead, the once hot and fervid eyes staring up at a sky he couldn't see. A woman near him, dead, her body shredded and mutilated, face untouched but for a bloody smear on the smooth skin. The children, dead, small bodies twisted. One child died as Rosie reached her. She let some closed off part of her mind acknowledge the death as Bennet caught up a woman who still showed some signs of life. Everyone else in the group was beyond help. Rosie looked around, started for a second group of tumbled bodies.

"It's coming back!" Bennet yelled at the Infantry as he ran for the transports. "Get ready!"

A young man, dead, the top of his head missing. A child trembling and crying near his feet, small body bloodied but arms and legs still there. Troopers all around her grabbing at anyone who might make it. Rosie snatched up the little boy. His blood leaked between her fingers. She ran, hearing the child's distressed whimpering over the scream of the fighter's engines. Someone, an infantryman, pulled the boy from her arms and pushed him into the transport. She spun on her heel and ran back to the dead and wounded.

Another child, dead. Another woman, dead, body curved around the child's, her back an open, bloody mess. Her backbone gleamed white in all the red meat. Dex, one of the troopers, his face creased with what looked like outrage at being blown to shards. Another woman. Dead. Another child. Dead.

And Grant, rolling over and trying to push himself up onto his knees, as Bennet had done a minute earlier, a lifetime earlier. Bennet reached him first, Rosie right behind. Between them, they hauled him up.

"Fuck," Grant said. His left hand was a mess of torn flesh and splintered white bone, the fingers gone.

Bennet held him up. Rosie took one more look around. No one else to pick up, no one else alive.

Run!

The first transport lurched out of the clearing just as the fighter came back. This time the infantry gunners were ready for it. It veered away from the ferocity of the return fire, banking steeply off to the right. The flechettes passed overhead to hit a barn on the far side of the clearing. Rosie slammed shut the door of the last transport and darted around to help Bennet with Grant. They scrambled up the side of the transport, feet in small toeholds, clinging to anything they could. Bennet hooked his left arm through a restraining strap, the other firm in Grant's belt, holding him against the side of the transport. Rosie reached around Grant to catch at a strap on his other side, Grant's spine hard and solid against the inside of her arm.

The transport lurched as it followed the others out of the clearing and into the relative cover of the trees, and Rosie had to grab at some webbing to keep herself stable. Grant, helpless between her and Bennet, took in harsh, distressed breaths.

Bennet glanced at Rosie. She gave a sharp nod towards Grant's left hand. The poor bastard needed help before he bled to death and she was on the wrong side of him to do it.

Bennet scowled at the mess. "Can you hold me on?" he asked the gunner.

The gunner shook her head but ducked down into the transport for an instant, shouting something Rosie couldn't hear. Another trooper pushed up into the gun turret with her.

"Can't stay up here." The infantryman leaned out of the turret, close to falling out headfirst, and loosened one end of a restraining strap. He threaded it through Bennet's belt and tied it to a handy strut, his movements sharp and precise despite the transport's lurching. He got another strap and secured Grant as well as he could. He dived back into the transport for an instant, reappearing with several loose field dressings in his hand. He thrust them at Bennet. "I'm needed down there. Can you take care of the boss?"

Rosie glanced up, looking for the fighter. She could hear it, close overhead. She couldn't see it. Flechettes ripped through the trees to the right, missing them, but making the transport shudder. The gunner cursed, and started the laser cannon. The hot air made Rosie wince away. Too close. She tightened her hold on Grant. "I've got him secure, Bennet."

Bennet worked his right arm free. Rosie tensed, bracing Grant in case he fell, but his head came up, and Grant, swallowing hard, wound the end of a strap around his right hand.

"Okay?" Bennet tucked the dressings in between the fastenings of his jacket, to keep his hands free, using the first dressing as a rough tourniquet.

"What the fuck do you think?" Grant said, but there was no malice in it. "Fuck."

Rosie twisted her hand through the loop on a restraining strap, tightening her grip as the transport lurched over the uneven ground. "Don't look at it. Look at me instead. I'm prettier."

Grant choked and somehow managed a laugh. Bennet took hold of the maimed arm and wrapped what was left of Grant's hand. It wasn't possible to be careful and gentle, not riding on the outside of a transport tearing across marshes pursued by the Maess. Grant had his teeth showing, clamped hard, and still he whimpered more than once. Rosie tightened her grip on him.

"Next time, I won't hold onto my bloody laser when shells are going off all around me." Grant's dark skin had greyed over. He glanced once at Rosie, his mouth working, before going back to staring at what Bennet was doing. His pupils had almost swallowed up his irises, leaving just a rim of brown around the black. "Bloody thing blew up in my hand."

The transport veered from side to side, heaving itself over tussocks of reedy marsh grass. How in hell Bennet kept his footing defeated Rosie. Both his hands were occupied in getting the mess into field dressings, and the bleeding under control.

"Left handed?" Rosie asked.

"Not anymore." Grant's laugh sounded more like a sob. "Shit, it hurts."

"That's the best I can do until the medics can see to it." Bennet hooked his left arm around the securing strap and used his right to cradle Grant's arm just below the elbow, keeping the injured hand from banging against the side of the transport. He glanced up. "It's coming around again."

Rosie scanned the skies for it. "They don't give up."

"Neither do we," the gunner said, tracking the fighter on the sensor pad. "I'll get the bastard this time. Duck!"

The gun barrel swung over their bowed heads, spitting the intense white laser pulse. Either it or one of the gunners in the other transports caught the fighter as it came around on another pass. The Maess ship sheered off, engines screaming. The pitch had Rosie's ears ringing.

"I was thinking about joining your lot," Grant said, as the fighter vanished into the cloud cover, trailing smoke. "Guess I blew it."

Bennet grimaced at Rosie behind Grant's back. "Not necessarily."

"Don't be daft. I'll lose it, I reckon. Fuck, it hurts!"

"I can't give you anything here."

"I know." Grant's eyes, clouded now and not quite focused, met Rosie's. "I'd have liked to join Shield."

She hoped her smile was reassuring. "Even after five days of watching us at work?"

"Hey, I always wanted to do some swashbuckling. You get all those sorts of jobs."

"Tell me about it," Rosie turned the grin onto Bennet. "We're the best there is at swashing buckles. Of course, Bennet being the perverse beggar he is, he buckles swashes."

"Huh?"

"Ignore her," Bennet said. "She likes to think she's funny."

"You're funny. I'm amusing." Rosie strained to hear the fighter. Silence, followed by a tentative scraping noise as the insect chorus started up again. In a second or two, the marshes sounded like they had before the Maess came, as if nothing touched them, as if nothing but the green water and insects were permanent.

Bennet grunted. "You know it's 'buckler', and not something that helps hold your belt together and your pants up?" Both of them stared at him. He frowned back at Rosie. He pulled his free hand out of the strap and gestured to his temple. "All right? You're bleeding."

Rosie touched her temple and winced. It was sticky. Now he'd told her about it, her head started to hurt. A nick, that was all. She nodded at him to tell him she was all right.

"A buckler?" Grant asked in a small, exhausted voice. His head drooped.

"A round shield," Bennet said. "Appropriate, when you come to think of it."

Seven cutters waited at the landing site, including the one from the *Hype*, guarded by a circle of Infantry troopers. The Infantry Colonel had at least had the sense to set up some field laser cannon.

The transports skidded to a halt. Bennet and Rosie got Grant down between them. His skin was very grey now, his eyes glazing. His arms and legs shook. He'd have fallen if they hadn't been holding him.

Rosie looked around her, one arm around Grant, the weight of her laser in her other hand. Across the clearing lay a row of still figures, mostly khaki-clad, some civilian. An infantryman, the paramedic who had given them the field dressings for Grant, climbed out of their transport carrying a child. He took it to the line of bodies and laid it down, straightening small arms and legs. Two others in the line were as small.

It wasn't one of Rosie's rescues. It had to be one of Bennet's. She glanced at him, sorry to see how tired he looked, how much his eyes were dulled with grief for a child whose name he didn't even know.

"Are we leaving them?" she said.

Bennet took off his helmet to run a hand through his hair. Right on cue, the moment the helmet came off, those dark cowlicks of his sprang up. He scrubbed the hand over his face, jammed his helmet back on and straightened up. "We'll be lucky to get the living out."

He was right there. Anyway, the dead wouldn't care.

Rosie grinned encouragement at Grant, as the lieutenant got his head up. The paramedic arrived and lifted Grant's arm, focused on the blood-soaked stump of a hand.

"Shield Captain!" The Infantry colonel jogged over to them, her face grim. "A Maess drone transport touched down to the west and we've got more incoming. Your cutter's the fastest. Can you hold here while we evacuate?"

Bennet nodded, and the colonel hurried away, shouting orders into the tumult.

"I guess someone has to be last out," Bennet said, after a second or two.

Rosie rolled her eyes. Shield was always left to do the dirty work.

Grant forced a faint grin as two of his own platoon took over from Rosie, helping him stay upright. "Good luck, you two. Be sure to turn off the lights."

"That's our job." Rosie kissed his cheek. "See you later, Grant." She watched them take him to the nearest cutter. Halfway there his legs gave out. One of the troopers dipped a shoulder to get Grant over it and jog trotted off, the second trooper running alongside to hold Grant steady. "He'll lose that hand."

"He already has."

"Better than being dead."

Bennet nodded, looked around the clearing. "We'll be spread thin. Let's get them out there."

She ran to do his bidding, getting the fourteen remaining Shield warriors ranged around the clearing. They were armed with handheld cannon from the *Hyperion*'s cutter, enough to bring down a Maess fighter if one came their way. She could hear one in the distance, but it was at a tangent to them. Heading up north into the hills towards the mines, maybe.

Cutters took off behind her, struggling up into the dubious safety of the skies. With the Maess up there, this could well be an end game for them all at last. No one in Shield had ever been captured alive. Every one of them would go down fighting, making sure the colonists got the best chance they could. Her gut gave an odd little lurch and she drew three or four sharp panting breaths to calm the jitters. No time for more.

A group of warriors seeded the western approach with explosives, some strung between the trees at chest height—chest height if you were a two-metre-tall Maess drone—and scattering tiny but efficient mines over the ground. She watched them and the approach at the same time, gaze flickering from one side of the clearing to the other and back again repeatedly.

A line of Infantry ran for the last cutter, running in an orderly fashion that struck her as incredibly funny and heartbreakingly sad. No words would explain why to anyone who wasn't Shield. Bennet would get it.

As soon as the cutter lifted off, they could be gone, leaving this hell-hole to the Maess drones. It couldn't be soon enough.

Bennet jogged over to her. He'd taken a handheld sensor left by the retreating Infantry. "This thing's jumping like crazy. A couple of fighters, and ground troops from the drone transport."

"How long?"

"Minutes. Three or four, maybe." He swung around in a half circle, eyes on the sensor display. "Make that three."

Tense now, Rosie looked behind her again. "They're closing up the last cutter."

"Then let's get the hell out of here." The grin Bennet gave her, more of a grimace really, betrayed that he, too, was tense and nervous.

She grinned back. Sergeant Tim was at the other edge of the clearing, watching for her signal. She called him over the com, waving at him for good measure, and within a second, Tim yelled the orders to get the troopers running for their own cutter. They weren't as tidy about it as the Infantry had been. But they were faster.

She tilted her head to listen. A fighter. Coming their way.

She ran for the cutter, making sure the troopers were in front of her. Only the two mining the clearing were still behind her and out of the corner of her eye, as she glanced back, she saw them start running. The first troopers were inside.

She reached the cutter before the fighter did. Tim had set up a field cannon, and had it firing when the fighter came into view over the trees, traversing the laser with expert skill as the Maess ship went overhead. The all-too-familiar twin lines of flechettes from the fighter bracketed the cutter on either side, mercifully missing anything vital.

"Fucking hell!" she said, buffeted by the abrupt changes in air pressure following the explosions.

One of the two remaining troopers went down, screaming. Bennet, almost behind the illusory safety of the gun, spun on his heel and ran back.

"Go!" he shouted at Rosie. "Get them out of here!"

The second fighter was so hard on the heels of the first the paint on its nose must have been blistered by the afterburners. It came in firing. The flechette hit. For a second Rosie saw Bennet's body silhouetted against the explosion's brilliant white glare, as he was hurled backwards to land sprawled face up on the grass, a still black figure spread-eagled against all the poisonous green.

CHAPTER THREE

32 Primus 7488: Sais City

Joss was out when the news came.

He'd had one of his lonely days and he went looking for comfort from a warm body, dancing and laughter. Bennet wouldn't blame him. Bennet knew it meant nothing. A substitute, that was all. A consolation prize.

He'd had a good night. It had been fun.

When he got home with the dawn, the sky to the east was just cooling from its first rosy blush into a clear blue. The tall buildings ringing the park across the road stood outlined in a splendour of gold edges and mauve shadows, hard against the sky, looking like they were holding it up.

The Shield officers were waiting. They had to have been watching for him, maybe from the dark hovercar parked in the street outside the apartment building. He barely had time to get from his cab to the street door when someone, a stranger, called his name. When he turned, he only saw the uniform. The face above it, a pale blur with a solemn expression, spoke in a quiet, hushed voice. Joss listened with his head bent, his hands clenched around his keys. When the little pain made itself known, he opened his hand and the keys were imprinted on his palm, pale white shadows pressed into his skin.

He was Bennet's legal next of kin. He was the one to be told there had been a laser shell on some scrubby little outpost, that they'd left Bennet there, lying on his back and staring up at the sky. They'd left the carrion for the Maess. Of course, they didn't phrase it in quite that way, those soberly dressed military types, when they explained Bennet had gone back for an injured trooper and been hit himself. It had to have been instantaneous, one of the Shield officers said, tone earnest. Painless. A mercy.

Joss shook his head. He couldn't believe it. Pain and carrion, that's what it was.

He closed the door on them, in the end, refusing their offers of assistance and counselling. There was no one for them to call to come and comfort him. There was no comfort to be had. He walked into the apartment great room, skirting the big glass sculpture that was its centrepiece, to reach the display cabinets in front of the wide windows.

It should be there, in the second row. Yes. There it was—the heart scarab, carved from gleaming, polished bloodstone, its dark green shot through with yellowy-white threads and a twist of scarlet running its entire length. Taken from who knew which long-dead, mummified husk of withered flesh and hard bone wrapped in resined linen, but a beautiful piece. Museum quality.

Bennet had loved it.

Joss's hands shook. He took three tries to turn the key, open the case and close his fingers around the scarab's cool stone sides. He could feel every edge of the crisp carvings with his fingertips— furled wing cases, the tucked-down head, the hieroglyphs on the underside a prayer for the beloved dead.

The comlink shrilled at him. He turned his head towards it, but didn't move. It went to voicemail. Meriel, Bennet's mother, choking on sobs. "Joss, oh Joss! Call me. Oh, Joss. Joss. I can't bear it. Bennet—no, Liam, what are you doing—"

It clicked itself off. Joss waited, but Meriel didn't call back. Nothing else. No other messages. He turned back to the scarab and tilted it towards the window until it caught the day's new light. It had warmed in his hand, the scarlet glowing against the dark green.

Bennet would never warm him again.

37 Primus 7488: Sais City

"Here." Meriel pushed the glass into Joss's hand. She was so like her son, Joss's chest tightened even while his gaze traced the familiar high cheekbones and wide grey eyes. Meriel's eyes and nose were red. She'd worn herself out doing what he couldn't do. He couldn't cry.

"It won't help." Nevertheless, he took the glass anyway and a sip of the liquor in it, because he liked her and, despite everything, they were friends. After Bennet and Caeden had fought with such deadly venom and Bennet had come to him, Meriel had refused to let Bennet go, fighting to keep her family as intact as she could, mediating between the warring factions. She was, Joss thought, less absolute than Caeden, more open to compromise. Definitely more pragmatic.

"I love my son and I refuse to lose him," she had said once, in the early days. "I'll do anything it takes to keep Bennet as close as I can." She'd smiled then. "And what that means, Joss, is that you and I will just have to get to know each other."

It had been a promise she'd kept. Over the years, Joss and Meriel had got to know, respect, and accept each other. Even to like each other. After all, these last few years they'd both been military spouses, spending long weeks alone. It drew them together. Sometimes he thought Meriel understood Joss's fears better than he did himself. It made for a bond that Joss, at least, hadn't expected.

Meriel seldom came alone, usually bringing one or more of Bennet's siblings with her. Althea—Thea—came most often, before marriage and motherhood had claimed her attention. Joss liked Thea. She was the most like Bennet of all the family, and didn't demand more of Bennet than he wanted to give. Sometimes Liam and Natalia came with them, the two young ones indifferent to Bennet's unorthodox living arrangements. At least, Natalia had been until she'd gone to the religious school Caeden had chosen for her. Since then she'd been cooler. Liam, though, had grown closer to Bennet over the last two or three years.

Thea was out of town with her husband and child, but Joss had listened to her grief-filled message on his answer-machine. Natalia hadn't come. So only Liam had driven his mother into the city centre for this... this what? This ritual of bereavement, Joss supposed, so she could do what he couldn't do, and cry for her son. Liam stood with his back to them, staring out of the windows, leaving them to talk.

"I was worried, when I couldn't reach you." Meriel sipped at her own liquor.

"I was out when the news came." The young man he'd picked up was beautiful, and Joss had been pleasuring himself in his dark sensuality while Bennet... he choked, and took a drink. The glass rattled against his teeth. He gulped down the liquor, welcoming its harshness against his throat. When he could, he said, "I was out. They were waiting when I got home, to tell me."

Meriel's hand closed over his, to help him still the shaking. Tears trickled down her face. He wished he could cry. But he couldn't. Instead, he put his hands onto the package that had come for Bennet only that morning, thinking the touch might bring Bennet closer. But Bennet was five days dead and he'd never open it now. Meriel glanced at it, and he said, "Printer's proofs."

"Yours?"

"His. The Thebaid asked him to revise one of the volumes of the History." He ran his hand in a long sweeping caress, but this time it wasn't against the body he'd loved all those years ago and all the years since, but against the hard-edged package of data discs. "He was a scholar, too."

Meriel smiled, blotting at the tears with a handkerchief already sodden with them. Joss watched, fascinated. Relieved. It had been worrying him, nagging at him like an aching tooth. At last the rituals had been observed: there was a scrap of linen, at last, to do duty as a burial shroud.

"He loved all that," she said. "I didn't realise he still did work for the Thebaid."

"He always has. He never cut his ties there. It's what he should have been doing, what he wanted to do. What I wanted him to do."

"He wanted the military as well, Joss,. No one forced him into it. We weren't in a position to, don't forget."

Joss put down the glass and rubbed at his right temple. Gods, he was so damned tired. "Then he wanted it all, I guess. Do you think he got it?"

Meriel shook her head, tears close again. It fascinated him, this easy facility for grief, and he resented it.

After a moment, he said, unable to bear the silence and needing to tell someone, "We fought about it." He looked down at the parcel and touched it, smoothing the packaging. "Things have been a bit difficult. Did he say? We've been going through a bad patch over the last year or two."

"He never said anything."

"We fought about him staying in the military. I wanted him here, at home, where we could be together and he was safe." His voice shook. "Was that so bad? I wanted him safe. I didn't want this. We fought about it just before he left. The last thing we did together, and we were fighting."

Meriel touched the hand lying on the proofs. "No relationship is without its problems. It changes and grows up, Joss, as the people in it do."

He hadn't wanted Bennet to change. He'd wanted his scholar back. "He just wouldn't listen to me."

"Bennet was seven shades of stubborn," Meriel said.

"He'd have done it, if he'd cared. He'd have stayed here."

Her eyes widened. "Joss, he left us and everything behind to be with you. He lived with you all these years. I'm sure he loved you, very much."

"Yes." After another silent minute, Joss touched the parcel again. "It isn't his best period. He's an early history expert, you know, but he did a good job of this. He's going to do some—" He bit at his lower lip. "No. Not now."

"He might still be alive." Liam's voice crackled with tension and anger. "He might be. We don't know."

"No one's going back to find out," Joss snapped. "That's not the military way."

Liam said nothing. Joss heard him move away to circle the room, restless, putting distance between them. Meriel shook her head, blotting at her eyes again with the scrap of linen.

This time the silence went on so long, Joss couldn't bear it. "I meant to call... I mean, I would have..." He stopped. He had to fight back the bitterness. "I suppose they told you before they told me."

He hadn't been able to call her. He hadn't been able to do anything. He had meant to, but it had been easier to just sit and wait for something to happen. In the end, she'd come to him. He'd known she would.

"Caeden knows everyone in the military, Joss. And the Supreme Commander is Bennet's godfather, after all. General Martens told Jak, Jak told Caeden, Caeden told me."

Joss nodded. He couldn't say he really knew Caeden. The few times they had met, Caeden had been stiff and proud towards the man he considered had corrupted his son. Joss didn't know how that stiff pride would react, but surely, the father in him overrode everything, at the end. "How... how's he taking it?"

"It's breaking his heart." Meriel blinked back more tears. "I had to tell the children. Oh Joss, I had to tell them. Caeden wasn't there to do it." She broke off, and cried again, hiding her face in her hands.

Anguished, helpless, Joss twisted in his chair. Liam was back at the huge window, staring out over the city, standing where Joss had kissed Bennet for the first time over the case with the bloodstone scarab. Joss couldn't see the boy's face, but the rigid back spoke volumes of grief and loss.

"Liam." He didn't know what to say. "Your mother."

He saw Liam's shoulders slump in a sigh, then stiffen again, and Liam turned to face him. All the brothers had in common was the thick mop of unruly dark hair, and their colouring. But Liam's eyes were vivid blue, not pale cool grey, and he didn't look like Bennet. Liam looked like Caeden.

Disappointed, Joss turned away again. Liam came to put his arms around his mother and let her cry. Joss listened to Liam's clumsy, heart-felt attempts at comfort, and he felt both useless and helpless, because he could neither grieve nor comfort.

But most of all he thought about the husk of bone and linen that Bennet had become.

A heart scarab and a long-dead mummy had brought them together in the first place.

Joss's laboratory on the seventh floor at the Thebaid Institute had been cool even in the hot summer of 7479, the aircon ramped up as high as it would go to keep the mummy at the optimum temperature to prevent damage. Joss had set the spotlights on their stands to bathe the mummy with unshadowed light.

"Here," Joss had said. "Can you feel it?"

Slender hands, smooth inside the skin-tight protective gloves, had moved over the intricate bandaging on the mummy's chest. "I think so."

Joss put his own hand over Bennet's, moving it into place. He pressed down, keeping the pressure light, letting Bennet feel the amulet where it lay on the mummy's rib cage. "Here. Just here. Got it now?"

Bennet's eyes lit up with delighted wonder. "Yes! A heart scarab?"

"Well done." Joss took his hand away. "The sensor says this

one's made from solid gold." Joss had a collection of amulets back at home in his apartment. Nothing as elaborate or fine as this one promised to be, but a nice little collection. "That's unusual. Most are carved from stone…" He stopped and arched an eyebrow at Bennet.

"Bloodstone, or jasper, or basalt. Hardstone, anyway." Bennet's hands moved over the bandages in a caress. "Are you going to remove it?"

"No. The museum has hundreds of the things, and we're archaeologists, not treasure hunters. It's better where it is."

"Oh." Bennet sounded disappointed. "This is the closest I've ever been allowed to a mummy. I've never had the chance to open one up."

Joss laughed, unsurprised that even this privileged young student hadn't been allowed to touch a mummy. The Thebaid Institute would hardly let a teenager loose on its best assets. Mummies were precious beyond belief, and good as Bennet was, he had a lot to learn yet.

Joss had been as impressed as anyone connected with the Thebaid when the kid most of them stigmatised as a scrubby little schoolboy had snatched the Jancis Scholarship, the most prestigious academic prize it offered, from under the noses of several promising scholars. Of course, the schoolboy in question had spent every spare hour at the Thebaid for years—first in the museum, hanging around until all the curators knew his name and who he was, and later allowed back behind the scenes when the youthful passion for history hadn't fizzled out. When Joss had returned to Sais and the Thebaid after a couple of years' absence, he had found Bennet already installed as the Dean's protégé. Even with that advantage, no one had expected Bennet to try for the prize for another year or two, or to take it with such ease that several scholarly noses were severely out of joint.

Still, Joss was breaking the rules, allowing Bennet into the lab while he was working, but Bennet had a way of begging with those big grey eyes that would take a stronger backbone than Joss's to resist. He was often around when Joss was at the Thebaid. Did

Bennet watch and wait for him? Probably, if the way the kid lit up was any guide.

Bennet hung over the mummy as if over a lover, his expression rapt and intent, one finger tracing the interlaced linen bandaging. He looked up and smiled. Did Bennet have any idea at all of how pretty he was? A face with cheekbones to die for, and skin so smooth Joss doubted if he even had to shave much yet. A strong mouth, that probably would taste... Joss stopped short.

No. He's too young.

"Why aren't you at school, anyway?" he asked, checking the tray of instruments set up to extract the tiny sample of DNA he needed for his tests.

"I am eighteen, you know. I've left school."

Legal, then.

"I would have thought you'd want to spend the summer with your friends."

Bennet shrugged, face reddening. "I'd rather be here." He added in a low mutter, "With you."

Joss didn't look up from the mummy, although he allowed himself to smile down at the bandaged face he held between his gloved hands. It took some effort, but he ignored the provocation. Not for the first time, he wondered just what Bennet was proposing to study next.

Well, he wasn't Bennet's teacher. Not in any real and academic sense. The amount of money he gifted to the Thebaid each year gave him a quasi-formal position there, but he wasn't on the teaching staff. He risked no professional standards if he gave in to temptation... He shut down on that thought and let a faint amusement into his tone. "Well, if you want to spend your days locked up in here with old mummies, who am I to stop you? Do you want to help me take a DNA sample from young Amthoth, here?"

Joss turned the mummy onto its side, and then its face, marvelling, no matter how many times he'd handled one, at how light these husks of once living men and women were. Bennet helped him get the mummy into position.

Bennet looked up at him and smiled. Joss's breath caught in his throat, and he had to turn the choke into a hurried cough. There was unmistakable admiration in that gaze. More. An invitation, perhaps, or a hint of a complicity. Not for the first time, he wondered what he might be called upon to teach. It was an effort to turn his attention to taking the sample and returning Amthoth to his coffin.

"It's the awards ceremony this weekend, isn't it?" Joss pulled off the thin protective gloves and dropped them into a nearby waste bin, grimacing at their greasy feel.

"Mmn." Bennet glanced at Joss and, when Joss nodded permission, began to reseal the mummy case.

Joss watched those slender hands at work. Bennet had an aptitude for this. Long fingers smoothed down the new seals, almost sensuous in the way they touched the delicate, fragile cartonnage of the coffin, drifting over the exquisite painting, careful not to damage it. It was a pleasure to watch Bennet work. Joss was particular about hands. His own were one of his vanities. One of his many vanities, if he was honest.

"Nicely done," Joss said when Bennet was finished. "You've got the touch for this sort of work."

Bennet blushed, and muttered something Joss wasn't meant to catch. He smiled. He was enjoying this little game, charting its growing intensity over the last few weeks. Bennet was new to it, but playing valiantly.

"You can leave it now. The porters will take it back into storage." Joss watched Bennet step back. "So, is the whole family celebrating with you?"

"No. They're not bothered."

Joss blinked. "Not bothered?"

"Dad won't be back for months, and Mama's got a committee meeting for the *Gyrfalcon* Family Support Group or something.

Thea's pleased, but she's away at med school until after the awards ceremony and the other two are too young. It's not important to them."

"Oh?" Joss said, taken aback.

"I mean they've got my life mapped out for me." Archetypal teenage bitterness laced through Bennet's tone. "I'm meant to go to the Academy in the autumn, and then follow Dad into Fleet. This is just my little hobby."

"I see," Joss said. "And the Jancis Scholarship?"

"It doesn't fit with the Academy, now does it?"

"Do you fit with the Academy?"

Bennet glanced at him, eyes hot with anger, and something else. Slyness. Yes, that was it. Slyness. The brat was up to something, and not just testing his wings in a mild flirtation. "No. I've got other plans. I just haven't told Dad yet. I'll tell him when I'm good and ready."

Joss didn't smile at the bravado. He wouldn't want to go up against 'Dad' himself. He was acquainted with Commander Caeden. His father, now dead, had known Caeden well. They all belonged to the elite, made up of Albion's best families, unrelated except by wealth, class and political affiliation. Incredible as it was, both Joss and this skinny kid had the right to the 'Seigneur' before their names, although Joss never bothered with his title and Bennet, presumably, had yet to grow into his. Caeden didn't use his title either, but then in Caeden's mind, the title of Commander was probably by far the most honourable he could bear. The man didn't have blood, he had liquefied service and honour and duty instead. That could be hard for his son to stand up to.

"You want to come here, to the Institute instead, and take up the scholarship?"

Bennet nodded and came back to Amthoth's coffin, leaning over it to study the painted vignettes. "I want my chance at this. Professor Bachman wants to teach me, and I can't miss out on that."

"It might mean a fight with your parents if they want you in the military."

Bennet looked sly again. "Oh, that's all right. I've applied for a place with SSI for when I finish here."

"And that is?" Joss had an academic's contempt for anything outside his world, enhanced and augmented by the gay socialite's contempt for anything outside his.

"The Strategic Studies Institute. It's a sort of fast track to the military and they only take ten or twelve people a year. It's only a year-long course, so I wouldn't waste any time at all. I'd gain a year, in fact. It takes four years to get through the Academy. If I come here first, I'd still have my commission in three."

"Why would you want to? If you break free, why not break all the way free?"

Bennet frowned, looking uncertain for the first time. "I'm not sure I don't want to be in the military. I think I do. I just know I want this as well."

"Oh well," Joss said, shrugging. "There's nothing wrong with wanting it all. I always do."

"Do you get it?" Bennet asked, with one of those unpredictable changes of mood that had Joss mildly on edge in a frisson-y, rather exciting way. Flirting again, overlaying his tone with a deep significance that once again invited Joss to be complicit, to know what Bennet meant without him actually saying it.

"Usually." Joss certainly had the money and the leisure to get anything he wanted, when he wanted. That was normality, the way things were. He laughed. "Yes, I do."

"Then I'll have a go at getting it all, too."

Joss smiled and watched him. Bennet went back to studying the coffin text paintings, lips moving soundlessly as he read the hieroglyphics. Gods, but he was more than pretty. He was beautiful.

"So," Joss said, with an effort, trying to turn the conversation back to where it started. "Who are you taking to the awards ceremony, then?"

Then he laughed to himself, because he wasn't turning the conversation at all. Wasn't he giving Bennet an opportunity, testing him, seeing if all this was, was the mild flirtation of a young man trying to find the limits of his attraction, teasing someone twice his age, or whether it was something more significant? It was like sending a little bolt of energy through the charged particles of a tense atmosphere and seeing where the lightning struck.

"No one," Bennet said. There had been a pause, long enough for Joss to have seen the upward glance from the face bent over the coffin, to have seen the flash of silvery-grey through the thick black lashes. "Unless you'd come? I'd like that."

Joss smiled as the lightning crackled around them, invisible, but no less potent for all that. *Bang on target.* "Thank you. So would I. I'd be delighted to come with you."

Bennet smiled that sly smile again.

Of course he'd gone. Foolish of him, but he'd gone. It was foolish to take Bennet back to his apartment after the awards ceremony, too. But then, life was too short to be wise.

"This is amazing." Bennet looked around the apartment's main living space with bright, inquisitive eyes. "Brilliant." He walked up to the glass sculpture dominating the huge main room. It changed shape and colour depending on the angle it was approached. It was one of Joss's favourite pieces. He was on the verge of issuing a warning when Bennet reached out to touch it, but he remembered how sensitively those hands had touched Amthoth's fragile mummy case two days ago. Besides, he could always commission another.

"It's by a new artist, called Ailion," Joss said. "She's going to be very collectable someday."

"It's lovely." Bennet put his prize, an engraved plaque, onto a nearby table. "I don't remember you coming to my house. I don't remember ever seeing you before last year, in the library at the Thebaid. You were reading the Lexus Scrolls."

Joss almost laughed aloud. Bennet and his intentions were as transparent as the glass sculpture behind him. "Come on. I promised to show you the amulets." He beckoned Bennet over to the showcase near the window, the panoramic window showing the city spread out before them. The dome of the Thebaid shone at him across the park, lit with soft milky light. He'd paid for that himself. It gave his apartment spectacular views.

Bennet leant on the case, hands on the wooden frame to take his weight. Joss watched him, smiling. "They're lovely. I like the heart scarab." Bennet pointed to the bloodstone scarab. He had taste. It was the best of the collection and something the curators at the Thebaid would covet. "Good carving."

"It's not bad." Joss moved away from the case and stood to take in the view across the park. He never tired of it. Had the air conditioning given up? The apartment was so airless. Bennet's reflection in the window glass looked unsure, murky somehow. "The view's nice from here."

It was all the invitation Bennet needed to join him. "Am I keeping you from doing something else?"

"Not especially. Why?" It hadn't been strictly true. It had been the first weekend for years that Joss hadn't lorded it at one of the many bars in downtown Sais, in the area where most of the gay population gathered, when he hadn't come home with some willing and beautiful young man to share pleasure with… but then, maybe things hadn't been so different, after all.

"It's what you said about me being a kid. I guess I'm in the way."

Transparent as glass.

Joss had turned away from the view and had put his hands on Bennet's shoulders. Beyond him, the bedroom door had lurked, a siren call both he and Bennet could hear. Joss had smiled. "You really are the most dreadful tease, Bennet," he had said, and kissed him.

And so he was lost, he supposed. Then and forever.

That's how it began.

Funny, but when you start out on something like that; you think you know how it will end, tomorrow or the next day. You watch long slender hands move over a husk of dry bone and linen, six thousand years dead, and you listen to the wonder and delight in his voice when he realises what's lying beneath his hands, what knowledge and secrets lie under his probing fingers. And you think all those weeks of mild flirtation are leading up to something significant after all, that they're leading to a beautiful young man trying his wings and you're going to be the one to help him spread them wide. Of course, it will only be until tomorrow or the next day, or the day after that, and then it will be as empty as that linen-wrapped husk and you'll see the next one to catch your eye, to flirt with, to spread wings with.

That's how they always are. That's how it's always been. So you start out on something where you don't think beyond tomorrow or the next day, but then suddenly there's a day after that, and a day after that, and you don't see the ending. Or it's a different ending, defying your experience and expectations. Because this one isn't like any of the others. This one has sticking power. This one doesn't leave.

This is the one you don't want to leave.

And that's something that has never happened before and you thought never would. The affection you felt for him, overlying the sexual attraction, catches you by surprise, laughs at you, and your pretensions and your sophistication, and transforms itself into something deeper without you even realising it's happening until it's done. One morning you wake with him curled up warm beside you, breathing so softly that only your heart can hear it, and you never want it to be any other way.

It's quite the trick he pulled on you; flirting with you over the silent witness offered by the long-dead man in the ornate linen bandages. Getting into the big empty space that was the centre of you and that couldn't be filled with playing at archaeology by day and dancing away every night, or by being the rich man, or the art patron, or any other of a couple of dozen ways you had of hiding. He took you by surprise, and with the soldier's skill that was his inheritance, he made the most of it, infiltrating every corner of the space, setting his forces with a tenacity a siege couldn't dislodge. He was clever about it, letting you teach him how to please and give. And he was generous about it, giving you the freedom to roam when he wasn't there and to come back again when he was.

You can't help but come back. What started out as his admiring the rich, sophisticated, older man inducting him into pleasure and you being flattered by a young man's lust, has changed somehow. You never thought there was much more to life than lust and pleasure, because until he came, you'd never found more and you thought you were too old, jaded and cynical for love. But he was truly clever about it, and while you taught him about pleasing and giving, he taught you about love and devotion, and because he was hungry for it and sating himself in you, he opened you right up for more. And he was heart-generous about it, being there, quiet and steadfast even when you roamed, knowing it meant nothing, and you'd be back because he'd filled that space and no one else could.

It's as if you're standing in the Field of Reeds, eyes widening against the light, his hands on your shoulders; and when you ask what it all means, he holds up a scarab carved in jasper or cornelian or lapis lazuli, and he laughs as he holds your heart carefully in those long hands; holding it for you, safe.

You expected none of this. And before you can turn around, blinking with the surprise, there's soft breathing and new bone and warm flesh and hot blood in the husk, and the dead man's gone.

Until now. He's back now, nine years later.

The dead man. The husk.

Because that was how it began and this is how it ends. He's gone, leaving nothing behind him.

Not even a scrap of old linen pressed into new service to wrap the corpse.

CHAPTER FOUR

37 Secundus 7488: the dreadnought, *Gyrfalcon*

Two Hornet squads curved in to cut across the bow of the destroyer following in the *Gyrfalcon*'s wake, turning to chase after the dreadnought and heading for her aft landing bays. The other ships of the First Flotilla, the frigates and corvettes, were further back behind the destroyer *Patroklus*, lit only by their faint navigation lights and little more than greyish shapes against the bright star-field. Nearer to hand, only a few miles away, one of *Patroklus*'s own patrols curved in from the other side, heading back to their cramped quarters on the destroyer.

It hadn't been a joint patrol. The small squadron on the destroyer rarely flew patrols with the *Gyrfalcon*'s own, although if it came to a pitched battle and the entire First Flotilla was committed, they flew and died together then. Under less terminal circumstances, there was a more-or-less friendly rivalry, characterised on the *Gyrfalcon*'s side with a kindly pity. The poor sods on the *Patroklus* weren't dreadnought pilots. Although, First Lieutenant Flynn conceded in one of his more generous and egalitarian moods, he supposed even a lesser pilot could aspire to greatness.

"But not, of course, reach it," he said to his best friend after they'd brought their squads into *Gyrfalcon*'s cavernous starboard bay, dismissed their pilots, given the obligatory report to their captain that 'nothing is happening, Sim, and it's boring, boring, and did I say boring?' and were settling into the Officers' Club for a quiet drink before dinner.

"Mmmmm," Cruz said, concentrating on the big plasma screen set into the wall.

Flynn gave the screen an idle glance. They were an intrusive and bad idea, he said, adding he'd rather take the time to be quiet and relax after a patrol.

Cruz's mouth opened into a perfect O, before tilting up into a smile. "Quiet. Certainly sounds like you, Flynn."

"Serious, here."

Really, ladies should not snort like that. It wasn't elegant. Cruz, when this was pointed out, snorted again. "The only time you're ever quiet is when you've been gagged with your own flight jacket and we've jammed your helmet on backwards over the top to muffle the squealing."

Flynn opened his mouth to protest, and closed it again without speaking. Cruz might have been right, once. Before the *Gyrfalcon* had been commandeered by the Shield Regiment, before he had met Shield Captain Bennet or brought him back from the infiltration mission on T18 and all that had followed, before he had loved Bennet. Before all that, Flynn would have been very loud indeed if he wasn't the focus of every heart and mind around him. Not now. Now he often let inattention slide.

For a minute or two, there was silence. Cruz had turned her attention back to the large screen and Flynn couldn't find enough motivation to be annoyed her focus wasn't where it should be. On him.

The internal vid-channel screened ship's news, items on everything from the orders of the day to the games played in the *Gyrfalcon*'s own Tierce league—Flynn and Cruz had just cruised home in the ship's mixed Tierce championship, defeating a hotly favoured security team—motivational messages from Commander Caeden who at least could be inspirational, or, the gods help them all, from Colonel Quist, who was Galactic Master at inspiring terror.

But on the hour, every hour, the screen broadcast the main headlines from AlbionNews. Flynn turned a lacklustre eye to the screen in time to see a reporter's enthusiastic announcement that President Maitland's daughter was engaged to the son of a major industrialist whose main investments were in power generation and military equipment.

Cruz grimaced. "Sold to the highest bidder, poor girl. The President's been raking in political donations there for years. Payback time."

Flynn shrugged. The screen flickered onto the next item. One word had him looking up with more interest. Nathan, star political reporter for AlbionNews, stood on the Praesidium steps reporting on a recent election in one of the colonies "… the Khartz colonial administration has now formally handed over the reins to a new government dominated by Phoenix League representatives. PL chairman, Seigneur Vines of Thorn, will attend the investiture of the new government next week. This is, of course, the third colony in this round of local elections to vote to install a PL government, although only on settlement planet Thorn, the birthplace of Phoenix, does the League have an absolute majority and can govern without having to negotiate a coalition with the smaller parties in the colonial legislature. Thorn is, of course, the site of a major incursion from the Maess a generation ago…"

"I was born on Thorn," Flynn said.

Cruz gave him a modicum of attention. "You were? I thought you were Macedonian."

"My mother was. The gods alone know who my father was. Not Macedonian, though. He must have been white, given my colouring. My mother came back to Albion when I was two, after the Maess attack on Thorn. I don't know what happened to him. She would never talk about him, but I've always thought he must have died in the attack." Flynn shrugged, losing interest again. He hadn't been back to his native colony since the day he'd left it. He had no memories of it.

On screen, Nathan wittered on about the impact on Albion's revenues with a major settlement planet and three colonial governments now in the Phoenix League camp, all elected on a ticket that included a reduction in the proportion of taxes handed over to Albion to fund the war with the Maess. Cruz returned her attention to Nathan's smooth segue to a think-piece on the Phoenix League's policies for a smaller military machine. Flynn looked away and focused on his drink. He only looked up again when Cruz made another of those unladylike snorts.

"Bloody Phoenix League would yell loud enough for help if the Maess came at them. Let 'em try saving their colony by lobbing a tax referendum at a drone. Idiots." She sighed. "Seems to me all we do these days is fall back while the Maess advance. If we give up much more space, we'll all end up sitting on each other's laps."

"Huh?"

She waved a hand at the screen, where Nathan had given way to his sidekick, Alexis, reporting on the loss of another planet to the Maess. The news cameras were set up at the main spaceport on Albion, filming the arrival of the refugee ship from whatever nearby world had been used as a quarantine staging post. A group of infantry walked past the cameras, turning their heads away.

"They've released the Telnos evacuees from quarantine. Remember it? We just walked away from Telnos and let the Maess take it. A few weeks ago now." Cruz's eyes were shadowed. "We're not winning, Flynn."

"If I remember right, it was small beer. It wasn't a legal colony or anything. I mean, it was only a few hundred farmers, wasn't it? Not like giving up a settlement planet—Cissante, say, or Woodstock, or Thorn. Or even one of their colonies. We couldn't afford to lose those. Maybe the bosses back home decided Telnos wasn't worth it."

"I don't think we can afford to give up any of them." Cruz took a swig of her drink and sank in her chair until she slouched as much as Flynn did. She didn't look happy.

Flynn let her be for a few minutes until AlbionNews gave way to internal *Gyrfalcon* messages. "Hey! It's us!"

The wide screen showed yesterday's moment of supreme triumph when he'd trounced the security team on the Tierce court. He admired the dexterity with which he twisted in mid-air to take the ball, even as Dafed, definitely the best player in the opposition, reached for it, and the graceful way he slammed it into the topmost hole in the court's wall, the Trinity, to take the game and the championship. Cruz had helped, of course.

"We were good," Cruz said, perking up.

Flynn grinned. "You were good. I was immense."

Cruz just laughed as the coverage of the most important thing to happen on the ship for months switched to more mundane ship business to do with prosecuting a long and occasionally boring war. "Shame the commander couldn't get to the game. He usually does. He even missed ship inspection last week. We haven't seen much of him for weeks if you stop to think about it. Quist's done all of it."

"Do you think Quist carried out a secret coup to take over the *Gyrfalcon* and murdered the commander?"

"And stuffed the body in a closet somewhere on the command deck?"

"Don't be daft! There'll be a regulation somewhere forbidding service personnel keeping bodies in their closets on the grounds it's untidy. She'd never breach regs. She'll have pushed him out of an airlock."

"You could be right." Cruz laughed and nodded at the screen, and its bland announcement that the commander would be off-ship the following week. "They may not know how true that is."

"Wonder where he's off to?" Flynn stretched and got comfortable.

"He goes back for meetings with the politicians, doesn't he? Poor sod." Cruz shrugged. "Don't get too comfy, Flynn. We should get in some Tierce practice before dinner."

Flynn's mild curiosity about the commander's comings and goings melted away in the face of more immediate things. "What? What the heck for? The season's over. We won."

"And I'm going to make damn sure we win next season, too. This is no time for slacking. We've a reputation to uphold."

Flynn grinned. "Hadn't you noticed? Mine's not the upholding kind."

"Good game, Flynn, Cruz."

Flynn started. He hadn't noticed Bridge Captain Omar sneaking up on him. It shouldn't be possible to have missed the man's approach—Flynn didn't have to look up to many people, but Omar was six-foot-six if he was an inch. He had to be a Bridge Officer. He wouldn't fit in a Hornet without being concertina-ed in.

Cruz glanced at Flynn, her mouth making a kind of pout and her eyebrows working overtime to convey her surprise. "Yeah, well, the best team won."

It wasn't usual for Bridge Officers to join pilots in the OC. The *Gyrfalcon*'s officers tended to work and socialise within their functional groups: techs with techs, pilots with pilots, Bridge with Bridge. Relations between the groups were cordial and easy, but not fulsome, based on a mutual respect. But you lived, ate and drank with the people you were closest to, the ones who watched your back out there when there was nothing between you and the cold of space but the thin metal shell of a Hornet's cockpit. More than that, Omar was just like Commander Caeden: well born, a scion of one of Albion's first families. He didn't have a lot in common with the likes of Cruz and Flynn.

Omar folded himself into a seat. "That's not what Colonel Quist says."

"I thought she looked sour when she handed over the cup." Cruz gave Flynn one more quirked eyebrow before allowing them to return to their natural position. "She didn't have money on Daved and Lily, did she?"

"Regulations," Flynn said. "Remember the regulations. They're tattooed on the woman's heart. In microscopic writing, of course, as befits so small and insignificant an organ. The Regs discourage wagers."

"Oh, she doesn't gamble." Omar was ill at ease, shifting in his chair as if something was poking into him. "At least... not with me, anyway. I know she and the commander have what they call tactical discussions. They toss to choose a team to support for the game, and then they discuss the chances. I've never seen money change hands."

Flynn stared. "I suppose tossing the coin could be exciting. If you squint."

Omar hunched one shoulder. "Whatever. Anyhow, the commander's not been up for it, so Quist picked on me to have the last discussion of the season. I won. She lost."

This unusual confidence from a Bridge officer merited a follow-up. And Cruz was just the girl to do it. "It has to one of the drawbacks of Bridge duty, having impassioned discussions with Colonel Quist about our brilliance. We were just saying the commander seemed a bit pre-occupied lately. We've not seen much of him for a few weeks."

Omar straightened up, looking relieved. "He has been distant recently. I didn't work it out myself until I saw today's news lines. He's not been himself for a while."

There was a short silence while the Flynn and Cruz exchanged more glances and raised eyebrows at each other, and Omar sipped at his drink.

"Are you going to tell us, or are you expecting Flynn to go and look it up?" Cruz asked at last. "I should warn you he only reads the more scurrilous news lines, and that's just because they have pictures of women with no clothes on."

"He can read?"

"The slackly hanging jaw helps. It gives me enough space to stick my tongue out of the corner of my mouth while I work out the big words." Flynn frowned. Why had Omar started to hint something, and then shied off? He'd handed out his hint, and didn't look disposed to say anymore. Time to push. "Assume we're too illiterate to go and scan all the news lines, and too pushed for time anyway, when we don't know what we're looking for. Why not just tell us?"

Omar hesitated, looking at his drink, not them. Then he shrugged. "I thought you might have picked up on it. You're right. The commander's been distant for the last few weeks, just not himself. I mean, he's not exactly jolly at the best of times, but he's approachable. But lately he's been like a block of ice. Colonel Quist's been covering for him, to give him some time to himself." Omar hesitated again, and Flynn had to fight back the urge to kick him, to get him just to cough it all out. "I didn't see the first announcement. Astonishing, when you think who the commander is. I'd have thought the media would have made a real splash of it. He must have used some influence to keep it out of the news lines. They only seem to have picked up on it now the quarantine's over for the rest of the Telnos refugees." Omar tossed back the last dregs of his drink. "The notice of the memorial service next month was in this morning's obituaries."

Years ago, the first time he'd ever done a simulated crash landing, the plunge down felt like it had left Flynn's stomach behind in the upper atmosphere. It had been hard to draw breath. Just like now.

He put down his drink, almost surprised to note his hands were steady. "Bennet?"

"I wondered if you knew." Omar pulled at his jacket, tugging it first one way and then the other. He'd probably thought long and hard before betraying what he'd learned about the commander. The command staff were as protective of each other as the pilots were of their squadron mates.

What instinct had brought Omar to tell them, of all people? Flynn had been so discreet it had been downright unnatural. He didn't think many people on the ship knew. Only Cruz, of course. Powell had guessed but he was long gone, transferring to the Third Flotilla as soon as they got back into Albion space from the T18 mission. Omar couldn't have known.

"No." Cruz's hand settled over Flynn's, warm and comforting. "We hadn't heard. I don't think many of us read the obituaries."

"I know you were friendly with him when he was here for that mission and Flynn gave him the ride home from T18. I thought you'd want to know." Omar paused, looking from one to the other. "I didn't have a lot to do with him, except for the morning he spent on the bridge with the commander. He seemed okay."

Flynn swallowed against the lump in his throat. He had to do it twice, and when he spoke, his tone was flat, wooden. "He was. He was okay. What happened?"

"I don't know the details. The obit only gave the time and place for the service."

"Killed in action?"

"I think so. I'm sorry. I hoped I wouldn't be the one to tell you, but I suppose it's not likely the commander will say anything. He's a very private man and Quist's certainly the only one he's spoken to. But when I realised what was up... I remembered how well you'd all got on with Shield Captain Bennet and I thought you should know." Omar raised his glass, grimacing when he saw it was empty. "Will you pass the word? Discreetly."

Cruz had liked Bennet, too. Not as much as Flynn had, maybe, but still. She nodded. "Yeah. Sure."

Omar stood up to leave. "Thanks, Cruz."

"Thanks for telling us. We appreciate it." Cruz watched him go, and turned back to Flynn. She grimaced at him, her mouth turning down.

Flynn scrubbed his hands over his face and looked up. "I think I'll pass on tonight's practice, Cruz, if it's all the same to you."

"Flynn—"

"No. Leave it. I really don't want to talk about it. I just…" Flynn stopped, shrugged. He hunched over to get control, hollowed out to the backbone. "I think I'll just head on back to my quarters."

"You don't want to be on your own!"

"But I do," this strange, calm Flynn said. "Really, Cruz, I do. I'm fine."

"Flynn. Please."

Flynn stood up. "I'll see you later."

"Call me if you—"

"Sure. Sure I will." Flynn smiled at her and left, head high.

But of course, he wouldn't call. Never had, never would.

It was easy to find now he knew what to look for. It took Flynn about two minutes, sitting hunched over the keyboard of the monitor in his quarters.

A small notice, announcing the time and place of the Midnight Watch, to be held on 4 Tertius. Not the big Temple of Thebes in the city, Flynn noted, but what had to be the local family church in Mendes, the wealthy coastal suburb of Sais. The notice didn't say very much.

'In loving memory of Bennet, much-loved partner of Joss… '

Bennet hadn't talked much about Joss. Enough that Flynn knew Joss was older than Bennet, that they'd been together since just after Bennet turned eighteen, that their relationship, at least on Joss's side, was an open one. But having said that much in the cramped cockpit of the Mosquito, fighting their way up out of the atmosphere of T18, Bennet hadn't mentioned his lover again.

Bennet had said that although he and Joss had that arrangement, a free and easy 'let's not be too lonely when we're apart' arrangement, Bennet had never taken advantage of it before, not until Flynn. So maybe Joss was a better-loved partner of

Bennet than Bennet was the much-loved partner of Joss? It sounded unbalanced, Joss wanting his cake and eating it, and Bennet constantly cutting him an extra slice. Flynn couldn't see why Joss would want anyone else when he had Bennet, or why Bennet allowed it.

Who knew? Who could know anything going on inside someone else's head or someone else's life? All anyone could go on was what they said and what could be interpreted from what they did.

'… beloved elder son of Caeden and Meriel… '

Bennet had spoken of his mother with obvious affection. Nothing to worry about there, no conflict left unresolved to haunt the living. Flynn was less certain about the commander. Bennet had talked about that too in the Mosquito on the way back up from T18. Cramped and in pain, he'd talked about anything to take his mind off his discomfort, even his difficulties with his father. Of course, Bennet had still been discreet, and it wasn't until later Flynn had put all the clues together and worked out that the angry, disappointed father outraged at his son's homosexuality was the same man as the grave, measured, respected and revered Commander Caeden.

But he thought it had ended all right. He thought the commander and Bennet had reached some sort of understanding while Bennet was on the *Gyrfalcon*. There had been the blessing Caeden had bestowed, just before Bennet left to infiltrate T18, his hand on Bennet's bowed head. That had to mean something significant. And when it was all over and Bennet was going back to his own ship, the commander had come down to the starboard deck to say goodbye and he'd hugged his son in front of all of them. That was an unusually emotional thing to do for the rather remote man who commanded the *Gyrfalcon*, an unexpected thing, and Bennet had looked surprised. But pleased.

So that was all right then.

When the Mosquito had gone, Caeden had looked at Flynn as if he could see through the solidity of flesh and bone to the tiny shield clutched in Flynn's hand and the ache in Flynn's chest.

Perhaps they'd had that ache in common. But the commander had turned away without saying anything, then or since.

Beloved son, beloved lover. Yes. They had that in common.

'... brother to Althea, Natalia and Liam, and uncle to Sairy...'

Bennet had mentioned a brother, years younger than him. What was it he'd said? Something to Nairn, wasn't it, about Liam interrogating him about the jobs he'd done for the Shield Regiment, and there'd been amusement, affection and pride in Bennet's voice. Yes, he was fond of his brother, at least. Odd he hadn't mentioned the sisters. Flynn glanced at the screen again, to remind himself. Althea and Natalia. One of them had to be Sairy's mother.

Bennet had been different things to different people. The funeral notice was for the Bennet who had been the much-loved partner, the Bennet who was a beloved son, or brother, or uncle. But there was nothing in there about being the first and only person Flynn had ever loved. He added that for himself.

The Bennet who'd taught him how to make love to a man rather than just have sex with one, the Bennet who'd kissed him and held him in the storeroom on the starboard deck, the Bennet who'd slipped the tiny silver Shield into his hand as they said goodbye—that was the Bennet who'd loved him. What Flynn didn't know was if he had been much-loved, or better-loved, or just a little bit, let's-not-be-lonely loved.

Now he would never know.

Colonel Quist was not inclined to let Flynn through to see the commander. "This isn't a good time, Lieutenant. I'll deal with it."

Flynn kept his head down and his tone respectful. "With respect, ma'am, it's personal. I won't take up much of his time, I promise, but I think... I think he'd want to know this." He looked up to let her see something of himself in the glance.

Quist gave him a long, considering look. He endured it as best he could.

"I don't ask for stuff like this as a rule, ma'am. I wouldn't bother him if I didn't think I had to."

Quist was hard but fair, Flynn would give her that much. She had to know this was about Bennet. "I'll ask him. But I can't guarantee he'll say yes. This really isn't a good time. Wait here." She must have been persuasive. It was a few minutes before she came back out of the bridge Office, but she held the door and nodded to Flynn to go in. "In you go, Lieutenant. And this had better be good."

She ushered him in and let the door slide closed behind him. Caeden sat at his desk, working through piles of datapads and reports. It was a minute or two before he looked up.

Flynn came to attention. "Sir."

"At ease." Caeden frowned. "Yes, Flynn?"

"Sir... I'm sorry to bother you, sir, but there I've just seen the news lines, and I wanted..." Flynn hesitated again and shook his head. Just spit it out, man. "I wanted to know if it's true."

"Bennet."

"Yes, sir."

The commander was always serious and reserved. Distant. He looked more than that now. He'd lost weight and crows' feet pulled at the corners of his eyes. As he picked up a framed holopic from his desk, his mouth thinned and turned down. Just for a second, Flynn thought he was going to be blown out of there, but Caeden put the holopic down again and waved Flynn towards the conference table in the centre of the room. "Sit down, Flynn."

"Sir?"

"Take a seat." Caeden got up, as Flynn looked at him in faint bemusement. "Do you want a coffee?"

Flynn shook his head. He sat stiff in the chair. "No, thank you, sir."

"You won't mind if I have one?" Caeden poured himself a cup

from the heated carafe on a side table.

"No, sir. Is it true, sir?"

"Yes." Caeden joined Flynn at the table. He put his hands around the mug as though to warm them.

Flynn let out his breath in a long sigh. He had to look away until he got it under control. "I don't want to intrude. It's just... I liked Bennet a lot, sir. I can't tell you how sorry I am."

"You don't need to. I should have thought to tell you, Flynn. I'm sorry." The commander's mouth twisted into a wry grin. "I should have remembered that Bennet... that you and he... well, even if you are the most troublesome pilot in the entire First Flotilla, I should have remembered you could claim friendship with him. I'm sorry for not thinking of that." The grin widened, became less forced and more as if the memory amused him. "He certainly fought me hard enough over you and that damned T18 mission."

Flynn nodded. "He told me you had some interesting discussions, sir."

"You have that effect on people." Caeden sipped at the coffee. "Bennet out-manoeuvred me about the mission, all the way down the line. But he was right about you. You saved him then and you gave me the chance... well. I'm grateful, and I should have remembered."

Flynn had lived through one excruciatingly embarrassing apology from the commander after T18. He didn't need another one. "The news line didn't say very much. I figured it was the Telnos thing last month?"

"Yes." Caeden put down the cup, careful not to spill it. His voice was very controlled, but Flynn could hear the shaking underneath it. Caeden shook at the same frequency, the one keyed into shock and grief, that he did himself. "The Maess attacked the landing area. Bennet's people were holding it, to get the last of the Infantry and colonists out. A fighter shelled the area as cover for advancing ground troops. You can guess the rest." He stopped, swallowed, and a sort of greyness came over him.

58

Flynn most certainly could.

"It wasn't an infiltration raid and they weren't wearing shield-suits. They were far more vulnerable on the ground than usual. As I understand it, they still had tracer units built into the helmets of their battledress. Bennet's... Bennet's stopped." The commander stopped too, forced into silence.

Flynn flinched. That was sharp and it hurt. He put a hand into his pocket and brought out the shield. He clenched his fingers around it until they ached. "Thank you for telling me, sir. I won't bother you any further. I know... I know..." He opened his fist, looking down at the shield, curving protective fingers over it. It hurt to give this up. But it was the right thing to do. Flynn took a deep breath and held out his hand. "Bennet gave me this when he left. I thought you might like to have it."

Caeden stared for a moment at the tiny silver badge. His fingers trembled as badly as Flynn's when he took it.

"It belongs to his family really, sir, not to me." Flynn got up. "Thank you for seeing me. Please accept my condolences, both you and your family."

"Flynn."

Flynn was almost at the door, but he paused and turned, obedient to the note of command. Caeden pushed back his chair and joined him. Flynn waited, enduring the scrutiny. His eyes stung and he couldn't quite get things into focus.

"Thank you, Flynn." Caeden held out the shield. "But Bennet gave this to you, as a keepsake. I'm certain his mother, if she were here, would like you to keep it to remember him by."

"I won't forget!" Flynn said, on a choke.

"No. There's no comfort in forgetfulness." Caeden put the shield back into Flynn's hand and closed Flynn's fingers over it. "But thank you, Flynn. I appreciate it."

Flynn's lips shaped the words, but no sound came out.

"Yes, I'm sure." Caeden forced a slight smile.

Flynn nodded, unable to speak.

Caeden put a hand on Flynn's shoulder. "He told me at T18 that you were the only one of my pilots he'd have in Shield. I don't think he could have offered you a greater compliment. So keep it safe. It was precious to him, and he wouldn't have given it to you lightly."

Because, as they both knew, Bennet never did anything significant lightly.

CHAPTER FIVE

39 Secundus 7488: Sais City

It was several weeks before Joss was able to go back to the Thebaid Institute.

He didn't go out. He didn't have the energy for it. If Meriel hadn't taken to calling on him every other day, he wouldn't have done much eating. He ignored the meals the maid prepared for him, but Meriel seemed to find some outlet for her grief in mothering her dead son's lover. Whenever she visited, she sat with him to make him eat. He was too apathetic to argue. It tasted of ash and dust.

He'd roused when Meriel told him what Caeden had done to keep Bennet's death out of the news lines. She'd meant it to comfort, but instead it irked him that Caeden's focus there wasn't on Bennet as himself—not the scholar, or the Shield warrior or, the gods forbid, Joss's lover—but on his status as Caeden's son. Joss had tried to write an obituary to put things back in the proper perspective, make his own claim paramount. He got as far as *much-loved partner of Joss* when he had to stop, sitting with an open datapad for hours, not getting past that first little phrase. Meriel had finished it. She had cried as she wrote, scored it all out, and wrote again, cried again.

He supposed it had been cathartic for her. There still was no catharsis for him.

The day he found enough energy to go out, he walked to the Thebaid, across the park from the empty apartment. The security man at the main entrance had the usual respectful greeting for him and he nodded back. The huge, man-high head from the colossus of Ramesses Usermaatre sat where it always had, on the first landing of the main staircase, the millennia-old carved granite face smooth, serene and perfect beneath the double crown, supercilious in its immutability. He walked through the mummy room, his gaze flickering over the decorated coffins, the amulets, the bandaged bodies.

Everything familiar and normal.

How was it, nothing seemed changed when in reality, everything had changed? Even the laboratory on the seventh floor was different. It had been his for years, his haven. Now it was quiet with loss and grief. It smelled musty. A film of dust overlaid scanner and table, and the pile of datapads on his desk were grey with it.

He ran a finger through it. Mummy dust.

He didn't even pretend to work. He stood beside the trestles where Amthoth's mummy had lain in its cartonnage coffin, everything coming to a halt again. The laboratory was haunted. Images of Bennet came with so much clarity, Joss could have been Amthoth, lying in his coffin with Bennet's hands resting on his empty chest.

There was no peace there. Maybe the library, where once he'd looked up from reading the Lexus Scrolls and found himself under the intense gaze of the Dean's favoured scholar. Maybe there.

He ran into the Dean, as he came out of the lift on the ground floor. Bachman looked astonished, and then uncomfortable, coming to shake hands. "My dear Joss, I'm so sorry. So very, very sorry. How are you?"

Joss nodded, marvelling at the scope of human reaction, the continuum along which you could plot people according to how much they'd loved Bennet. The Dean was sorry, Liam was grieving, and Meriel was broken-hearted, while Joss, himself, was wretched and desolate.

"Such a waste. One of my best students." Bachman let go of Joss's hand with a final pat. "I saw the notice for the Midnight Watch."

"Yes. I'm arranging it with the family. It will be at the local family temple in Mendes." Joss's voice sounded rusty, even to his own ears. He cleared his throat and managed a tight smile. "They're reclaiming him, you see. He wouldn't care about a Midnight Watch."

Bachman inched away. "Well, I... I suppose it's natural for a family to want some sort of ceremony to mark... to celebrate Bennet's life. He could have achieved so much! Such a loss to scholarship and to us all."

"Yes."

"I'd like to be there. And so would many of the faculty."

Joss nodded again, the way he'd just nodded agreement when Meriel asked him about a service for Bennet. Whatever they wanted. It didn't matter. Except, he realised now as the Dean murmured further condolences and platitudes, it would be a Theban affair, a Caeden family affair; another reclamation of Bennet back from reality into a chilly perfection that tried to erase the parts of Bennet's life they didn't approve of. This, too, was for the son of the commander.

But not for Joss's lover.

Bachman though, would be welcomed by Caeden and family. He represented the respectable aspect to Bennet's life. Nothing there to cause scandal or offence.

"My dear Joss," Bachman protested, when Joss said as much. He looked uneasy as he patted Joss on the arm and let him go at last.

Joss turned into the library. When he'd seen Bennet for the very first time in here... which library carrel had it been? Joss stared at them. This one. He'd been using this one when he'd first seen Bennet. It was vacant. Joss settled into the chair and raised his head to look over the wooden barrier between it and the desk opposite. No Bennet there today, staring at him with the intent, expectant expression on his face that had intrigued Joss so much.

No Bennet anywhere, now.

Joss was almost alone in the library but for one of the Thebaid's tutors sitting beside a student discussing harvest records following the first landfall on Albion. They kept their voices low to avoid disturbing him. Letting him remember, unencumbered.

The library had seen some seminal moments in their relationship. Significant. Life-changing.

He hadn't only seen Bennet here for the first time, but it had been here… Joss twisted in his chair to look about him. Yes. In that book bay there, by the west window. That's where Commander Caeden had found them. If not quite in flagrante delicto, then not far off it. Bennet had sought him out for comfort after telling Caeden he didn't intend taking a place at the Military Academy. His poor Bennet had been reaping that particular whirlwind ever since. Caeden had not taken it well. So far, though, Bennet had stood firm in the face of Caeden's fury and disapproval. Bennet had quite a backbone, even at only just eighteen. Caeden should have been proud, not complain that SSI graduates were usually non-combatants and it only counted in the military if you were being shot at. Not a concept Joss adhered to— keeping Bennet safe behind a desk was the only thing to reconcile him to SSI and a military career at all.

The debacle when Caeden found them… Bennet had been kissing him, there was no possibility of pretending innocence and Caeden had been incandescent with rage. Bennet had stood up to his father well until Caeden, far more versed in the art of warfare than his son, landed the killer blow. What was it he'd said?

What you want, what you are… filthy and disgusting… You make me sick. And so help me if you've ever touched Liam, I'll tear you apart. I don't want your kind anywhere near the children.

Something like that. Something designed to maim and hurt. It had maimed and hurt Bennet.

His poor Bennet had lost that battle, but there was some consolation in knowing Caeden hadn't won it. Joss had. Bennet had walked out of the library with Joss and never gone back.

He pushed the memory away before it could fester. It didn't matter now. No one was the victor now.

He didn't look at the Lexus Scrolls. Instead, he reread the obituary he and Meriel had written. The Midnight Watch might reclaim Caeden's version of Bennet, but the public notice of it had made Joss's claim paramount. Caeden would be forced into some sort of acceptance, whether he liked it or not.

'… much-loved partner of Joss…'

He stabbed his forefinger at the screen, jabbing at the five little words. His, not Caeden's. Never Caeden's. Hadn't been for years. Bennet was his.

The burst of energy drained away as quickly as it came, left him feeling tired and sick. Anger and resentment didn't make him less wretched, but it might just pull others closer to his end of that strange continuum of loss.

Then it mightn't be so lonely.

After the Battle of the Library, Joss hadn't seen Caeden again for three years, not until the day Bennet had graduated from the Strategic Studies Institute.

If his graduation from the Thebaid the year before had a been a triumph of academic excellence and a celebration of scholarship, Bennet's graduation at SSI was all crisply ironed uniforms and gold braid and a band playing military marches. SSI kept it short, not as rigid with ceremony as the Academy passing out parade immediately preceding it. No sword of honour here, no chief cadet to be feted, but all the same the military machine didn't want to lose the twelve men and women who'd survived the rigours of SSI. Not every SSI graduate took his or her commission—a fleeting hope Joss had clung to until the very last minute—and the top brass sat through another militaristic ceremony to show their support and encouragement to those who did. Caeden sat with a bevy of Fleet Commanders on one side of the Supreme Commander, with several infantry generals and one imposing Field Marshall on the other. General Martens of the Shield Regiment sat apart, austere in black and silver. As Joss said rather wistfully to Meriel, one direct hit and the Maess could have won the war.

Joss endured the short ceremony with Bennet's mother and siblings. With her usual ruthless charm, Meriel had appropriated him when he arrived at the joint Academy-SSI parade ground and swept him up with her into the VIP seats. When the graduating class appeared, her hand gripped Joss's arm.

"Good grief!" She turned her head to look at Joss and smiled. She had a wicked smile. "Caeden'll have a fit!"

Joss finally abandoned hope of persuading Bennet not to take his commission. "That's probably Bennet's intention."

Alone in the graduating class, Bennet had worn Shield Regiment uniform. He looked tall and too thin in all the black uniform, and far too young to be offered up on the altar of the war with the Maess, but he wore the ceremonial sword Joss had designed for him and his expression was solemn as he took Shield Oath. When the ceremony was over, Meriel gathered Joss up with her brood and swept him off to the stand where the top brass and the graduates were. Caeden stood beside another Fleet Commander, looking at Bennet with a most peculiar expression on his face, as if dismay was warring with something else. Who knew what?

Joss himself had felt lost. He'd wanted so desperately that Bennet wouldn't take an active, fighting commission. He'd lost the battle.

But maybe not the war. Not yet.

Taking Shield didn't change anything. Caeden's expression throughout the ceremony had been as stony as those of the leaders who'd led their people to the Albion from Earth, and who'd immortalised themselves in almost indestructible granite.

"He thinks I chose Shield for all the wrong reasons," Bennet had explained later. "I'll be home often, you see, between missions. Far more often than if I'd gone into Fleet, the way he wanted. He thinks that's selfish of me."

Bennet's gesture wasn't enough, then.

But Bennet made it anyway, despite the war of attrition Joss waged, despite Joss begging him to stay at home and be a scholar at the Institute where he belonged. "I don't know why you're bothering," he'd said—how many times? Dozens of times. "It won't make him any happier about you."

"It's not for him. It's for me. It's what I want to do. It means I can do something to help stop the war and spend lots of time at home with you. It's the best of both worlds, Joss."

And then the scene changed, moved forward. Bennet wasn't a sweet-faced boy anymore, but twenty-four years old, more than six years Joss's lover, more than three years of working on 'jobs' behind the lines that he never talked about, but sometimes returned from, looking twenty years older than Joss, eyes haunted. This time, Bennet had almost not come home at all, and Joss was rehashing old arguments, frightened, saying it repeatedly. More than dozens of times.

"I want you out, Bennet. For the gods' sake, love, you nearly died!"

Bennet had shifted uncomfortably in the hospital bed, his hand on the new bionic rib they'd implanted the week before and they were having such trouble with. "But I didn't. I could get killed crossing the road to the Thebaid, Joss. Nothing's safe. But this is what I want to do. It's what I have to do."

"He's not even here. He's not even here to impress."

Bennet had sighed. "Please, Joss, give it a rest. How many times do I have to tell you, it's got nothing to do with him? It's my life, and I'm living it the way I like."

"Having it all."

"Yes. Isn't that the way you like it?"

Sure it was. Only once you'd got it all, you sometimes wondered what it was you'd got and why the hell you'd wanted it in the first place.

SECTION TWO:
TELNOS

31 Primus – 04 Tertius 7488

.

CHAPTER SIX

31 - 34 Primus 7488: Telnos

Every breath, every intake of air, felt like it scraped out the inside of his skull.

Someone had been using his head as an anvil, the hammer pounding out pain and agony with every heartbeat. He couldn't move. Everything hurt.

When he opened his eyes, eyelids tacky and sticky, the light was the dark purple of dusk and shadows gathered beneath the trees. He was pinned down. Something leaden lay over him, something bonelessly heavy, not able to take its own weight anymore. A leg draped over his the way a lover's might, an arm over his chest, something else crushing down his right shoulder. His right arm was numb. He pushed with his left hand at what he thought was pressing him down, protesting at what he thought was being demanded of him. He couldn't shift it. He closed his eyes again as a pair of drones marched past the human bodies piled chest high.

It hurt even to mumble.

"Not now, Joss."

The man's voice was so loud it shocked him awake. "Fuck, this one's alive!"

He couldn't get his eyes open. They were stuck, hurting. He reached up, his hand closing on air.

"Ifan! We've got a warm one!" Someone caught his hand. Held it. A woman, her tone sharp with alarm. Her voice boomed and pounded at Bennet like the hammer on the anvil. "Hell, these flies!"

More voices, closer and louder. Something tugging at him. It hurt.

It hurt.

"A Shield." Another man this time. The voice was in his ear almost. "Anyone else breathing?"

Something wet and lukewarm washed over his face. He couldn't get his hand free to push them away. He couldn't—

"Steady," the second man said in the darkness. "Steady. We've got to clear the blood away to see how bad it is. Anyone else, Alice?"

"No," the woman said. "Nothing."

And then he was lifted up, fireworks exploding in his head behind his tightly closed eyelids. Someone was moaning. Not close. A long way away.

"Shit," the second man said. "More than five years since I left the military and I'm still carrying a bloody officer."

When Bennet did manage to get his eyes open and keep them open, he was lying on a narrow bed in the lower half of a bunk. The upper level was only a couple of feet above his face. He stared up at wood slats, rough-cut, a pleasing golden brown colour. The knots made nice patterns, curved and interlinked, something to concentrate on while his mind, skittish and uncontrollable, flashed from image to image, thought to thought.

"Awake?"

He turned his head. The savage pain had faded to a dull ache, centred on his right temple.

"Ifan." The big man sitting beside the bed waved a hand at himself.

Bennet thought about it.

"It's my name." Ifan rolled his eyes. "You officers haven't improved any since my time. Thirsty?"

It would be safer not to nod. His mouth was dry. "Yes."

"Good. Don't try to move and I'll help you lift your head up. Got it?" Ifan slipped a hand under Bennet's neck and cradled the back of his head, supporting it up a couple of inches.

Even that little movement started the hammer beating at his temple, and a wave of nausea rushed over him. Ifan tipped water into his mouth when he opened it to complain. The water wasn't as cool as he'd like, but refreshing. Ifan let his head down again, slow and careful. After another minute or two, the hammers went away again and the dull ache came back.

"And you are?"

Bennet licked dry lips, grateful now for the water. "Bennet."

"Shield Captain?"

"Yes."

He squinted down at himself, trying to see the damage. His right shoulder was heavily bandaged and his arm felt odd, but he couldn't see anything else. Both legs were there, and he could move them, and he could lift and use his left hand.

"You've been out of it for a couple of days. Three, counting the one you must have spent at the landing site." Ifan settled back in his chair.

Bennet frowned.

"Telnos," Ifan said, helpfully. "You were evacuating the farmers, remember?"

"Yes." It was, quite suddenly, true, like someone switching on a light. Bennet did remember. "The Maess got here."

"They sure-as-fuck did. We were in a transport with a couple of infantry when they arrived. We didn't make it to the landing site—they blew the transport to hell, five miles short. By the time those of us who made it out of the transport got to the landing area, there wasn't a cutter in sight and the place was crawling with Maess drones."

"I got hit?"

"I guess so, yes."

Flashes of memory. Smoke and screaming. A man with a beard. A child whimpering with pain as her head lolled helplessly against Bennet's shoulder. A hand, half blown off, and his own hands wrapping the mutilations into reddening field dressings. Someone carrying a dead kid to a row of bodies. Nothing connecting, nothing linking one thing to another, but somehow they made some sense.

"I got left behind."

Rosie! Did Rosie get away with his people? Did she get them away safe? She must have done. No cutters, the man had said. Please the gods she got herself and everyone else out.

"Looks like it," Ifan said. "We waited until the Maess pulled out and went to see what we could salvage. We found you under a pile of bodies."

Bennet blinked at him. "Why were you looking?"

"We hoped we might find more weapons. We have some, but more wouldn't hurt. I've got your laser." Ifan looked away and back again, as if embarrassed. "And we could see there were some kids there. We thought we'd bury them, at least, and get them away from the flies."

Someone carrying a dead kid to a row of bodies... Ifan didn't have to be embarrassed about wanting to bury them. It wasn't anything to be ashamed of.

"You took a bad hit to the head. Luckily, for you, your helmet took the worst of it. How's your arm and shoulder?"

"Dead. Numb. I don't think I can do much with them."

"After we got you back here, I dug some shrapnel out of your shoulder, but I don't think I got it all. I could only carve out the bigger bits. There's probably some shit in there pressing on the nerves."

Bennet swallowed. Well, damn. "What is this place?"

"This is our mine, the Chryseis mine." There was a note of pride in the big man's voice.

"I thought we'd got all the miners."

Ifan grinned. "Let's just say the Chryseis isn't one of the bigger mines. Isn't one of the most legal, either. The troopers couldn't find us to tell us what the fuck was going on."

A small illegal mine. That meant a hidden mine, one it wouldn't be easy for the Maess to find. And it meant an unshielded mine, a more dangerous operation where the miners took out the solactinium as fast as they could do it before the radiation caused irreparable damage to their health. A mine the Maess couldn't touch. In an unshielded mine, a drone would close down within minutes, the radiation too much for its delicate circuitry. For once, the weaker human body could withstand more than its metal copies. They could be relatively safe here for a while, at least.

Bennet lifted his head and blinked to focus. A couple of Infantry troopers sat side by side on a bunk a few feet away, watching. One of them, female, raised a hand to acknowledge him. Beyond them were more men and women, clustered around a closed stove throwing out a welcome heat. They were somewhere underground, in the mine. Trailing wires had been pinned to rough walls hewn from the rock, feeding power to a row of overhead lights. The light nearest Bennet was dim, the bulb encased in dust. But this place had power. It had to have its own generator, probably solactinium-powered.

Ifan offered him more water. This time, the hammers weren't as merciless.

"How many?" he asked, when Ifan let his head down on the pillow again.

"Twelve. Me and eight of my people, you and the two troopers. The troopers have been doing what I've told 'em for the past couple of days, but they'll look to you now you're awake."

"You're ex-Infantry? Sergeant?"

"Corporal." Ifan rubbed at his nose, and added, "I never made sergeant, for some reason. I never understood why those officers had such a downer on me." He grinned at Bennet. "How'd you know?"

"You're not Shield. I'd know another Shield anywhere. And you'd never fit inside a Fleet Hornet. You have to have been a mudbrain."

Ifan grinned and touched his forehead in ironic salute.

"What have we got? Transports? Weapons?"

"We all have hand lasers and we have a couple of laser rifles we used for hunting. The troopers have their rifles. No transports. The drones blew up everything they could find at the landing site and the transport we were in was toast. All we have left are horses, and luckily I'd left them up here when the Infantry found us and got us out." Ifan looked over to the people at the other end of the living chamber. "We carried you back here."

"Thanks." It must have taken hours. The mines were at least twenty miles from the landing site. Bennet was grateful they hadn't just decided it was too much trouble to lug his carcass around.

Ifan shrugged, then added, in a low voice, the lament of every non-com and officer Bennet had ever met after a battle, "I lost too many people in the transport. Too many."

"Me too." Bennet might, technically, have been the one who was lost, but it cut both ways.

They wouldn't be back, Fleet or Infantry, or even Shield.

Albion had abandoned Telnos, and they wouldn't be back.

08 Secundus 7488

"We'd better find shelter," Ifan said. "You're getting the shakes."

Bennet wound his left hand into the horse's rough mane, his good hand, tightening his grip against the surges of light-headed dizziness. It was as bad as having a dose of Alrian influenza and about as debilitating. "I thought I'd be over the worst by now."

"Not a chance. It takes more than a few weeks to acclimatise to this little paradise." Ifan glanced up at the sky. "We won't get back to Chryseis tonight, and I don't think there's a farm we can get to before you fall off that horse. We could find a thicker copse to hide in."

"That's your idea of shelter?"

The big miner shrugged. "It's the best we'll get."

"Too many years deprivation, if you think three trees are as good as a house."

"I had a bloody good reason for being in this hell-hole. I was only about a year away from being rich enough to retire to some pleasure planet with lots of friendly ladies. Bloody Maess." Ifan nodded over to a stand of trees. "Over there."

Bennet kneed his horse to make her follow after Ifan's, letting the mare pick her own way through the shallow pools. He loosened his fingers from her mane, keeping the thin leather reins in a tight grip. For a few minutes, he sat watching the splash of water from under the hooves of Ifan's mount as the bigger grey cob led the way, losing himself in the rhythmic rise and fall of hooves and the relentless swishing of the cob's tail against the ever-present gnats.

The horses were a stroke of luck. When the troopers had found the Chryseis mine and evacuated it, Ifan hadn't had time to free the stocky horses and ponies the miners used for transportation. Horses had been a necessity on Telnos. They coped with the damp climate and the marshes in a way machinery couldn't. Amazing how they and cattle had survived the ending of Earth—fertilised ovum scavenged from some agricultural colony as humanity had fled, according to the histories, carefully hoarded and used, and new in vitro stocks created every generation. Even surrogacy breeding using similar animals found on Albion after Landfall and probably thousands of planets visited en route, left them relatively little changed from the ancient descriptions.

If you discounted little things like spines on the cattle and some breeds of tail-less, mane-less horses, of course.

Ifan's horses had still been in their paddock on the day, almost two weeks ago now, that Bennet had made it out of the mine under his own steam. They'd been an invaluable tool to help find the surviving settlers.

As they entered the trees, Ifan slowed the grey, letting the smaller mare come alongside. "We'd better get right into the middle."

Bennet nodded and let him lead on. The patch of dry land, lush with marsh grass, was thick with trees. Ifan was right. It was as good as they'd get when it came to shelter.

Ifan grunted, and pulled up. "At least the horses will get something to eat tonight," he said as the cob tossed its head, testing the reins, trying to get free enough to get its head down to crop at the grass.

Bennet slid from the saddle. He pushed back the wide-brimmed hat he'd found in a deserted farmhouse and rested his forehead against the pommel, holding on to the saddle with his good hand to counter the weakness in his knees until he caught his breath. His legs trembled.

"I'll take care of them." Ifan said, voice rough.

It was enough to make Bennet start. He'd almost drifted off where he stood. There was a dark stain on the saddle leather where his forehead had rested, and sweat stung his eyes. Fucking fever. He couldn't shake it.

He let Ifan take the reins. Three or four uncertain steps brought him to a tree. He turned his back to it and slid down. He'd have fallen over without the rough bark at his back and it took a real effort to stop shivering. It was so bloody warm and sticky, so humid, it was stupid to be shivering.

Ifan chuck-chucked at the horses, taking them a few yards off to a clearing so small, the two animals barely fit. Bennet leaned back. Damn. It wasn't fair to leave everything to Ifan. He lifted his useless right hand, manoeuvring it to drop it into his lap, and set his teeth against the jabbing pain in his arm and shoulder. He tilted the hat brim down over his face to discourage the gnats and closed his eyes, listening to Ifan unharness the horses, setting them on a short hobble line to graze.

"You're getting worse," Ifan said in the same rough tone that Bennet had come to realise masked concern.

"I've got off lightly, so far." Bennet scratched at his three-week growth of beard.

"Yeah. But one bad bout, and it'll clear for a few days. You'll feel better afterwards." A small pause. "It's for your own good."

Tilting up his chin to see from under the hat, Bennet stared. "No. You haven't turned into my mother, but hell, for a minute there, you sounded just like her."

Ifan grinned, and bustled about the campsite. He dipped a can into the brackish water of the nearest pool and set it on a patch of ground scraped clean of grass.

Bennet shifted slightly to get his laser out from under his belt, putting it down on the grass near his left hand. He'd been damn lucky the Maess hadn't found his backup laser, jammed into the back of his pants, under his jacket. The drones had taken the other, before throwing him onto the heap of bodies at one side of the landing point, where Ifan and his group of miners had found him the day after the Maess arrived.

Ifan gave the side of the can a short, controlled burst from his own laser pistol. The water bubbled, boiling out the worst of the impurities before he poured it into a wide-mouthed bottle fitted with a filter. Ifan would have to repeat the process a couple of times before they'd have enough clean water to drink. He glanced at Bennet when he started on heating the second can. "I may need to find some witch grubs if you get any worse."

Bennet pulled a face. He'd seen the grubs in use. "I'd rather have the fever, thanks."

"I thought you lot in Shield didn't do queasy."

"I got left behind and I'm hardly properly dressed." Bennet wore Ifan's only spare shirt, several sizes too big for him, tucked into his uniform pants. "I think that means I'm off duty. Where those grubs are concerned, I'm doing queasy."

"You might be all right and never have to use them." Ifan took a small enamelled cup and a bundle of rags from his saddlebag. He tipped about a third of the hot water into the cup, and reached for one of the rags. "Let's see to it."

Bennet sighed. Wonderful climate this. The whole damn planet reeked of infection.

Ifan was almost as big as the horse he rode, but he was gentle. He checked the scar on Bennet's right temple first, nodding with satisfaction. "That's good. It's healing pretty well. There's less pus." He helped Bennet half-shrug out of the borrowed shirt, undid the crude bandages on his right shoulder and upper arm and laid the rag he'd had steeping in the hot water over the angry red shrapnel wounds. "This is looking better, too. It's closed up at last."

Bennet hissed through his teeth at the pain, then sighed as the warmth spread through his shoulder, bringing a momentary relief. "I normally heal a helluva lot faster than this."

"It's this bloody climate. Place stinks." Ifan concentrated on cleaning up the wounds that Bennet could barely stand to look at, some days. "How's the hand?"

Bennet glanced down at his right hand lying heavy on his lap. He could move his arm with difficulty, a little more every day, but his hand was still almost useless, numb and lacking sensation. Three weeks after the debacle at the landing area, and his fingers were already curling over on themselves, twisting like the fingers of an arthritic, a hundred years his senior. It took a huge effort to straighten them, so much effort and strain he could feel the sweat trickling down the back of his neck.

"About the same." He let the straining muscles relax and prodded at the back of his right hand. He could see the flesh depress, whitening under the pressure, but he could feel very little.

"As soon as you figure out a way of getting us all off-planet, the medics will fix it."

"You have more faith in me than I do."

"You're the one drawing a captain's pay," Ifan said, and grinned. He pulled the shirt back up over Bennet's shoulder.

"No pressure, then." Bennet managed a grin back, when what he wanted to do was hit something and yell.

But, of course, he had to have useable hands to hit anything. So instead, he settled the hat back over his eyes, drew his knees up and rested his left arm on them, and his head on his arm, and tried to relax until Ifan had enough hot water to thin the disgusting concentrate the emergency rations manufacturer had peddled as a nutritious soup.

Maess!

He struggled up again out of the dark, pushing at whatever was pinning him down. His right arm was heavy, useless. He pushed against the weight with it, choking back a gasp at the pain lancing through his shoulder. He could only push at Joss with his left hand—no, not Joss. Whoever who was holding him down, sprawled over him with limp arms and legs, heavy as death.

He couldn't open his eyes. They were stuck and sticky. And they hurt.

Something, lots of somethings, tracked down over Bennet's face, clustering around his closed eyes, stinging and tickling. He managed to get his left hand to his eyelids, rubbing at them. Soft little bodies brushed against his fingers and were gone again. He had to scrape at his eyelids before he could get his eyes open. The harsh morning light of morning burned into them, making them water. His fingers were the first thing he focused on, browny-red with drying blood.

He could just turn his head to the left. Everything else was pinned down.

A woman's face, so close he could kiss her, the forehead gashed open to the grey brain beneath. Flies crawled on the gaping wound, and over her open eyes. She stared at him. She couldn't see him, not for all the flies.

He closed his eyes quickly so the flies couldn't crawl over them.

A hand closed over Bennet's left shoulder, and he jerked awake.

Ifan knelt beside him. "You were dreaming."

Bennet stared at him through the dusk until he remembered he wasn't buried under a pile of corpses. "Sorry."

"Not a problem. Here." Ifan handed him a cup of vaguely meaty-smelling liquid. "I don't know what flavour it's meant to be, but it's better than yesterday's."

Bennet leaned back against his tree, and took a mouthful of the soup. He didn't quite trust Ifan's culinary recommendations, but after three weeks of eating nothing but emergency rations, he didn't care anymore. It didn't matter.

CHAPTER SEVEN

09 Secundus 7488

Ifan woke him at dawn, handing him half a cup of water and a dry biscuit. "Time to think about moving out."

"Thanks." Bennet levered himself up with his left hand, and took his unappetising breakfast. At some point last night, Ifan must have helped him lie down, and covered him with a thin blanket and the netting that kept the worst of the midges at bay. The night's rest had done him good. He felt better. The fever had ebbed away again for a time, leaving him with a dull headache.

Ifan turned to his own meagre breakfast. Beyond him, the horses cropped at the lush marsh grass, tails swishing against the early morning assault from the gnats.

Ifan put their stuff away into the drawstring saddlebags. "Shoulder?"

"Not too bad, this morning." Bennet's arm was still heavy and useless. "I've got pins and needles, though. Good job I'm left-handed."

Grant had said something like that, hadn't he? Back then, back a lifetime ago when Bennet had wrapped a maimed hand in reddening field dressings, Grant had said something about it to

Rosie. Please the gods Bennet no longer believed in, they'd both made it. Sometimes he woke up in the night, his gut clenching with anxiety about Rosie.

Ifan nodded. "Maybe it's a good sign, and the nerves are getting back. Hopeful. Get us off-planet and the medics can probably fix it."

"I'm working on it."

Bennet walked off into the bushes. When he got back into the campsite after relieving himself and taking a sketchy wash in the one of the shallow pools bordering their little island, Ifan was on his feet, saddling the horses.

"I don't think we'll find anyone else," he said as Bennet approached. "We haven't found anyone for days." He heaved up the mare's saddle. "No one else has either."

One of the Brethren they'd rescued had been induced to make a map of all the farms and settlements he knew. Bennet and Ifan were working their way through the list. So far, on this trip, though, they hadn't found anyone to save.

All they'd found were bodies, whole families butchered where the Maess found them. Or empty farmhouses left in ruins after the drones ravaged their way through them, and no sign of the humans at all. That was possibly even more disturbing than the too-small bodies of children, little lives crushed out before they'd had a chance. Where had the Maess taken the missing families? What did they want with them?

Ifan slapped the saddle over the cob's back and kneed it in the stomach so he could tighten the girth, threading it through its wooden ring ties and pulling tight. The horse grunted and threw him a reproachful look, showing the whites of its eyes. Knotting the girth securely, he said, "Mind you, I didn't reckon on ever finding as many as we have."

Three intact families, twenty-three people in all. Counting the troopers and the nine surviving miners, three dozen people were hidden away from the Maess. It amazed Bennet they'd found so many that the drones had missed. He pushed away the thoughts of failure and concentrated on that small victory.

"And at least they've stopped quoting scripture at me." Bennet couldn't do much, one-handed, but he rubbed the grey's ears, and got the hackamore bridle on. Big brown eyes rolling at him innocently, the horse blew greenish, grassy saliva all over him. Bennet grinned. These thick-hocked working horses wouldn't have seen the inside of the stables where his mother kept her thoroughbreds, out at the country house on Albion, but he was developing quite an affection for them.

"There's always a good side," Ifan agreed, grinning. He swung up into the cob's saddle.

Bennet got onto the smaller mare with less grace, hauling himself into the saddle. He looped the reins around his left hand, settling the right on the saddlebow. "We'll head back to the mine tonight. I don't think there's anyone left to find."

They ran into the Maess patrol mid-morning.

They had no opportunity to avoid it. Bennet's mare stepped into a small clearing at the same instant the Maess drones, four of them, marched into the open space from the opposite side.

Fucking hell!

Bennet hauled back on the reins, bringing the mare to a complete, rump-scraping stop. Ifan, still in the trees behind him, had more warning. He was alert, anyway, and cautious enough to stop the cob while he was still in cover. The only indication Bennet had he was there at all was the almost subliminal whine as he readied his laser pistol.

Bennet froze into place, holding the mare steady.

The four drones marching in single file across the glade, heads moving from side to side, were of the older, less sophisticated type. Their arms were photon rifles with only rudimentary hands to mimic their human enemies. There was no urgency in anything the cyborgs did, nothing suggesting they were looking for anything.

They just marched along at a steady pace.

With all the speed of treacle moving over ice, Bennet leaned down along the mare's neck. Anything that meant he wasn't as big a target...

The drones stopped and faced him. He stared back at the blank silvery-grey masks, the travesty of human faces these things wore over circuits and microchips and the few organic cells that powered everything, watching as they processed the information they were getting. He barely breathed, ready to fling himself out of the saddle if need be, sliding his feet out of the cured-leather stirrups.

The lead drone tilted its head to one side and then the other. In a human, it would have been curiosity. With this thing, who the hell knew what it meant?

The whole world stopped.

The sounds of the marsh faded away. The buzz of insects had muted down to the faint sound of a saw in the far distance. Even the usually sharp cries of the bird-like flyers were dulled. Only a fast, erratic thumping sounded loud in Bennet's ears. The entire world focused down to the blank oval head appearing to be look intently at him, weighing him up, analysing the data its sensors had amassed.

The drone lifted its arm. Bennet froze, staring down the bore of the built-in laser rifle. It looked big enough to swallow the world. Sweat prickled on Bennet's forehead, running down to sting his eyes. He didn't want to blink. He couldn't.

The head tilted again to one side. The drone's arm dropped. It turned almost before Bennet had time to register it, and the drones resumed their original course and marched on.

Sweet fucking gods in fucking heaven.

He watched them until they were out of sight. Only when the last silvery body vanished into the trees did he take a full breath. Many breaths, fast and loud. The hand he raised to wipe his mouth shook with palsy. He blinked the sweat out of his eyes.

Fuck. He was going to throw up. And gods, did he need to piss.

Ifan edged the cob out from the trees. "What the fuck happened?" He sounded almost shrill. If a groundout whisper could sound shrill.

"I d-d-dunno." Bennet straightened up. It took two breaths to get it out. Fuck, his stupid stammer was back. He hadn't done that in years. He shook his head, and, looping the reins around the pommel, got his left hand up to rub at his eyes. "G-great d-day in the morning. Why didn't they shoot?"

He jerked his head towards the trees, and backed the mare into the cover under the lush leaf canopy. Ifan followed, looked as wrecked as he felt.

"That," Ifan said, "was a helluva lot closer than I ever want it to be."

"No shit." Bennet blew out a noisy breath. The need to piss died away. He leaned out of the saddle to get his feet back into the stirrups. Ifan brought the cob and secured the right stirrup for him. Bennet's hands were still shaking. He felt clammy, the shirt clinging to the small of his back. Why wasn't he dead? "They were older drones. That was lucky."

"What difference does it make?"

"Not as sophisticated as the new ones. Not as advanced. Not as clever."

Ifan brought the cob closer until he and Bennet were knee to knee. He took a small flask from a pocket and offered it. "Take a swig of that. It'll settle your nerves."

The liquor tasted like nectar. Bennet coughed against the harshness in his throat, but the warmth spread through him, chasing out the cold feeling in his chest. His next breath was steadier. Normal. Ifan took a swig himself and smacked his lips in appreciation. Bennet glanced at him sidelong, just as Ifan looked at him. Ifan's mouth twitched. That was all it took. Bennet laughed until he coughed again, until his chest hurt so much he had to hunch over and take some big, whooping breaths. Ifan's laugh was a roar.

"Hell, but we were lucky," Ifan said, grinning, when they'd calmed down. He proffered the flask.

Bennet took another welcome mouthful of spirits. Lucky? That only just began to describe it. "The only thing I can think of is they're not programmed to kill all organic life. They're only programmed to kill humans. Their sensor mechanisms are a mystery, but maybe they just didn't see me."

"Huh."

"They'd pick me up in an instant if I were on foot or in a transport, because that's what they're programmed to do. There's a big difference between organic human and metal transport for example—composition, power signatures, infra-red signatures... But there isn't a huge difference between the pony's core temperature and mine and we're both organic." Bennet straightened up. That could be it. A hole in the drones' programming. "And we're lucky the saddles have so little metal. Maybe all they saw was a single four legged animal. They couldn't differentiate between me and the horse."

"Whatever it was, it saved your skin."

Bennet laughed. "All that machine efficiency, all that sophistication, beaten by something as primitive as a man on a horse! That's useful to know."

Ifan looked alarmed. "What do you mean, useful? How in hell can that be useful?"

Bennet grinned. "Oh, you never know when something like that will come in handy."

"Oh fuck," Ifan said. "Bloody officers."

They reached the farm in the early afternoon.

It looked deserted. The farmhouse stood at one side of the clearing, surrounded by an overgrown garden the marsh was already reclaiming as its own, a ramshackle building built on stilts to get it above the marshy ground. The crawl space underneath was boxed in to keep snakes out of the living quarters. The barn was better built and cared for. No surprises there. Every farm they'd searched over the last couple of weeks had shown more care for the livestock than for the people.

Maess drones had been to the farm.

Bennet opened the door to what had to be the kitchen, and walked in on what the Maess had left behind. For an instant he stared, before jumping back out onto the veranda. There was nothing in his stomach but water and dry biscuit, but he did his best to rid himself of it, clinging to the veranda rail to hold himself up.

"Bennet?" Ifan was there immediately. "How many?"

Bennet spat out the bile-tasting saliva, trying to get his churning guts under control. "Two."

"I'll take care of it."

Bennet leaned against the veranda post. Oh, but 'you lot in Shield' could definitely do queasy. No doubt about it. At all. He listened to Ifan's subdued cursing, trying not to think about the two sprawled bodies on the kitchen floor, grotesque shapes given new life by the heaving mass of grey insect larvae covering them like a moving skin over the gleam of picked bones.

"I threw a couple of blankets over them," Ifan said, from behind him.

Bennet turned to see Ifan wiping his mouth, a sour look on his face. The big ex-trooper had seen a lot in his time, but nothing had inured either of them to the reeking, rotting horror the human body could become. And in this climate, it took only a few hours.

Bennet edged his way back into the kitchen. It wasn't a sophisticated set up, a fireplace for cooking, long since cold, a table and chairs. At one side, a larder door stood open, with a chair in front of it. The larder was empty. Ifan pushed past him, into the rest of the little house. Two more rooms, that was all. The few sticks of furniture were tumbled and half-destroyed, beds and mattresses ripped to pieces. No more bodies.

"Nothing." Ifan came back to where Bennet leant against a wall trying not to see that the blankets Ifan had used to cover the two corpses were undulating. Ifan moved the chair to one side and check out the larder shelves. "Not a lot. A few emergency bars." He filled his pockets as he spoke. "The rest's rotting."

Bennet grimaced. Another bloody failure. "Then I guess we give it up and head back."

"If we start back now, we'll be home by nightfall."

Home. Bennet turned the grimace into a faint grin, and followed Ifan out to where they'd left the horses. "We'd better check the barn."

Bennet half-dreaded they'd find the starving cattle that had greeted them at most of the other farms. But the animals were in good condition with access to feed, and a plentiful supply of water from a stream diverted to flow into a header tank before being channelled out of the barn..

"What about the animals?" Ifan looked over the cattle.

"I don't think much of our chances of moving them more than twenty miles."

Ifan laughed, though it was rueful. Their previous efforts at herding the independent-minded cattle had ended in ignominious failure.

Bennet grinned back. "I hate to see that much fresh meat get away from us, but it's better if we turn them loose. Next time, we'll bring a couple of the farmers with us."

Ifan snorted. "If you can get them to lay off praying." Then added, all practicality, "There's a couple of calves. We can take them back. There'll be enough for a couple of good meals."

"You get to shoot them, then. I'm too soft hearted."

"Officers!" Ifan rolled his eyes.

Ifan had the first dead calf over the front of his horse, tying its feet together with rope under the cob's belly, soothing the spooked horse with his hand, when Bennet put his finger on what was bothering him.

The animals were far too well cared for. Those disgusting horrors in the house had been dead for three weeks at least, but the animals had been well fed and the stalls were reasonably clean. Someone had been caring for them. Who needed to put a chair in front of the larder? Both the bodies in the kitchen had been adults. They hadn't needed a chair to stand on.

Bennet caught at Ifan's arm as the big miner straightened. "There's someone here."

Ifan frowned. "Wha—?" Bennet explained, and Ifan's frown deepened. "You think it's a kid?"

"I don't know. I don't know if any of it makes sense, but there's something just niggling at me."

"No one in the house." Ifan turned in a slow circle, scanning the thick vegetation. "And a million places to hide. Maybe if we wait, they'll come out."

"I'm not leaving a kid behind. No arguments." Bennet had a sudden clear memory of scooping up an injured child, a small head lolling helplessly as if the neck was too weak to support the weight, making the sort of whimpering no child should have to make. She'd died in the transport, the small body unable to take the shock and trauma of gross injury. He'd had her blood all over his tunic. "I can't."

Because he'd failed so many kids on this bloody planet. *Too many.* There was too much blood on his hands. Ifan shook his head, but kept silent. Wise man.

Bennet looked the house over. Not a prepossessing sight, made from wooden planks rough with brilliant green and yellow lichen, the gaps between them caulked with something… mud? There was plenty of that, anyway. Resin leaked down the boards in dusty trails, weeping its way out of the wood. He started up the veranda steps… paused. *Ah. Of course.*

He beckoned Ifan over. "My family has a country house, where they can pretend to get back to the simple life. It's an old place on my grandfather's estates, up in the Caledonia region."

Ifan blinked, either at the change of mood or at what he evidently saw as an unexpected confidence. "And I'm sure it's very nice, too."

"The house looks like this one. Bigger, but very like this. When I was kid, our farm manager made me a den, a hidey-hole just for me, to let me get away from my sisters and my kid brother. Mostly my brother." Bennet backed down the step. "He cut a door in the boarding under the veranda, and let me get into the crawl space. I kept all my treasures in there, where Liam couldn't get at them."

He stepped back, scanning the boarding. There. Just to the left of the steps.

"Worth a try," Ifan agreed, when Bennet pointed it out. He leaned down and opened the door, letting light flood into the dark space. "Well, there's no way in hell I'll ever fit through there."

"Not even if I greased you." Bennet held up his hand for silence, and listened. A faint rustling noise, that was all. "Snakes? Does this bloody planet have snakes?"

"Snakes don't scuttle." Ifan's grin was pure evil. "Could be rats, I guess." Bennet gave him the hard stare he'd long ago learned from his father, and Ifan's totally unintimidated grin broadened. "Hey, the rats eat snakes."

"The other way around, I think. You'll have to help me in." Bennet grasped one edge of the doorframe and, with Ifan supporting his shoulders, slid into the space.

It was dark and shadowy, striped with long thin bars where the boards had warped and the shaft of bright sunlight coming through the door. Bennet knelt, letting his eyes adjust to the dimness, the top of his head brushing the underside of the veranda.

Something moved over to his right.

"Hello?"

No answer, other than more scuttling and movement, less stealthy now. Bennet saw something darker than the grey dimness around him.

"Hello. I'm Bennet. Who're you?"

"Light." Ifan offered a small battery operated flashlight from those ever-useful saddlebags.

Bennet took the torch and jammed it under his heavy right hand. "I'm going to turn on a light. Don't worry about it. It's just so you can see me better." He flicked the switch with his left hand, and let the glow of the light illuminate him. "See? I'm not going to hurt you."

More silence, more faint scuttling. It would have been better if Ifan hadn't mentioned rats. Bennet didn't like them. But whatever was moving down there was far bigger. He settled down for a long wait, resisting the temptation to flash the light around the space and flush out whoever, or whatever, was hiding there.

"I won't hurt you. Ifan and I are from the mines, in the hills. It's safe up there."

More noise in shadows for a response, but Bennet grinned, because that was no rat or snake, but something gloriously human.

"I really won't hurt you. I'm here to take you somewhere safe." He lifted the torch. "Let's see you, huh?"

He swept the beam over to the source of the noise, taking it slow. He'd been right. The kid couldn't be more than about eight, thin and filthy, eyes gleaming in the torchlight. A boy, probably, although it was difficult to be sure through the dirt and the tangled hair.

"Hey," Bennet said, gentle as he could make it.

The kid crouched on a pile of filthy quilts, ready to jump and run, his arms outstretched, hands clutching his bedding. His hands clenched and unclenched, bunching up the quilts. He breathed heavily, staring back at Bennet.

Bennet moved the beam to one side, careful not to get the child in the eyes with it. "This is brilliant hiding place you've got here. I had one like this, when I was your age. What's your name?"

Silence.

"My name's Bennet, and that's Ifan outside. He's a bit too big to get in here. Ifan's a miner and we're living up in the hills in his mine. Have you ever been in a mine? It's dark, like here, but Ifan's smart and he's got lights fixed up and everything. And there's some other kids there."

To his delight, the kid spoke. "Those things?"

Which things did the child mean? The Maess drones or the decomposing awfulness the kid's family had become? Bennet kept up the same cheerful even tone. "The drones? They've gone."

"Mama told me to run down here and hide when they came."

"That was smart. But the drones aren't here and you can come out now. We'll take you up to Ifan's mine, where it's safe."

"They didn't get up again when the things went."

Bennet stiffened. Now the kid was talking about the dead horrors above their heads. "No. I know."

"They don't look right. I stopped going in."

Thank the gods for that, too. "I'm glad. They'd be glad too. What's your name?"

The kid unclenched his fists from the quilts and, still crouching, moved forward a couple of feet. "It's not them now. They've gone, haven't they?"

Oh shit.

"Yes," Bennet said. "Yes, they have. They're not really there anymore."

"Gods." Ifan spoke so quietly it was like a prayer. The miner appeared to be clearing his throat with unusual vigour.

"They've gone to be with the gods." Bennet took his cue.

"Oh," the child said, and his voice wobbled.

Bennet held out his arms as wide as he could, forcing even the useless one into service, and the kid rushed him, scuttling on all fours to fling himself into Bennet's lap. Bennet dropped the torch and got his good arm around the child. The kid clung hard, but he wasn't crying.

"It'll be all right. I promise it'll be all right." Bennet sat for a long time, murmuring what he considered inanities, but it seemed to comfort the child. When the boy stopped shaking, he stroked the dirty hair. "Let's get out of here, shall we, and get out into the sun where I can see you properly. Ifan will help."

He manoeuvred the boy towards the door, but the kid clung like a limpet, refusing to speak and refusing to let go. The door had been a tightish fit on the way in. Bennet with attached child just would not fit back through.

"I'll never get both of you through that little door," Ifan said. Ten minutes of fruitless cajoling on Bennet's part had the boy clinging harder than ever. "Hang on. I've thought of something."

The kid lifted up his head. "Where's he gone?"

"To find something to get us out." The gods knew what. It would probably involve high explosive somewhere. Bennet's experience of Infantry troopers had taught him they were rarely subtle. "What's your name?"

"Luke."

"Good name. My parents nearly called my little brother Luke, but in the end, my father opted for a different prophet. Dad was going through one of his religious phases at the time, and Mama couldn't shift him. She wanted to call my brother Achilleus, mind you, so Liam's always been grateful to Dad for standing his ground." Bennet grinned down at the dirty face near his.

"Bennet," Luke said, testing it.

"That's right." Bennet looked around when Ifan stuck his head through the open door.

"Found a crowbar in the barn," Ifan announced, and before Bennet could say anything, the miner applied the crowbar to the boards. It took him less than a minute to more than double the size of the door.

"I think you'll have to come with us now, Luke. Ifan appears to have opted for a bit of house demolition and ruined your hideout."

Ifan was unapologetic. "You're the one being soft hearted about not forcing the kid to let go. And as usual, you need me to get you out of trouble."

Even with Ifan's house renovations, it was still hard to get out with an eight-year-old clinging on with arms and legs. Ifan had to help. It was as well he was a big man. He physically lifted Bennet and Luke out, careful, despite his scornful tone, not to pull too hard on Bennet's injured shoulder. Within a few seconds, Bennet was sitting on the steps with Luke on his lap.

Bennet made the introductions. "This is Luke." He glanced at the house. "Can you go back in there and see what you can find? Something to remind him... holopics, if there are any, of him with his parents and whatever official papers you can lay your hands on."

"I get all the nice jobs." Ifan reached into the crawl space to retrieve his precious flashlight, and squeezed past them to get into the house.

"What if those things come?" Luke asked, while they waited.

"Ifan and I have got lasers, and we're faster than they are. We'll shoot them."

"Good." Luke pulled back and studied Bennet's face. "You're not a Brother. You're not Saved."

No, he wasn't. Not even with a three-week growth that would barely register on Rosie's Religious Beard Scale.

"I'm a soldier. In Shield. See?" Bennet touched the tiny silver shield pinned into his borrowed shirt. At least Ifan had been able to salvage it from the jacket and tunic ripped apart by shrapnel. "We were here to get all you people off before the Maess came. We didn't get everyone, and I got hurt and left behind. Ifan rescued me."

"Does Ifan look after you?"

"He likes to think so," Bennet said, as his rescuer squeezed back down the steps again.

"Of course I do. He's an officer. You always end up looking after them. They wrote it into the Regs somewhere, to make sure of it." Ifan patted a pocket and said to Bennet, "Found a few holopics, but that's it. Not much in the way of official paperwork. But I picked up a couple of shirts that should be a better fit for you."

"You just want yours back."

"Correct. Listen, I'll go set the animals free and get the other calf, and we'd better get going. It'll take us three, four hours to get back and the day's wearing on."

Bennet glanced at Luke. "Have you been feeding the animals?"

Luke's small chest puffed out with conscious pride. "I did my chores when it was dark and the things couldn't see me if they came. Sometimes I stayed in the barn."

"Well, we're going to have to let them go free." The gods alone knew what the kid had been eating. Bennet suspected the animal feed he'd seen in the barn had formed a major part of Luke's diet. It would be difficult if Luke took badly to them slaughtering the calves he'd cared for. "We've had to kill the calves, Luke. We need to feed a lot of people back at the mine."

But Luke was a farm boy. He just shrugged. Besides, other losses put everything into perspective, even at Luke's young age.

Ifan reappeared with the second dead calf. "Time to go, Bennet."

This time Luke consented to be set on his feet, although he clutched at Bennet's shirt with both hands and walked so close beside him, Bennet was as hampered as he had been before. Somehow, they persuaded Luke to let go long enough for Bennet to get up on the mare, the boy scrambling up behind him as quickly as he could.

"I didn't say goodbye." He wrapped both arms around Bennet's waist.

There was no way in hell Bennet would let him back into that house, to see the writhing, sinuous movement under the thin blankets. "They won't mind. They aren't really there, you know."

Ifan looked up from securing the second calf in front of Bennet's saddle, and scowled. For all his bluster, Ifan was softer hearted than Bennet.

The child seemed very accepting. Maybe it was just relief that he didn't have to fend for himself anymore, that he could be a child again. He didn't protest and insist, he still didn't cry. Instead, he asked, so innocent that a Liam-trained Bennet had all his antennae quivering, "If Ifan looks after you, are you going to look after me?"

"Man traps ahead!" Ifan swung into his saddle, starting the cob.

Bennet could recognise a trap for himself when he saw one, thank you. "Until I can get everyone off this planet and get you home, and I find you some family."

Luke rubbed his cheek against Bennet's shoulder, and seemed satisfied. "Good."

Ifan shook his head, eyes rolling. Bennet grinned back. Well, maybe he had one foot caught in the trap, at that.

CHAPTER EIGHT

39 Secundus 7488: Telnos

"They've got more sense than us humans," Ifan said, "choosing their main area up in the hills. If you'd done that and we hadn't had to go driving twenty miles to get to a cutter that left before we could reach it, we'd have got away from here weeks ago."

Bennet lay face down just below the brow of the ridge, watching the Maess in the valley. What they could see of the base was well established, built around the mouth to the largest solactinium mine on the planet. It was all low key. Drone recharging stations built in the mine's mouth; the landing field taking up most of the flat valley floor, with more than a couple of dozen ships, including several ground-space fighters parked around one of the larger drone transporters; tanks of some sort of volatile chemical off to one side of the field—What did the Maess use that for? Fuel? Their laser flechettes? Something the drones needed? Should have trawled the T18 data to find out—all enclosed by a simple fence patrolled by drones. Very low key. The Maess evidently felt secure here. It was a worrying indication of just how far back Albion's forces had fallen.

"It was about where our targets were. There were more farmers than miners."

"Yeah," Infantry Private Janerse said, on Bennet's other side. "And you lot weren't exactly leaping up and down saying 'here we are!' Shy and retiring, maybe?"

"We had reasons for wanting to keep a low profile."

Janerse had a wry grin that lit up her face. She used it now. "Beats getting arrested for illegal mining, any day."

Ifan had developed a grand passion for the sardonic, cynical Janerse. "You found us in the end, Jan. You saved me." He puckered up his lips in invitation, smacking them together and spreading out his arms.

Rolling her eyes, she made gagging noises.

Bennet put down the field glasses Ifan had dug up from the bottom of a storage box and reached for the datapad. Recalled to his duties, Ifan steadied the pad, allowing Bennet to draw a quick sketch map with the stylus.

Bennet made a note of all the ships he could see at the landing pad. "Still no sign of human prisoners."

"They may not need them in a shielded mine." Ifan took the pad and closed it down, slipping it back into his pocket for safekeeping. "No need for slave labour if the drones can do it."

"Doesn't make sense to me," Janerse said. "Why'd they work themselves if they can get us to do it?"

"Machine efficiency." Bennet rolled on to his back and looked up into a sky that, if he squinted ever so hard and pretended, was almost the blue of Albion. He brought up his left hand to massage the constant dull ache in his right shoulder. "They're stronger than us, they don't get tired, and they only need to recharge every couple of days. They couldn't do it in the Chryseis, since you were mining there without shielding, but they can do it here."

"They don't need humans here," Ifan said.

"No. That's why mostly what we found was corpses."

But not the right number of corpses. The estimates for the settler population, the number they'd managed to evacuate and the number they'd found since, dead or alive... well, it didn't tally. It just didn't tally.

Many people were missing. The gods alone knew what had happened to them.

"Remind me not to get captured, then," Janerse said.

"Very wise. It wouldn't be a good idea." Bennet blew out a breath and rolled back onto his stomach, reaching for the binoculars. "I'd give a helluva lot for some solactinite right now."

Ifan turned his head. "Yeah?"

"Yeah. I like big bright explosions."

"They'd know we were here."

"Not yet. When we leave, as a parting shot." Bennet turned his attention to the base. "Or if they find us. I'd like to take them with us."

"We're sitting on a mountain made of solactinium," Janerse reminded them.

"Unrefined solactinium's no use to me." Bennet settled back down to silent watching.

After a while, Janerse glanced at her wrist chronometer and slid down the side of the ridge to the little copse where they'd left the horses, going to check on the animals and get more water. When she was out of earshot, Ifan said, "I could maybe do something for you, to get your big bang."

"Commercial explosive? I thought of that, but I'm more used to solactinite. Getting the quantities and timing right would be the trick."

"I didn't mean commercial." The tips of Ifan's ears reddened. "I have a bit more than that salted away. Something more useful."

Bennet frowned, and rolled onto his side, as intent now on Ifan as he had been on the base. "Is that a hint you have solactinite?"

"I'm telling you I had customers who didn't ask questions and who supplied me with the equipment and chemicals needed for processing the ore, if it meant they could take the stuff and not have to refine it themselves."

Bennet waited.

"Jacks," Ifan said, referring to the common name given to the small bands of pirates and smugglers who made a living out of preying and trading on the edges of Albion's space. "They didn't worry about whether the solactinite I sold 'em had a government license or not. They helped finance us."

Bennet grimaced. He had killed very few men in his career—mankind had managed to unite to escape a common enemy when they'd fled Earth, and war between humans was so far back in their past, most people thought it was just as legendary as Earth itself—but he'd come up against and killed Jacks. They were predators, for all that a man could, in a purely academic way, admire the courage that had them dodging about the same bits of space the Maess were trying to control. "I didn't think you meant the official Quartermaster's Office. This is more than just a bit illegal, Ifan."

"My whole mine's more than just a bit illegal." Ifan fidgeted for a second or two. "When you're a grunt, and they decide they don't want you anymore, the pension's not exactly going to keep you in style, you know."

"Uh-huh."

"It's a lot less than you'll get."

"Ifan, I likely won't live to get my pension and we both know it." Bennet gave him another long, level, calculating stare. "How much do you have?"

"A lot."

"Where have you been processing it?"

"Side cave, a few hundred yards further in." Ifan rubbed at his nose, looking rueful. "It has a hidden entrance."

"Timers? Electronic detonators?"

Ifan nodded. "The arrangement with my customers was to provide it ready for use. They provided the technical supplies.

There's a lot of solactinite there, Bennet. I was about to make a shipment when the Maess arrived."

Bennet grinned. Coming up against a Jack raid was one thing. Looking at a whole heap of solactinite with which to wreak havoc with the Maess, was entirely another. Looking relieved, Ifan grinned back.

"You will, but not to the Jacks. I think we'll sell this lot to the Maess." Bennet let the grin widen. "Congratulations, Corporal Ifan. You have just joined the Shield Regiment."

That wiped the grin from Ifan's face, double quick.

As evening drew in, they prepared to head back to the Chryseis. Janerse had been muttering to herself for some time, and as they finally gathered everything together, her self-restraint gave way. "We've been watching that place for a couple of weeks, Bennet. Why are we bothering, if there aren't any prisoners there? There's no one to rescue."

"Because it appears Ifan has a substantial stock of solactinite, and whatever else happens, I'm blowing the base." Bennet grinned at her sour expression. "I'm Shield. I blow shit up. It's what we do."

Janerse's snort sounded remarkably like one of the ponies.

Bennet laughed and let himself slide a few feet down the hillside, not attempting to stand up until he was well below the ridgeline. They slithered and slid down to the horses, their lifeline here. Bennet's little theory about the short sightedness of drone programming had been borne out more than once. They'd never deliberately ridden a horse at drones, but they'd all sat their horses to one side, leaning down along the horses' necks as a patrol had plodded past them. Nervous work, but it proved the cyborgs didn't see a human on a horse, but only a single entity.

Half way back, Ifan edged the grey cob closer to Bennet's mare. "What are we going to do, Bennet? We can't hang about forever waiting for something to happen, and I don't think there's anyone left for you to rescue."

"I suppose I try and think of a way to get us off-planet."

"That'd be neat," Janerse murmured. "I was kind of hoping we'd just hang on until the drones got all the solactinium and moved on."

"That'll take months," Ifan objected. "Maybe even a couple of years. These foothills are almost solid solactinium ore."

Bennet couldn't argue with that assessment. "And we can't live in an unshielded mine forever. We can withstand it better than the Maess drones do, but not months, much less a couple of years. Especially the kids."

"But we'll be behind their lines by now," Janerse argued. "Way behind. How can we get out?"

"Shield operates behind the lines all the time."

"Sure, but there's only one of you."

"And a helluva lot of civilians," Ifan said. "It's the kids that bother me. The mine isn't good for them. Maybe we should head north into the mountains. Unless you seriously think you can get us off-planet?"

"I don't know." Bennet looked down at his hand, lying heavy on the saddlebow. "Given the right bits of kit, I'm sure I could fly one of their smaller ships. I don't know if I could fly anything big enough for thirty-six of us."

"You can fly one? How come?" Janerse gave him a sceptical look.

"The techs in the Strategy Unit have taken more than one captured small transport apart. I've helped put together a flight simulation for them. We know the bigger ships carry drones and maybe even a real Maess sometimes. They have cockpits and cabin space—not like fighters, which don't have any free space inside at all. The key thing would be disengaging the cyborg control unit..." Bennet stopped. Shook his head. "There's one piece of equipment I'd need to hack into the controls. I don't have it. I can't make it.

End of story. We have to find some other way of staying safe."

Pie in the sky, even thinking about it. Without a Link to merge into the control board, he had no chance of hacking into a transport ship. He'd be able to disconnect the control unit, maybe, but with no Link, the transport would just sit there. Biggest paperweight in the galaxy.

They were screwed. They were fucking screwed and he couldn't think of any way at all of getting them off-planet. Not one.

He raised his half-numb right hand and rubbed at the headache gathering in his temple.

Ifan raised an eyebrow. "You know a helluva lot about this stuff."

T18.

Hours spent huddled in a computer room in a base far behind enemy lines, on T18. A year and a half now since the night he'd slugged home across a desert to where Flynn and the Mosquito waited for him, his belt pouch full of little data crystals worth more than T18's planetary weight in gold. The techs were still translating and analysing the data, and would be for years to come. Flynn... No. Don't go there. There's no point.

Bennet allowed through a small, twisted grin. "Must have been something I picked up."

The entrance to the Chryseis was little more than a cave mouth in the steep valley side, carefully camouflaged to give no sign of human activity. The only giveaway was the paddock, hidden amongst trees for extra security, and even then, the horses were brought inside each night and stabled. With luck, no one would guess there were humans within a hundred miles of the place. While that might once have hidden an unauthorised Jack operation from the authorities, it now hid them from the Maess. There were small mercies to be had in associating with those whose deference to legal authority was less than Bennet's own.

The miners had taken on responsibility for the mine's security. They took turns to stand guard at the cave mouth—it was Alice, tonight, and the burly Illurian whose name Bennet just couldn't pronounce—while a third, Pietr, came out with one of the farmers to take care of the horses. Bennet was relieved to hand over the mare and trudge inside, hoping someone had kept food aside for them.

Once inside the cave entrance, the mine tunnel itself meandered half a mile and more into the side of the ridge, with many a side passage. Deep in one such side turning, protected by partial shielding against the solactinium emissions, Ifan and his fellow miners had made their living quarters, shared now with the farming families and the three military survivors.

Well, 'shared' was maybe too optimistic a term. The farmers had been glad enough to be rescued, but they viewed the miners and the military as tainted, polluted and beyond redemption. The farming families had elected to live in overcrowded near-squalor at one end of the cave. It made for some interesting social dynamics that had only resolved themselves by the two groups having the minimum of interaction.

"They're religious. They like dirt," Ifan had said, dismissively, when all their overtures of friendship had been rejected. He bristled with offence at being prayed over, and Bennet had prevented an altercation only with difficulty. Mainly by putting himself between Ifan and the offending farmer, and hoping Ifan wouldn't hit him while he was injured.

Janerse had sniffed with equal disdain, for once on Ifan's side. "They also like our rations and our protection."

Bennet let the farmers be. They weren't any use to him in attempts to rescue others, or get off-planet. They were just so much baggage he was responsible for. As Rosie had reminded him weeks before, he didn't have to like the people he was paid to protect with his life. He just had to get on with it.

Luke was different. Nominally, in the care of the least

unfriendly of the farming families, he had attached himself to Bennet with all the tenacity of a limpet. Bennet let him. One of the hardest wrenches in his life, an unforeseen consequence of Joss, had been Bennet's estrangement from his siblings. Luke was younger than Liam had been back then, but not by much. Looking after Luke felt as if he were making up for something he'd failed at with Liam.

So it had become routine, Luke waiting in the shadows just inside the entrance for Bennet to get back. Ifan and whoever else was with them would take the horses, and Luke would tuck his hand into Bennet's and walk with him back through to the living area, chattering every step of the way.

Equally routine for Bennet to wake every morning half crowded out of his narrow bunk, Luke curled up beside him, despite having been put to bed each night at the other end of the living quarters, where the three farming families had set up base. After the first week, even Leah and her dour husband, Abram, had given that one up as unwinnable, despite misgivings about Bennet not being among the Saved Elect.

Bennet was storing up problems. If he were sensible about it, he'd ease Luke's dependency on him, but a large part of him believed they'd live—or most likely, die—on Telnos, and the folly of allowing an orphaned child to see him as a surrogate father seemed academic. The reality was that a small kid had found his only security in a half-paralysed Shield officer, as trapped on this planet as any of them. Bennet couldn't deny him that.

"Why d'you keep it?" Luke twisted on Bennet's lap right in the middle of Bennet's patient explanation of the proper way to remove a mummy's internal organs. His fingers played with the communicator around Bennet's numb right wrist.

"It's my comlink," Bennet said, for about the fifteenth time in the last couple of weeks.

"But who's going to call you on it?"

Bennet paused, and shrugged. "Who indeed." He unbuckled it and fastened it around Luke's arm, instead. "Here. You can keep it for me. Just don't lose it, and if it ever starts to vibrate, you come and tell me, okay?"

"Okay."

"Right," Bennet said, rubbing at his wrist. The pressure of his fingers was faint, but there. Feeling was coming back as the nerves in his shoulder recovered. Thank the gods. "Now then, once they'd got the heart out…"

Graphic depictions of mummification techniques neither prevented Luke from falling asleep nor troubled his dreams later. Bennet rolled him in a blanket and shifted him to the foot of the bed. Luke didn't stir. Bennet lay down in whatever space was left. Being crowded was a small price to pay for having someone here to be fond of.

The opportunity for reflection and self-analysis was one of the disadvantages of being marooned. He'd had many quiet moments to realise he wasn't created to be on his own, that he needed something and someone, even a kid, to look after and worry over, that he clung to a few people too much and probably for too long.

That he'd clung to Joss too much.

And for too long?

Ifan's voice rumbled somewhere above his head. "Awake?"

Bennet opened his eyes. The memory of Joss' face hovering over him, eyes locked on his as they made love, faded into the reality of a dim cave smelling of too much humanity and too little soap. Near his feet, Luke made an unappealing sniffling noise and turned over, kicking at Bennet's legs. Further away, one of the farmers coughed in his fever, and spat into a cup. Joss's patrician nose would have wrinkled with fastidious disgust.

"Just thinking," he said, half smiling at the expression Joss would be wearing if he'd been there.

"Home?"

"Yeah." Bennet scooted up the bed to sit with his back against the rock wall of the cave that acted as the headboard.

"You don't talk about your home."

"No." And after a second, to soften that bleak monosyllable, he added, "It's been more than five weeks. They must think I'm dead."

And maybe they were right. Bennet and everyone else, even little Luke, were dead but just hadn't realised it yet. They were dead the day the Maess took the planet and all that was left was the last unquiet kicking of the corpse.

Screwed. We're all fucked up with nowhere to go.

Janerse and Randle hovered behind Ifan. Bennet arched an eyebrow. "What is this? A deputation?"

Ifan nodded. "That'll do to describe it, I guess. Thing is, Bennet, you're not going in there on your own."

Bennet couldn't say he was surprised. Touched, and proud of them, but not surprised. "Have any of you ever been inside a Maess base?"

Ifan shrugged. "No."

Janerse and Randle both grinned.

"Don't be daft," Randle said. "Sir."

"Well, as someone pointed out to me once, it's my job to walk in and out of Maess bases every day of the week."

"With one useable hand?" Randle asked.

He couldn't take them. They were the only protection the civilians had. "I'm left-handed. I'll manage. I'm the only one who knows what to expect."

"You don't have a shield-suit here. That means you're just as liable to be seen as anyone else." Ifan raised a hand as big as a meat platter. "I've got two hands. I'm going with you."

"Ifan, you're very comforting to have around—"

"Huh?" Janerse widened her eyes, pantomiming shocked

disbelief.

"Well, he's big enough to hide behind, I suppose," Randle said.

Bennet talked over them. "But you're too big to sneak. You aren't exactly light on your feet."

"He lumbers." Janerse's sniff was probably calculated to goad Ifan into further indiscretion.

"I'm going," Ifan said, folding his arms over his chest.

Bennet saw the flat determination in the ex-trooper's expression. Despite the protests, he'd rather have Ifan along than just about anyone he could think of—bar getting the *Hype* and her crew back, of course. "If I agree, you'll do as I tell you, understood?"

"I'm coming along to help, not bloody re-enlisting!"

"On my terms, or not at all, Ifan."

"You shouldn't be going in there at all, with that hand." Ifan scowled. "All right. Although this is my mine and my solactinite—"

"And it'll be your jail sentence when we get back," Janerse said, glittery bright.

Ifan reddened. Sniffed. Sat down on the side of Bennet's bunk and squirmed until his substantial hind-end took up almost as much room as Luke. He folded his arms over his chest again. "When?"

Bennet managed not to let the smile show. "One dark night. We'll go then."

04 Tertius 7488

Bennet had enough solactinite prepared within a couple of days, but it was several more before he moved on the base. He and Ifan would be vulnerable without the protection of shield-suits and the fields they generated to disrupt detection. A dark night with as little moonlight as possible might be nothing more than an illusory protection, but it was all they had. Four days after preparing the charges, Telnos's main moon had waned, and the two smaller, more distant ones were hidden behind cloudbanks.

"We go now," Bennet said, as soon as it was full dark.

"Where will you leave it?" Janerse asked.

"The chemical depot, inside the mine entrance, the buildings, attached to some of the ships they have on the ground." Bennet watched her stow the prepped solactinite into backpacks. "When I'm ready, we'll blow it all."

"And when will that be?"

"I don't know. I just want to be ready."

"The gods alone knows what for." Ifan scowled as if he were regretting the whole idea and whatever impulse had had him volunteering to try an infiltrate a Maess base for the first time in his life.

But he didn't back out. Not that Bennet had expected him to, of course, but it was reassuring, three hours later, to have Ifan beside him in a shallow depression a few feet from the Maess fence. Janerse and Randle waited on the other side of the ridge with the horses, prepared to act as backup.

"Try not to put that to the test, okay, boss?" was all Randle said about it.

Inside the fence, drones walked predetermined routes. Steady pace, no deviation. Still mostly the older drones, the less sophisticated kind. Once an EDA drone marched across the gap between buildings; a small diversion from the familiar pattern.

"They're keeping to the same patrolling pattern as during the day," Ifan said, breathing it into Bennet's ear.

"We'll have to time it right."

"It's not much of a fence, though."

Bennet indicated the parallel beams of light lancing across the spaces between the fence posts, the white beams at eighteen-inch intervals. "We break one of those beams and every alarm in the place will go off. It's hooked up to their sensor net."

Ifan grimaced. They'd already discussed it, how they'd have to dig a shallow scrape under the lowermost beam to get inside the perimeter fence. Discussion was one thing. Being there, on the ground, was something else entirely.

"This isn't going to work, Bennet. I can't dig us under the fence. This shale's too loose." Ifan probed at the jagged little slabs of loose scree they were lying on. "It'll cave in on us. If we have to leave in a hurry, I don't want to have to be digging my way out from the inside."

"Nor do I." Bennet rolled over onto his back, and stared up at the sky for a minute or two. Well, he'd thought from the beginning there was only one easy way in. "We'll have to try the other way. Go and get our horses, Ifan."

"Oh shit," Ifan said. "Do you really think it will work?"

Bennet went through the arguments again. "They should see a single entity they've already dismissed as harmless. They've far more chance of seeing two-legged men running about if we try to sneak. You're too big for it, and I'll be slower. No shield-suits. The horses will work."

"It's damn risky."

"Everything we do is risky. Go get the horses and we'll just ride in."

"Fucking bloody hell." Ifan hefted the short handled spade he'd brought with him and sighed, then trudged back up the slope. He was back within a few minutes, riding the grey and leading Bennet's mare. Bennet could hear him long before he saw him, the horses slipping down the side of the ridge with the metallic ring of hoof on stone. One of them snorted its displeasure. He got to his feet when Ifan brought the horses between him and the fence, pulling himself up into the saddle, slightly off balance with the pack on his back.

"Jan agrees with me. She thinks you're crazy." Then with quiet satisfaction: "I think she's worried about me."

"The gods help us," Bennet said. "Straight in, through the fence, then just follow my lead. Ready?"

"Of course I'm not bloody ready!" But Ifan followed Bennet anyway.

The mare was skittish, rolling her eyes at the bright bars of light, but Bennet pushed her on, letting her dance her way through the 'fence', trying to let her have enough of her head to act naturally. She broke into a canter, skittering off to one side for a few yards before he brought her to a stop. The grey cob followed.

"I thought you said the fence was alarmed," Ifan said, when no klaxons sounded.

"We think the drones are linked in like monitors to a network. The alarms don't need to be audible." Bennet loosened the reins and let the mare graze. He leaned down along her neck, making himself as small as he could. Ifan followed suit. Bennet dropped his voice to the merest breath of a whisper. "Here they come. We just have to sit it out."

One pair of drones marched towards them from the north, another pair from the mine mouth. Bennet, the side of his face pressed against the mare's rough mane, gathered the reins into his hand, holding her steady, letting her know he was still there and still in charge. She tossed her head as the cyborgs marched up to them. Beside him, Ifan held the cob under a tight rein.

Bennet didn't dare close his eyes, although he wanted too. This was madness. It was so stupid he couldn't believe he'd ever even dreamed of doing it.

The drone was so close he could touch it without even reaching out, standing stock still before him. The blank oval of a face was eyeless, but it seemed to be contemplating him, weighing him up, and processing the data collected by its sensors. It raised one of its stiff arms. Drones had only rudimentary hands, greyish-silver metallic parodies of a human hand bigger even than Ifan's, the palms little more than a ring of metal around the black round mouth of the laser rifle built into a drone's arms. The drone touched the mare with a tentativeness that astonished Bennet. She snorted and danced back a few steps. Bennet let her, but he didn't let her get too far away from the cob.

The drone watched them for another few seconds, each one as long as a lifetime, then turned and marched away with its companion. The other two drones moved back, and after a few more minutes, returned the way they'd come.

"Fucking hell," Ifan said, quieter than a breath, and his face was a pale blur in the darkness.

"Ssshh." Bennet brought the mare alongside the cob, still leant forward low along her neck. He kept his voice down to that ghost of a whisper. "We wait."

"For how long?"

"As long as it takes."

It took four hours.

Bennet made them wait at least an hour before setting the first charge, letting the horses drift in the direction of the chemical dump, grazing as they went. A drone patrol passed close to them once, but ignored them, and it was a long time before Bennet set the horses on their slow, careful drifting again, towards his first target.

Setting the solactinite was the easy part, with Ifan sitting the cob to block the drones' view of the mare, while Bennet slipped off her back to work his way through the cache of huge metal tanks. Even one-handed, it took only a few minutes to set the charges on half a dozen, scattered across the dump where one exploding tank would ignite the ones around it. He set the charges low, tucking them behind phalanges on the tank supports where they would sit in shadow.

When he was back on the mare, they started another slow drift towards the mine entrance, another few steps in the intricate dance, until all the dancing was done and it was time to leave the ball.

SECTION THREE: MIDNIGHT WATCH

04 Tertius 7488

CHAPTER NINE

Mendes, Sais City

"You must be Shield Lieutenant Rosamund."

Startled, Rosie jumped up. She had been sitting with her hands in her lap, looking down at them, and hadn't heard his approach. She came to attention, saluting. "Commander Caeden."

The commander smiled at her. It was a thin smile. Strained. "There's no need for formality here, Lieutenant. This is unofficial." He held out his hand. He had long, elegant hands. Like Bennet. "I'm glad you came. Please come through to my study. I've asked Hanna to bring us coffee."

He tucked her hand under his arm with a rather old-fashioned courtesy and escorted her out of the room the housekeeper—at least, Rosie assumed it had been the housekeeper—had called the Yellow Saloon, and across the wide entrance hall. The house was huge. Rosie had known what sort of family Bennet had come from, of course, but she hadn't translated that into a house quite this grand. It was built into the cliffs overlooking the western ocean, and appeared to be mostly made of glass. The sea and sky must dominate the view from every window. It looked like something showcased in an upmarket interior design programme—not that this family would ever do anything so vulgar as to allow any

HoloTV company, no matter how prestigious, to feature this house in one of their programmes.

The commander's study was smaller than she expected, given the luxury she'd seen so far. Three walls were lined with books in floor to ceiling bookshelves. Real books with decorative bindings, not electronic datapads. There was a faint tang of leather and old paper on the air. The desk faced the fourth wall with its wide windows, and looked out to sea. She'd never get any work done at it, herself. She would be forever looking up to watch the play of light on the sea or catch a glimpse of the lighthouse on Mendes Point.

The commander led her to a leather sofa at one side of the room and gestured to her to take a seat. He dropped into a chair at right angles to her, facing the window. The light wasn't kind to him. His face was familiar from the news lines and press interviews, of course. He was a popular go-to source for the journalists who wanted a comment about this or that aspect of the war. One of the hazards of leading the First Flotilla, she supposed. It was a surprise to see he looked older in the flesh than he appeared on AlbionNews. His shoulders were hunched, as if he were closing over himself, and he seemed tired, rubbing a hand over his face in a gesture so familiar, her heart thumped.

She found herself ticking off the similarities and differences, working through a mental checklist. She'd never thought Bennet looked like his father. Oh, there were undeniable similarities, of course there were. They were the same height, for one thing, and maybe one day Bennet would have filled out to the same build. But their faces weren't alike, and Caeden's eyes were a dark blue rather than Bennet's pale grey. The similarity in the shape of their hands had surprised her, though, and she looked closer, searching for other things they shared. The commander's hair, white now, was as thick as Bennet's and, like Bennet's trademark cowlicks, threatened to escape the stricter control the commander kept over it. The shapes of their ears, too, had similar lines. But that gesture, the way Caeden put his hand over his lower face and rubbed his thumb and forefinger along his cheekbones and closed his eyes… that was pure Bennet.

Rosie tightened her mouth hard against its tendency to tremble. Her eyes stung.

"Thank you for coming, Rosamund." He made a question of her name, seeking permission to use it.

It took a moment for her to be sure her voice wouldn't shake too much. "Bennet always called me Rosie."

"And may I?" He smiled at her nod. "Thank you, Rosie. I'm grateful for your time."

"That's all right. I'm glad to help, if I can. I can't tell you how sorry…" Her voice trailed away.

Caeden nodded, but before he could reply, the housekeeper arrived with a tray of coffee and macaroons. Laying the tray on the low table in front of the sofa and leaving it to Caeden to pour the coffee, she gave Rosie a tight smile. She closed the door behind her.

Rosie took her coffee black and unsweetened, and she refused one of the proffered macaroons. They looked homemade and delicious, but she'd have to choke it down and it would probably taste like ashes in the mouth. She sipped her coffee while Caeden sifted big brown sugar crystals into his own and stirred it. He had his head bent, focused on the little task and his fingers trembled on the spoon. Perhaps it wasn't that he was older than she'd thought, but that grief had aged him quickly and he was still trying to adjust to it.

"The one advantage I have in this is who I am, Rosie." The small smile he gave her seemed to seek her indulgence. "I asked for all the mission logs and reports, yours and the Infantry's, so I've a good idea of the official version of what happened on Telnos. The Supreme Commander is—was—Bennet's godfather, did you know that? He made sure I had access to anything I wanted to see. And, of course, I received your letter. My wife and I appreciated your kind words. Thank you."

Rosie winced. She'd laboured for days over the letter she'd sent. It had occupied the time while they were in quarantine and she'd been strung between not wanting to believe Bennet was gone, and the need to write it all down because he was owed a proper accounting. She'd locked herself away, cried, and wrote, and then cried some more. At the end she'd thought the letter too stilted and formal, but she sent it anyway. She couldn't find the energy to try again. "I wanted you to know how devastated the crew is."

"It meant a great deal to us. It comforted Bennet's mother and I'm grateful for your kindness. Meriel—my wife—would like to thank you herself, but I know you'll understand how difficult things are for her at the moment. I hope you'll be at the service tonight?"

"We're all coming. The whole crew, now we're out of quarantine. Lieutenant Grant's out of hospital, too, and he wants to be there, if that's all right. He was in charge of the Infantry platoon supporting us on Telnos. He and Bennet got on really well."

"He'll be welcome. Well, I hope tonight, after the ceremony, you'll allow me to introduce my wife, and I will be in your debt if you could speak to her. It will only be for a moment or two, I promise you. I realise how uncomfortable it may be for you, but I hope you'll agree."

Rosie could only nod. It was impossible to refuse, no matter how much she wished she could.

Caeden sipped at his coffee. "What the official versions don't tell me is what Telnos was really like or how Bennet was in those few days you were there. What it felt like, what you did there, what Bennet said and did, just what happened—" His voice rose, letting the emotion through. He stopped, tightening his mouth.

"You want me to tell you about Telnos?"

He unclenched his jaw enough to speak. "And what you did there. Please."

"Oh." She picked up her cup and sipped at the coffee. It was very good coffee.

"I'd appreciate all of it, Rosie," he said. When she looked up, it appeared all the controls all back in place. She wasn't fooled, though. The commander wasn't as monolithic as he liked to appear in public, as untouched.

"All right." She paused, gathering her thoughts. "It stank," she said, after a minute. "I don't mean that in any other way but that the whole place just smelled bad. We were in the marshes all the time and the mud was disgusting. It was slimy, it stuck to everything, and it smelled like..." she hesitated, and feeling her face heat, she went on, "Bennet said there was something in it that had been dead for a very long time."

She winced at the social faux pas of mentioning death in this house of mourning. But Bennet had said it, so it was to be remembered and treasured, the way she tried to remember and treasure everything about him. She thought this was what the commander wanted.

Caeden just nodded. "What else?"

"It was hot and muggy in the marshes. It rained all the time. Well, not exactly rain. More like a kind of drizzle, you know? The air was always damp and heavy, and you never felt dry. Or clean. And the flies!" She ran her hand through her hair to dislodge the memory. "The flies were awful. Every time we stopped moving, they'd try to eat us alive."

She drank more coffee, relishing the warmth it gave her. She found herself smiling, remembering. "Bennet hated it. He hated the smell and the heat, and he really hated not ever being quite clean. That sort of thing always annoyed him. I've seen him come back from jobs covered in crap and mud and blood, and I'd ask him how things went and all I'd get was a grunt, because all he could ever think about was getting into a shower. Most times, the only way I got to find out what he'd been up to was to be—" She stopped and her face was hot again. She gave Caeden a sidelong glance and said, hurriedly, "Be right outside, yelling questions at him."

"Ah?" The quirked-up smile he gave her was friendly and non-judgmental. "I know, of course, that Shield ships are very small."

She smiled back. "Yes. They are. We shared quarters for three years." She shrugged, still smiling. "Well, all right. I'd have to get in right there with him and ask. It didn't mean anything, you know.

We were friends and I loved him very much."

The words just slipped out. But the truth of them was someone reaching out to wipe the smile from her face, dragging down the corners of her mouth with a rough, careless hand. The little stab of pain under her chest left her nauseated. She put the cup down, and blinked down at it to get the stinging out of her eyes.

Oh, Bennet.

"I think that was mutual." Caeden's voice was kind.

She knew. She knew Bennet loved her. It just wasn't enough, and not the right way. It didn't matter, not now. Nothing mattered now.

As soon as she could trust her voice, she went back to the story of Bennet's last days. "We were in the marshes because we were sent in to find the farming families. You know they were there illegally? Some religious reason behind it."

"The Brethren are a small, but extreme, sect."

"Bennet was so angry with them. He hated that they were so close-minded and suspicious. They didn't believe the Maess were coming and they had to leave. They were so hard to convince. They thought it was some kind of plot by the government." She managed a wry grin. "Not that I think the Ennead cared what they did, of course, but the farmers were convinced they were being persecuted. Bennet said they were looking for martyrdom and they saw us as a heaven-sent opportunity to embrace it. He wasn't sympathetic."

"He wasn't religious," Caeden said, without condemnation.

"No. I think he got a bit of enjoyment out of poking fun at them. But not the first day. We were too busy chasing them all over the planet for that. The first time we came on a settlement, everyone in it scattered into the marshes as soon as we appeared. It took us hours to round them all up and oh! Did we all stink by the end of it! Bennet was furious. He swore worse than any of the Infantry troopers, and believe me, they were creative."

Caeden's mouth twitched. "I can imagine."

"But still, they had less of a problem with him than they did with the rest of us. Especially with me. They didn't like women running around with laser rifles. But Bennet could talk to them about what they believed in and he was very good at using the Book to find reasons for them to do what he said." Rosie smiled. "One of the advantages of a religious upbringing, he said, was always knowing which verse to quote. He didn't like them, though. He could forgive a lot of things, I think, but he hated wilful ignorance. And it cut at him, the life the kids had there. All work and prayers, and no fun. No real childlike things. He didn't like that." She clasped her hands together in her lap to stop them from trembling. "We had a fight about it. I thought he was looking down on them for being, you know, working class. He was angry about what he saw as child abuse."

"Did he stammer?"

Rosie stared. "No."

"Then he wasn't angry with you."

It made her grin, despite everything. "I know. He was angry with the parents. He loved kids." She hesitated again, sifting through what she could or should say.

"Please," he said. "Please go on."

"We spent five days on it. We were clearing a settlement when the fighter came. A lot of people got killed in the first strafing run. There was a little girl… I had to pull her out of Bennet's arms, and he was covered all over with blood from her." Rosie pressed her lips together hard. The child had been so tiny. "She died in the transport on the way to the landing area."

"That must have upset him."

"Yes." Rosie sighed softly. "But he had a job to do, you know, so he just got on with it. And he was good at it. He was Shield, through and through."

"Yes. I was very proud of him."

Well, Bennet didn't think so.

She supposed she couldn't say that aloud, though. She

contented herself with giving him a doubtful look. "When we got to the landing area, the Maess were only minutes away. We were last out, as always." Her lip curled. "Shield gets all the dirty jobs. We got the Infantry out and the settlers, and we were running for the cutter." She took another gulp of coffee. They were coming to it. When she spoke again, her voice shook and she couldn't stop it. "Javier, one of our people, went down. Bennet went back for him." She looked up at Caeden, at Bennet's father. "Did he know? I think he did. It was the last thing he ever said to me. 'Get them out of here,' he said, as if he knew he wouldn't be able to do it himself. Do you think he knew?"

"I don't know, Rosie," Caeden said, after a minute, his voice thick.

She couldn't look at him then. She pulled a handkerchief from her pocket and dabbed at her eyes. "I think he knew," she said, muffled by the linen.

"Then he probably did."

"I saw him get hit." Rosie crushed the handkerchief between shaking fingers. She couldn't stop them trembling. She tried to close her eyes against the image of Bennet spread-eagled out on the marshy ground. "I saw him."

Caeden grimaced. "I'm sorry. It's just that his mother needed to try…" He shook his head. "We're just trying to get something of him back, to understand what it was like for him those last few days. It might sound odd, because some of the things hurt, but it helps to get whatever scrap we can of him. I'm sorry if I upset you."

"It's all right."

Caeden sat back, watching her. "Are you sure, Rosie?"

She looked at him squarely. "I was quite some distance away when he went down, otherwise I wouldn't be here either. We weren't in shield-suits, just ordinary battledress, but we could still track everyone. We all wear tracers, Commander, built into our helmets. Bennet and I had command helmets. They let us track everyone else's tracer during a firefight, letting us know where they all are and where we might need to do something fast. His tracer blinked off."

Caeden sighed. Nodded. Looked away, his mouth tightening.

Rosie felt a stab of sympathy for him. It hurt so badly to lose Bennet, and there had been nothing between them but love and friendship. What must it be like, when there was guilt and remorse instead? "What you said, about wanting to know the details, to get something of him back? I can understand that. It makes sense. It's crazy, but I know what you mean about the picture being made up of little details. Things you normally wouldn't notice or care about."

Still, she hesitated.

Caeden leaned forward and touched her clasped hands. "Don't censor yourself. Don't worry if you think you're going to say something you think I won't want to hear. Every crumb is important right now, every tiny fragment that gives us a better picture of him. It truly does help."

Well, he seemed to mean it.

"Remember we were friends. And being in Shield, the sort of jobs we do make that important. They're very small ships, Commander. It's hard to have secrets. We rely on everyone else on the ship being Shield, too, and that means they'll have our backs and won't let us down. Shield is family and Shield looks after its own."

He nodded. "Every little detail, Rosie."

Rosie nodded. "All right. Everyone on the ship knew about Joss. Nobody much cared who Bennet slept with when he got home. All we cared about was where it counts, in the field, he was Shield. One of us. I don't think, though, anyone other than me knew much about you and his family." She had to swallow against the lump in her throat. "He trusted me, you see. We really were friends. We talked about things. I know he left home to be with Joss when he was quite young and that caused a big breach with you. I know he was close to his mother and he stayed good friends with Thea, but he didn't see as much of his kid brother and sister.

He missed them and he wasn't happy about not being as close to them. It made him feel… He said once it was like being something that had been left over. Superfluous to requirements, is how he described it. Closed out."

"He was never that. Never."

"I only know what he said. I know he and Liam are closer now—were closer—but things were more distant than he liked with Natalia. I just wanted to say he seemed easier talking about you after the T18 job. He said things were getting sorted out. I think it did you both good, didn't it?"

Caeden actually laughed. "Yes. Yes, it did. It gave me the chance I thought I'd never have, to make things right with him. We got a good distance down that road, thank the gods."

"Yes. He said things were good. He was happy about it."

He looked away from her, staring past her to where the sea tried to satisfy its insatiable hunger by pounding against the cliffs beneath the house. After a moment, he passed his hand over his face. "Thank you, Rosie. Thank you. That helps a great deal, to know he felt the same. It eases my mind. I'm glad he had you to trust in and talk to."

"As I said, we were good friends."

"It's hard for me to think that for a long time he and I weren't good friends. But he was always my son. And in the end, that's all that matters."

Greatly daring, she patted his hand, the way she had sometimes patted Bennet's. She gave him a minute or two, letting him stare out to sea and, hopefully, get some comfort there.

"Thank you, my dear. I'm sorry to put you through that. I'm afraid when you meet his mother tonight she may seek some of the same information." His smile was rueful, unamused. "It helps so much to have a picture of his last few days. It brings him closer. Every scrap helps mark who he was and what we've lost."

Rosie winced and nodded. "I wish…"

He tilted his head towards her and waited.

She drew a long breath. "I wish I could have brought him home."

The silence lasted for a long time. Rosie stared down at her coffee cup. She couldn't see it clearly and her eyes ached. Her throat was tight and her nose felt stuffed up, as if she had a head cold. Everything ached and hurt and complained.

She'd failed Bennet there. She'd failed him, she'd left him behind, and nothing could ever make that right. Shield prided itself on looking after its own. It felt wrong to have abandoned Bennet, even if the dead were past caring if they went home or not.

Caeden's voice sounded rusty and rough when he spoke again. "Your duty was to the living, Rosie. Bennet wouldn't have that any other way."

"No. I know. It doesn't make it any easier."

"I know. I do know. I feel helpless, too, and a failure." He raised his hands, then let them drop into his lap. "Bennet trusted you, and I'll honour that by trusting you too. It's too late. That's the thing. Too late to for me do something for him to show him how much he wasn't superfluous or left over. That's hard."

Rosie froze. "Oh."

Caeden gave her a sharp look. "What is it?"

It was a chance. Not much of one, maybe, but a chance. She had her own amends to make and maybe… She moistened her lips, choosing her words with care. "There's one way, maybe. Listen. Bennet was beyond angry with those farmers for not believing us and slowing us down, because he knew we hadn't got everyone off. It wasn't really to do with him bucking against religion. He was too smart for that. There were missing miners and farming families. Even some of the Infantry didn't make it back. He was mad as hell over what would happen to them, especially for the kids' sakes. He would hate being here and knowing he'd left kids behind to die. He'd hate that. It would have eaten him up."

Caeden sat back. She thought he was thinking over what she'd said, that he was taking the right message from it. He nodded. "Yes. I see."

"It would mark the kind of person he was. He'd like it."

Caeden's mouth twitched. "Is this how Shield operates? Sneaking?"

Her throat tightened further. She nodded. "Maybe. Yes."

Caeden excused himself and went to the window. She doubted he saw much of the sea beyond, but he was standing straighter than when he'd greeted her in the salon, more upright. "I see," he said, again. "Rosie, have you ever met the Supreme Commander?"

She was surprised into a laugh. "Not likely!"

"You'll meet him tonight. I'd like to introduce you to him. I want you to tell him about those families that got left behind, all right?"

He turned his head and they looked at each other. He had understood, then. She nodded, the laughter gone as fast as it came. She could only hope Caeden's influence would be enough. That someone—please the gods let it be the Hype—would be sent back to look.

"We'll leave it there for now." Caeden detoured to his desk to collect a small parcel before coming back to his chair. He smiled at her. "There's another reason I wanted to see you today. I wanted to give you this. Bennet wanted you to have it. He left it to you in his will."

He handed over the little parcel. Startled, Rosie took it.

"Open it." While she struggled with the packaging, he added, "It belonged to my grandmother's family. She died when Bennet was about thirteen or fourteen. She wanted him to give this to the girl he was going to marry. Well, we both know that was never going to happen."

The wrappings hid a rather shabby, red velvet jewellery case. She had to fiddle with the clasp, an odd little mechanism she had to press in, before she could open it. Inside was a note from Bennet. She'd know that scrawl anywhere. And underneath... Rosie drew in a sharp breath.

"Oh," was all she could say.

Caeden smiled. "They're good diamonds and a fine sapphire, but you'll appreciate it isn't of any great monetary value. Maybe a few thousand credits. For Bennet, its value was purely sentimental."

"He was. Sentimental, I mean. Although he tried to hide it." Rosie picked up the note from Bennet and glanced again at the pendant beneath. The diamonds flashed and the deep blue stone in the centre glowed. The note was short.

For the only girl who could have straightened me out.

The commander was very considerate. He let her bawl for several minutes, only patting her shoulder or handing her another handkerchief when hers was sodden. He made her drink more coffee, fastened the pendant around her neck and waved away her incoherent protests.

"But you said it was a family piece! I can't—"

"But didn't you say Shield was family?" Caeden closed her fingers over the box and Bennet's note, holding her hands between his. "He left it to you, Rosie. He wanted you to have it. Take it with his love, and his mother's and my best wishes and thanks."

"It's lovely." She smoothed Bennet's note, fingers caressing the untidy writing, and folded it, slipping it back into the jewel case. The case went into her pocket. "Thank you."

"I'm glad that despite everything, he had someone to give it to. And I'm glad it was you, Rosie."

She had to use her handkerchief again, and he let her be until she was dabbing her eyes. She sniffed, wishing Bennet's message hadn't been so damn ironic. But it put her in mind of something else. "I tried to contact Joss when they released us from quarantine, but all I got was a stock response from his lawyer. Is he all right?"

"I just got in on this morning's shuttle from Demeter, so I haven't seen him myself yet. He'll be there tonight. Do you know him well?"

"Not well. We met a few times." Her mouth snapped shut because this was something that maybe she shouldn't say.

"Meriel says he's devastated."

Rosie snorted. "I just wonder where he was when Bennet—" She stopped, choked, then said, more temperately, "I'm sorry. It's none of my business. But if you want to know what other things were on Bennet's mind on Telnos, then I can tell you that Joss was. They weren't very happy, you know. He didn't make Bennet happy."

Caeden said nothing for a moment. "We can't really know, I suppose. But I'm sure Joss is grieving deeply. Perhaps the service tonight will help him draw a line under it all."

"Will it help you draw any lines?"

She saw his eyes gleam with tears. "For one third of my son's life we were estranged from each other, and for the other two thirds I was barely there, a part-time father for a few weeks a year. What do you think?"

She looked away, flushed. "That I'd better go. You'll have a lot to do, Commander, if you just got in from Demeter. I'll be pleased to meet Madame Meriel this evening and talk to her, if you think it will help her." Rosie stood up and held out her hand. "Forget what I said about Joss, please. As you say, only those two could tell what was really going on and I know Bennet loved him."

Caeden got to his feet, and took her outstretched hand. "Yes."

"And what I think is that some people can draw lines and some of us don't get any benefit from them."

Caeden held her hand in his for a second and put the other over it just as he had when they met. "I agree, my dear. I don't think that some of us understand what they are."

CHAPTER TEN

The Thebaid, Sais City

Joss didn't return to the Thebaid until the morning of the Midnight Watch.

He spent some time before he left the apartment choosing the right amulets. The heart scarab was easy of course, but the others took some consideration. In the end, he chose a djed and a tet made from carved lapis lazuli and an udjat, the eye of Horus, of yellow gold inlaid with white and black enamels. He wrapped them in a silk scarf he'd once bought as part of a campaign to make his Bennet into an elegant man about town—a pointless exercise, since the soldier would insist on pushing through the civilised veneer, but he'd had fun shopping. Bennet had laughed and allowed himself to be indulged, but Joss didn't think he'd ever worn the scarf.

He should make another sacrifice of something he loved and that Bennet had loved, for Bennet to take with him. Thinking about what might be suitable had filled his days for the last week. He'd combed through the apartment, picking up this artefact or that, considering each one. But they were too small, too insubstantial. In the end there was only one choice. The glass sculpture Bennet had admired the first night they had together, lay in shards on the living room floor when Joss closed the door on the apartment and walked across the park to the Institute.

It took the porters perhaps half an hour to locate the mummy in the storage vaults and bring it to him. He used the time to prepare. When the porters arrived, the coffin went onto the trestles he'd got ready while he waited, and they stood to one side while he opened seals that hadn't been touched for more than nine years. Once he'd moved the lid aside, they lifted the elaborately-wrapped mummy out of its quiet coffin and laid it on the examination table.

They left him alone, then, with Amthoth.

He had agreed the time and place for the service with Meriel, allowing her the comfort of the local family temple and the priest who'd carried out Bennet's naming ceremony. It didn't matter. Like Bennet, he'd been brought up in the faith, and like Bennet he'd fallen away from it.

For both of them, anything to do with Thebes was the Institute, not the church. Bennet hadn't been inside a temple for years and he'd have laughed at the thought of several Theban priests getting pious for his sake. But he might have enjoyed it, sitting beside Joss, the pair of them tracing the ancient rites in the modern service, seeing the long chain of ritual binding the Midnight Watch to Amthoth.

Reminded, Joss turned back to the mummy on the table. The bandages had shrunk over the millennia so that something of the features could be discerned, the sharp nose echoing the high cheekbones. Bennet had had wonderful cheekbones and he'd been beautiful. Joss wondered if Amthoth had been beautiful. He wondered who'd loved Amthoth, six millennia ago.

He laid his hands on Amthoth's chest, on the husk of dry bone and old linen.

Resentment flared like the ache in an old wound when the cold air hit it. He'd wanted Bennet out of the military. He'd wanted Bennet to himself. If Bennet had been at home where he belonged then he wouldn't have been killed and they'd have been happy.

They'd have been together. There would have been no need for those frequent short-lived flings he had to keep the loneliness at bay when Bennet wasn't there.

"I don't know why you feel the need to sleep with people you don't care for," Bennet had said once. "What's in it for you? I can't see it."

"It's just sex. You're permanent. You're the one I love." Joss had kissed him, relieved that he was back again and unhurt, and Bennet had pulled Joss down onto the bed and demonstrated it wasn't just sex with him.

Joss said it again now, to Amthoth. "It's just sex. And I get bored to tears with just sex. It was different when you were home."

It was true. The nameless ones who lasted a week or less were to pass the time, dropped the instant Bennet got home, picked up again sometimes when Bennet was away, petty substitutions for the Bennet who was the permanency who wasn't just sex. And now the permanency was gone and all he'd have to remember Bennet by would be a few lines of an obituary in one of the quality news lines and some cold, High Theban church service.

With candles, though. He could almost hear Bennet laughing. *Light one for me.*

Joss could do that. He reached for bronze dish packed with incense and put it on the table, a few inches from the top of Amthoth's head. Two further dishes of incense, one at each side at the hip, and a fourth dish at the feet. He and Bennet would have their own private remembrance here, with Amthoth, where it all began.

He dissolved natron in water and rinsed his hands and mouth, as the priests would have done six millennia before, when this rite was performed for Amthoth. A pinch of the dry salt in each nostril and, like the priests, he had purified himself in the eyes of the gods, saying the prayers to himself in the old Theban only scholars could read or speak now. When everything was ready, he took the amulets from the case in which he'd carried them. Later, he would bury them in the Thebaid's grounds, wrapped in the silk scarf.

Joss lit the incense and breathed it in. It was sharp, biting at the back of his throat. It felt right. Bennet might laugh, but he'd prefer this to the genteel and chilly service his family were preparing for him. He'd see its significance.

One by one, Joss laid the amulets on the mummy, reciting the proper prayers. Last came the bloodstone heart scarab, the one Bennet had admired the first time they'd been together and that had been one of Bennet's favourites ever since. He laid it on the mummy's hollow, heart-less chest. He put his hand over the scarab, in the exact spot where he'd once put his hand over Bennet's.

"I have come in order that I may be thy protection. I gather together for thee thy bones, I draw together for thee thy members, I have brought for thee thy heart..."

When it was all over, he'd gathered together the amulets and replaced Amthoth in his coffin with eyes that could hardly focus. The mummy weighed so little, so much had wasted away.

He closed the lid on the decorated box where Amthoth slept in peace, the last substitution for Bennet.

The very last.

Mendes temple, Sais City

"Friend or family, sir?"

Joss stood and stared, disoriented by the question. What did he mean, this priest in his white linen vestments?

He had driven out to Mendes to the small local temple in which Bennet had sat out many a bored childhood hour, going straight there rather than to a house where he had doubted his welcome. A long time ago he had crossed that threshold, taken by his father in one of his attempts to get Joss interested in politics—and to try and marry Joss off to a political ally's niece—but Joss would have been blind to a dozen nieces dancing naked on the table. He smiled at the irony of his father never knowing that one day he'd seduce and love the political ally's eldest son.

He'd dithered right until the last minute about whether to come at all. What use was it to him, this family and establishment service? He'd said his goodbye already through the medium of Amthoth.

But in the end, he couldn't stay away. Anything else would be an abandonment and he'd abandoned Bennet all too many times already through those substitutes he'd played with. Each one had been an abandonment, a betrayal. Even Amthoth had been that. And even though Bennet was almost six weeks dead and he'd abandoned Joss now—the supreme, irrevocable abandonment— Joss couldn't do it again.

The empty space would allow no further substitutions.

"Friend or family, sir?"

You think about it.

You look into the main body of the temple, to the rows of pews set before the altar, the candles, the gold and the crimson that make a pale and unconvincing echo, in this constricted place, of the grandeur of the main Temple sitting on the edge of the park a few hundred yards from the Institute. This smaller and meaner temple is already crowded. The left hand of the nave is full of uniforms, one whole contingent of more than thirty in funereal black, the ones who failed to bring him back this time.

Like you, they come to celebrate failure and emptiness and silence.

At the front of the right hand side, there's the shock of white hair to mark where Caeden sits, the leonine head framed by the crimson of the altar cloth. You wonder what failure and abandonment demands his atonement.

You pulled Bennet apart between you, you and Caeden. He tried to please you both, and ended up pleasing neither. And it angered you, that he should still be trying to win Caeden's approval, to live a life strung out between what you wanted and what the Great Commander wanted.

If he'd loved you enough, he wouldn't have wanted to do that. He wouldn't have wanted anything but the life you had together.

But he didn't love you enough. He didn't. *He only loved you enough to compromise, and what comfort is there in the compromise that killed him?* Only the comfort that death took him while he was still yours.

Cold comfort, but it's all you have.

It's as if you're standing in the Field of Reeds, eyes widening against the light, his hands on your shoulders; and when you ask what it all means, he holds up a scarab, intricately carved in bloodstone or faience or lapis lazuli; he holds your heart in those long hands.

And you watch as he holds your gaze with his, the grey eyes sad and remote and regretful, and he shakes his head. He drops the scarab, unheeded, to the ground and the lips brushing yours are cold and loveless as he says goodbye.

The priest waited, a patient and helpful expression on his face.

"What?" Joss said.

"Friend or family, sir? So I know where to direct you to sit."

"Oh." Joss looked past the priest into the temple, seeing again the whiteness of Caeden's head. "I'm family. I'm the only family he's had for years. I know where I'm going to sit."

Head high, he brushed past the priest and marched up the aisle to the front of the chapel. He was conscious of people glancing at him as he went past them, but he recognised only a few. General Martens was there, near the front. When Bennet had first joined Shield, he'd had no trouble describing what the general looked like, but he'd struggled to get across what he'd called the 'more important' things. She was the epitome of Shield, Bennet had said;

quiet, reticent and watchful. Her greatest quality was a kind of stillness. Joss had been disappointed when he finally saw the general at an awards ceremony. He'd been expecting something monolithic and imposing, and couldn't reconcile Bennet's description with the small woman sitting quietly at the side of the dais. Not for the first time, Joss had proof he and Bennet hadn't always seen things alike.

Ah, there was Rosie, in the familiar black and silver. Joss looked away. The uniform brought too many memories of Bennet. A young black man, face gaunt, sat beside her in a different uniform, not Shield, his left arm cradled in a sling, a slash of white linen against the bright scarlet of his tunic. His arm looked foreshortened with no hand visible. He wore a black armband on his uninjured arm.

Rosie stared at Joss as he went past her. Jumping up, she put out a hand to stop him. "Joss!"

He paused, allowed her to approach. She pulled him into a hug. Her eyes were wet when she stepped back.

"Oh, Joss."

Could everyone in the universe cry more easily than him? His eyes burned and burned, but that was all he could do. He allowed to Rosie embrace him and cry on his shoulder and he had to hear the words she choked out, words about Bennet and regrets and *Oh gods, I had to leave him, Joss, and I'm so, so sorry*. He allowed it because Bennet had… had loved her, he supposed. He had never understood what Bennet had seen in her. She was a scrap of a thing with no beauty and even less animation. Her eyes were red and she sniffled into a handkerchief.

When she drew back, he patted her shoulder. He disengaged himself without speaking, and went on up the aisle. He could sense her gaze on his back, intent and sombre. He passed Felix, Bennet's partner at the Strategy Unit, on the way. Felix didn't jump up to detain him. He nodded at Joss instead, his gaze as grave as Rosie's.

As he drew level with the front pew, where the family sat, Joss heard Meriel say something to Caeden, caught his own name, but he ignored them for the moment. He had his own rituals to finish. He'd brought a candle with him, pure and white and unsullied, just like the precious thing Bennet had given him more than nine years ago and which he'd spent the last nine years wasting. He'd dipped it into the natron solution with which he'd honoured Bennet and Amthoth, trying to marry together their two worlds. He lit it carefully and set it into the candelabrum, beside the dozens of others already burning there.

Beside him someone in a gold-braided uniform chose a candle from the box on the altar and lit it, setting into a holder beside Joss's. Joss listened to the murmur of a prayer of remembrance.

Yes. He should mumble something so the form was observed, the ritual intact. But not this rite.

He said, softly, in old Theban, "Thou shalt come unto the Field of Reeds and bread and wine and cakes shall be given to thee at the altar of the God. Thou shalt be nourished by it and thy body shall be like the bodies of the gods. Rejoice thou in it."

The man next to him glanced at him, eyebrow shooting up to his hairline, but he said nothing, going instead down the aisle to take the first seat on the left hand side. When Joss turned, he saw Caeden had got up and gone to join the gold braid, talking to him quietly. Rosie, too, had been beckoned forward to join the conversation, her face pink.

Thea waited a few feet away. She held out her arms and gathered him in. Joss liked Thea the best of all Bennet's family, even more than Meriel. She and Bennet were very alike, even down to the wide grey eyes. Joss avoided looking at her eyes now. They were too much like Bennet's.

"Mama wants you to sit with us, with the rest of the family." Thea rested her forehead against his. "Joss. Oh, Joss."

Someone else who could cry so easily that Joss felt a dull envy. He patted her back and let her go into the first pew to retake her seat beside her husband, whose name Joss could barely remember. Alain? Something like that. They must have left the child at home.

There was a space beside Meriel, on the outside of the pew.

She held out her hand, and he allowed himself to be drawn into the seat beside her.

"Joss," she said, her voice thick.

He kissed her cheek, and nodded at Liam and Natalia sitting further down the pew. Both were in cadet uniform. Two more of Caeden's sacrificial lambs on the altar of duty and honour and service.

"Hey," Liam said, subdued.

"How are you?" Natalia was polite and cool as always.

How the hell did she think he was? Joss didn't answer, except by shaking his head. He glanced over at Caeden. Both Caeden and the gold braid had turned to look at him. He couldn't hear what was being said, and he turned away to watch the preparations by the altar. Almost time.

Caeden came back a few minutes later, squeezing past Joss to sit between him and Meriel. He gathered his wife's hand in his and Joss was surprised, when Caeden turned to him, that his eyes weren't as cold and calculating as usual. Instead, they acknowledged, accepted.

"I'm glad you came, Joss," Caeden said, and he seemed to mean it, even though he'd probably have to explain later to those friends and family who didn't already know—and Joss suspected that Caeden had kept everything as quiet as he could—just who Joss was, sitting up there in the front row with them as though he had the right.

Then a horn sounded and they were silent, and the service for the beloved dead began. The choir, piercingly high and remote, sang of death and resurrection. It was glorious, and so beautiful it made Joss's throat ache. And when he could bear no more of the austere beauty, and the tears came at last, despite his attempts to be as still and quiet as the man he sat beside, it was Caeden's free hand that settled on his arm in comfort.

He cried because of how much he'd wasted, because of the petty substitutions, because Bennet had been beautiful and strong and good for him, and because Bennet was gone. And he cried because he couldn't laugh as he imagined the shock on Bennet's face to see him and Caeden weeping together, with Caeden's hand on his.

CHAPTER ELEVEN

The dreadnought *Gyrfalcon*

Fleet Lieutenant Flynn was not a religious man. His orphanage had enforced attendance at church while he was growing up, of course, so he could give regular thanks for the inestimable blessings rained down upon him by the social cohesion services department of the Albion state. With no other opportunity to enrich an otherwise emotionally deprived life, any religious impulses had faded fast. Besides, Flynn wasn't made for religious devotion. He had found his own way in this, as in all other things. His views of the gods and religion were a touch unformed and required no sort of formal observance. It was more convenient that way.

He had been here before, in this quiet section on Deck 1 near the prow of the ship, but not to worship, and not to give thanks. In more than four years of service on the *Gyrfalcon*, Flynn had been to the Theban chapel often to honour and remember the dead.

At a quarter of an hour before midnight, Deck 1 was deserted. He hadn't seen anyone on his way to the chapel.

It was a small room, the plain altar and the huge candelabrum beside it set before a view-screen taking up an entire wall, showing the twisting energy streams of hyperspace. Somewhere up ahead were the stars and systems towards which the *Gyrfalcon* travelled. Dredging up the memories of the religious instruction that his orphanage had given him, he understood the symbolism of putting the chapel here, of providing the view of what lay ahead—a representation of the soul's journey to the gods, of course. Not something he subscribed to within his incoherent thoughts about religion, but it looked pretty. More to the point, Flynn liked to look where he was going straight in the eye.

The chapel was sparsely furnished and decorated with restraint, unlike the main Theban temple in Sais City. Flynn couldn't remember now why he'd wandered in there on a home leave once. Probably because it was cool inside and he'd thought, when he was capable of thought at all, that the richly stained windows would cast a dim and soothing light. He had been nursing a doozy of a headache, he remembered, still recovering from the excitements of the evening before when he'd had a streak of luck at the gambling tables that was likely still talked about in hushed tones in Sais's casinos. All he wanted was somewhere quiet where the light wouldn't hurt his desperately hung-over eyes. What he had found was a vast space that appeared to have been attacked by some maniac with an unlimited supply of gold leaf and crimson paint. As a hangover cure, it hadn't quite made the grade.

This little room was clean and barely decorated. A few of ancient hieroglyphics had been picked out along the tops of the walls, a frieze of symbols in greens, blues and ochre. He had no idea what they meant. He walked down the aisle to the plain altar and the great candelabrum set beside it. It was a good room. Comforting.

He'd attended far too many Midnight Watches, for far too many friends. Mind you, not that the lost pilots had all been High Thebans. They would have been content with a short memorial service. They were low church types, who, if they'd thought of religion at all, wanted it simple and direct and over as fast as possible.

He thought that simplicity would appeal to Bennet, too. What was it Bennet had said, almost two years ago now? Something about Flynn not missing much by not being a church-goer, except maybe the sung High Service. Well, Flynn couldn't do the hymns and the prayers, but he could and would light the candle on the stroke of midnight, and he'd remember.

He'd remember a cramped and smelly Mosquito cockpit, Bennet jammed in behind the pilot's seat, and the sudden heat and weight of a hand on his right shoulder as Bennet made his move: shyly and circumspectly, because it was Bennet and the way he did things, but an unmistakable offer. Flynn had accepted without words, bringing his left hand up and putting it over Bennet's.

Yes. I want you too. Yes.

Bennet's thumb had rubbed little circles on Flynn's skin, feather light, subtle. The restraint set the entire pace of their time together—with one regrettable lapse on his side. Not the hot and animalistic sex he was used to, but unhurried and leisurely lovemaking. They hadn't had very long together, but he treasured and cherished every minute. He hoped he'd been as special in Bennet's life as Bennet had been for him.

Almost time.

He took a candle from the box on the altar. White for remembrance. He glanced at his chronometer, counting off the last minute. As midnight struck, he lit the candle at the eternal flame at the altar.

Clutching the tiny silver shield in his left hand, he added the candle to the half-melted pile of wax on the candelabrum, and remembered.

"How long do you think we'll have?" Flynn had asked, licking his way down the side of Bennet's neck, tasting the salt.

"Dunno." Bennet had tilted his head back to give Flynn easier access. He had smoothed his hands over Flynn's back. Flynn was settled comfortably between Bennet's legs. "They'll call when they've arranged a rendezvous."

"I hope it's not for about a zillion years," Flynn muttered, licking his way up the other side of Bennet's neck.

"Don't worry about it. Make the most of what we've got." Bennet's eyes widened as Flynn's cock pressed up against him.

Flynn chuckled, using his hands to trail a five-fingered teasing pattern up Bennet's sides. Bennet laughed and wriggled, caught Flynn by the back of his neck and kissed him.

Flynn liked kissing. In fact, Flynn considered himself something of an expert in the art. He'd tried it in all its forms, from the first tentative pressing together of juvenile lips that had you wondering what all the fuss was about, to the discovery that if you just opened your mouth and, you know, kind of moved everything, your tongue suddenly had a lot more positive uses than just allowing you to articulate clearly and swallow things without choking. Flynn got the hang of it, ran with it, and never looked back.

Soft kisses and hard kisses; kisses that were wet and slobbery with people who didn't know exactly how to hold their lips to get the best and sexiest effect, and wet and sexy kisses with people who did. Kisses that turned the blood to molten lava and kisses that cooled you as you came down. Kisses that inflamed and kisses that soothed; feverish kisses and languid after-sex kisses. Kisses that meant only good fellowship and casual affection, and kisses that were desire incarnate.

Flynn had not only tried them all, he'd made them his own. He was considered by all the relevant authorities to be rather a specialist in the area.

Flynn really liked kissing. He had been gratified by the discovery that Bennet liked it too. Because now he could add slow kisses to the repertoire. Kisses so leisured and intense the world came to a stop while a hot tongue moved over his lips, explored each and every tooth down to the last molar, while teeth pulled at his bottom lip, biting it gently until it was swollen and hot and heavy, and he had to lick his lip to cool it and met Bennet's tongue with his. Only then, would Bennet's mouth close over his and start a real in-earnest kiss that lasted several more centuries. Those were kisses Bennet seemed to specialise in.

Flynn was always willing to take tips from another expert. A man should always try to extend his technique.

Later, when he had his breath back, Flynn contented himself with the cooling kisses, the little kisses that fluttered always on the edge of drowsiness, the ones that meant satisfaction and peace and weren't about sex at all. But they sure as hell weren't just good fellowship and casual affection kisses.

"I'm impressed," Bennet said in his ear, breath warm and moist. "You're hornier than a seventeen year old."

Flynn blinked to keep himself awake. Unlike his previous lovers, Bennet wasn't there just for some quick sex, and rather to Flynn's surprise and gratification, put as much energy into all the other elements of the relationship as he did the act itself. After-sex talks might not be profound—certainly not deep discussions about theology or philosophy—but every conversation helped create something. Flynn wasn't sure what, but he liked the unusual sensation of someone being as interested in his mind and personality as much as they were interested in making pleasurable use of his gonads. A refreshing change.

"I get inspired," he said.

"Oh?"

"The way you kiss me. Do you realise that kiss would be illegal, even in private between two consenting adults, in seven out of the nine provinces and would carry a government health warning in the other two?"

Bennet laughed, the vibration in his chest making Flynn vibrate in kind. "Which ones wouldn't have banned it?"

"Well, Galatia for a start. Galatians are flighty."

"True," Bennet said, nodding. "You have to think a people whose national dress consists of a few feathers and two stick-on rhinestones, can't be the deepest thinkers on Albion."

"Yeah, but they're too flighty to appreciate a good thing when they get it. A kiss like that needs serious application. The Nicaeans now are a different proposition altogether. Those Nicaean courtesans pay good money to be trained to kiss like that. You might want to bear it in mind if ever you want a change of career."

"And what would you know about Nicaean courtesans?"

"Oh, I may have had dealings with one or two in the past." Flynn raised himself up onto one elbow and looked down into Bennet's flushed face. "But if you give me something, I promise I won't ever do it again."

"What should I give you, then?"

"Well, let's start with another one of those kisses, and see where that leads us, huh?"

Somehow, neither of them had been surprised when it led to exactly the same place as all its predecessors.

No, it wasn't hard to remember. It was harder to remember and keep calm, to stop everything overwhelming him and his gut tearing itself into knots. That was harder.

Flynn found his way to a seat, the one in front of where Cruz sat. She must have followed Flynn down here, stalwart and silent, the sister Flynn had never had, loving and undemanding and the prop of normality in Flynn's life. She put a hand on his shoulder, but said nothing, letting him grieve in silence.

Flynn sat with his head bowed. On the altar, the candle flame guttered, flickered, and went out.

Cruz leaned forward until her breath ghosted against the side of Flynn's neck. "All right?"

"I will be. Sorry."

"You don't have to be sorry." Cruz's hand tightened on Flynn's shoulder. "You needed that, I'd say."

"Mmn. Thanks for being here."

"That's what friends are for." Cruz left her seat and moved forward a row to join Flynn. "I didn't want to disturb you, but I didn't want you to be on your own, either. You aren't on your own,

Flynn."

"You did it just right. Thanks." After a long silence, he glanced at his wrist chronometer. "It'll all be over on Albion, too, by now. It's not much, is it, Cruz? You're born and grow up and live and have fun, and you go to work and get shot at and you blow things up, and it's all exciting and amazing, and then one day it comes to an end with a candle and a few hymns. It doesn't seem right." Flynn struggled with it. "I mean, it's out of proportion. It's too small, a paltry kind of thing to say it's all over."

"It helps people. To have a service to mark it all, I mean." Poor Cruz. Her forte was in silence and support at a time like this. She didn't know what to say.

"The commander will be there, I guess, and Madame Meriel. I saw a holopic of her on the news lines. She's beautiful. You can see where he got his looks from. His brother and sisters will be there, and the people from his ship, and the Shield General and the Supreme Commander, I bet, and loads of the top brass for the commander's sake." Flynn let his voice fade away.

And Joss. Joss would be there, the one who had the right to mourn in public because Bennet had belonged to him.

Much-loved partner of Joss...

But Flynn had been the one in the store room, just before Bennet left, where Bennet had almost said he loved him. Flynn was the one holding the silver shield in his hand.

"And here it's just me and you."

"Flynn," Cruz said, helplessly.

"It's all right. Everything's all right. I lost him last year, really. We knew we'd never meet again, but at least as long as I thought he was okay, I could bear it." He paused, and thought about it, hard. "Now I don't know that I can."

Cruz sighed and retreated to what she was good at. Her hand slipped into Flynn's and held it, and they sat in silence.

The Midnight Watch, the great and terrible and sublime service to honour the memory of the beloved dead, was over.

SECTION FOUR:
FROM THE LION'S MOUTH

17 – 21 Tertius 7488

CHAPTER TWELVE

17 Tertius 7488: Telnos

If ever Bennet was to have a wish granted, it would be that whichever prophet the Brethren had followed to Telnos had been punished by a Divine infliction of every calamity known to mankind. The man deserved to suffer. A few old-fashioned plagues would be in order. Fleas, maybe. That was a good one. Or even better, boils .Imagining the man covered from head to foot in weeping pustular sores was gratifying.

"It's just the fever," was Ifan's diagnosis, when Bennet shared this comforting thought. "And you've had it worse."

Bennet grunted a response and plodded between the beds belonging to the farmer families to reach the field kitchen. There was always hot water on the cook stove. Ifan went with him and stood to one side, watching, before shaking his head in pitying fashion and slapping Bennet's hands away from the kettle. The big jar of grubs and the leafy twigs they lived on sat on a nearby shelf. The little buggers had almost stripped the twigs bare of leaves. Ifan picked out the three biggest of the thick-bodied white maggots while Bennet grumbled and leaned up against the stove, relishing the warmth.

The grubs squished against the sides of the tin cup with the help of a spoon, juicy and gelatinous. Ifan gave them a thorough mashing before adding boiling water. A few pinches of allspice and a sprinkling of herbs from the cooking stores followed. The herbs and spices had no medicinal effect whatsoever, but people claimed they made the slimy liquid more palatable.

They lied. The muck was disgusting. It was the epitome of disgusting.

Bennet let his shoulders slump in the hope he looked pathetic, but Ifan was all business and little sympathy. They all had to drink the grub tea at some time or other when the constant low-grade fevers flared up. Bennet's latest bout was well on its way out of his system, thanks to the grubs, but he wouldn't be averse to some coddling. Sadly, ex-troopers didn't do coddling very well. At all.

"Here. It should have steeped enough by now." Ifan's big hands were surprisingly deft, straining the tea into another cup and setting the dregs aside with more hot water. There was enough to make another, if weaker, dose and they couldn't afford to waste any of it. Bennet would probably be made to drink it later.

Bennet hesitated, his gut roiling at the thought of trying to drink the crap. "Who do you think tried the grubs in the first place?"

Ifan shrugged, then grimaced. "The gods alone know."

"I can't work out what sort of cockeyed madman would even think about it. I mean, who looks at a tree full of maggots and thinks, 'Hey! If I eat them maybe I won't get the fever.' Who does that?"

"Maybe one of them had a vision or something."

Luke appeared at Bennet's side. "Leah said to drink it up," he ordered. "While it's good and hot."

Dear gods, could Shield officers do queasy!

Bennet groaned aloud, took a deep breath and tilted the cup up, choking down the thick liquid in a single go. If he stopped, he would never find the fortitude to try again. He had to press his lips together hard against the nausea threatened by his rebellious stomach. Ifan, grinning, handed him a cup of water to rinse his mouth. Nothing could take the taste away.

Luke watched with interest. "Leah and Abram pray for you every day. Did you know?"

"That's almost worse than the grubs," Ifan said. "Insulting."

"If it's a choice between the insults or grubs, then I'll take the prayers." Maybe he'd keep the grubs down this time. He allowed himself to relax, and started back towards his own bunk at the other end of the cave, Luke sticking like a burr, as usual. It seemed a long way to walk. Ifan, still grinning, went with them. The unsympathetic bastard.

Luke tucked his hand into Bennet's. "She made me pray for you, too."

"You don't have to if you don't want to."

"Oh, I don't mind," Luke assured him.

"That's nice of you, Lukey. But I'd rather have a cup of tea than a prayer. Real tea."

Luke lit up at the prospect of being useful and darted away. Bennet blew out a long breath. He collapsed onto his narrow bunk, aching. Everything ached. Ifan pushed Bennet's legs to one side and appropriated far more of the bunk than he deserved. Bennet didn't have enough energy to protest.

Luke sidled up to them, carrying a tin mug in two careful hands.

"And where's mine?" Ifan demanded.

Luke guided the cup into Bennet's hand. "I can only carry one," he said, settling down beside Bennet. "I'm too little to carry two."

"Couldn't you have brought mine, instead, then?"

Luke grinned and shook his head.

Bennet took an ostentatious mouthful of his tea. It washed away the last lingering taste of slimy herbs. "Lovely."

Luke preened. "I helped Leah make it." He held out his arm, and shook his hand rapidly. "Oh!"

"What's the matter?" Bennet asked. "Did something bite you?"

"It tickles." Luke laughed. Twisting, he thrust the offending hand at Bennet, shaking it again as if trying to shake off something stuck to it. "It tickles!"

"What does?" Bennet couldn't see any distress on the child's face. Whatever this was, didn't seem serious.

"My special chronometer. The one you gave me."

Bennet froze. "The comlink?"

"Uh-huh."

Bennet put down the cup down with great care. "Let me see, Lukey."

Luke obliged, unfastening the comlink with Ifan's help, and dropping it into Bennet's outstretched hand. Bennet closed his fingers over the comlink.

"Can I have it back, though?" Luke asked.

"In a minute." Tightening his grip on the link, Bennet waited.

"It's a proximity alarm." Bennet held up the comlink so everyone could see it. "The comlink's not transmitting at the moment, just receiving. Shield ships transmit in subspace bands, at a modulating frequency that mimics natural transmitters like pulsars. It lets any ground operation stay in touch with the ship."

"How close are they?" Janerse took the comlink from him. Her eyes widened when it vibrated in her hand. She smiled.

"It's a strong signal. They've dropped out of hyperspace, probably somewhere on the edge of this system, and are in range of any signal I send. I just have to tell them I'm here."

"And you're hesitating? Why?" one of the farmers demanded. Abram, Leah's husband.

"Because the Maess probably can't detect the incoming frequency, but for me to contact the Shield ship and explain what we need them to do means a conversation of several minutes. And the comlink is limited. I can't send with the same sophistication of frequency modulation a ship's comms desk has. The chances are the Maess will pick up my transmission."

"So if you contact the Shield ship from here, it could lead them straight to the Chryseis." Ifan nodded as he got it.

"Yes. It's a risk." Bennet looked around the gathered adults. "That's why I'm telling you all. I think you've the right to know, and be prepared. This is our only realistic chance of getting everyone off this planet and home, but it isn't coming free. We may have to fight our way out."

"You've got their base mined," one of the miners said.

"Yes, and as soon as I can hook up with the ship, we'll agree a time for blowing it."

"Why not blow it now as a distraction?" Randle asked.

"Because if I do and the Shield ship can't take us all, then the Maess will definitely know we're here. That's our safety net gone. And it'll bring any Maess ships in the area here at light speed. I've got to be sure either the Maess are going to get us and there's no way out, in which case I'm taking them with us, or I've got everyone away who can be got away and we blow the base behind us."

"Too complicated for me." Janerse handed back the comlink. "Basically, I'm a blow them up and run for it kind of girl, but you're the boss. I'll do whatever you want. Just tell me what that is."

"Me too." Ifan straightened out his customary slouch. "What do you want us to do?"

Bennet grinned at them. They weren't Shield, but at the moment it didn't matter. Experience over the last couple of years had shown him that first Fleet, and now the Infantry, were every bit as skilled and professional as the Shield Regiment. They did what they did differently, but they did it well. He was lucky to have them.

"I want you all to start getting ready to evacuate. I'll get them to bring the cutter in as near as I can to here, but the timing's going to be tight. Be ready to run, okay? Make sure the kids know what to do. Ifan, you come with me. I want to be a couple of miles away from here before I contact them. It's not much, but it might misdirect the drones long enough for us to get out."

"I'll get the horses." Ifan left, running. The big man did lumber, Janerse was right there. But he could lumber to some purpose and with surprising speed.

"There won't be room to take much," Bennet said to the two troopers. "What people stand up in, and no more. Have everyone by the mine entrance, okay?"

Janerse nodded. "Will do. Good luck, sir."

Bennet glanced at the other side of the cave, to where Luke sat on his bed, ignoring the other children playing and squabbling a few yards away from him. Luke knew something was up, and he was focused on Bennet to the exclusion of all else. Somehow, now, those stored up problems Bennet had been ignoring were coming back to bite him. There was no time to prepare Luke now.

He smiled reassurance at the child, and looked at Janerse. "And look after Luke for me."

By the time Ifan brought his horse to a standstill, at a point a couple of miles and two ridges from the Chryseis, the evening had deepened into dusk. Colour had leached from the world, leaving a dim twilight the same purple as the bloom on a grape. The cob stood blowing out noisy, frothy breaths, its sides heaving.

"Far enough?" Ifan asked.

"Should be." Bennet slid from his mare's saddle, and tossed Ifan the reins.

He took the comlink from the breast pocket of his shirt. Several times on the wild ride across the hills, he'd felt it vibrate. The Shield ship was still close by. Closer, if the increasing rate of the signal was any guide. He strapped it back into place on his right wrist, brought his right arm up across his chest and opened up the link. He hesitated only for a second, before hailing them. He used a voiceless signal, one any Shield ship should pick up on instantly.

Signal once. Pause for three seconds. Signal again. Pause again for another three seconds, counting them by soundlessly. Signal for the third and last time. Wait precisely ten seconds, and repeat. Signal. Pause. Signal. Pause. Signal.

He couldn't have said it any louder and better with words. *Here I am, and I'm in trouble. Come and get me!*

"They should have got that," he said.

"What will they do?"

"Call me." Please the gods, let them call. Let the comms desk officer be awake and realise one of their own is here, asking for help. "They should home in on my frequency, and call me."

The seconds ticked by. Ifan sighed, sagging in the saddle. The big miner looked sick, his face white and sweat beading on his upper lip. Bennet noticed the details in a detached kind of way, the way he noticed Ifan's eyes were brown and his hair was thinning. Little details to concentrate on to help him deny his own stress as long as he could. It wasn't successful. He couldn't stand still, fidgeting as badly as a nervous horse. He echoed Ifan's sigh.

"Come on!" He stared at the comlink, trying to will it into life.

He started the sequence again. Signal. Pause. Signal. Pause. Signal. Wait for precisely ten seconds and repeat. Signal. Pause. Signal. Pause…

"This is Captain Tarrant of the Shield ship *Hyperion*." The comlink crackled into life. "Identify yourself."

Bennet's mouth dropped open, his heart hammering under his ribs. For a second he stared at the comlink, nonplussed, before forcing his brain into action. He had to wipe his hand on his pants before he could be sure of touching the comlink without his finger slipping from the button.

"Identify yourself," Tarrant repeated.

Tarrant? Oh great. And Rosie? What had happened to Rosie? Hadn't she made it, after all?

"This is Shield Captain Bennet. Also of the Shield ship *Hyperion*." He had to fight to keep the tremor out of his voice. "Repeat ident."

There was a second's silence, then *Hype* came back at him, but it wasn't Tarrant. It was Rosie, it was his lovely, beautiful Rosie, her voice cracking with disbelief and delight. "Bennet! Oh Bennet! You're alive!"

He had to stiffen his knees to hold himself up. He caught hold of Ifan's stirrup for support. Ifan's hand closed over his shoulder, and the big man grinned. Bennet nodded back. He had a chance to get these people out. Oh gods, he had a chance to get them out.

"Of course I am. Calm down, Rosie, and listen to me. Right now, I need help to get people off-planet. I need the cutter. Are you locked on my signal?"

"We are." It was Tarrant again, tone cool. He must have wrested the comlink back from Rosie. "Modulate to seventy-six."

"Done." Bennet ignored the faint hostility, flicked the comlink onto the new frequency. "Right, then. The rendezvous point is two miles east of me, bearing oh-two-eight degrees. Get that cutter down here as fast as you can do it."

"How many of you are there?"

"Thirty-six. Fourteen of them kids."

"The best we can do is pack twenty into the cutter, maybe twenty-five with the kids, but we'd be close to overload. Modulate to eighty-two."

Bennet complied. It wouldn't do to snarl. He settled for a pointed acidity. "I know the capacity of my own cutter, Captain. You'll have to do two runs. Have you launched her yet?"

A pause, then Tarrant said, stiffly, "She'll be on her way in five minutes under Lieutenant Rosamund's command."

"Good." Bennet grinned at Ifan. The miner gave him the thumb's up. "Tell Rosie to bring as many sidearms and laser rifles as she can carry. ETA?"

"About forty minutes," Tarrant said, still cool. "We're coming in from behind one of the moons and we're not in orbit yet. Modulate to eighty-seven."

Again, Bennet flicked the comlink onto the new frequency. "Fine. That'll give me time to get back to our hiding place and get ready to blow the Maess base. What about Maess ships?"

"Nothing on our scanners in this system except what's at the base—"

"Small drone transports and a dozen fighters. Nothing bigger."

"Excellent. If you blow the base, that should buy us some time."

"I'm banking on it. I'll blow the base when the cutter arrives. I'll signal again on this frequency in forty minutes, to give you something to home in on. Bennet out."

He snapped off the comlink, pushing away the annoyance that Tarrant—*Tarrant!*—had had the temerity to take his ship, and concentrated on the job in hand.

Bennet swung back up into the saddle, and started the mare back towards the Chryseis. He twisted often in the saddle to look towards the valley that hid the Maess base. If a reaction came to the transmission, it would come from there. He divided his attention between the base behind him and the skies above him. All serene.

Maybe they'd got away with it.

After a few quiet minutes, with no sign of a reaction, Ifan rode the grey up close. "We're on our way home."

Bennet cast one more glance over his shoulder towards the Maess base. Yes, thank the gods. He'd get most of them home. He would get the kids home. Luke would be safe.

But even if the Maess had missed the transmissions, or had lost them in the frequency changes and didn't think them important, there was no way in the gods' heaven they were going to miss the cutter.

He wouldn't be putting a great deal of money on the chances of survival for those waiting for the cutter's second run. Not on his own chances, or Ifan's, or the two troopers', or anyone else they made stay behind.

Didn't matter. He'd get the civilians out, and a Shield couldn't ask for more.

He re-established contact exactly forty minutes later. "Where are you, Rosie?"

"Three minutes. We've got you pinpointed. Close down."

"Out."

He, Ifan and the troopers were in the open, on the long slope leading up to the entrance of the mine. The miners and farmers clustered in the mine mouth behind him. Eleven would have to stay back for the second run.

"Leave it to me," Ifan had said as they rode back. "At least we can get all the farmers off. I wouldn't trust any of them in a tight spot when we need shooting, not praying. There's nine of us miners and three of you, so we'll draw lots to see which one of my lot gets to leave on the cutter and misses all the fun."

Bennet made no protest. He suspected most of the miners were Jacks, or ex-Jacks. They'd be able to handle themselves in a fight. It was best not to ask where they'd acquired the skills. Still, he'd rather have them at his back than one of the farmers, that was for sure. Ifan had been brisk when they got back with the news. The miners, more than one looking rueful, had gathered to one side of the farmers.

"The Maess'll pick up on the cutter, won't they?" Janerse said.

Bennet nodded, scanning the night sky and the hills. "This close in? Yes."

"That'll make waiting for the second run an exciting experience."

Ifan leered at her. "Never mind. I'll be here to take care of you."

She looked sick. "I'd rather shoot myself. Or you."

"Not now, you two." A star dropped out of the heavens. Bennet pointed. "There she is! Jan, Randle, get them ready to run. I want to turn that cutter around in seconds." He snapped on the communicator again. "Rosie?"

"I'm here."

"We're ready to start loading them as soon as you land. Just get the door open and the ramp down, and stand back."

"We can't take all of them, Bennet."

"I know. I'll stay for the second run. We've got enough volunteers to stay with me."

"Uh-huh. Shut up for a minute while I land this thing."

The cutter came down at the bottom of the slope a couple of hundred yards away, where the ground was even. Gods, but that functional little ship was the most beautiful thing Bennet had ever seen.

He glanced back at Janerse and Randle. "Go get 'em."

The two troopers jogged back to the mine. The cutter was down, and within a second or two its door opened and the ramp was out. Rosie ran down it before it had the chance to hit dirt, racing up the slope to reach Bennet. Behind her, Sergeant Tim lugged a fair amount of armament to the head of the ramp. Rosie slowed when she got to him. Her eyes were bright, and the smile on her face would have ignited stone.

"Bennet," she said.

Just for a minute, thoughts of Joss and anyone else were tossed into oblivion. Bennet pulled her in close with his good hand, and kissed her. Properly. Like he meant it. There was nothing in the least bit brotherly about it and he was surprised to realise he had wanted to do that for a long time. He was very surprised when she kissed him back.

"Oh Bennet," she said. Her eyes filled with tears. "I left you behind."

"You did what I told you to do."

Her face twisted. "You look like hell in a beard."

He gave her shoulders a shake to get her focused again, and released her. "There's no time now, Rosie. Let's get these kids off."

She hugged him again and stepped back, dabbing at her eyes. The farming families streamed past them, chivvied by Janerse and Randle. They headed for the cutter with the same speed as they'd head for salvation.

Which, of course, the cutter was.

"Bennet!" It was a wail.

Luke stopped beside him, hands reaching out to clamp around Bennet's waist. Bennet had managed to find only a couple of minutes to explain to Luke that they were leaving, that Luke would have to go first and Bennet would follow. The child hadn't cried until now. He'd sat clutching his blanket to his thin chest and watching Bennet over the top, his eyes wide. But now he clung and cried. Leah paused and turned and came back, sending her own brood of six onward.

Bennet got his arm around Luke and the child swarmed up him like climbing a tree. Bennet hugged him hard. "It'll be okay," he promised. "I want you to go with Leah, and take care of her for me, all right? You're going up to my ship, Lukey, where it's safe, and then as soon as I get there we'll take you home."

"Noooo," Luke wailed as Ifan pried him off Bennet. "I want to stay with you! You promised you'd look after me!"

"I'll be there as soon as I can, I promise." Bennet detached the last clinging hand and nodded to Ifan. The miner ran for the cutter, Leah beside him. She carried the big glass bottle of grubs, Bennet noticed, but his attention was on Luke's despairing face as Ifan passed the child to Tim at the cutter hatch.

"Shit," Bennet said. What a damn mess.

"What's wrong with your arm?" Rosie demanded.

"Shrapnel damage, I think. Never mind that now. You'd better get moving."

"You're injured. You should be on that cutter."

"Do as you're told, Rosie." Bennet glanced southwest where the Maess base was, narrowing his eyes to focus. Was that a fighter taking off? "The Maess will be on their way and I can't hold here once you've lifted off. I'll have to take to the edge of the marshes and get under cover. We'll need covering fire from the Mozzies."

"They launched twenty minutes after I did. They'll be here in a couple of minutes."

"Great. As soon as you've taken off, have them plough us a road. Two roads. Get them to go due south and due east of here. I'll cut into the marshes on a diagonal, straight down the middle of 'em." Bennet indicated the comlink. "I'll signal again an hour after the cutter lifts off. That should give you time to unload it and turn it around."

"I'll be right here with you." Rosie sighed. "No, don't argue. I'm not leaving you behind again, and Tim knows what to do."

Bennet turned to see Ifan jogging back towards him, carrying the huge holdall of armaments. Tim was closing the airlock door. "Rosie," he said, protesting.

She hefted her laser in her hand. "Shield looks after its own, Bennet."

No time to argue it. The cutter ramp rose up into place across the airlock door. Too late now, to send Rosie packing. Besides he was so glad to have her with him he could have genuflected his thanks to his father's gods. She smiled. She knew.

Ifan straightened up from the weapons cache. He shouldered one of the heavy-duty plasma rifles "All right?"

Bennet nodded. "Better than I felt an hour ago. The kids have a chance now."

"Yeah. Not bad going—for an officer."

Bennet laughed. "Why did you never make sergeant?"

"Mouth's too big." Ifan took a small transmitter from his pocket and handed it to Bennet with a flourish.

Bennet took the transmitter just as the cutter, shuddering against the pull of gravity, clawed its way up into the atmosphere. Within a moment or two, the cutter was one star amongst the others. He wasn't at all sure they'd get out, but he was going to take the Maess with him no matter what. He grinned at Ifan, satisfied, and pressed the button.

An instant later, the ground heaved beneath their feet, moving in a series of shudders, like an animal trying to dislodge something that irritated it. Miles to the southwest, a huge dust cloud boiled into the sky, lit from beneath with dark red flames sooty black around the edges. He and Ifan watched it, shoulder to shoulder.

"That? Makes it worthwhile," Ifan said when the ground stopped shaking, grinning down at him.

Rosie came to his other side. "The base?"

"Toast." With all the solactinium ignited underground, it should burn for years. Bennet smiled, satisfied. If nothing else, he'd taken most of the bastards with him. "That should help keep them busy. Now's our chance to get under cover." He turned to Ifan. "Time to get the horses, Sergeant."

Ifan blinked and grinned and Bennet would be eternally damned if Ifan didn't pull off the neatest salute he'd seen in a long time.

Sweet.

CHAPTER THIRTEEN

17 Tertius 7488: Telnos

"Horses?" Rosie suppressed a shudder. She didn't like horses. Big brutes that rolled their eyes at her and always looked as if they were working out which pile of manure to drop her in. "What's wrong with walking?"

"They're faster." Bennet hauled himself up onto the horse's broad back. "We discovered Maess drones don't see us as humans on horses. They don't take any notice of us and every little helps." He looked rueful. "I'd offer you a hand up, but I don't have the hand to spare."

"I can manage." Rosie squirmed up to ride pillion. It was not an elegant manoeuvre. "Oof!"

"Okay? Hold on." Bennet gathered up the reins. "What brought you here, Rosie? I thought this place would've been written off by now."

"It was your father's idea," Rosie put her arms around his waist and rested her cheek on his back. He was alive. Her eyes stung and her voice wavered. "Oh, Bennet." She choked, grimaced, said his name again as a sort of talisman. "Bennet. I didn't expect to find you, much less for you to be alive. No one did. But your father was taken with the idea you'd want him to do something about getting out any survivors. A tribute to your memory sort of thing."

"It's the sort of noble gesture he'd love."

Two Mosquitoes whined overhead. Rosie glanced up but they were invisible in the cloud cover. "Yes. I got that about him. You two are rather alike, you know. Anyhow, when I suggested we came back, he got it at once. He can take a hint. Which is where you two aren't at all alike, come to think on it."

"When did you see him?" Bennet touched his heels to the horse, getting it moving. The miners, most of them doubled up on the horses, were halfway down the slope. Bennet let the horse pick its way in the rear of the little group. The big miner stuck with him, off to one side.

"The morning of the Watch, and then at the funeral, of course. I wore a black armband and your pendant, and I cried myself silly. We all did. They held the Watch in your parents' local temple and it was lovely. Your mother was very sweet to me when I went to tell her how sorry we all were. You look a lot like her."

"So I'm told."

"Anyhow, before the Watch started, your dad had me talk to the Supreme Commander to persuade him it wasn't a good idea to leave people trapped on this little hell-hole. And after a week thinking about it, they sent us back here to see what we could find. It took us a few days to sneak our way in. This sector's hot with Maess now and well behind the lines. We took it slow and took the long way around. The last thing we wanted was to be noticed. We didn't know what we'd find when we got here, but we didn't expect it would be you and you'd gathered all the survivors together."

"Not all. I don't think I got them all." There was an odd note to his voice she didn't quite get. Regret? Guilt?

"You did damned well." Rosie squirmed again. She tightened her arms around Bennet and squeezed. "Oh, Bennet. I never thought to find you. I really didn't."

"A gladsome surprise for all of us, then. Except maybe for that dickhead, Tarrant. Whose idea was it to give him my ship?"

An eye roll was safe, since he couldn't see her. Bennet and Tarrant had never got along. Too alike and too competitive. "The general's maybe? We thought you'd bought the farm."

"Well, I may have done a spot of renting, but I'm not looking to purchase."

"I was sure you were gone. Your tracer…" For a moment she rested her forehead against his back and just felt him breathing. He was warm and alive. She touched her lips to his shoulder, where he wouldn't notice it. No one would see, not in the near-dark.

Bennet turned and brushed his hair back. A thin scar ran just below his hairline. "The bit of shrapnel that almost destroyed my boyish good looks put paid to the tracer. Ifan said my helmet was shredded."

"It was," the big man said. He had the female Infantry trooper behind him on his horse. He had one hand over hers where she had them clasped around his waist. "You were bloody lucky not to get your head ripped off."

Rosie shivered and once more tightened her grip. Bennet grunted. She choked out an apology. "Sorry. I'm so sorry, Bennet. I got on the cutter without… I thought you were gone."

"Don't be daft, Rosie. I gave you an order to get out of there and I'd only be mad if you'd disobeyed it. I was lucky Ifan came by." He nodded towards the big man. "This is Ifan, by the way. He's an ex-Infantry corporal. You can tell, because he couldn't follow an order to save his life without bitching and whining about it. He may also be an ex-Jack, although I'm not putting too much money on that 'ex'. And whatever you do, don't ask where he got all the solactinite we used to mine the base, because it's likely I'll face charges for colluding in a felony and I'd hate to take you down with me." Bennet's tone softened. "I couldn't have managed without him looking after me."

"There are a lot of people who'll owe you for that, Ifan." Rosie nodded at Ifan, hoping it conveyed how grateful she was.

"Probably not in a good way," Ifan grumbled, but Rosie had already pegged this one for a devotee. She hadn't missed the pleased flush and the salute when the base went up. Hadn't Bennet called him 'sergeant' then, though? She smiled. A field promotion.

Bennet's own right hand was heavy over Rosie's, mimicking Ifan. "That's Janerse with him, allowing him liberties with her hand in a way that will come between me and my sleep for a week. She and Randle are Infantry. The transport they were using to get Ifan's people to the landing site was targeted and they got left behind."

"We knew we hadn't got everyone. That's why we're here, to get out anyone who managed to avoid the Maess." Rosie added, for Bennet alone, "We thought, as well, that we might find your bod—" She broke off with another grimace. "Find you and bring you home."

He turned his head. His smile was warm, and he didn't complain when her hold on him tightened again. "Shield looks after its own."

She nodded. "Yes. Yes, we do. We're a bit late getting there sometimes, but we do."

The Maess fighter crossed the marshes a couple of miles to the west of them, heading south. Bennet had been right when he said he'd thought he'd seen at least one take to the air before the base went up. Rosie frowned at it. There may be other drones around, too. Quiet and careful as Bennet's people had been for the last few weeks, the Maess knew now they were there. The fighter drone had dodged the Mozzies so far.

"Do you think the drones will look for us? If there's no organic Maess directing them, I mean." She glanced at Bennet, but his only answer was a shrug. Not encouraging.

Bennet had chosen a clearing on the edge of the marsh as a landing site for the cutter when it got back. The ground was firm, not the morass of mud and slime deeper in the fens, and the open space was certainly big enough to take the cutter. The trees gave reassuring cover. Any sense of safety was illusory without shield-suits to hide them from the fighter's sensors, but Rosie would take what she could get.

"Tarrant's cautious." Rosie made a fair effort at ignoring the fighter in the distance, listening instead for the Mozzies. The fighter appeared to be quartering the marshes. It probably was looking for them. "It shouldn't have taken us as long to get here as it did, but he didn't want to hurry. There's a lot of Maess activity in this sector, but the nearest battleship's a couple of hours away. We should be able to make it, though we'll have to run like hell for home."

"It depends on what the Maess have left on the ground," Bennet said. "And if they still have some direction in their programming. I'd hoped to catch them all in the base."

"They might have patrols out still," the other trooper said. Randle, Bennet had called him. "They spend a lot of time in the marshes, looking for survivors."

"To work the mines?" Rosie asked.

Bennet's mouth thinned to a grim line. "They don't need workers for the mines here."

Rosie shivered, despite the close, fetid air.

Ifan tossed the saddle into the undergrowth and slapped his horse on the rump. It followed the rest of the horses into the trees. "I'll miss them."

"They're better off free," Bennet said.

In ten minutes, the cutter should be back. In nine minutes, Bennet would start signalling again. Rosie settled down at the base of a tree to wait it out on one side of Bennet, Ifan on the other. The others were all within a few feet, quiet, watchful and ready; all armed, all tense. The only sound was the thin high whine of the gnats, and the occasional slapping noise as someone dealt with them when they settled. Rosie sighed. Some things never changed. She scratched at her hairline, pushing back her helmet. It was as if the last seven weeks hadn't happened.

Bennet laughed, bumping shoulders with her. "I'd forgotten

how much the flies like you."

"I'd forgotten how much I hate them." Rosie screwed up her face and rubbed at it, to dislodge the sweat and the flies congregating on it, seeking the salt.

His free hand, clumsy, closed over hers. What had he done to it? He could barely use it. "Thank you for getting everyone out. I knew you would."

"Except you." She pressed up against him. Stupid to keep going over that. He had to know how sorry she was to have left him. "We got everyone else home. It was exciting, getting past the Maess ships and back to the *Hype*. I thought a couple of times... still, we got home. Grant made it too, by the way. I'm going out with him, a bit."

"Are you? A bit? Does that mean it's not serious?"

Well, that was the question wasn't it? Grant was a good guy. Better than some she'd dated in the past. But he wasn't Bennet. "We'll see. I like him. He's a bit down right now, what with losing the hand and because they're talking about retiring him out of the Infantry." After a second or two, she said, quietly, "You haven't asked me about Joss."

"No." Bennet stared out across the clearing. After a minute, "Have you seen him?"

"At the Midnight Watch." She frowned. "I'm maybe not the fairest judge, you know. He never really liked me much, and if I'm honest, that's mutual. But I felt heart sorry for him that night. He looked terrible."

"Oh," Bennet said, tone flat and unemotional.

"His clothes were hanging off him and he looked haggard. Old. He didn't look like he's coping too well."

Bennet drew his knees up, lifted his right arm to lie across them and rested his chin on his arm. He said nothing, appearing to concentrate on the clearing ahead of him.

"He'll be all right when you get home, I guess." Rosie couldn't keep the sympathy in her voice. Her tone was touched with cynicism again. "He'll have you back again."

"Who's Joss?" Ifan asked.

Bennet slapped at his neck to dislodge a midge. "My partner."

Ifan didn't seem the type to let that bother him. "Good to have someone to get home to," was all he said.

Bennet's shoulders twitched. "I don't know. Joss has wanted me out of the military for years. He's going to be as mad as all hell when I get home."

"Ultimatum time?" Rosie asked.

"I wouldn't be at all surprised."

"Well, then." Rosie breathed it against his ear. "Now's your chance."

She frowned at Bennet's silence. She tilted her head back to rest it against the rough tree trunk, transferring the scowl to the tree canopy above. The night sky beyond was laced with clouds.

Maybe she just couldn't be unbiased where Joss was concerned, but she could almost see the great reunion unfolding. She couldn't deny Joss had looked dreadful at the Midnight Watch, nor that his grief was genuine. He'd looked every inch his age. More. Very unlike the elegant, fashionable man she'd known. But he would use his grief to his advantage when Bennet got back. She could see it. He'd stand there in the clothes that were hanging off him, pleading, wearing his misery and pain like the badge of the suffering he went through when he thought Bennet was dead, waving it like a banner to get attention. Joss would likely use every weapon he had to persuade Bennet to resign his commission and stay at home. And what a damn waste that would be!

No, she couldn't be unbiased where Joss was concerned. He was such a bloody drama queen.

Ifan said something, and wandered off to a nearby tree to sit with Janerse. How tactful of him. Unexpected. She said so.

In the dim light, she could just see the corner of Bennet's mouth turn up. "Surprises me too. He's normally as subtle as a runaway Transport shuttle. He probably just wants to flirt with Jan."

Rosie sighed and pressed in close. It was hard to hold back and not tell him he'd be a fool to let Joss force him back into the trophy boyfriend role he'd had at eighteen. But it wasn't her business. Damn Joss for having Bennet and not appreciating what he had. The man was a fool.

Bennet spoke so quietly she could barely hear him. "I do still love Joss, you know. But I love him because of all the compromises, the ones that make sure I can be myself rather than getting swallowed up. Joss loves me despite them."

"We said it weeks ago, didn't we? You've changed and grown up and he hasn't."

"I tried not to think about him, not to wonder what he'd be doing and feeling. Maybe it was because I didn't think I'd ever get home to see him again and maybe..." Bennet stopped and shrugged again.

Men. They were useless at talking about feelings. Too much testosterone or something.

"It's just that... look, Bennet, don't you think every compromise must come to an end at last?"

Bennet's smile was crooked. "Oh yes. Yes."

It was very wrong of Rosie to feel cheered by that, and to hope. But she was, and she did.

"The boat's on its way down." Rosie had used her own comlink. Bennet needed his usable hand for his laser, and he'd allowed her to handle the comms. On Bennet's nod, she started signalling. The response was immediate. Tarrant was efficient, though Bennet would never admit it, and he'd turned the cutter around with all possible speed.

"Good," Bennet said. "We might even get out of here. Keep the locator on a one second burst every ten seconds. If we have to move fast, they should be able to track us."

"So can the Maess," one of the miners observed. "If there're any left."

"There's at least one fighter." Bennet glanced up at the cloud cover and frowned. "There may be drones. It's a risk we have to take."

Rosie scanned as much of the sky as she could see above the tree line, reminded this might not be as easy as just walking onto the cutter and heading home.

The miner's grimace was mostly a defiant grin. She looked tough as hell. "Well, I guess it adds to the excitement."

"You could say that." Bennet got up. "Into position, everyone."

Bennet had already given his orders. The military there fanned out to ring the perimeter of the small clearing—Bennet, Janerse and Randle, Ifan and Rosie herself—staying just inside the tree line. A Mosquito screamed overhead, firing at a target a mile or so beyond them.

"Escort," Rosie said. "The cutter can't be far behind."

But what had the Mosquito found to fire at, and where had that Maess fighter got to?

"Here she is," Janerse said, as the dark shape of the cutter broke the cloud cover. "Oh gods, she's beautiful!"

The miners cheered, and more than one stood up, shading their eyes with their hands, watching the cutter drop towards them out of the night sky.

"Stay sharp!" Bennet ordered. "We aren't out yet. Don't forget that fighter!"

With obvious reluctance, they settled back into cover, attention not on their surroundings but on the sky above their heads. Bennet shook his head and Rosie, as relieved as the miners, hid a grin. He wouldn't relax, probably, until he was on the *Hype*'s Bridge arguing with Tarrant about who got to sit in the captain's chair.

Rosie gave the approaching cutter the same attention as every other part of the three hundred and sixty degree scanning she gave to the entire clearing. It dropped down to treetop level, and came down in the centre of the clearing, to the sound of muted cheering. Tim had the door open almost as it landed.

"Hurry it up, Boss!" he yelled. "We picked up a fighter on the scanner!"

"Go!" Bennet waved at the miners.

They didn't need telling twice, running for the cutter ramp. Bennet and the others backed up, covering the miners' retreat, bracketing the cutter within the defence of their guns. Rosie tightened her grip on her laser.

Almost there. Almost the— Wait. What was—?

"Incoming! West!" She swung around, firing at the moving shapes in the trees, the big laser rifle in her hands making the familiar deep booming sound as the chemical reactants exploded in the chambers, expelling the high impact laser-guided bolts.

Bennet swerved around the bottom of the ramp and ran to her, Janerse beside him. Rosie retreated backwards, firing at a mass of heavily armoured Maess drones pushing through the thick brush towards them.

"Shit!" Bennet joined her shoulder to shoulder, firing his hand laser.

Ifan lunged in from the other side. "They're all in!"

"Everyone into the boat!" Bennet shot a drone in the head as it got clear of the undergrowth. "Everyone in!"

A Mosquito swooped down to fire at the Maess, and the explosion from its shells shook the clearing and everything in it. From further back in the trees, the Maess drones fired on the cutter, trying to hit something vital to disable it. The air above Rosie's head was charged as a laser shot missed her by a few inches, spitting with spicules of light and heat. Her skin tingled. She shook her head against the stinging, glancing behind her quickly to check the ramp.

Randle was in and safe.

Janerse was a couple of feet behind Randle. A laser bolt caught her mid-body. She went down screaming, tumbling off the ramp to land at Ifan's feet. The big miner dropped his rifle, caught her up and ran for it, leaping onto the ramp and charging up to where Tim held the door, giving him covering fire. Rosie and Bennet retreated up the ramp more slowly, covering Ifan's back.

Then Bennet wasn't there anymore.

Rosie fired off a fusillade of shots, terrified and yelling. Bennet had been knocked off his feet, thrown onto his back. He lay half on the ramp, half off, his head dangling over the side. His laser had gone flying. Rosie kicked it aside to get to him.

Bennet!

Rosie gasped, the breath pounded out of her by shock and fright. She took out the nearest drone, stooped and grabbed Bennet's arm pulling him back onto the ramp. "Bennet! Bennet!"

"Nnnn," he said. "Nnnnn."

Then Ifan was there, looming over Rosie and shouldering her aside. He grabbed Bennet, pulled him up and half turned him, big hands under his armpits to pull him upright to be dragged up the ramp like a piece of luggage. Bennet screamed. Ifan just kept going, half-running backwards up the ramp, pulling Bennet along with him. Bennet's head lolled against Ifan's shoulder.

Rosie ran behind them, swearing. Bennet's eyes were open, but he looked past her, frowning. She spun around, firing at the Maess drones marching towards the cutter, trying to disrupt their aim. The Maess fighter appeared over the treetops, firing, a Mozzie in pursuit.

"Ramp coming up!" Tim yelled.

Ifan gathered Bennet up and hurled him bodily towards Tim. He spun on his heel, grabbed Rosie as if she'd been a doll and threw her after Bennet. Tim shrugged her off as she stumbled into him, his attention on getting Bennet through the hatch. As the ramp came up, Ifan catapulted into the airlock after her, knocking her down with the impact. She staggered up, clutching at the side of the lock, Ifan's hand closing over her arm to haul her up and steady her.

Tim already had Bennet over the lip of the inner airlock door, dragging him across the floor. Rosie bent to help, only to be shouldered out of the way by Ifan.

The cutter shuddered in the percussion as the fighter fired at it. She looked up, heart thumping and breath coming short, but the shielding held. Tim let Ifan take Bennet and slammed his hand against the inner controls for the door, sealing them in.

No time to get into a seat. No time to get strapped in. Ifan dropped down onto the floor beside Bennet and hooked an arm behind one of the miner's knees to brace himself, using the other to pull Bennet up against his chest.

Rosie spared a glance at the pilot. "Take off! Take off!"

The cutter juddered again, this time from the strain as the engines had it clawing its way up. Rosie staggered against the fierce acceleration; it threw her off her feet for the second time in less than a minute. She rolled towards Bennet to help protect him, to cushion him, and wrapped herself around the other side of him, face to face with Ifan over the top of Bennet's bowed head.

Was he breathing? Oh gods, was he breathing?

Willing hands caught and held them. The miner whose knees Ifan had braced himself against grunted and leaned down, clamping his hand around the top of Rosie's arm. "Hold on."

And then everything was lost in the roaring in her ears. She was ground into the cutter floor, unable to speak or breathe, the weight of the world crushing her down.

"Bennet? Bennet?"

He was breathing at least, but with difficulty, each breath catching in his throat. He was unconscious, eyes closed, head lolling as if his neck was too weak to hold it up.

Just as well, given the damage.

Rosie pressed her cheek against his. He was still alive. Tears stung. She blinked them back. Later. She'd cry later.

Tim struggled to reach the medical kit, battling his way to the front up the steep incline as the cutter fought its way up into the sky. "I'll be there in a minute."

"Hurry!" Rosie smoothed back the long hair falling into Bennet's eyes. She pressed her lips together hard when her fingers brushed over the long scar on his hairline. She shouldn't have left him. Shield looked after its own, and she'd let him down. She shouldn't have left him.

Ifan let Bennet go, sliding out from underneath him as the cutter levelled out. He glanced up the aisle to the seats where Janerse was lying. Randle sat on the other side of the aisle, staring at his feet.

"I'll take care of him. You see to Janerse," Rosie said, following the direction of Ifan's gaze. She turned her attention back to Bennet, grimacing at his right knee. The joint was a mess of charred bone and burnt, torn flesh. Only the cauterising effect of the laser stopped him from bleeding to death.

"No need." Ifan looked down at Bennet, and, very gently, moved him into a more comfortable position. "There's no need."

"Oh." Rosie looked again to where Janerse was. Scuffed boots, surprisingly small, hung limply over the edge of the double seat. Shocked and sorry, she glanced at Ifan. She didn't like the look on the miner's face. It was safer to look at Bennet, smooth his hair back again and try not to think it might have been Bennet's boots dangling over the edge of a seat, and her sitting in Randle's place, staring at the floor. And she tried very hard not to think it might still be.

"How bad is he?" Tim slid to a halt beside her, saving her from having to find something to say, helping her focus on what was most important.

"Laser bolt, straight through the knee. I can't see anything else."

"That's bad enough. Let me in at him." Tim worked fast, enclosing the shattered joint in a protective capsule, holding the leg together.

"We're out!" the pilot yelled. "Escort formed up. We'll be back on the *Hype* in twenty minutes."

"Good." She didn't lift her gaze from Tim's competent hands snapping closed the capsule's locks.

They all had basic paramedic training, but Tim was the most experienced and the most skilled. Ifan sat beside her, very quiet, his hand curving over Bennet's wrist, feeling for a pulse. She kept her eyes on Bennet's white face, what she could see of it through the obscuring beard. Tim was too busy now to keep her from having to speak to Ifan, from having to say something, and in the end, she had to. She touched Ifan's hand, the one that sat, rock steady, on Bennet's wrist.

"I'm sorry," she said. Damn that was a stupid thing to say! Stupid. Of course she was sorry. Everyone was sorry.

Ifan's attention was fixed on what Tim was doing. He held Bennet's limp right hand steady while Tim got an intravenous line into the back of it. Only then, when Tim sat back, did Ifan answer her.

"So am I," he said.

CHAPTER FOURTEEN

20 Tertius 7488: the dreadnought, *Gyrfalcon*

It started out as one more patrol, just like all the others; like the one he'd done yesterday and the day before, and the one he'd do tomorrow and the day after that.

Not that 'routine and mundane' was a problem. He didn't have to think too much. Just let the training take over, and coast along inside it. No thinking, no feeling. It got him through the day, anyway.

"I get that," Cruz had said, when she'd suggested Flynn ask for a few days leave of absence and he'd tried to explain why it was a bad idea to stop flying. "It's something to cling to. I do get that it's sort of... sort of grounding you. Something stable."

Women. They always wanted to analyse stuff and talk about feelings.

Flynn didn't want to talk about feelings, not even with Cruz. All he wanted was to get his feet under him again.

Flying gave him the chance to get away from people. There wasn't much privacy in the military. He always had do something or be somewhere. The day ticked along to the beat set by the commander and the colonel, and the poor saps who had signed up for their commissions marched along to that beat. But there was always someone marching alongside a man—going to the same briefings, beside him in the barracks or the ready room or the gym, muscling into his company in the officers' club or the commissary, talking to him all the bloody time. Some days the only time he got to himself was to lock the toilet door and sit there, quiet, and even then, some big-mouthed wit would yell to ask if he needed laxatives or something.

Some space was a good thing, now and again.

The Hornet gave him that. He could sit in silence, letting his squad chatter around him, or join in if he wanted to. It was comforting to have the choice. They were a good bunch, too. They let him talk or they let him be quiet, and they let him call which one it was going to be. None of them chivvied him, none of them questioned him. Even when he was silent this was still his place, he was still included.

Cruz had probably had a word with Carson, Flynn's wingman. His squad and Cruz's often patrolled closely together. She'd be looking out for him, as usual. He couldn't do it without Cruz. She was pure gold. Pure, pure gold.

This particular patrol started out like any other. He and his squad had taken off on the second wave, five minutes after Cruz's people. Their course was a wide arc that took them around and behind the First Flotilla, checking the port flank was quiet, that nothing was sneaking up on them in hyperspace—the close in pickets looked after normal space. Cruz's squad mirrored Flynn's on the starboard side. The two arcs met at a point several thousand miles behind the last corvette in the Flotilla, the Hornets sitting a holding pattern amid the swirling colours of hyperspace while he and Cruz exchanged a few words.

Nothing significant. Just the usual military exchange anyone could listen in to, a formal report on the outcome of their patrols so far—*we dropped into normal space when we thought we heard a transmission from that asteroid belt, but it checked out; or there's some sort of anomaly here and the Isometrics desk wants another set of close-up readings to confirm the ones we took; or there's a blip in the ion stream at these co-ordinates, so don't get too close or it'll fry your sensors*—then a couple of minutes on the private channel that, equally, anyone could have listened to since it consisted of little more than Cruz talking Flynn into some extra Tierce practice when they got back. It was easier just to agree, and it would fill up an hour or two. Then with ritualistic and ribald com noise casting mutual reproaches upon the looks, virtue and sexual tastes of their respective mothers, the two squads passed each other; Flynn to make his way home on the starboard flank, Cruz to patrol the port side.

Nothing significant. All profoundly ordinary, in fact. But it showed Cruz looking out for him, making sure he knew he wasn't on his own.

He rolled his shoulders, forcing himself to relax as they headed for home.

Carson broke the silence. "What are you up to when we get back? We're planning on getting together with Cruz's flight."

Flynn roused himself. Hell. They'd expect him to be sociable. Still, it filled up another couple of hours. "It'll have to be after the Tierce practice I've just arranged with her. But I don't see why not."

But the *Gyrfalcon* had other plans for him. They were half way back when the call came. It was the captain himself, ordering Flynn to hand over command of his squad to Carson and get back to the ship, on the double.

Flynn blinked. Stared at the comlink.

"Lieutenant Flynn. Respond."

Impatient beggars. He worked the tiny navigational computer on the console. "ETA forty minutes, GyrLeader."

"Make it thirty," Simonitz said.

Flynn frowned at the comlink. "Sim, what's going on?"

"All I'm allowed to tell you is you're wanted back on board," Captain Simonitz said in the tone of voice that made it clear whoever had put the prohibition on him was still within earshot.

178

Flynn scowled as he listened. That was bad luck. In other circumstances, Simonitz would have told him what was up, but the captain, presumably in the presence of senior officers, had to appear intent only on getting Flynn back as fast as possible. "Move it, Flynn. We're tracking you on Isometrics."

Why? In case he ran away? What the hell was this all about?

Flynn duly moved it. He handed over to Carson, adding a private set of instructions to tell Cruz what had happened in case he was otherwise engaged when the other patrol got home, and kicked the engines up a notch, sending his little fighter hurtling back to the *Gyrfalcon*.

An invigorating flight, made all the more interesting by his increasing anticipation. What was going on? He couldn't be in trouble. He'd been so good over the last few weeks, since… since then. He should be handed a damned halo. Besides, even when he wasn't being good, he'd never been in trouble so deep they had to call him back to yell at him. What in hell did they want him for? Better pick up the pace. Maybe make it back inside the recommended thirty minutes. Even without the Simonitz's warning tone, the curiosity was enough to kill him.

He brought the Hornet into position to take his usual flight path into the starboard deck and hit the comlink for the landing routine. "Bridge, this is Alpha Squad 2 leader. Am coming in to approach starboard bay. Permission to land?"

A flurry of static, then. "Permission denied. Please await further instructions."

What. The. Hell?

He slowed the Hornet so hard she stood on her nose. "Come again?"

"Approach to starboard bay denied. Am sending you an approach for the cutter deck. Please acknowledge and comply."

Flynn watched the data stream flash from the comlink to the navigation computer. "Data input functioning and executed. Approach to cutter deck confirmed."

Why in hell send him to the cutter deck? It just meant someone would have to move the Hornet later. The gods knew what they were all smoking up there on the bridge, because that made no sense at all. Not that the bridge ever did make much sense, but still. It was stupid.

The cutter deck sat amidships, between the two Hornet flight bays. He let the navigation computer take control over the flight-board and take his ship in on automatic. He took control back to follow the floor lights to a parking bay over to one side.

No one met him on the decking. No Simonitz to explain. No other officer. The port Deckmaster, Chelle, had command of the cutter deck that day—it alternated between her and Maire, the starboard Deckmaster. Chelle glanced at him but turned away almost immediately. She didn't even yell at him for cluttering up the deck with his Hornet. Whatever this was about, wasn't anything to do with her. At least no one from security was waiting for him. Not that they had reason. For once, his conscience was so clean it squeaked.

The deck was busy, with a group of techs preparing a cutter for a flight. Well, nothing out of the ordinary there. Cutters came and went all the time. Chelle stood to one side yelling at the techs, and that too was the status quo, if her reputation for a fiery temper and a vocabulary that would shame a trooper was anything to go by. Flynn's ears burned, and he'd thought he knew all the swear words in the lexicon. The techs wouldn't be able to obey her instructions without complex surgery.

Still nothing to explain why he was there. Flynn stood beside his Hornet, helmet in hand, watching all the activity for a clue and feeling like a spare part the techs had forgotten. He paged the bridge.

"I'm here," he announced, in as inviting a tone as he could manage. "Would somebody like to tell me where I'm to go next?"

"You're to stay put, Lieutenant."

That was the unmistakable voice of Colonel Quist, and even over the comlink it had Flynn's spine stiffening out of its customary slouch and straightening into a vague approximation of a military posture. That woman had one helluva effect. She had them all conditioned to jump when she so much as raised an eyebrow. He gawked at the comlink.

"Yes, ma'am," he said, and closed down the link, sharpish. The last thing he needed was a conversation with the colonel. "Staying put, ma'am," he added to the uncaring flight deck.

If all he was required to do was wait, then wait he would. It wasn't something he wasn't good at. Made him nervous, standing around with nothing to do. Not fun, being left to one side one side like this. Disrespectful, too, standing around awaiting someone else's convenience. What if they forgot about him? What if five days later, someone said, 'Hey, where's old Flynn?' and discovered him faint from hunger and thirst, gamely waiting for orders in some forgotten corner of the cutter deck?

He kicked at the decking with one boot. On his own and with nothing to do, without the routine to sustain him, his thoughts had a bad habit of going in one particular direction.

No. No, not that. Don't think about that.

He blew out a noisy breath, turned his back to the main part of the ship and stared out across the deck, back out through the transparent force fields to the stars beyond. He could just see the grey shape of the *Patroklus* behind them. That was distraction enough. He shifted several feet to one side for a better view. What would it be like, serving on her? Frustrating, likely. Destroyers were all very well, but they were second best, and all the time the best of the best—the *Gyrfalcon* and her pilots—would be constantly in front of you, proof the gods were mocking you and your ambitions. Dangling the prize and snatching it away again. *Yeah. Frustrating.* Almost as damn frustrating as waiting around on the cutter deck for something to happen.

"Flynn," Commander Caeden said, from behind him.

Flynn jumped and spun on his heel, his mouth dropping with surprise. The commander had been back on board for a week or so, but Flynn hadn't seen him. He'd wondered if Caeden would call him in and tell him about the service on Albion, give him more details than he'd been able to glean from the sparse news line reports, but had shaken his head at his own naiveté. Of course the commander wouldn't single out Flynn like that. It wouldn't be right.

"Sir." He made it both a greeting and a question. He switched his helmet to his other hand and saluted.

The commander was different. For weeks, he'd been subdued, as if he'd been greyed over, the spark gone. Now the energy and eagerness were back, like someone had switched the lights on. For an instant, Flynn stared. Then joy and hope had the blood pounding in his ears until he was dizzy with it, his heart thumping. He dropped the helmet, unheeded, to the deck.

It couldn't be.

Caeden smiled at Flynn. He smiled, damn it.

"I need a pilot to take me to Demeter, Flynn. I thought you might do."

Oh gods, oh gods. "Bennet?"

"Bennet." Caeden caught Flynn by the arm, frog-marching him across the deck to the cutter. "Come on. We need to get to Demeter."

The Deckmaster, unaccountably ladylike, waited by the cutter to hand it over to the commander and his pilot. Whatever discussion Caeden had with her passed Flynn by. He saw their mouths open, and sounds came out, but what the hell they said… who knew? Made no sense at all.

Bennet.

Oh gods. Bennet!

Caeden grabbed his arm again and bundled him into the cutter. He'd end up with bruises at this rate. "I think I'd better take her out of the deck, at least. I've had a little longer to acclimatise to the news."

Flynn nodded. Anything the commander said. He couldn't stop

smiling and he couldn't remember how to speak. He sat where Caeden put him, looking down at his hands clasped loosely in his lap, while Caeden disengaged the cutter from the anchor mechanism and took her out and into hyperspace.

Bennet was alive.

"Course locked in." Caeden turned in the pilot's chair. When Flynn looked up, the commander's voice sharpened. "Over it?"

Flynn nodded, making himself concentrate. "Sorry, sir."

"Don't be." Caeden stood up and indicated the pilot's seat. "Yours, Lieutenant."

He scrambled into the chair. Not that there was much to do with the course already locked into the navigation computers. "Yes, sir. Sir? What happened, sir?"

Caeden settled himself into the seat behind Flynn's. "What happened was that I persuaded the Supreme Commander to send in a Shield team—Bennet's own ship, as it happens—to see if they could find any human survivors on Telnos."

"The Supreme Commander?"

"He's Bennet's godfather. They're very fond of each other."

Flynn stared. "Right," he said. Fond of the Supreme Commander? Only in Bennet-world. "Did you send them to look for him, then, sir?"

"No," Caeden said, after a minute. "No, I didn't. I thought he was dead, Flynn. What I was told by his people, the people who saw him get hit… I thought he was dead. I didn't think they'd find anyone, and I was sure they wouldn't find Bennet."

He'd done it, Caeden said, because Bennet would hate leaving a job undone, and he'd wanted to honour his son's memory in a way Bennet would have liked. But Bennet had finished the job himself. He'd collected more than thirty other survivors, many of them children, and with one regrettable casualty he'd got them all safely off-planet, blowing the main Maess base as they left.

Flynn laughed. "Of course he blew it! That's his job."

"Yes." Caeden's smile faded. "They had to fight their way out, and the Shield ship took some damage. They weren't able to get a coms link until a couple of hours ago when they crossed back into our space and were able to relay through the bigger coms array at Joaquin starbase. The Supreme Commander called me straight away. The good news was that he's alive, but Jak told me he's been injured and they're taking everyone into Demeter to ship them home. So get me there, Flynn, because we won't have long between the Shield ship docking and the transfer to an Albion-bound ship, and I want to see my son."

Flying cutters wasn't top of Flynn's list of things to do. Might as well ask a racehorse to pull a coal-cart—it got the job done, but it was an unconscionable waste to make a fine, highly trained thoroughbred do something any donkey could do. But flying this cutter... well, Flynn flew it as if it had been crafted out of melted-down gold credits. He was honoured. And scared. What in hell had possessed the commander to let him in on this? The gods bless him for doing it, but why?

Because Caeden didn't explain further. He didn't explain his reasoning for asking for Flynn. He gave no hint, other than this extraordinary request for Flynn to pilot for him, that he knew or even cared what Bennet's relationship with Flynn had been. He didn't indicate either consent or condemnation, leaving Flynn to deduce for himself that the very fact he was there meant it might not be condemnation. Of course, it was probably light years from consent, too. Didn't mean the old man would break out the sparkling wine and the orange blossom.

The commander left him alone after that first speech, never commenting on the number of times Flynn had to wipe his eyes, or blow his nose, or make some other sign of turbulent emotion. Flynn spent the flight veering between happiness and apprehension so intense both hurt like fury; he was strung out so tight between the two his chest ached.

Bennet was alive. Bennet was injured, Caeden didn't know

how badly. But Bennet was alive. He was injured. He was alive…
hell, it was a seesaw. Up one second, plummeting down the next
because they didn't know how bad it was. But Bennet was alive.
He was alive. It was all that mattered.

Caeden was a silent, brooding presence. Maybe consideration
had him turning a blind eye to Flynn being a complete wreck on
that damn seesaw. Maybe he was too intent on his own worries to
see it. And maybe he regretted saying as much as he had. Indeed,
every time Flynn glanced over his shoulder to where Caeden was
sitting, the commander was quiet and still, his eyes often closed,
hands folded on his breast. Praying, it looked like.

That wasn't a bad idea. Flynn tried it. It wasn't a bad idea at
all. For a novice, Flynn found he was quite good at it.

21 Tertius 7488: Demeter Transfer Station

Two hours out from the station, the commander stirred for the first
time in their seven-hour flight, coming to sit beside Flynn in the
co-pilot's seat to use the comlink. It was something to see, Caeden
being not only the commander of the *Gyrfalcon* and the First
Flotilla, but the patrician blue-blood Seigneur who expected
everything to be done exactly the way he wanted it, when he
wanted it.

And, of course, it was.

Demeter's commander was called to the comlink, Caeden's
apparent assumption being that station heads sat around in their
offices waiting for calls from him. Well, maybe they did. Colonel
Luiz certainly didn't keep the commander waiting.

Caeden greeted him with affability—another one of the Elect,
surmised Flynn, another member of the club to which all these rich
and influential men belonged. But a junior member. The greeting
was polite, but then Caeden moved straight into demands for
information, and for immediate and willing assistance. Caeden's
attitude presupposed all of this would be granted without
discussion, much less protest. Colonel Luiz seemed to share the

same set of cultural mores. He neither discussed nor protested.

Privilege was a wonderful thing. The commander had so much of it, the man didn't even realise it. For Caeden, this was normality. Did he have any idea of what was normal for most people, those who didn't have his blood and breeding to call upon?

"The Shield ship got in two hours ago and transferred the miners and farmers to Docking Bay 12, where the hospital ship, the *Peregrine*, is berthed," Colonel Luiz said, as soon as Caeden made his requirements clear. "We're waiting for a shuttle from Cetes, bringing in some seriously injured casualties from a skirmish there. As soon as they've been transferred, the *Peregrine* will leave for Albion."

"My son is a Shield officer and will be on the *Peregrine*. Shield Captain Bennet. Can you get me any word on his condition? The Supreme Commander was only able to tell me he'd been wounded in the final evacuation from Telnos."

Not to mention whatever injuries he had from the first evacuation, when he'd been left behind. Flynn shook his head at his reflection in the screen. Bennet was alive after more than seven weeks of being dead. That was all that mattered.

Caeden went on, "Jak had no details, and the *Hyperion* went back into comms silence."

Flynn held his breath, but was disappointed.

"I'll see what I can do, sir. I have no details here either, but I'll make enquiries."

"Thank you, Colonel. I appreciate your help. When do you expect the Cetes shuttle?"

"Four hours, Commander."

"I see." Caeden frowned at the comlink. "Then I should have time to see Bennet. Our ETA is—what, Lieutenant?"

Flynn glanced at the console. "We'll drop into normal space in about ninety minutes, sir."

"Ninety minutes, Colonel. I'd be grateful if you would clear dock 11 or 13 for me."

Flynn gaped.

"Of course," Luiz said, blandly.

CHAPTER FIFTEEN

21 Tertius 7488: Demeter Transfer Station

Eighty-seven minutes after the commander spoke to the colonel, Flynn brought the cutter into Gate 11.

He didn't look at the commander when they were given their approach path. What could he say about it? It would save time, and when they had so little to spare it would be agonising to waste precious minutes working their way from elsewhere in the station to reach the *Peregrine*. But he couldn't help wondering what ship had been unceremoniously moved to accommodate the *Gyrfalcon*'s cutter. No. To accommodate the *Gyrfalcon*'s commander.

He brought the cutter in, turning her side-on to the station to bring her outer door against Gate 11's airlock, manoeuvring until she faced the big hospital ship. He closed the systems down and waited for the airlocks to synchronise, glancing once at the profile beside him as Caeden gazed at the screens showing the *Peregrine* looming over them. He said nothing, waiting for orders, swallowing back the nausea. Luiz hadn't come back to them with any information. Flynn was still in limbo when it came to news on Bennet's condition.

Caeden got up. "Come with me, Flynn."

Oh thank the gods. He wasn't going to be left behind.

Flynn followed, keeping as still and quiet as he could. Restraint, that's what mattered now. Restraint. His presence depended on the commander's good will, and he'd do nothing to jeopardise it.

Luiz stood on the other side of the decontamination chamber door; a short man in a command uniform similar Caeden's in colour and decorations, and comically unlike Caeden's in the way it failed to flatter the colonel's stocky body. As soon as the brief formalities were over the colonel gestured to a turbolift. "I've got a travelpod held for you, sir."

"Thank you." Caeden followed him into the elevator, Flynn tagging along behind. "Bennet?"

"I wasn't able to get much." Luiz set the pod in motion. "All the *Peregrine* would tell me was that he's in surgery."

Flynn held his breath for a second. In surgery? That didn't sound good. Of course, hospital ships were fully equipped to deal with anything, but were usually just a more comfortable sort of transport home to real medical facilities. That meant it had to be a real emergency. He glanced at the commander out of the corner of his eye.

Caeden had stiffened up again, donning the cold and distant protective colouration that might have fooled Flynn if it hadn't been for the day he'd offered Caeden the shield. He'd seen behind the mask then. What he was seeing now... Well, it didn't look good. The commander was worried. Flynn shifted his weight uncomfortably from one foot to the other, but held it all back, unwilling to draw attention to himself.

"I've got some of the *Hyperion*'s people waiting to see you," Luiz added.

Caeden nodded. "Thank you. I appreciate the kindness."

"Anything to help, sir."

The travelpod stopped. Luiz led them out, down another turbolift, and through the airlocks into the *Peregrine*. A medical orderly ushered them down a deck to a comfortable cabin where two people waited: a woman in Shield uniform and a big civilian. A very big civilian.

"Commander!" The woman jumped up from her seat.

Caeden surprised Flynn then. From the look on her face before she vanished into the commander's embrace, Caeden surprised the Shield officer too. The commander caught hold of her shoulders and pulled her close, dropping a kiss on her forehead.

"Thank you, Rosie," he said. "Bless you, child. I can't thank you enough." He kept hold of both her hands.

Rosie. Rosamund. Bennet's Lieutenant, Flynn remembered. Bennet hadn't talked much about his job in Shield, but he'd mentioned Rosie with love.

"He's in surgery," she said. "Did they tell you?"

Caeden nodded. "But not what's wrong, or how serious it is."

She bit at her lip, and something in Flynn's chest contracted in pain. She was worried, very worried. "He was hit as we got onto the cutter, a laser bolt through the knee. We did what we could on the way back, but we're not equipped to deal with anything that serious, and all Tim could do—Sergeant Timon, Commander; you met him at... at the service, if you remember. He's our best paramedic as well as our top sergeant. All Tim could do was keep him sedated so he was comfortable. They took him straight into surgery when we got here." She swallowed hard. "They're trying to save his leg."

Flynn winced, the contraction in his chest becoming a hard thumping. His hands were clammy, and he wiped them on his pants legs. His fingers shook, like palsy.

Caeden looked down at the deck for a second, then smiled at her. The smile didn't take the anxiety from his eyes. "He's alive, Rosie, and his mother and I will never forget you kept your promise and brought him home." He kissed her again, and looked at the civilian.

"This is Ifan." Rosie freed a hand from Caeden's grip, and

beckoned Ifan closer. "Ifan ran one of the smaller mines on Telnos, sir, the one where they gathered all the survivors. He was Bennet's right hand man down there. He saved Bennet's life. Twice. He found him alive at the landing area and got him out before the Maess came back, and he got him onto the cutter on Telnos."

Caeden held out a hand. "Thank you, Ifan," he said, simply. He turned back to Rosie. "Did they say how long they'd be?"

"They've been in there for hours. They said it could take a long time." She drew the commander down into a seat. "They have his shoulder to see to, as well."

"Shrapnel," Ifan said. When Caeden and Flynn both looked at him, he added, "He was hit in the head and right shoulder at the landing site, when he got left behind, and some of the crap's still in there. He couldn't use his right hand much. I reckoned he has some shrapnel pressing on a nerve, but we had no way to check."

Flynn grimaced at this extra, unwelcome information. Rosie sighed and shrugged. She glanced at Flynn, raising an eyebrow.

"This is Flynn," Caeden said. "He's a friend of Bennet's."

Her eyes narrowed. "Really?"

Flynn gave her a tight little grin and settled into a chair on the other side of Caeden.

Quite deliberately, Rosie leaned forward to peer around Caeden and stare at Flynn. He stared back, and she said, "From the *Gyrfalcon*?" He nodded, and her frown smoothed out into a slight, knowing smile. "Well, then. I guess that explains it."

Caeden, withdrawn and possibly praying again, ignored them. Flynn shot him a quick glance, and when he looked at Rosie, she too glanced at Caeden before nodding at Flynn and sitting back. After that, he couldn't see much of her at all unless he leaned forwards or backwards to catch a glimpse of her and wonder what the hell she was talking about.

And hope she wouldn't talk about it anymore.

Time dragged.

Colonel Luiz had left them to it after a while. Presumably, he had a station to run and work to do beyond dealing with invading Fleet commanders demanding his time and attention. Caeden stood to shake hands with the colonel and thank him for his help. Flynn let his lip twist into a cynical little grin. *Noblesse oblige*, and all that.

Then Caeden surprised him. The commander had being doing that a lot recently. "I don't know whose ship you had to move to let me in this close, Colonel, but please thank them for me. I'd like the captain's name before I leave, please, to apologise in person."

Luiz nodded and murmured something, and let them be. Caeden resumed his seat, and took Rosie's hand in his again, patting it. He looked beyond her to where Ifan sat, big as a mountain.

"How did you find Bennet, Ifan?"

"Sergeant Ifan, Commander. He's ex-Infantry."

"I was a corporal. It was his idea of joke."

Rosie smiled. "Look on it as field promotion, Ifan. It was his idea of a compliment."

Ifan sniffed, and said, to answer Caeden's question, "Day the Maess got there we were late getting to the site, Commander. A fighter got our transport, and we had to do the last few miles on foot. No one there but Maess drones. They'd piled all the bodies up at one side of the site, and when they left, next day, we went looking for survivors and weapons. We weren't expecting to find any, but there were kids there, and we... well, we didn't want to leave the kids out in the open."

"But Bennet was alive."

"Just. He had a bad head wound and he was out of things for a couple of days, and he couldn't do much for nearly a week with the concussion. The shrapnel in his shoulder was a bother, too. I dug out everything I could see while he was unconscious, but I'm not a doctor, and"—he held up a huge hand—"these are a bit big for fancy work."

"Thank you, Sergeant," Caeden said. "I can't tell you how grateful his mother and I are."

"You're welcome. He didn't say much about home, but I'm not surprised he turns out to be a commander's son. The minute he woke up, he started giving orders."

"And you took them," Rosie observed, sweetly.

Ifan's melancholy face brightened. "It's all the training they gave us. They end up conditioning us. What choice did I have?"

Time really dragged. Minutes stretched and stretched, until each felt a year-long.

The knot of apprehension in Flynn's gut sent him to the bathroom a couple of times. He couldn't throw up. He tried, but all that came up was spit and acid, and the lead weight in his stomach was unaffected by it. He hung over the pan, retching and spluttering and the lead just sat there, weighing him down.

Being locked in a cubicle away from the commander's eyes at least meant he could let loose for a few seconds. He couldn't be sick, but he could dab at his eyes without anyone noticing.

Dear gods, a pile of corpses. Bennet had been found in a pile of corpses.

He was alive. They may be working on him, but he was alive. He was back. He wasn't in that pile of bodies. He was back.

But even if Bennet was back, he still wasn't Flynn's.

Time to get back to the waiting room. If the surgeon came out to tell them how Bennet was and he missed it… Time to get back. He splashed his face with cold water and raced back. No surgeon, no news, just three strained faces turning to watch him slow down and return to his seat.

"Sorry," he said, and dropped back into his chair beside the commander.

"I should give you this back," Rosie said, out of nowhere. She reached inside her collar and pulled on a fine chain. Flynn hadn't realised that Shield personnel, even officers, went around wearing diamond pendants, much less one as fine as this. The star sapphire in the centre caught the light with a flash of deep blue.

She reached up to undo the clasp, but Caeden was too fast for her. He put his hand over hers, stilling them.

"Keep it, Rosie. Bennet meant you to have it." He smiled at her. "He won't want it back. It meant a lot to him, and he doesn't give things like that away lightly."

Rosie nodded and let her hands drop. Flynn reached up to his collar ran a fingertip around it to touch the tiny silver shield he wore hidden inside it.

No. Bennet never did anything significant, lightly.

That was hopeful.

They'd been through it all, a potted history of the last seven weeks. Ifan finding Bennet. Bennet starting the search for survivors. Bennet and Ifan finding Luke ("Poor little Luke," Rosie said. "He's devastated because Bennet was hurt. We let him see Bennet once on the way back, but it upset him too much."). Bennet and Ifan infiltrating the base to mine it (Caeden laughed, but Flynn was horrified. On *horses?* The man was mad. He had always said Shield officers were mad.). Luke's timely revelation about the communicator tickling his wrist. The last horrendous few minutes on Telnos (Flynn battled nausea again).

Everything that led to them sitting there, waiting.

Now they were talked out, sitting in silence, none of them

inclined to further conversation. All, guessed Flynn, too caught up in worrying about Bennet. The shuttle from Cetes was due soon. It might get there and the *Peregrine* would leave for home and Bennet would still be in surgery, and they just wouldn't know how he was or get to see him.

Except the commander wouldn't allow the *Peregrine* to leave. There had to be considerable benefits to being privileged.

"Commander?" It was Colonel Luiz again. "This is Doctor Shannon. I've explained that you're awaiting news of Shield Captain Bennet."

Caeden couldn't sit straighter—his back was ramrod straight already—but he did tense. "My son?"

The doctor smiled. "He's in the Recovery Room, Commander Caeden, and we're cautiously pleased with his condition. He came through surgery well."

Flynn let out pent-up breath in a long sigh, and slumped in his chair. Rosie turned to Ifan on her other side, and hugged him so hard the big man's eyes should have bulged.

Caeden bowed his head for a second. "Thank you, doctor. How is he, please?"

The doctor pulled up a chair. "We couldn't save the knee. The laser bolt destroyed it, and, to be honest, we had a hard time getting enough useable bone in the femur and tibia to graft in a bionic joint. It will be a long time before he's mobile again."

"How long?"

"Months. Maybe a year."

"But you've saved his leg," Rosie said. "That's all he'll care about."

The doctor's smile was thin. "I'm more concerned about his medical history. There is a risk he might reject the graft. You know that three years ago he had a replacement rib, of course. Although the graft eventually took, he was on anti-rejectants for weeks. Because of the antibodies his system created last time, the reaction now is likely to be worse. We've started him on the anti-rejectants as a precaution."

"Still, that should work, shouldn't it?" Rosie said.

"We hope so," the doctor answered, with the kind of professional bonhomie that had all of Flynn's hackles rising. "It'll be an unpleasant few months for him, though. It's a shame he's one of the small minority who have this sort of difficulty."

"His shoulder?" Ifan asked. "I couldn't get all the crap out of it."

"We did. Several pieces of shrapnel had pressed on the nerves. Again, it will be some months before he has full use of the arm, but he should recover at least some manual dexterity."

"Some," Caeden repeated.

"The damage was extensive. He'll need intensive physiotherapy and he may never recover full use of the hand. But we never know—he just might."

Caeden nodded, and passed a hand over his face. "Is there anything else I should know about before I call his mother? Will you be quarantining him?"

"Quarantine? Oh, for the Telnos fever? No, there's no need for that. The first batch of people were quarantined, of course, until we were certain there wasn't any risk. The fever's a recurrent amoeboid infection. The infection vectors are blood-feeding insects, which carry the amoeba on their mouthparts and transfer them into their victim's bloodstream. There's no possibility of human to human contagion."

"Does he have the fever?"

"Yes," Ifan said, before the doctor could speak. "We all did, even those of us who lived in the hills. Those damned midges would fly for miles if they thought they'd get a good meal."

"We'll find a cure for it, eventually." The doctor glanced at his chronometer. "It's unpleasant, but not dangerous."

Ifan frowned at the man. "What about the solactinium? We were in an unshielded mine."

"We've already started a course of decontaminants to leach out the solactinium. As we will with all of you. I don't think any of you were exposed long enough to cause any serious damage." The doctor looked at his chronometer again and stood up. "The Shield Captain is still very heavily sedated, Commander, and won't be responsive, but you may have five minutes with him. Please excuse me. A shuttle of wounded has just arrived from Cetes and I'm needed for triage. The orderly will take you to him."

The doctor bustled off, and Caeden stood up, looking uncharacteristically uncertain, as if he didn't quite understand what he'd heard. He turned to meet Flynn's eyes.

"I won't be long," he said.

"He'll recognise him, at least," Rosie said, wiping her eyes. She glanced at Flynn. "Tim got the beard off him on the way back. Bennet must have hated that."

"We all did." Ifan ran a hand over his own clean-shaven chin. "We didn't have water to spare for personal grooming. Only those religious freaks wanted the hair."

Rosie laughed, and cried again. "And didn't they annoy the fuck out of Bennet!"

Flynn turned his head and watched the door. They were talking about stuff he had no part in. Rosie and Ifan had Telnos in common, and it seemed a lifetime since Flynn had sat in the OC, yawned his way through an AlbionNews report on the evacuation and announced that whatever happened on Telnos had nothing to do with him. Ironic, really. He should give up on irony.

He looked at them when silence fell, to find Rosie watching him, her eyes wide and candid, so innocent looking the threat was almost visible. Ifan stared at the ceiling.

"So," she said. "A friend of Bennet's."

"Uh-huh."

"From the *Gyrfalcon*."

Flynn sighed and nodded. She was starting that again, was she? Well, they did say Shield never gave up, never gave in. Ifan focused on him for an instant, but didn't appear to be interested. The big man's sad gaze flickered away again.

"Mmn." Rosie's stare, though, was intense. Hard. "Good friends, I expect."

Flynn wasn't about to let her faze him. He smiled his best smile. "I expect so."

"Mmn," Rosie said again. "The deprivation that was good for his soul, I wonder?"

What the fuck was she was on about? "So do I. Wonder, I mean."

"Oh, I expect you are. Seems likely." She leaned forward and touched him on the knee, and he was suddenly faced by a tough and very competent soldier. "What matters is Bennet's expectations. Don't mess it up, airhead."

Flynn blinked at her. "I probably won't get the chance," he said, surprised into honesty.

She cast another look at the door as it opened, and came over all female and inscrutable. "We'll see. Commander! How is he?"

"Alive," Caeden said, with deep and obvious thankfulness. He turned to Flynn. "You can have a couple of minutes with him, Flynn. That's all. Then it's Rosie's turn."

Flynn was out of the door before the commander could change his mind and definitely before Rosie could say anything. The medical orderly pointed him to a room down the corridor. He hesitated, as terrified as he was delighted, before opening the door and plunging in before he could change his mind. The room was quiet and dim, crowded with medical equipment.

Bennet was the only person in it.

He looked small, in the bed. A stupid thing to think, because he was only half an inch shorter than Flynn, but here he looked small and thin. Vulnerable. The equipment didn't help, dwarfing the bed with its monitors and lights and making constant beeping sounds. A cradle kept the bedcovers from weighing on the injured leg.

Flynn took Bennet's right hand in his, careful not to disturb the tubing and valves of the intravenous line inserted into the vein on the back. A clear liquid dripped into the tubing, and Flynn watched it for a second or two, timing the drops and wondering what it was.

Bennet's face was so white that all Flynn could focus on were the black smudges of hair and eyebrows against the white pillow. His eyes were closed, and his breathing deep and even, as if he were merely asleep. Flynn smiled. Bennet had slept like this in the little cabin on the *Gyrfalcon*, a still constant in the bed with Flynn fidgeting around him all night. Bennet only woke up when the fidgeting resolved itself into true wakefulness and the opportunity for another long slow lovemaking. Off duty, Bennet's radar was switched off for anything less, as if he were making up for all the nights when he was on a job and sleep was a luxury.

Flynn leaned forward. Nothing he did would wake Bennet right then, no matter how much he fidgeted.

It was a gentle kiss, an undemanding kiss, a kiss that thanked the gods, whole heartedly, that Bennet was alive, a kiss that shouted joyful thanks that the lips under his were warm and living, not cold and dead. A kiss that gave Flynn the courage to say what he could never have said if Bennet was awake.

"Welcome back, Ben," he said, using his free hand to trace the line of Bennet's face. "Love you."

SECTION FIVE:
ASCLEPIUS

26 Tertius – 38 Quintus, 7488

CHAPTER SIXTEEN

26 Tertius – 5 Quartus: Military Hospital, Sais

Long ago, when Bennet was still new in Joss's life and not so grown and mature that he couldn't still take pleasure in some childlike things, he'd persuaded Joss to go with him to the annual summer fairground held on the outskirts of Sais. Bennet had taken his hand and pulled him into a ride where he'd been forced into a tiny car that swooped up and down a narrow track, labouring up from the bottom of sharp, upright curves to tremble for an instant on the top, perched a hundred feet above the ground, before hurtling down the other side again. Joss remembered, clearly, the hollowness in the pit of his stomach and the wind rushing in his face too fast and hard for him to breathe.

Getting Bennet back was just like that—a wild dizzy ride he couldn't control, rushing him from despair to that trembling instant of a joy so exquisite it was excruciating, only to hurl him back down into a careworn unhappiness. And all without giving him the chance to catch his breath.

How had the impossibly joyful reunion he'd dreamed of, been reduced to sickness, pain and bad temper?

When the medical staff had taken Bennet out of the life-support pod in which he'd travelled home and returned him to the loving bosom of his partner and his family, he had barely acknowledged any of them. The pain and the fever seemed overwhelming. Three days of living at the hospital with him hadn't improved matters. Bennet, very sick and very bad-tempered, had no qualms at all about taking it out on anyone who came within shouting distance.

It was a relief to be turned out of Bennet's room for half an hour by the medical staff. Joss allowed Meriel to take him off to join the rest of the family in the café, where Liam and Natalia waited. Thea took a break from ward rounds to join them. It was hard not to complain. Joss did understand Bennet was in a lot of pain, and was sick and worried about his leg. But still. Bennet had no thought for how they'd all felt, thinking him dead.

Hence, Joss on the downward plunge again.

"I thought it would be all right. I thought…" He picked at the pastry Liam had brought him. Hospital food, even in the coffee shop provided for visitors, was limp and unappetising. It couldn't possibly be nutritious. A hospital should know better. "He doesn't seem to care if we're there or not."

Meriel stirred cream into her coffee. "Joss, darling, he's always horrible when he's sick. Remember a couple of years ago when he had the rib done?"

"I'm not used to him being like this." Joss crumbled the pastry and pushed the plate to one side.

"I am. With Caeden away so much, I saw all four of them through every childhood crisis single-handed, everything from a chipped tooth to the time Liam broke almost everything breakable falling off a roof where he had no business being in the first place." Meriel poked Liam as she spoke.

"I didn't do it on purpose," Liam said, grinning.

"You shouldn't have done it all."

"He did it for the attention, Mama," Natalia said in her usual snippy tone. "Youngest child syndrome."

"I dare say. Bennet may not have fallen off roofs, Joss, but he had his share of childhood ailments. He's been a dreadful patient since infancy. Prepare yourself for squalls."

"Can't you do something, Thea?" Joss appealed to the one sibling he thought Bennet might listen to.

Thea glanced up from the datapad in her hands. "Do what? I'm not on his care team. I'm a trauma surgeon. I'd have been perfect for his treatment on the *Peregrine*, but he's past that stage and now he needs the sort of specialist orthopaedics work he'll get from Doctor Harald. Of course, I wish I could look after him but the hospital is quite right to keep me out of it." She put down the datapad and tapped the screen with one finger. "I've taken a look at his notes and all things considered, he's not doing too badly. He's in a lot of pain and that darn fever won't let go, of course, and the anti-rejectants for the bionics are fierce. But it could be worse."

"It was worse." Meriel' hands trembled, the coffee cup rattling in its saucer. Silver threaded through her hair now, and the lines around her eyes hadn't been there before Telnos.

Of all Bennet's siblings, Thea looked like him the most, with the same long-limbed body, but she had a grace and spontaneity he lacked. She moved in an instant to stoop over her mother and rest her cheek against Meriel's hair, while Liam looked agonised and Natalia looked the other way.

Joss's comlink buzzed. He glanced at the message and pushed the link away into his pocket. The damn press again. They'd hounded him for three days. AlbionNews, this time, wanting a statement about the astonishing developments of the Telnos story and this return from beyond the grave. What in hell's name did they expect him to say? His Bennet had been dead and was back, when Joss had given up all hope. Of course he was ecstatic, delighted, in raptures. What else did they expect him to be? They could write the damn story without his help.

"It scares me," Joss said. "It scares me that he's so sick. I thought if ever I got him back then everything would be all right, but it's not and I'm frightened."

Meriel took Joss's hand. "He'll be fine, Joss dear."

"He's not the same. He's changed." Why in hell couldn't

Bennet have just listened to him? If he'd cared enough, he would have left the military years ago. "I couldn't bear it if he loses that leg."

"Don't worry," Liam said. "You've still got both of yours."

Joss and Meriel spent every day at the hospital, with Thea, Liam and Natalia in regular supporting roles. Joss only really counted Thea. Natalia was always distant, and he and Liam hadn't yet got past the patently insincere apology Meriel had forced out of her younger son for that inappropriate remark.

Bennet, in his more disgruntled and unpleasant moods—all too frequent, Joss grumbled, and it didn't help to have Meriel laugh and say she thought Bennet rather enjoyed them—appeared to find their constant presence as difficult to bear as the drug regimen designed to save his leg. Joss agonised over Bennet's temper tantrums, but the family regarded them as both therapeutic and inevitable. 'Bless him,' Liam had added fondly, expounding this theory in his helpless brother's hearing at the height of one such episode. Liam had shown some nimble footwork dodging the pillow Bennet hurled at his head.

At least Caeden wasn't there to add to Joss's burden. He sent— and required—daily emails about his son's progress, but it would be weeks before he could get home to see Bennet for himself. The *Gyrfalcon* was caught up in major exercises and manoeuvres, and with Bennet out of danger, Caeden put duty first. Typical of the man, of course, but no one in the family appeared to expect anything different or be one whit fazed by it. Bennet had managed a faint grin when Joss mentioned his father's absence and a 'Hell, if he came running home, I'd think I was probably dying!' Which had Joss wincing and changing the subject. Fast. He even welcomed another bad-tempered spat a moment or two later, as welcome proof that Bennet was very much alive.

Bennet was better behaved when outsiders visited, although Captain Felix of the Strategy Unit, an early visitor, was treated as if he were family in that regard. Felix did not appear to resent it and left grinning, promising to bring some work with him next time.

"If you have this much energy to expend in bad temper, we might as well usefully channel it into Albion's defence." Felix had paused in the doorway, returned to the bed and delivered a brisk and, to Joss's eyes, unsentimental hug. Bennet, he noticed, didn't complain.

Bennet was positively angelic when, a week after he was brought home, General Martens came to welcome her prodigal captain, bringing with her the Supreme Commander in all his glory. If Bennet had later demanded painkillers against the effect of the glare of gold braid on his eyes, he was the epitome of quiet respect throughout the visit. Bennet had snorted at his family's obtuseness. Of course, he was polite. He certainly wasn't out to annoy the Management and get posted into the Strategy Unit as punishment.

He gave Joss a wry grin. "I'll have to be content with annoying you and Mama, to make up for my restraint with His Nibs."

Meriel laughed and kissed him. Joss sighed, and endured.

Bennet had been retching all day, hands clenching on each convulsion, even his damaged right hand twitching. The IV unit dripped the anti-rejectant medication into him, fuelling the reaction. When he woke after a short sleep following his overlords' departure, it was to the next dose of medication and an almost instantaneous bout of sickness. Joss had never thought he'd learn to cope with holding Bennet's head while he retched and puked, but he soothed with hands and voice, and wiped Bennet's face when it was all over.

"Want some water?" Joss asked when Bennet finally quieted and focused on him.

Bennet's eyes were red, and his voice was thin with exhaustion. "No."

"I think you'd better have some," Joss said, firmly.

Bennet took it without further argument. He didn't even

complain at having to take the water in a dreadful infant's feeding cup with a spout. He moved his head away when he'd had enough. "Where is everyone?"

"Your mother went home, Thea said she'd be by later before she goes off duty and I assume the other two are at the Academy where they belong." Joss straightened the bedcovers, twitching them into neatness despite the way Bennet grumbled and tightened his mouth at him. He settled back into his chair beside the bed.

Bennet frowned, staring at the ceiling, his fingers twisting in the sheets until he had them as wrinkled as they were before Joss straightened them. After a while, his eyes closed, his breathing levelling out. Joss let himself droop for a moment or two and went off to find some coffee. He needed a restorative. Coffee would have to do.

Thea was there when he got back. He could hear the murmur of their voices beyond the half open door. He hesitated.

"How bad is it?" Thea asked.

"It hurts like fuck and I wish to the gods they'd cut the fucking thing off."

"No, you don't," Thea said, scornfully.

"Maybe." A short pause, and Bennet's voice was tentative, anxious. "Will they take my leg, do you think?"

Thea was far too direct for Joss's peace of mind. "I think it's chancy. The bionics won't grow in without the drugs to stop you rejecting the transplant. So I think it's grin and bear it time, little brother. Once the bionics are in and bone's grown over the graft, you'll be fine. It'll be all right."

"And if it's not?"

How Althea could laugh was beyond Joss. "Then at least you can be grateful it's only one leg, and not both."

A short silence, while Joss dithered about going in.

"Thanks, Thea," Bennet said and he sounded like he meant it. Joss, who had been the butt of so many sarcastic remarks for the last week whenever he'd expressed loving concern, couldn't help feeling it was unfair. Thea had hardly been what he would call comforting. "What's up between Joss and Liam?"

It astonished Joss that Bennet had noticed, he'd been so self-absorbed since he got home. In Thea's place, Joss would prevaricate. Thea had no such delicacy.

"Things were fraught, a couple of days after you got home. Liam was... well, he upset Joss."

"A family failing."

"That's different. Liam was rather harsh and said something he shouldn't. We all know how hard it was on Joss, thinking you were dead, and he's still finding it hard coping with you being ill now. Liam knows better than to make smart-arse comments. It was not helpful."

Joss raised his hand to push at the door and announce his presence.

"Joss fusses too much. At least you don't cry, or pat my hand, or wipe my face, or straighten the bedcovers more than three times a minute."

"Bennet, that's unkind. Joss just wants to take care of you."

"He's mad at me."

"Whatever for?"

"Surviving," Bennet said. "It was much easier to forgive me when I was dead."

Joss let his hand drop again. When Althea came out of Bennet's room five minutes later, he was standing by the nurse's station discussing the unseasonable weather and conveying, he hoped, absolutely nothing of the man who had just had heard his lover mock and deride all his loving concern.

Two weeks after Bennet's return, a miner appeared at the hospital.

He said he'd been on Telnos with Bennet, and much as Joss hoped to put Telnos well behind him in a past he would never willingly revisit, he couldn't refuse permission for this Ifan person to visit. Not with the way Bennet's face lit up when his name was mentioned.

The day Ifan came to the hospital, Bennet was flushed and sick with another bout of the fever. His mouth had thinned right down, making his mouth a whitened slash across his pale face, as though keeping his lips pressed together was all that stopped him from yelling at the pain or at them when they tried his limited patience too far. It hadn't been the best of days. Joss had had his hands slapped away several times when he tried to help. But Bennet cheered up when Ifan appeared.

Which was galling.

Ifan looked just like Joss had expected a miner to look: big, rough around the edges and not someone he would like to meet in a dark alley. Bennet was pleased to see Ifan, though, even laughing when they shook hands, so there had to be more to him than his looks suggested. Ifan was bluff and hearty, although his voice shook when he talked to Bennet about a trooper who had died on the second evacuation of Telnos. Meriel and Joss withdrew to the window, giving Bennet and Ifan privacy to talk about the dead soldier.

"He's too like his father," Meriel said. "He has to be responsible for everything, just like Caeden. At least Caeden's old enough to know it's impossible. Bennet still thinks death and pain can be defied and held back because it shouldn't be allowed to happen on his watch, and it's his fault if it does."

Well, there wasn't much Joss could say to that. Besides, Meriel was right. Bennet was far too like his father for Joss's comfort.

They re-joined the conversation when it became more general, focusing on Ifan's plans to reenlist—"To get a few of those fu... damned drones, for Jan's sake."—and news of the other survivors.

"Have you seen Luke?" Bennet asked.

"A few days ago. He's gone to his mother's sister, did you

know?"

"I know someone in Child Welfare who was able to tell us what happened to him," Meriel said. Bennet had fretted himself into a fever about the child. He held himself responsible for Luke, too, and Meriel had exerted herself to get the information needed to set Bennet's mind at rest.

"The kid's settling in and his aunt said they'd found a good counsellor for him," Ifan said. "She's not one of the Brethren, and she's doing what's best for him, not what some cockeyed fanatic thinks is best for the gods."

"I miss him," Bennet said.

Joss blinked. "We aren't adopting him, are we?"

"I don't think they'd let us."

Alarmed, Joss tried to nip that one in the bud. "It's just that I'm not at all maternal."

"You don't have the figure for it, dear." Bennet smiled, reaching out to stroke the back of Joss's hand. They were the first kind words he'd had for Joss since breakfast, and, despite everything, Joss relished them. "I'd like to see him, to be sure he's all right."

Meriel looked alarmed. "I don't think that's wise for either of you. You can't adopt him, sweetheart, and he has a family. You've got to let him settle with his aunt. He needs some stability."

Ifan nodded. "I think you're right there, ma'am. He's not yours, Bennet. Let it go. The kid will be all right."

"I know. I got fond of him, that's all. He reminded me of Liam, Mama."

"Not as destructive, I hope. Liam at eight was Something Appalling." Meriel sounded ridiculously proud. "He still is."

Joss managed not to snort. He wouldn't be arguing with that.

"Luke's a nice kid," Ifan said. "But his aunt's right in trying to put Telnos behind him. I wasn't welcome when I went to check on him. I think she'd seen the coverage on AlbionNews."

"What coverage?" Bennet asked.

Joss grimaced at Meriel. She looked horrified, grimacing back. They'd agreed not to worry Bennet about this. One of them should have remembered to warn the miner.

"What coverage?" Bennet was persistent as ever.

"Well, sweetheart, you didn't think the Telnos rescue would get by them without a mention, did you?" Meriel's tone was light.

"Given who your father is," Joss said, silky smooth.

"No," Bennet said.

"Well then." Meriel shrugged.

"And?"

"Okay, on the whole," Ifan said. "I mean, they got me down pat. Handsome, dashing, heroic—"

"Illegal?"

"I think they missed that." Ifan's big, sad face softened into a smile.

"Mama?"

Meriel sighed. "It's nothing, really. AlbionNews dug up the fact you live with Joss, and were snide about it, that's all."

They hadn't just dug it up. They'd leapt on it, shrieking with joy, delighted at the chance to get in some digs at Caeden's public image of the devout, religious, upright man.

"Gossip column stuff. It wasn't a real news item, just slid in at the end of a bulletin. Some light relief after all the real news, the deep stuff about the war or tax protests or the gains the Peace Movement has made in politics. That had proper, solemn treatment, and then the main news anchor, Nathan, and his skinny sidekick, Alexis, took pot shots at us for laughs." Joss added in a mincing, affected tone, "Wouldn't we have liked to have been flies on the wall when the eldest son of our leading High Theban family left home to live with Professor Josiah, one of his tutors at the Thebaid Institute, the *minute* he reached the age of consent? We can only imagine some of the family discussions that day! Do you think they prayed, Alexis?"

Bennet slumped onto his pillows. "Oh."

"That was the flavour of it." Joss glared at Meriel for the shushing motions she made at him. "AlbionNews had a wonderful time."

"Pretty rich, really, for Alexis to try and take the moral high ground," Meriel said, "since she's never out of the gossip columns. She has a child, I believe, and has never named the father."

Joss snorted. "Presumably because she didn't know who it was. What's more, Nathan is hardly the most heterosexual man on the planet. I've seen him in far too many gay bars over the years, looking for pretty boys. You'd think he'd have more loyalty, more integrity, than to run the story on those terms. It was infuriating, Bennet. I had enough to worry about here with you, without guttersnipe journalists suggesting I was your tutor and there was something improper about us."

Bennet held out his hand for Joss to take. "What did you do?"

"Why do you think we pay lawyers?" Joss took Bennet's hand in both of his and squeezed. "Mine finally earned his keep pointing out the blindingly obvious—I am not Commander Caeden's son and my private life is precisely that."

"We issued a statement about how proud we were of you," Meriel said. "Liam suggested we add a line about being proudest of the fact you were one of the few men on Albion who couldn't lay claim to being the father of Alexis's son."

Bennet laughed.

"I wish I'd thought of it," Joss said. "A pity your father vetoed it."

"I met your dad," Ifan said to Bennet. "He arrived in Demeter a couple of hours after we did."

Bennet looked tired now. The visit was wearing him out. He wasn't fit enough for miners to come along and upset whatever precarious balance Joss had managed to create for them.

"I know. Poor Dad. He must have spent hours in a cutter, and I wasn't even awake when he got there."

"Eight hours there and back again, according to the pilot he brought with him," Ifan said. "More than my dad would have done for me, always supposing I'd known who he was."

"He took a pilot with him?" Bennet grinned at his mother. "You'll have to have words with him, Mama. He's getting delusions of grandeur again."

"I think he's entitled," Meriel murmured.

"Entitled or not, I'm sure he hasn't forgotten how to fly his own cutter!"

"I think he just wanted to give your friend—wotsisname? Flynn—a chance to see you were okay," Ifan said.

Bennet's smile vanished. He looked like a spasm of pain had hit him. "Flynn? He had Flynn pilot him to Demeter?"

Joss straightened in his chair. He kept it light. "Who's Flynn?"

Bennet shot a quick glance at Joss, and lay back against his pillow, breathing rather fast. He pulled his hand free. "He's…" Bennet hesitated. "He's the pilot who brought me back from the job I did with the *Gyrfalcon*, the year before last." His grin looked forced. "I wouldn't have got back without him."

Joss made his mouth curve up. "Then we owe him a great deal."

"He'd have been great in Shield. I should recruit him."

"Uh-huh," Joss said.

"He's far too much a maverick for Dad's peace of mind, though. Definitely not one of Dad's favourites."

"Well," Joss said. "It looks like Flynn and I might have something in common there."

Bennet was quiet after that, taking little part in the latter part of the conversation. Ifan and Meriel had, of course, assumed he was worn out by the visit and Ifan, all consideration, cut it short.

Bennet did tire easily it was true, and he'd been unwell all day. It was a quite reasonable assumption for them to make. Joss didn't make the same assumption. The pilot. Something to do with the pilot... Bennet had said too much to cover for it. Far too much.

Joss said his goodbyes to Meriel, who intended to drive Ifan back to his hostel. He waited for a few minutes after they'd left, enjoying the peace and quiet, listening to Bennet's quiet breathing.

Too quiet and too even to be true. He didn't believe Bennet was asleep.

He took hold of Bennet's left hand, studying it for a long minute, seeing the little scars and calluses that hadn't been there the day they'd flirted across Amthoth's corpse. Those had come later, as Bennet had learned to wield a laser. Bennet opened his eyes and smiled at him. It was a thin pale thing, that smile.

"Who's Flynn?"

"I told you. One of my father's pilots."

"Yes. I know. We've done all that." Joss waited, then said, when it was obvious Bennet wasn't intending to say anything more, "Bennet?"

Bennet shook his head. "A pilot. That's all."

"One your father decided to take to Demeter with him. Why did he do that, do you think?"

"The gods alone know," Bennet said, and there was no doubting his sincerity.

"I wondered. I wondered if there'd been something. You've not been the same over the last year or two. I thought it might be because you'd made things up with your father, but now I don't know."

"We all change." Bennet sounded bone weary. "I'm getting older, that's all."

"Trite, but true. Especially if someone else changes you— whoever it was you met while you were away. Not your father after all, then, the catalyst for this change. This Flynn, maybe?"

Bennet didn't confirm or deny anything. "There's nothing for you to worry about."

"No?"

"Joss, I'm here. With you. Please let's leave it at that."

"Would you leave it?"

"I do," Bennet snapped. He pushed himself up, half sitting against the bank of pillows. "Always! Every time you fuck with someone else, I do. I forgive you every single time, and believe me, I'm beginning to wonder why."

"Bennet!"

"Look, I liked Flynn, okay? He got me back when no one else could, and he saved my life, and he was fun and, hell, can you imagine how difficult it was for me on my father's ship, knowing what the old man thought of me? Flynn was a good friend all the time I was there, while I was trying to sort things out with Dad and do a bloody difficult infiltration run at the same time. But he's on the *Gyrfalcon*, and I'm here. I'm *always here*, Joss. I always come back to where you are. It's been nine years and that means a hell of a lot to me. How much does it mean to you?"

"How can you ask that?" What was Bennet playing at? This wasn't how it was supposed to go.

"Because all you do is pull at it, like picking at a scab." Bennet fell back, breathing harsh and difficult. "Because you aren't satisfied with it," he said, in a quieter voice, "and I don't think you ever have been. And that worries me, because I can't give you any more, and it's not enough."

"But I love you," Joss said. Bennet had never complained before. He'd only laughed wryly and insisted on having Joss to himself when he was at home. "I do!"

"Do you? Yet you can't ever wait for me to come home, can you? There always has to be someone to fill the spaces." Bennet's voice hitched and he turned his face away.

Bennet's shoulders shook. Shocked, trying to tell himself illness and weariness caused it, Joss put his arms around him. "But

214

they don't mean anything! They're just substitutes. It's you I want really. I'm sorry. I'm sorry. I love you, and I thought you'd gone and it nearly killed me. I'm sorry. I do love you, I do…"

Bennet got his arm around Joss's neck and shook some more. So Joss kissed and soothed, and choked with remorse, until at last Bennet fell asleep, his face pressed into Joss's neck.

Joss was out-manoeuvred and out-gunned. A scholar had no chance against the trained military. No chance at all.

It's just sometimes they didn't realise it until later.

You watch him sleep, the one who has returned, unlooked for, from the Field of Reeds; re-embodied, whole, the living flesh banishing the dry husk you'd thought you were left with.

For him you made the sacrifice of things he'd loved, so they'd be there with him in the dark for his pleasure, his forever. For him you'd burnt the incense, recited the prayers, made the ritual gestures, finding some peace in the gestures and the words. The ancient ceremonial was for the living as much as the coffined dead; to let you find comfort and rest your mind and spirit in ritual, to have the ceremony take over the daily effort of living, to let it take the place of thinking and remorse.

It comes as a rude surprise when you find it was a waste: a waste of a sacrifice, a waste of good incense, a waste of heart-felt prayers.

A useless gesture.

He moves in his sleep, frowning. He's still beautiful, even with his too-thin face and the pain it wears too often. You can stroke his hair while he sleeps like this, take the heavy hands in yours and he won't strike your hands away and tell you to leave him be. Or worse still, let you do it and all the time you know he's humouring you, he's telling himself he has to allow you to do it, that he's submitting out of some misguided sense of duty.

Once you would have given worlds to have him back home and

safe; and now, surely, you can be reassured that this time there'll be no going back. It will be months before he'll walk properly again, if ever, and the military won't want him, crippled. He's home now, for good. That has to be a cause for rejoicing.

But all you can think of is that it is all a waste, a useless gesture.

The paper covering the cracks is as thin and worn as tissue. It's starting to let the truth leak through.

There's nothing for you to worry about.

Your back twinges and you shift in your chair to ease it, watching his sleeping face.

He didn't say 'He was just a pilot. I barely remember him.' Which you just wouldn't believe.

And he didn't say 'He really was just a friend. I didn't sleep with him.' Which you'd find hard to believe, although you'd try.

And he didn't say 'Nothing but a substitute, just like the ones you have.' Which you'd like to believe, because it's hurtful, but acceptable.

All he said was 'There's nothing for you to worry about.'

Another useless gesture.

CHAPTER SEVENTEEN

13 - 14 Quintus 7488: Sais

More than eight weeks after being rescued from Telnos, Bennet was allowed home at last. Liam came to do the honours, indignant at the suspicion with which his family greeted him—"No, I did not skip lectures! I got permission!"—and drove his mother, Joss and Bennet back to the apartment in the centre of the city with Thea waving them off from the hospital front door. Natalia wasn't there. She had the sense of responsibility Liam lacked, according to their mother.

It was true that Tallie wasn't one to slide out of Academy classes, even to collect her elder brother from the Military Hospital. But her dislike for Joss was at least part of the reason for her absence. Bennet wasn't even sure she liked him, much. He couldn't connect to her the way he did with Liam and Thea.

The journey home took them through the Old City. It wasn't the most direct route, but Liam claimed his sense of direction was off that day and he took them down several side roads and past all the places and buildings Bennet loved, before crossing the park to the neo-classical apartment buildings lining the wide avenue on the other side. Once he glanced behind to the back seat to meet Bennet's gaze, his own eyes bright. He was a good kid. Even if he did sneak out of lectures.

The underground parking garage was one advantage of an expensive apartment in the centre of the city. Liam had no difficulty finding a parking spot near the elevator, close to where Bennet's own car sat under its protective tarp. Liam and Joss between them got Bennet into and out of the elevator, Meriel bringing up the rear, fluttering and full of anxious advice.

The apartment took up the entire top floor of the building. Bennet paused on the threshold of the living room—bigger than the *Hype*'s landing bays—and took it all in, everything from the latest of Joss's artistic acquisitions to the breath-taking view.

It didn't feel real. It felt more like a stage set.

He hadn't expected to ever see it again. He swallowed against an uncomfortable lump in his throat and his eyes stung. He glanced at Joss. Ah, yes. Joss was, of course, about to cry. Any minute now.

Joss's hands were trembling when he took hold of Bennet, and kissed him. "Welcome home," he said, and pulled Bennet in close, ignoring or not hearing Bennet's gasp of discomfort, and started crying all over him.

Bennet grimaced into the side of Joss's neck and patted his shoulder.

It still didn't feel real.

Natalia turned up just as Bennet—having had what his mother insisted on referring to, brightly, as a refreshing little rest—started on a round of inspection to see what had changed in the months since he'd been home last. Joss greeted her with the same degree of coolness with which she met him. They didn't like each other much. Bennet was surprised, though, when Tallie gave him a swift hug. That was unexpected.

There was one obvious change to the décor. A delicate glass sculpture had always stood in the centre of the polished floor. It was gone. A large bronze stood in its place.

Bennet nodded towards it. "What happened to the Ailion piece?"

"Which one was that?" Natalia asked.

"The glass sculpture." Joss watched for Bennet's reaction. "I broke it."

Bennet stared at him. "Deliberately?" At Joss's nod, he asked, "A propitiatory sacrifice?"

Joss smiled, and inclined his head. "There's my clever scholar."

"Well, if I'd been in the afterlife, I would have been impressed," Bennet said. Shame. He'd liked the Ailion piece.

"It seemed appropriate." Joss winced. "I'm thinking about commissioning another."

"Sometimes," Meriel said, "I don't have the faintest idea what you two are talking about."

Liam, lounging beside her on the sofa, twirled his forefinger at his temple and grinned.

"I'll miss it." Bennet turned his back on his aggravating little brother, and looked towards the display case in the window. Years ago, he'd hung over Joss's amulet collection admiring the scarabs before ensuring that Joss seduced him. Bennet looked at Joss, then hobbled over and checked the case. They weren't all there. "Where's the heart scarab?"

Joss laughed. "I'll have to dig it up again. I buried it in the Institute gardens along with two or three others."

Bennet turned, still awkward on his crutches. He jammed his uninjured hip up against the display case for extra support. "You did that?"

"The whole thing." Joss swept up his hands in a helpless gesture, shrugging. "I couldn't get through it any other way. Amthoth helped me."

Liam did a little more finger twirling. "I don't know what the heck they're talking about either. I think they're both touched in the head, Mama."

Bennet sent a rude gesture Liam's way, but kept his attention on Joss. "That's… that's scary, Joss."

Joss shrugged again. "It helped me cope." He came to join Bennet at the window. "I kissed you for the first time, right here."

Bennet smiled. Poor Joss. He didn't deserve to be the target for all of Bennet's bad temper, and the gods knew, he'd given up his life the past few weeks to be at the hospital. He deserved better than this. "I know. Did you think I'd forgotten? I do hope it wasn't a one-off sort of thing."

Joss laughed. "Transparent as glass," he said, and kissed Bennet. It was their first real kiss since Bennet had come home. They ignored Liam's ribald comments, Natalia's pink face and Meriel's quiet laughter. Joss's eyes were bright. "Welcome home, love."

Bennet smiled at him, then frowned as he processed what Joss had said. "Who's Amthoth?"

Joss administered the drugs, as the hospital had taught him. He put down the hypospray. "Do you really not remember the Amthoth mummy?"

"No. We must have studied hundreds. Was Amthoth an important one?"

"No," Joss said, after a minute. "Not at all."

Ouch. Bennet had put his foot in it there then. He turned to apologise, to make it up somehow for forgetting the mummy's significance, when the first surge of nausea hit him and he had to close his eyes.

In the scale of things, mummies weren't that important.

He turned onto his side and retched.

Day one of freedom started in the same way as all Bennet's days in hospital.

The IV was attached every night to a permanent catheter in the back of his right hand—a doubtful way to make the semi-useless appendage useful again. But he was grateful each night for the sedative that relieved the feelings of nausea and allowed him to rest. At seven in the morning, precisely, the IV switched from painkillers to anti-rejectants, shooting the dose into Bennet at a greatly increased drip-rate, pre-set to get the full dosage into him within a few minutes.

He woke about fifteen minutes later, dazed and disoriented as the first wave of nausea swept up over him, bringing the cold, queasy disgust with it. He moved, his leg heavy in the encasing capsule. A warm, naked body pressed up against him, spooning into his back. Joss had an arm thrown over his side, the hand against the base of his sternum.

"Bennet?" Joss said.

Bennet couldn't answer. He head swam and his mouth filled with saliva, mirroring the sweat prickling on his forehead and in the corner of his eyelids. The slight pressure of Joss's hand was too much. The first dry retch came, as always, from his feet up, convulsing him and ending in a cough deep-chested enough to make his ribs ache. A sharp pain flashed across the small of his back as his muscles contracted.

Joss moved quickly, raising himself on one elbow. "I'm here. Just relax."

He brushed Bennet's hair back just as the second convulsion hit. Bennet's hands clenched, and he half raised one arm to push Joss away. He let his hand fall back again, forcing himself to accept, to endure. He closed his eyes and set his jaw, closing his lips tight on words that would only tear and rend if he let them out.

"I'm here," Joss said over and over. His hand smoothed over Bennet's hair.

Bennet's resolve fled. He opened his mouth and let the words loose to do their worst.

26 Quintus 7488: Sais

Bennet wriggled to get the left crutch in exactly the right place and started across the room. At least this time, Joss made himself sit still and just watch. He twitched, true, and half rose while Bennet negotiated one of the large sofas, but subsided again when Bennet's gaze caught his. Bennet would have brushed off yet another solicitous offer of help and comfort he didn't want, damn it. He was tired of holding back. He wasn't an invalid and he'd be damned if he'd let Joss make him one. They'd fought too much over Joss's tendency to fuss since Bennet had come home from the hospital. Joss forever made little dabs at him, it felt like; smoothing his hair, putting a hand on his brow or cheek, rubbing soothing circles on his lower back when the nausea was at its worst. It took everything Bennet had not to strike Joss's hands away and growl at him. Joss wasn't cut out for nursing any more than Bennet wanted to be nursed.

He lowered himself into his chair, and after a glance at his wrist chronometer, smiled at Joss. "Not bad."

"What isn't?"

"The bedroom to living space handicap stakes. I've just shaved three seconds off my best time. By next week, I'll be doing the distance in less than a minute."

"Maybe we need a few obstacles in place, then, to make it a challenge?"

Bennet laughed. "It's challenging enough without a water jump, thank you!" His smile faded as Joss handed him a cup of bland milky 'invalid's food'. It was all he could keep down, but gods, he hated it. He sipped at it without enthusiasm.

"You'd better drink it. Liam will be here soon to take you to the hospital for your check up."

"Aren't you taking me?"

"No. I called Liam before breakfast. He should have got here twenty minutes ago. He's late."

"He's Liam. He's always late. What are you going to do, then?"

"I'm going to the Institute. I haven't been there for weeks." Joss looked expectant.

"Good," Bennet said, tired of living with a martyr. If he asked, Joss would drop the idea at once and take him to the hospital for his regular appointment with Dr Harald. But Joss would be so noble and self-sacrificing; Bennet's teeth would ache from grinding them down to the bone. "You must be bored with being at home all the time. Give my best to the Dean and tell him to stop bothering me about the printer's proofs. I'll finish them when I can."

Joss's lips tightened. "Fine. Do you want this?" He offered a datapad.

"Please." Bennet took the datapad in both hands. The right hand was much improved, but still clumsy. "There's a letter from Dad in my email box."

Joss barely looked up from a plate of pastries. *Damn him.* Bennet would have killed to be able to eat a pastry. "I thought we'd have heard from him before now."

"Not when they're on exercises. He'll have been too busy trying to fool whichever other Fleet commander he's pitched against, and I expect they were on comms silence for most of it." Bennet opened up the letter.

25 Quintus 7488

My dear Bennet,

I'm delighted to hear from your mother that the hospital has released you at last. Personally, I think they lost patience with your bad temper, but your mother assures me they didn't just throw you out into the street. I find that unlikely, but more than thirty years of marriage to her has taught me

> she is usually truthful, so I suppose I shall have to believe you were discharged rather than merely evicted.

Bennet snorted. According to his mother, Bennet had come by the bad temper honestly. Caeden had just got better at hiding it.

> There's an encouraging postscript from Liam—all the communication I ever get from him, by the way, and another instance of the two of you being more alike than is comfortable—to the effect that he got you all the way home from hospital and you refrained from throwing up on him. It pains me to say this about any son of mine, but there have been times when I've been tempted to throw up all over him myself. I'm torn between relief that you are evidently getting stronger, and a desire to tell you that you may act *in loco parentis* in that regard whenever he deserves it. I leave it to your discretion, but I do expect a full account of any incident you think will amuse me. The gods know Liam affords me precious few opportunities for amusement, and I'm prepared to take whatever I can get.

Bennet laughed aloud.

Joss sighed. "Another one of his more facetious letters, I take it? Does he always have to be so ponderous about it? His writing style's heavier than an elephant dancing on a pinhead."

"Of course it is. But that's the whole point. You know it's done for effect." Bennet frowned. What was up with Joss? He usually enjoyed reading Caeden's letters when Bennet shared them, as amused as Bennet by Caeden's style.

Joss sighed again. "If you say so. What's so funny about this one?"

"Dad just gave me his permission to throw up all over Liam."

"Why?"

"Because it's Liam."

"No. I meant, why is it funny?"

Joss was missing the point about elephants and pinheads, obviously. Bennet could only shrug. "Because it's Liam."

Joss huffed and returned to his late breakfast.

> The war games and exercises with Fourth...
>
> {several paragraphs deleted by the military censor before publication}

Bennet grinned again. "Oh, listen to this."

He started recounting the elaborate military trick Caeden had pulled during the exercises, but Joss just huffed again, louder, and poured himself another coffee. He never had been much interested in military stuff. Bennet broke off, his nose wrinkling against the smell. It made him queasy.

Joss sipped the coffee. He didn't drink it often. "He does remember who the enemy actually is?"

Bennet turned back to his letter. "He won't let himself be beaten."

> Otherwise, things are quiet at last. We've been in action or exercises now for well over a year, and the pilots are getting restless. We've decided it's time we allowed furlough. I'll be home myself for a long leave in two or three months. I wish it could be earlier—I want to see you very much. But we're giving those pilots whose leave has been delayed the first opportunity for a furlough at home. I expect the city's casinos will be particularly grateful at the return of one talented gambler; I've no doubt the rest will have their own ways of celebrating. They'll be arriving on the noon shuttle on the thirty-ninth, and Colonel Quist and I are counting the days.
>
> A letter direct from you won't hurt, you know.

I'm aware you're still having trouble with your right hand—although your mother tells me that's improving daily—but I'd remind you that you've been left-handed since birth. I believe that leaves you without a valid excuse.

My regards to Joss.

With love...

Bennet stopped breathing, the amusement gone. Joss said something. His voice buzzed, like a wasp trapped under a glass. Bennet's mouth was so dry he had to work it a couple of times.

"Bennet?" Joss sounded alarmed, his voice rising and sharpening. "Bennet?"

Bennet started breathing again with a funny little whooshing noise. "Huh?"

"Are you all right?"

"Fine." Bennet gave him a swift smile. "I'm fine." He pushed the datapad into his right hand and switched it off. It dropped onto the table before he could catch it. Damn! He swore over the stiff fingers of his right hand and shook his head when Joss picked up the datapad and offered it to him. "No. It's okay. I'll read it again when I get back. Liam should be here any minute."

Right on cue, his younger brother breezed in as if the place belonged to him. It wasn't much good remonstrating with him. Liam was young enough to think all of Albion belonged to him and rebukes were shed like water from oilskin. Bennet gave him a grin in welcome. It wasn't his job to discipline Liam and he wasn't a fan of lost causes. Besides, right then he could have kissed his little brother for being the distraction he needed.

"The traffic is foul," Liam said in hurried explanation for his lateness and haste, skirting around the table to find a cup and make an assault on Joss's coffee. "We don't have a lot of time if you aren't going to be late, Bennet." And to Joss, as he emptied the coffee pot, he said, "I thought you liked tea."

"I do," Joss said. "But today, I wanted coffee."

Bennet grimaced. "It's making me feel sick."

Liam downed the coffee in two gulps. "Sorry, I forgot you don't like the smell much. Ready?"

Bennet nodded, and got to his feet. Liam, bless him, sat back and let him struggle. Joss half got up. "I can manage," Bennet said, quite sharply, and Joss sank back down again. He looked sulky with his eyes narrowing and his mouth turning down at the corners.

Liam winked at him, and waited as Bennet fought to get upright. "Hurry it up. We'll be late. I don't want any more speeding tickets."

"What's the rush?"

"Hey, I just want to get you there on time. The sooner they fix that knee and get you back to work, the better for everyone."

Bennet's grin didn't falter, but Joss said, as sharp as Bennet had been a second before, "Don't be ridiculous, Liam." Still shard-sharp, he said, tone cold, "I could come, if you like."

Bennet smiled at him. "And miss out on telling Bachman where he gets off chasing me over the proofs? Shame on you. You know you'll enjoy being protective." He manoeuvred himself to the side of Joss's chair and leaned right down to plant a kiss on Joss's hair. "I'll be home in a couple of hours."

"I may not be back."

Bennet stooped a little further and brushed Joss's lips with his. "Love you," he said, very soft.

Joss blinked, and smiled back. "I won't be late."

Liam went to grab the door to the private elevator down to the carports in the basement. Bennet turned to make a final goodbye, to see Joss reaching for the datapad to read the letter.

Damn.

He turned away to the elevator and let Liam close the doors.

Bennet was in bed when Joss got home, propped up against Joss's pillows as well as his own, the proofs of volume sixty-three of the *History of the Theban Peoples* strewn all over the place.

"I'm not asleep," he said, as Joss hovered over him for a second. He grinned. "Hey."

Joss dropped a light kiss on the top of his head. "Where's Liam?"

"He was getting restless, so I sent him home." Bennet let Joss take the proof out of the way and sat up to return Joss's pillows to where they belonged.

"You look worn out. I knew I should have stayed with you. Liam is too much even when you're well."

"He's all right, is Liam. And you need to have time for yourself, you know. You don't want to be tied to me all day long, like we're conjoined twins." Bennet settled back again and patted Joss's side of the bed in invitation. "You shouldn't neglect your work at the Institute. Good day?"

"Nice to be back there." Joss held up a bundle wrapped in a soil-stained scarf. "Although I did have to spend some time scouting around the Institute's grounds trying to remember where I'd buried the amulets. What about the hospital?"

Bennet grinned. "Brilliant! They've scheduled me in for the fortieth, to lose the capsule."

Joss settled down beside Bennet. "That's real progress."

"It most certainly is." Bennet took Joss's hand. "They'll take me off the damned drugs too. I would just love to stop heaving up my toenails twice a day."

Joss's smile was thin. "Won't you miss it?"

"No." Bennet's fingers closed over Joss's. "There are other things I miss a great deal more."

"Such as?"

"You." Bennet got his hand up against the back of Joss's neck, and pulled on it steadily. Forcing Joss to go with the pressure and lean down. Bennet's lips moved against Joss's as he spoke. "I missed you, you know."

Joss allowed the kiss. "Did you?"

"I wanted to be home so badly, all the time I was trapped there." Bennet slid his right hand down the line of Joss's jaw. It was clumsier than usual, but he had life and feeling back in the hand. When Joss pressed his cheek against Bennet's palm, he felt it. "I just wanted to come home. I dreamed about you."

Joss kissed him. On the lips. No more avuncular head kisses. "Did you?" he said, again.

Bennet smiled up at him. "I thought, since you're home and I don't have to take my next hit for at least two hours, we could remind ourselves of what we were missing."

Joss blinked with surprise. "Are you mad?"

"No. I sent Liam home. I wanted us to remember. It's been a long time."

Joss shook his head.

"Please." Bennet couldn't keep the catch from his voice. "It's been all wrong since I got home, all upside-down and stressed. I just want to feel normal for an hour or two. That's all. Like it used to be."

"And will be again when you're well."

"That could be weeks yet." Bennet pulled Joss closer. "Think of it as the challenge we talked about this morning. I'm not going to be able to move much, so you can be dominant and demanding."

"Not my style, darling," Joss said, laughing.

Bennet plucked at Joss's shirt. "Come to bed."

"It's madness. I'll hurt you."

"Never." Bennet kissed him. "You never would. Come to bed."

Joss laughed and shook his head.

"Please," Bennet said. "I want you, Joss."

Joss took a moment to look at him, but whatever he saw there must have satisfied him. He got up to strip. Bennet liked watching him strip. Watching Joss get naked was almost the sexiest part of it. Joss hesitated. Bennet held out his hand, and smiled, and Joss laughed and continued. Bennet was already naked but for a thin tee, and when Joss slid into bed it was the work of seconds for Joss to get it off him.

Bennet managed to frame Joss's face with both his hands. "I love you, you know," he said, seriously, and kissed him.

He wasn't certain which one of them he was trying convince.

CHAPTER EIGHTEEN

26 Quintus 7488: Sais

Bennet decided against taking any pain killers that night, just setting up the IV to deliver his next morning's torment. He closed his eyes and lay still, breathing soft and quiet.

Joss loved long, slow lovemaking, using hands and mouth and tongue to arouse Bennet. When Bennet could bear no more, Joss helped him turn onto his side and slowly pushed into him from behind, his lips dusting Bennet's back and shoulders with constant kisses to soothe the burn. It had been a long time, nearly four months since they'd last been together. Joss moving inside him with familiar deliberate, unhurried tenderness reminded him how much he'd missed this, and how he'd missed Joss.

They'd lain quietly afterwards, Joss's hands on him soft and loving. At seven that evening, those same hands administered the second dose of the cocktail of drugs the doctors promised would save the leg. Joss held him through the next hour or so of painful retching, and for once Bennet let him, without complaint. He owed Joss that much. When it was over, he didn't want to do anything but doze, but sometime in the early hours, he unhooked himself from the IV and struggled out of bed.

"Bennet?"

"I'm just going to the bathroom. Sorry to wake you. I didn't mean to."

He spent a long time in there, looking at his face in the mirror, trying to see the truth in it. And when he finally gave up on that as unprofitable and came out, Joss was curled onto his side, breathing evenly. Bennet watched him for a minute, not able to face bed again. Instead, he got himself into the main room in something over the best time he'd recorded that morning, before his world had been turned upside-down in what seemed the fiftieth time in a few weeks.

He settled on the huge sofa set before the windows, the crutches on the floor, taking in the familiar view. The dome of Thebaid in the near distance, across the park, was beautifully lit. Joss had been a major contributor to the building's restoration appeal, and had been vocal on the charitable committee overseeing the work. In effect, Joss had secured a tasteful view from his windows by paying for it.

What in hell had his father meant by telling him? What was the old man up to?

"I read your father's letter."

Bennet jumped, startled. He hadn't heard Joss approach. "Well, you usually do. Did the elephant on the pin make you laugh?"

"Not this time."

Bennet said nothing.

"Are you going to do anything about him? It is him, isn't it? The gambler your father took such pains to mention. The pilot? Flynn."

"Yes," Bennet said.

"Did even your father know about you and him?"

Did he? Caeden hadn't shown any sign of realising what was going on, but that didn't mean he didn't have his suspicions. Caeden didn't miss much going on aboard his ship.

"He knew we were friends."

"Just good friends."

"You don't have to worry about it," Bennet said, too tired for denials. The room was cool. Too cool. He pulled a throw over himself, forcing himself to use his hand despite the clumsiness. The throw caught on the catheter in the back of the hand, and he winced at the sharp pain.

"That's what you said before." Joss stooped to help him. "I'm not worried."

"Fine."

"You're home and I never thought you would be, and I love you." Joss twisted the cord of his robe in one hand. "I just wanted to know."

"I never ask you." Bennet turned back to looking out the huge window, watching the city lights. Reflected in the plate glass before him, Joss raised a hand to his mouth.

"I need to be sure, Bennet."

"Are we asking questions now? Should I ask who you were with when word came through about Telnos? Mama said they couldn't find you. Were you with someone else?"

Even the reflection of Joss showed the flush on his face. Bennet shook his head, sorry he'd said it. It was true, but he'd created the arrangement himself. It was pointless to blame Joss for it.

"No," he said, before Joss could answer. "I'm sorry. You don't have to answer that. It's my own fault for even suggesting it. But it's supposed to be two way, Joss. I don't ever ask who you've been seeing."

"That's different!" Joss said.

"No. It isn't."

"Of course it is! I tell you anyway and you know they mean nothing, because I can do just sex and have it mean nothing. You can't. You're not like that. It always means something to you."

"Joss—"

"It's all your fault anyway! If you didn't keep going away… You know I don't like being on my own." Joss waited, but Bennet kept silent, too weary for this. "You kept quiet about this one. You've kept bloody quiet about this Flynn. Does that mean it meant something? You've never done that before. Never."

"I won't see him again. Please stop worrying."

"So you did sleep with him!"

"Yes."

"Oh," Joss said, as if someone had stabbed him. "Oh." Then, "Did you love him?"

Bennet answered with silence.

"Did he love you?"

Did he? That was the big question. Flynn hadn't had much experience of love. "I think so."

"So what was that?" Joss made a sweeping gesture towards the bedroom door. "You trying to convince yourself you still care?"

"I do care! We've had nearly nine years together. You know how much that means to me."

"And just what does it mean? Not enough to stay at home with me. Not enough to want to be with me."

"Please Joss, don't start that now. I really can't face another fight about my job, not now. Please."

"You don't care. Not enough."

"I care about a lot of things."

And then the circular dance began. Bennet sighed, because they'd go over it and over it, until there'd be tears and a reconciliation. The cracks would be papered over again.

Or maybe not.

"I never thought you'd do this," Joss said, back to twisting the cord on his robe.

"The agreement cuts both ways, remember? You do it."

"But I never thought you would!"

Bennet sighed. "No. I don't expect you did."

"Why did you, then?"

Bennet shrugged, thinking how transparent Joss was, how ironic his anger was. "I did what you've been encouraging me to do, Joss. I grew up."

Joss frowned. "You said you loved me. Do you? Do you really?"

Bennet closed his eyes for a second and sighed. "Yes."

"Why did you do it then?"

Bennet stared at the glass reflection, meeting Joss's gaze there. "Because," he said, "I wanted to."

32 Quintus 7488

"I haven't seen Joss for days," Meriel said.

Bennet had spent the last few minutes staring out over the city from the chair placed before the wide window. He turned his head and tried to smile. "Well, that makes two of us."

He was not one of nature's great optimists. He knew himself well enough, and the Shield psychs had taken him apart often enough to provide corroborative proof, to realise that while he didn't spend all of his time looking for shadow and darkness, he was never much surprised when they happened. He usually met them with a burst of energetic bad temper and a strong sense of ill-usage. The psychs found the analysis amusing. Wankers, every last one of them.

So, realist as he was, he doubted he and Joss had a future. Things were tense. He'd lasted out three days before decamping into one of the spare rooms with the savage declaration that if Joss wanted to indulge in high-decibel histrionics at three in the morning, he could do so without Bennet as the main audience.

Maybe he could have said it more temperately. It hadn't helped, that was for sure. He hadn't seen much of Joss since. He wasn't sure where Joss spent his nights, even. Joss headed out of the apartment each evening and didn't return while Bennet was awake to see or hear him.

He was surprised that he mostly felt relieved.

His mother, though, frowned. "It's quite difficult to be the detached kind of mother I ought to be and not ask too many questions. I know you don't like interference, and heaven knows you're old enough to expect privacy from your parents—"

"We're breaking up," Bennet said.

Bennet had never seen his poised, beautiful mother so blindsided. Her mouth dropped open and the delicate colour drained from her face. She looked older. "Are you sure?" She grimaced. "Sorry. That was a stupid question."

"The corpse is mostly dead. Sometimes it kicks, but I think that's just stubbornness. It's been dying for a while."

"You've never said anything." She rubbed at her forehead, frowning.

"No. I've been trying—" he broke off and shrugged. "I've been trying hard. But we've always had problems. We just pretended they weren't there. Joss never wanted me in the military at all, you know, but mostly we got by until I got hurt last time. Since then, he's never missed an opportunity to nag me about resigning my commission. This last year's been the worst."

"Sweetheart, he was out of his mind with worry then and broken-hearted when we thought you were dead. Of course he'd prefer to have you safe! Don't you think I worry about your father?"

"Do you nag him half to death about it? Do you make it so bad he'd rather stay out there fighting, rather than come home?"

"It's hard not to, sometimes. Oh dear."

"Joss can't cope with me being in the military, Mama. That's at the root of it. It helps I'm home often between jobs, far more often than Dad is, but it's not enough."

She had tensed up, and her hands closed and opened, closed and opened, but she tried to laugh, huffing out a half-laugh, half sigh. "It's not unknown, you know. Military marriages aren't easy. At least, given my family, I knew what I was getting into with your father. More than Joss did with you, I suppose. His family had no connexion to the services at all, did they? So he couldn't have any idea."

"He's had long enough to get used to it." Bennet frowned. "How do you and Dad manage it? He's away much more than I am."

"All marriages need work, darling. It's the nature of the beast. Military marriages need more work than most." She shrugged, lifting one shoulder. "You know what I do, Bennet. I work in welfare for other military families, and I run the *Gyrfalcon*'s family group. We're all in it together and that's a great help. I keep busy when he's not here and we spend a lot of time planning for when he is. We try and look forward." She smiled. "It gives you something to aim for, to cross the weeks off the calendar. The time your father is here at home... well, we make that matter. He doesn't allow even Int Com or the Military Council to intrude on his home leaves. You must remember how focused he is on us as a family?"

Bennet grinned, wryly. Too focused for his comfort, sometimes.

"Your father and I make the effort to keep in touch. Every couple of days, as it happens—"

"I'm usually on comms silence. Sometimes for weeks."

She gave him a small, tight smile. "I know. That isn't easy for Joss. Or me. We worry, you know."

He nodded.

She frowned, touched his hand. "I know about this... the feeling that everything's so hard when one of you is away so much. I knew what it was like for my mother and sister, so I was prepared. But it's still hard when it happens to you. It's like being chopped in half most of the time." She flushed. "I don't talk about your father and me much, because… well, because mostly it's got nothing to do with you children. I don't deny it's hard sometimes. He's way out there where I can't reach him if anything happened to him… and the first few weeks after he goes back each time, that's the worst. I get lonely, too. I know how Joss feels, Bennet. We're left behind and cut out of so much. It's horribly hard."

He'd never seen her so intense before, or so open. She looked small, somehow, not as indomitable as he always thought her. She had her lips pressed together and her eyes were wet. She dabbed at them with a handkerchief. She'd always been there, always. For the first time, he saw the cost. He took her free hand. He'd wondered, sometimes, at his mother taking Joss under her wing. He hadn't given any thought to how much they might have in common.

"Your father gets lonely too, you know. And it breaks his heart that he was never here very much when you all were children. He missed so much. Liam was almost six months old before your father even saw him."

Bennet squeezed her hand. "Not a great advert for military marriage, Mama."

"I'm realistic, darling. There are no easy answers and we've had our problems, your father and I. We're good and strong, but it's not perfect and we still fight, you know."

"I'll bet you fight fair, though. Joss will do anything to get me to resign my commission."

His mother sighed. "It may not be an issue. You have to face up to the possibility you won't get back."

Bennet stared, surprised. "Of course I'll get back! It might take a long time, but I'll get back."

She tugged her hand free and put both up to her face. "Oh dear gods, there is no denying you are your father's son! He thinks he can spin the world the way he wants it, too."

Bennet touched her hands until she allowed him to take them in his again. She looked tired, drained. "There's no point in being mad with the laws of genetics, you know. Half of it came from you. If I'm stubborn, I came by it honestly. I won't let this stop me, Mama. I will get back."

"Then maybe," she said, "You should think about whether you ought to. Which is more important, Bennet? The job, or Joss?"

He looked away, staring back out across the city. "It's not that simple."

"Then you've answered the question, haven't you?" She turned her hands in his to grasp his, palm to palm. "Poor Joss."

His mouth twisted into a grimace. "It really isn't that simple."

"Isn't it?

"No. It's more about getting lost, getting swallowed up."

"You don't think, then," Meriel said, "that loving someone means you get lost? I always thought it meant not being as self-centred. Thinking about someone else."

"Of course, but not to the point where you don't have a separate existence. Or do you think it should mean sacrificing everything you are and believe in, to keep someone else happy? That makes you resentful, Mama. And resentment's like vitriol. It burns."

"I don't mean that."

"That's what's being asked of me. The sacrifices come in small chunks. It's gradual, like whittling something down to a new shape, a bit at a time, and it's not a comfortable process. I have my doubts, sometimes, that it's worth it." Bennet looked out across the park to the Thebaid Institute's gilded dome. "Besides, the job's the constant complaint, the background noise. We have a more fundamental problem, me and Joss."

"It has to be fixable, sweetheart. You and Joss have had so much, you can't just let it all drain away."

"I don't think there's much left to fix. Joss won't even talk to me."

"About the something more fundamental?"

Bennet tried for a smile. It didn't feel very convincing from his side of it. "It's funny, almost like a philosophical question, the emotional difference between quantity and degree."

"I don't know what you mean."

"Which is the worst of two wrongs, do you think? Being asked to forgive and forget dozens of emotionless, goodtime bouts of sex or being asked to forgive one where it meant something?"

Meriel frowned. "There's been someone else?"

"Do you remember the pilot who took Dad to Demeter when I was in the hospital ship?"

"Oh, Bennet. You didn't!"

Bennet said nothing.

"Your father can't have known."

"I don't know. He knew Flynn and I became friends. But Joss, now he's found out—"

"What do you expect? The poor man was broken-hearted when we thought you were dead. He looked like a ghost at the Midnight Watch. I was so worried he'd have a breakdown or something. What in heaven's name do you expect?"

"That if I'm expected to forgive all the dozens he's had, every time I go away, then he can make the effort for my little lapse." She stared, her mouth dropping open and he added, sharper than he intended, "Do you think that Joss has been faithful to me, Mama? Then think again. I doubt if he can even remember how many there's been."

"I don't understand." He'd never heard her speak in such a small, diminished voice.

"It's not entirely his fault. I agreed to an open relationship for him, when I'm not here."

"All these years? Oh, Bennet." She raised one hand to her throat, a gesture of helplessness. "How can you bear it? Why in heaven's name did you agree to that?"

"Because I thought it would make him happier, and I would have done anything then to keep him. I worried he'd walk away from me, you see. That he'd find someone who was here all the time, who could give him what he wanted." Bennet tried not to let his mouth twist into a sneer, even one aimed at the foolish innocent he'd been. "I thought it would help keep us together."

Her hand closed over his. "Oh, my poor darling. Really? All that time?"

"Since I took Shield Oath, yes. I thought... oh, what does it matter what I thought then. I put up with it, because I loved Joss. But Joss, you see, is only just beginning to see how much it hurt me. How much it still does."

Both her hands clutched at his now. "I find it so hard to understand how you could have lived like that for so long."

"I loved him." Bennet shrugged.

"You never said anything."

"No. What could I say? It was mostly for him, the arrangement we came to. And I tried not to let it matter. But so far as he's concerned, all that doesn't count against four nights with Flynn. He thinks it's worse because I can't share his attitude to it all, that it's just sex and doesn't matter."

"Do you love this Flynn?"

Bennet hesitated. "I don't know. He meant a lot to me. Means a lot."

She shook her head. "I don't know then, Bennet. It's all wrong and cock-eyed, to me. In the scale of... of wrongness, I suppose I can understand Joss a little. Emotional involvement does make it worse. At least, it would for me. It's a question of significance. Everything else is sophistry."

"I still love Joss." Bennet rubbed his hands over his eyes. Gods, he needed some sleep. "I do. Not the same as I did, maybe, but I do. But I'm no more prepared to let him rule the way I live my life, than I would let Dad."

"I know Joss loves you," she said, uncertain. "If only you could have seen how he was, how hurt and grieving." She paused. "If you had to choose?"

Bennet shrugged.

"Oh." Meriel's eyes filled with tears. "Oh."

"I don't know that I'll ever see Flynn again. We decided there wasn't any future in it, that we couldn't be together. But that's not what matters when it comes to me and Joss, is it? Because no matter if I never see Flynn again, he's always there between us. Something I want and can't have."

"Oh dear."

"And I have tried, Mama. Truly I have. But neither of us has been happy, so in a way I'm almost relieved everything's come to a head at last." Bennet stared out at the view again, gesturing to the Thebaid's dome. "It's as dead as those mummies Joss is so bloody fond of. It's as dry and dusty, and no amount of incense and prayer will bring it back to life." He looked at her at last. His eyes stung. "I'm relieved. But I'm so sorry—"

She put her arms around him. "What are you going to do?"

"I dunno. I'm winging it. It's not like I've got a lot of experience of breaking up with someone. I mean, I don't even know how long these things are supposed to take."

His mother choked. "I don't think there's any set standard, darling. There isn't a checklist or anything."

Her tone was enough to make him smile. "I just meant it's taking a bloody eternity."

She sat and watched him for a few minutes. "You can always come home. Your room's still there. It's always been there for you. Come home."

Bennet looked around the apartment. He missed the glass sculpture that had always been in the centre of the big room and that Joss, being histrionic and dramatic about Bennet's supposed death had destroyed in his honour, but everything else was as he'd known it for nine years. Everything was familiar, from the case of amulets where Joss had first kissed him to the stack of the books, the volumes of the History his parents had given him when he'd graduated from the Thebaid. Everything meant something, from the chandelier down to the tiny stain on the rug before the fireplace. They'd made love there one night, just after that dreadful scene in the Institute's library with his father, and Joss had spilled some oil. In a fit of romanticism, Joss had had the mark carefully preserved. A rite of passage, Joss had called it, a shaking off of familial shackles, and worthy of remembrance. He wondered if Joss would remember it. Or if he'd just get a new rug.

"This is home," he said.

38 Quintus 7488

"Your friend the pilot arrives tomorrow," Joss said, apparently quite composed, breaking a two day silence. "What are you going to do about it?"

"I hadn't intended doing anything about it."

"Really? When your father went to so much trouble to set this up?"

Bennet sighed. "I don't know that Dad thought he was doing anything other than tell me a friend was visiting Albion."

The noise Joss made in response was vulgar, but left Bennet in no doubt about his feelings.

After a minute Joss said, tense and hard-mouthed, "What do you intend to do?"

"Nothing." Bennet turned a page on the old book he'd been pretending to read since breakfast. "I told you."

"Why not?"

Bennet stared at the page for a second. The words ran into a blur. He closed up the book and put it down. "Do you want a serious discussion or are you just winding up for another screaming fit?" Joss's lips thinned into a forbidding line, and Bennet raised a hand in submission. "Sorry. That wasn't helpful."

"No."

Bennet said in a careful monotone, "I never expected to see Flynn again. I don't have any future with Flynn and never expected I would have. I'm with you. When I left the *Gyrfalcon*, I came home to you, and I wanted that to work. I still want it to work."

"Because you want some sort of backup for what you can't have with him? Some sort of sad little substitute because that's better than nothing?"

"Because we've been together for a long time and I was—am—committed to you. Do you really think I want to throw it all away?"

"I don't know what I think."

"Then I don't know what to say to convince you, Joss."

Joss looked scared and determined, straightening up in his chair. The evening sun slanted in through the windows, picking out the silvering strands in his hair. "Promise me never to see him again."

Bennet shrugged. "I told you, I'm not planning on it."

Joss talked on over the top of him. "And I want your promise you'll give up this stupid idea that you'll go back into the military. Even if they fix your leg, you can't put me through that again. You can't."

"Oh god," Bennet said in real despair. "Please, Joss. Not again."

"Promise me that you'll stay at home."

It was like a ritual. You had to make the sacramental gestures, say the ceremonial words. But this one never came to any sort of conclusion, miraculous or otherwise. He tried to keep the scorn out of his tone. "Stay at home to do what?"

"Bachman's desperate to get you back. You can have a research fellowship tomorrow." Joss captured both of Bennet's hands in his. "I couldn't bear it again. I just couldn't. You don't know what it was like. I thought I would go out of my mind,

Bennet. Really, truly out of it. There was no point to anything. If you love me at all, the way you say you do, then stay at home with me. It can be just like it was before, when we were both at the Institute."

"It can't be the same. I'm not the same person."

"Because of him!"

"Because I grew up. Look, when we started this, when I was at the Institute, the only thing I cared about, apart from you, was the past. I loved it all, everything from a mummy case to a potsherd. It fascinated me then."

"It still does, doesn't it? You could do the work you loved."

"I'm doing work I love. Joss, I can't bury myself in the past all the time. I have to do something towards trying to make sure we have a future."

"And that's your father speaking."

"Maybe he's not wrong about that, at least."

Joss dropped Bennet's hands. "Are you saying you won't promise?"

"I'm saying that you want me to be someone other than I am. I'm not sure I can do it. And I won't make promises I can't keep."

"Balls!" Joss said, with unaccustomed crudity. "You would if you cared."

"Listen to me. I'm going to be home for a long time, months at least. Let's just take it as it comes, Joss. No pressure, no demands. Please, let's just try it."

Joss shook his head. "I don't understand you."

Bennet agreed silently with that diagnosis. "I'm sorry, Joss. Please."

"I never thought you were so selfish." Joss stood up. "I'm going out. I don't know when I'll be back. If I'll be back at all."

"Joss—"

"I'm still wondering what that was, the other night, when the letter came when you came on to me so hard. Guilt? Expiation? What?"

"I wanted you," Bennet said, knowing it had been desperation. A desperate attempt to convince himself he could make this work, to breathe life back into the corpse.

"I won't be any man's substitute," Joss said. "I couldn't have got less love out of it if I'd bought it. Is that what I've been doing all these years, Bennet? Buying it? So, what do I owe you for the other night?"

SECTION SIX:
TWICE FORSWORN

37 QUINTUS – 05 OCTAVUS 7488

CHAPTER NINETEEN

37 Quintus 7488: the dreadnought, *Gyrfalcon*

"So, d'you think you'll see him when you get home?"

"Dunno."

Flynn had crammed everything into his kitbag. Cruz had taken it out again, making tutting noises. She was gainfully employed in shaking out the creases and repacking Flynn's bag. Must be the thwarted maternal instinct or something. Quite heart-warming.

"Do you know where he lives?" she asked.

"No idea." Flynn hesitated to ruin Cruz's rosy-hued romantic vision of the world, but it would be kinder, for both of them. "It's not like I could just drop in for tea and cakes, you know. He does live with someone."

"Yeah," Cruz said with a snigger. "His tutor. And what did the guy teach, huh?"

"I don't think he was Bennet's tutor."

"AlbionNews got it wrong? Tell me it isn't so." Cruz picked up the datapad. Flynn had it set to the book he intended to take along to while away the journey. She raised an eyebrow. "Getting in some practice?"

"It's not pornography—it's art!" Flynn said, because protest was expected.

"A Soldier's Sexy Secrets. Yeah that's art." Cruz held up the datapad and turned it towards Flynn. The female soldier decorating the cover wasn't making a secret of her best weapons. "You're just reading this because of the size of her tits." Cruz gestured towards her own chest.

Flynn smiled as he mimicked Cruz, but with far more exaggeration. "Oh my, yes."

Cruz's mouth tightened. "You're a sexist jerk, Flynn. Women aren't recruited on the basis of their chest size."

"In real life, I hope not. I have every respect for your abilities as a pilot and a soldier, Cruz, and that has nothing whatsoever..." On dangerous ground, Flynn paused and widened the grin. "You get the idea. Respect. Every possible respect."

The look she gave him promised retribution, but knowing Cruz, it would be in her own sweet time and when he least expected it. She spoke in a pleasant tone and her smile was radiant. Not to mention frightening. "I will hurt you for that."

"I expect you will."

She shoved the datapad into the kitbag before returning to the previous subject. "Did you know about Bennet's partner?"

"Yes." Flynn got up and busied himself over at the tiny kitchen area, checking everything was clean and ship-shape. Cruz said nothing. Flynn wriggled his shoulders like a dog ridding itself of a flea. Gods, he hated it when she went quiet. It meant too much. And it worked every time. He gabbled anything to fill the silences. "Bennet was often away, you know, and the guy got lonely. So they had an arrangement that meant they were exclusive at home, and didn't ask questions about what they did when they were apart."

"Convenient."

"Mostly for him, for Joss." Flynn got over saying the name by rushing at it. "How many potential squeezes was Bennet likely to find inside a Maess base?"

"He found you."

"I think that was a unique occurrence. And I'll remind you, Cruz, that I was the one who found him."

"And you have the medal to prove it." Cruz raised her wrist and squinted at her chronometer. "Thirty minutes. We'd better head down to the cutter deck." She waited for a minute or two while Flynn dithered, pulling his bed straight and shutting closet doors. "You could ask the commander."

"Oh yeah! 'Sir, would you tell me how I can get hold of your son? Because basically I want to spend my entire furlough screwing him blind.' That should go down well."

"He took you to Demeter. Although I do see that you'd have to phrase your request with delicacy. You and delicacy would be a problem."

"He just needed a pilot to fly him to Demeter."

"Right. So he dragged you back off patrol to do it, when he could have commandeered any one of five dozen others. Sound reasoning, I must say. Very credible. If that's the best you can come up with, how come you're always so good at devising new gambling ploys?"

"You're good at what you're good at," Flynn said.

Cruz laughed, and laced the kitbag together. She tossed it to Flynn. "C'mon, time you got moving." She hustled him out of the door to the turbolift. At least once the lift was on its way to the cutter deck, she waited until the two other crewmen in it had exited on the Engineering deck before continuing. "It's not like it's going to come as a shock to the commander that his son likes men."

"Cruz, are you seriously suggesting I walk up to the commander and tell him Bennet and I were lovers?" Flynn felt his face grow hot, and hung his head in the hope that Cruz wouldn't guess he had virtually done just that. "He knows we were friends. That's why he took me to Demeter."

She narrowed her eyes at him. "Flynn?"

His shoulders rose up. "You don't have to escort me to the cutter, you know. I can find it on my own."

"Flynn!"

Flynn sighed at the odd mixture of suspicion and arch delight in Cruz's voice. That was the worst of having her as a friend. She always knew when Flynn had more to tell and she never gave up until he told her. Damn woman could run all over him like a runaway Transport shuttle.

"Ishowedimbennet'shiel," he muttered.

"What?"

Flynn cringed. "When Bennet left, after the T18 thing, he gave me something—"

"So I heard." Cruz sniggered again.

"Not that, you moron. He left me his shield."

Cruz's jaw dropped. "His shield?"

Flynn nodded, and turned back the stand-up collar of his flight jacket.

Cruz stared at the little silver shield, eyes wide. "But... but that's like getting engaged!"

"When I found out Bennet was... Well, we know now he wasn't, but at the time we all thought he was gone, I went to see the commander."

"You did what?"

"I went to see the commander. I offered him Bennet's shield. He told me to keep it. That's all. But he knew we were friends, so that's why he took me. It was good of him."

"I shouldn't have listened to you and left you on your own. You need a keeper, Flynn. I'm astonished he took you to Demeter and didn't stick you in the brig instead."

"It's all right. He was good about... Oh, about everything. I don't know what he thinks or knows, and I don't think he'll ever ask or say anything. He's okay really."

Cruz just stared. Abject astonishment was not a good look on her. He preferred his Cruz indomitable and unshockable.

Flynn sighed. He reached up to finger the little shield, the way he did every time he launched, for good luck and good love. He needed both.

39 Quintus 7488: Albion's main spaceport

Danae, the *Gyrfalcon*'s chief cutter pilot, had to have broken a couple of speed regulations to get them to Demeter in time to catch their connecting flight. Flynn spent the journey dozing and playing one-handed card games to pass the time, listening to the plans the other escapees had for seeing friends and families. He had neither to look forward to, and he wasn't sorry they were separated when they reached Demeter, directed to different departure gates to join the long lines of pilots and troopers from a couple of dozen ships, all heading for the transport home.

A sleepy sergeant stamped Flynn's leave papers without looking at them, and he scooted up the ramp onto a big, smelly and uncomfortable transport ship that delivered him at the main Albion spaceport near Sais the next day. Not exactly first class travel, but he was deposited in the huge arrivals hall at about noon, where he could shuffle down yet another line to get his papers stamped, eyes only part open, kitbag clutched in his hands, cursing the sun blazing down through the glass roof to burn the back of his neck. He hadn't slept well on the journey, and although ship's time and Sais time were identical and he should be bright eyed and full of excitement about the weeks ahead, he was tired and fretting.

He dug his papers out of the side pocket of his bag and handed them over to a guard sergeant at the desk, leaning up against the counter and closing his eyes. Almost there. A couple of hours and he could get some sleep at the hostel and wake refreshed and ready to hit the nightspots.

It was the long silence that alerted him. He straightened up, looking enquiringly at the sergeant. She stared at the leave docket, frowning.

"Problem?" he asked.

"I don't know, sir." She looked down the line of duty clerks checking in the returning heroes and raised a hand to catch the attention of one of her colleagues. Leaning her chair back on two legs, she showed him Flynn's papers. She glanced at Flynn then, and raised a questioning, sardonic eyebrow.

"Looks like," the other sergeant said.

Oh shit.

"Something wrong?" Flynn couldn't think what. It was legal. It wasn't like Flynn had had to use vanishing ink on someone else's furlough authorisation and forge the commander's signature. Colonel Quist had signed it in triplicate, and catch her getting anything wrong. Never happened. Stars would go out before the woman made a mistake.

"Oh, I don't think so, sir. We were asked to keep an eye open for you, that's all. This way, sir." The male sergeant beckoned Flynn to the end of the counter, and opened up the barrier. Flynn trailed along to join him.

"What's up, Sarge?"

"Please come through, sir."

Flynn heaved a sigh and did as he was told. It didn't do to diss non-coms. They had far too much opportunity to make an officer's life a living hell. Much easier to go along with this and try and sort it out without losing his temper.

The sergeant handed him back his papers. "The captain's waiting for you, sir. This way."

"Captain? What captain?"

"Well, I assume he's yours, sir." The sergeant rapped on an office door, and ushered Flynn inside, closing the door as soon as he was through.

Flynn took an uncertain step forward, dropping the kitbag to the floor. His breath came short. The sergeant had been right. It was Flynn's captain. At least, Flynn hoped so.

"Hey," Bennet said, cutting off further fruitless speculation by holding out his arms.

Flynn stepped right in.

"I can't believe it. I can't," Flynn said for the hundredth time.

He held Bennet as close as he could, but carefully. Bennet was pale and thin, looked worn and tired, and the hands holding Flynn's had little strength in them. It was obvious the last few months had been hard on him.

Flynn kissed Bennet again. It was a kiss just like the ones Flynn remembered. The ones whose memories had torn at his heart at that Midnight Watch. Long and deep, slow and exploratory, a tongue mapping out the shape and taste of his mouth again, teeth biting gently at his lips. He'd missed this. "How did you know I'd be here?"

"Dad told me."

"Are you kidding?"

Bennet shook his head. "He didn't say anything outright, but I knew he meant you." He gestured to his Shield uniform. It looked too big for his thin frame. "So I remembered a wise general of my acquaintance who once told me Shield could commandeer near enough anything. It worked. I've commandeered you. The noncoms out there think it's a secret Shield operation."

Flynn grinned. "Really?"

"Of course, the fact I bribed 'em had nothing to do with it."

Flynn laughed and showed Bennet the little shield badge he'd kept safe on the inside of his jacket collar. "I'll wear this on the outside then, if you think that will help."

Bennet touched it and smiled. "Let's go and talk. I've got a cab waiting to take us back into the city. The driver will wait a while yet, for the tip I promised him."

Flynn nodded, and let him go. Bennet had been leaning up against a desk, probably belonging to a real Transport Fleet captain who didn't greet returning pilots with frantic kisses, and for the first time Flynn saw that his right leg was still encased in a rigid healing capsule. A pair of crutches were propped against the desk alongside him.

Flynn made himself stand back and not jump in to help, unasked. The elbow crutch came first, designed to hold Bennet's damaged right arm in a horizontal cradle to ensure the strain was evenly spread along his arm rather than concentrated in his hand. It took a second of effort for Bennet to force his fingers to move and close on the right handgrip. The normal crutch was much easier. Bennet slid his arm into the clamp fitting, his left hand stretching down to reach the handgrip.

Flynn was relieved to see Bennet using his right hand at all, remembering the surgeon's less than whole-hearted conviction that Bennet would get back any dexterity. Bennet still looked too damned frail, though. He swallowed hard against the lump in his throat. "What is with you and crutches, every time I want to take you to bed and ravish you? Most normal people have rubber or leather fetishes."

"I always like to go my own way."

"I thought it might be a pirate role-playing thing. Trouble is, I don't want to hide my baby blues behind an eye patch."

Bennet laughed and started out of the office, Flynn dodging ahead to get the door for him. "When I get the chance, let me tell you about the seven weeks I spent associating with pirates and Jacks."

He thanked the desk sergeants prettily, and they made their way to one of the cafés, Flynn slowing his normal gait to match Bennet's progress. They found a quiet table tucked away in a corner. Bennet refused anything but water, and Flynn contented himself with the same. The girl behind the counter rolled her eyes at their extravagance.

"You're not doing too badly." Flynn had watched every painful step. "Of course, this means I can out-run you this time."

"Did you try, last time?"

"I ran," Flynn protested. "Of course, I ran straight towards you." He tapped the IV catheter in the back of Bennet's hand with a forefinger. "This has an unpleasantly medical look. How are you doing, really?"

"Better. I've got to see my surgeon again—tomorrow, as it happens—and if all goes well, I'll lose the capsule for good."

"Will they keep you in hospital?"

Bennet shook his head. "I'll be in for the day, but that should be it."

"I'll still come and see you and I'll bring flowers." Flynn tapped the catheter again. "And this?"

Bennet sighed. "I have trouble with bionics. I'm on anti-rejectants, twice a day, until they grow in. This gets the morning dose into me while I'm sleeping, that's all."

"Ah, that explains why you look like shit."

"You told me I was beautiful back there."

"I lied. I was undergoing an extreme emotional reaction, and I'll say anything in those circumstances. You scared me, you bastard."

"I scared myself." Bennet's grin was a thin, unconvincing thing. "I wasn't expecting to get back."

"Worse than our little adventure, then?"

"I was in deep trouble, Flynn, and I didn't have you to get me home."

Flynn thought of the moment he'd understood what Omar was trying oh-so-delicately to tell them; the moment when he'd learned what real desolation was. "Your Dad told me he'd sent in your own crew."

Bennet nodded. "I was glad to see them."

"Remind me to kiss that lieutenant's feet when I see her next," Flynn said. "She scared the hell out of me, but she got you back this time, and I owe her."

"Rosie? She scares all my men. I'm going to have to speak to her about that."

"Yeah, Rosie. And what do you mean, all your men?"

Bennet smiled.

"Hmmm. Well, I'm grateful to her anyway. Your dad took me to Demeter, did you know?" Flynn paused at the look on Bennet's face. "Are you all right?"

"I'll tell you about it in a minute. I heard you met Rosie there. The *Hype*'s company was back three weeks ago and I saw her then, while I was still imprisoned in the hospital. She told me all about meeting you at Demeter and handed out one helluva lot of unsolicited and unrepeatable advice. She'll be back again in another few weeks. You two should meet properly."

"Uh-huh," Flynn said, not to be diverted. "What's bothering you? Is your dad giving you hell about associating with me?"

"Not Dad, no."

"Oh." Flynn grimaced at the pained, stressed look on Bennet's face. "I'm sorry, Bennet."

"Don't be. It's been coming for a long time." Bennet choked and shook his head, rubbing at his eyes. "It's even harder than I thought it would be."

"I am sorry, though."

"You're the catalyst maybe, but you're not the cause. We haven't been happy for a couple of years." Bennet shrugged. "I'm too tired to keep on trying and pretending. I don't have the energy for it."

"If it's not me, then what?"

"I grew up. Joss hasn't changed in nine years and he can't cope with the fact I have."

"Have you left him?" Flynn tried to suppress the little jump his heart gave. It wasn't right to rejoice when Bennet was obviously distressed.

"It's more of a continuing process." Bennet ran his hand through his hair. It sprang up, as unruly as Flynn remembered it. "We haven't quite finished the demolition job. It takes a long time to knock down so many years. It's tiring me out, to be honest. I didn't get much sleep last night. We had a screaming fight that lasted until after three, and then he slammed out of the apartment. I haven't seen him since."

Flynn tried to look sympathetic and interested, when all the time his blood pounded to one particular rhythm: *Bennet's free, Bennet's free.* The details of how and why could come later.

"What are we going to do?" he asked.

"What do you want, Flynn?"

"You," Flynn said, instantly. "I want you."

Bennet stared at him for a second or two, unsmiling, the grey eyes unreadable. "I'm not free yet."

"I'll wait until you are. I'll wait as long as it takes."

"Will you?"

"I want you very much, you see. Still, and always."

"I almost didn't come to meet you. I thought how disloyal it would be to Joss to come, I tried to pretend... but then he said... last night, he said something that changed everything." Bennet stopped, and said, slowly, "So I changed my mind about meeting you."

"I'm glad you did." Flynn closed his hand on Bennet's for an instant, all he could allow himself in public. "I can't tell you how glad."

They looked at each other for a minute, and then Bennet smiled. "So am I." He added, very quietly, "I've missed you, Flynn."

Flynn nodded. It would be all right and there wasn't any need for words. They sat in silence for a few minutes, and Flynn wondered if the expression on his face was as dreamy and happy as the one Bennet wore. It made something in his chest feel tight. He didn't remember anyone looking at him the way Bennet did.

He said, to try and get his breath back, "Why did your dad tell you I was coming back?"

"Why did he take you to Demeter? I've given up wondering why the old man does anything. I'm not up to the exertion, yet. It gives me a headache."

Flynn's face grew hot. "Oops."

"Oops?"

"Er—I think I was a little less discreet than I might have been. Sorry."

Astonishingly Bennet managed to pale. Flynn wouldn't have thought it possible. "You told him?"

"Not exactly." Flynn squirmed on his seat. "The day I found out about Telnos, I was upset."

"Gratifying," Bennet said, in an un-encouraging sort of way.

"I went to see him. I thought he might like to have your shield."

Bennet stared, then shook his head. "He didn't, I take it."

"Not like that, idiot. He said I should keep it, because you meant me to have it. He was good to me, when I come to think on it, given how devastated he was. And he was devastated, Bennet."

"I know."

"So when the news came through that you were alive, he asked for me to fly him to Demeter. He let me see you there, for a couple of minutes." Flynn thought about those few minutes in the quiet little hospital room and how thankful he'd been for Caeden's gesture. "It was generous, don't you think? Especially since he doesn't approve of me much."

"I think," Bennet said, "that since he's gone out of his way to tell me you were coming home, he can't disapprove of you that much."

"Ha! He thinks I'm unreliable and a troublemaker, and I gamble and I have this bad reputation in the sexual department."

"He did once describe you as one of the banes of his existence." Bennet had brightened. Probably with amusement, the unsympathetic bastard. "I was impressed and, believe me, I approve. Dad needs a few banes to lighten him up, and it will do Liam good to realise he has a rival."

Flynn snorted, not entirely understanding the reference to Bennet's brother. "He was that polite? I figure he thinks of me as some sort of... oh I don't know, some sort of morally bankrupt scoundrel."

Bennet laughed. "The question is, are you my morally bankrupt scoundrel?"

Flynn sobered, leaning forward, indifferent to the dozens of people in the café who may see him. He'd waited almost two years for this. He touched Bennet's face with his hand and made his promise.

"Well, I'm damn sure I'm no one else's."

Bennet smiled.

CHAPTER TWENTY

39 Quintus 7488

Joss was home when Bennet returned to the apartment in the late afternoon, a robe over his nakedness. He looked frowzy and rumpled, as if he'd just woken. He flushed red when Bennet came in.

"You went." He glanced behind him to the closed bedroom door.

Bennet wouldn't let it touch him, the way Joss stood with hunched shoulders and his arms crossed over his gut. He wouldn't allow himself to feel pity. He had to stay detached, or be lost. "I thought that after what you said yesterday, it wouldn't matter to you."

"You lied to me! You went to see him. You promised you wouldn't!"

"No, I told you I hadn't planned on it. I didn't lie. I didn't intend to go. I wouldn't have gone, but you made it clear last night just what you think of me. All bets were off then, Joss, all promises. It's your own fault."

Joss's flush deepened. "I didn't mean it."

"Didn't you? You said it. And I thought you calculated precisely what it would mean for both of us."

Joss said, in tense voice, "Are you leaving?"

"Probably." Bennet manoeuvred the crutches to get past Joss to the kitchen. Although he couldn't eat much, he'd still missed out on the milky food supplement that did duty as lunch.

"Don't go," Joss said, choking, following him into the kitchen. "Please don't go. I love you."

Bennet fished the bottle he needed out of the cooler, and straightened up. He felt sick, and it was nothing to do with the medication.

He and Flynn hadn't talked for long. He'd been tired by the trip out to the spaceport. Flynn hadn't missed it, and had insisted on him coming back to rest—"I'm home for six weeks. Plenty of time."—and although six weeks weren't going to be anywhere near enough for him, he'd let Flynn have his way. They'd held hands in the cab back into the city, and the kiss he'd got when he'd dropped Flynn at the military hostel had held a world of promise. Six weeks might not be long enough but if it was all he had, he would make the most of it.

Seeing Flynn again had decided him. They might not have much of a future together, but it was more than he and Joss had. He looked at Joss for a minute, seeing him with eyes that were no longer dazzled, no longer in thrall. Joss was still beautiful, still thin and elegant, still desirable, but Bennet wasn't stirred by him anymore. It was like looking at Joss's reflection, and seeing only the pallid, thin, and insubstantial image of everything he'd loved; nothing more now than loving a memory.

Joss deserved an answer, even if not the one he wanted. Bennet put the bottle down. He couldn't face drinking it. "I love you, too. Still. But this isn't going to work."

"You can't love us both!"

"Oh, but I can. I do." Bennet moved to lean against the counter and take the weight off his knee. He paused, frowning, trying to find the words. "I think you got me too young, Joss. I don't mean that as any kind of criticism or accusation, because the gods know I didn't need persuading, and I wouldn't change a second of it. It was glorious and I loved you so much I thought I'd die from it. It's just a fact. What I mean is, that you got me when I was still growing. The trouble is I've grown into something that isn't what you expected or what can make you happy. We just don't want the same things anymore."

"Bennet—"

"Be honest with me, Joss. Every time this last year when I got home and called you from the spaceport, what did you really think? I know you'd be relieved I was all right, but apart from that, what was it? Dread? Fear? Wondering how you'd get through the next three weeks without another fight, without us screaming at each other? Longing for me to go away again so you can have some peace?"

"No!" But Joss wouldn't meet Bennet's eyes. "Love. Happiness. Relief. Wanting you..."

"Oh," Bennet said, not unkindly. "The sex has never been anything less than incandescent. But that wasn't what I meant." He reached out a hand, and rested it on the side of Joss's face. "I loved you more than I can ever say. You have been so much to me, Joss... given me so much. I'll always love you, I think. It's just that the way I love you has changed."

"Please." Joss pressed his face against Bennet's hand.

"The last two years haven't been too great, for either of us. I wish we could turn the chronometer back to before they happened, but we can't." Bennet levered himself up and put his hands on Joss's shoulders. "I've been with you for a third of my life. I wouldn't change that. I've been happier than not, for nearly all of it."

"Bennet, please." Joss's hands moved in a series of uncoordinated jerks, reaching out for Bennet and snatching back again. "It doesn't have to change. It doesn't."

"It's changed already. We can't stop it." Bennet bit back a sigh. Joss just wasn't getting it. "Joss, if you met me now, today, for the very first time, would you want to spend the next nine years with me? Or would it be something that would last a few hours or a few days?"

Joss flushed red again. His gaze slid away. "Of course I'd want you! Please don't do this!"

The bedroom door opened. A strange voice called through it. "Hey, Joss! Where'd you go?"

Joss, eyes wide, flushed scarlet. The colour drained away slowly, mottling his skin. He grimaced and hunched in on himself, shoulders rising and his head sinking down defensively, as if he were trying to make himself a smaller target. The reaction wasn't kind to him. He looked every year his age.

Bennet opened his mouth, then closed it again. He had known. He had always known, though it had been one more thing to lie to himself about. Of course Joss brought them home, the quick fucks he'd said meant nothing. Of course he did. Still it jabbed at him, right under the breastbone. His chest hurt. He let his hands drop away and took a step back until he had the counter to lean against again.

This one couldn't be more than twenty, not that much older than Bennet had been the first time. He was wearing one of Joss's shirts and not much else, strong brown legs bare. The shirt hem brushed his cock. It bobbed as he walked towards them. Joss raised a hand and rubbed at one eye with a forefinger. He wouldn't look at Bennet.

"Can I have some coffee?" Bright blue eyes looked Bennet up and down. "I love a man in uniform," he said, and laughed.

"You said that once," Bennet said, to Joss. "But you grew to hate the uniform."

"And all it stands for," Joss choked, ignoring the kid completely.

"And me?"

"No. Never you." Joss looked daggers at the date he'd brought home. "I'm sorry, Bennet. I shouldn't have brought him here."

"It's your apartment." Three words, but they cut the cord.

"Are we on for a threesome, then?" The kid dug Joss in the ribs. "I didn't know you had a boyfriend."

Bennet leaned forward and kissed Joss. He was careful. Gentle. Passionless. Joss tasted of salt, the tears tracking down his face. Bennet turned his back to the kid but the smile he had for Joss was kind.

"He doesn't."

40 Quintus 7488: Military Hospital, Sais

When his mother arrived in his hospital room, Bennet expected his surgeon wouldn't be far behind. And nor was he. Meriel was barely through the door when Doctor Harald appeared, flushed and solicitous, eyes gleaming with lust.

When he'd been incarcerated in a room like this for weeks, charting the development of the doctor's infatuation had been one of his few pleasures. The man was besotted. Bennet's mother had, of course, pretended to notice neither the doctor nor the derision of her ungrateful children. Althea was openly amused, Bennet held her accountable for his long stay in hospital, Liam made mocking threats to protect his father's honour and Natalia treated her to a great deal of old-maidenish disapproval. Meriel laughed at them all, but Bennet thought she was flattered by the doctor's attention.

She greeted Doctor Harald, and kissed Bennet. "No Joss?"

"No." Bennet lay back, obedient to the doctor's gesture. Harald and his team started unsealing the capsule. Meriel came to hold his hand, and he looked from the doctor to her, choosing his words with care in the presence of strangers. "No. It's done."

"Oh Bennet. I'm so sorry."

"Yes. So am I." Bennet changed the subject. "I wasn't expecting to see you. This shouldn't take too long, I hope."

"You'll probably be in for most of the day." Harald glanced up from his examination. "It's going to take a while to get the capsule off, and then we'll want to take a good look at it on the scanner and run mobility tests." He focused on Meriel for a second, and smiled. "It will be rather boring for you, Madame."

"I don't think it will be all that exciting for me," Bennet said.

"Well, I won't stay all day." Meriel made herself comfortable in the chair beside the bed. "I'll wait until the capsule's off, then go home. I'll come back this evening."

She held Bennet's hand throughout the procedure, though she winced and looked away when they started to remove the cage of metal rods that had held the knee together. Bennet didn't blame her. His knee was swollen, misshapen, tracked with long red scar-lines from all the surgery. Not a pretty sight. And it was painful. He was grateful for the local anaesthetic. He tried not to complain, but his poor mother's fingers must have ached from the grip he had on them. She didn't complain either.

"That doesn't look too bad," the doctor said.

"Really?" Meriel sounded surprised.

It looked appalling to Bennet's eyes, but he supposed he was biased.

"Not bad at all." Harald gave Meriel a warm smile, and then said to Bennet, "You'll be walking with a cane in a month or two, and walking normally by the end of the year. Even running, when we get your exercises and physiotherapy sorted out. Do you play sports?"

"I did a lot of running away from the Maess. Does that count?"

"You were very good at Tierce," Meriel put in.

"Years ago! I haven't played anything but the odd scratch game since I was in SSI."

"Champion team, though." She was evidently in supportive, proud mother role that day and Bennet could only grin and shrug.

"Tierce is good exercise," Harald said. "I don't see why you couldn't pick it up again in a few months. That knee will be as

266

good as the real thing, I promise."

"It'll make a handy target for my opponents to home in on, anyway." Bennet flexed his right hand. "Could I play with this hand, though?"

"You know, I think you'll get some reasonable dexterity." Harald took Bennet's hand in his and pressed back on the fingers, testing the reflexes. "It's a lot better than I expected at this stage. When you're overtired and overstressed, you'll likely notice an impact on dexterity and maybe even mobility"—he tapped Bennet's knee—"but otherwise things look good. I'll revise that. The hand and knee look good, the rest of you looks terrible."

"It's been a difficult few days," Bennet said, more to himself than either of them.

"Well, try and relax now. I know that wasn't pleasant and I'm sorry I couldn't give you anything for it, but I need you alert for the rest of the day. I'll give you a half-hour or so to get your breath back, and then we'll start. You're not to move until I come back, understood? I don't want you putting any strain on the joint."

"Sure," Bennet said. "Thanks."

Meriel waited until the medics had left. "How do you feel?"

He didn't pretend to misunderstand her. "I don't know."

Meriel tightened her grip on his hands. "What happened, sweetheart? I thought you were going to try."

"I'm tired of trying. We decided yesterday. At least, I did. And then of course we were up most of the night talking and… well, it got a bit fraught." Bennet's free hand twisted in the sheets. "I hadn't realised it would be this messy, even when it's the right thing to do. I want it over, but gods it's not easy and it hurts."

"Oh dear." Meriel bobbed up from the chair to give him a comforting kiss. "How's Joss taking it?"

"Not well."

"I wrote and told your father that things weren't good. I didn't mention Flynn."

"It was coming anyway. It has nothing to do with Flynn." Bennet wasn't certain he believed that himself, and his mother merely raised a cynical eyebrow. "And please don't let Dad think it's Flynn's fault. It wouldn't be fair."

"I've got a letter for you on my datapad. He sent it to my mailbox. I don't think he wanted anyone but you to see it, and he knows Joss has access to your mail."

"Later, maybe." He'd have to change that, change his passwords.

"I don't suppose he's said anything different than in his letter to me. He said to me that I was to make sure you knew he was sorry, but that he trusted you to know your own mind best. He'll support you in whatever you do, Bennet. And he said twice in his letter to me that if you needed it, your old room's still there." When Bennet looked at her, startled, her answering smile was shaky. "We've never changed anything in it."

"I'm too old to come running home."

"The offer's there. What are you going to do? Immediately, I mean. Will you go back to the apartment tonight?"

"No," Bennet said. "I can't do that to Joss. I sorted out a hotel earlier this morning. I can live there until I find an apartment of my own."

"You can't do that! Come home instead."

"I don't know, Mama. I've not been there for so long. I don't think I can come back."

She grimaced. "Maybe not. Perhaps there's no turning back that particular chronometer. Not permanently."

"It's a bit pathetic, too, grown men running home to mummy."

She winced and laughed. "Well, yes. In normal circumstances. But things are not normal and you aren't well. You can't live in a hotel, darling. If you were well, then I wouldn't worry. At least, I wouldn't worry quite as much. But I can't let you do that when you're still recovering. I just can't. Come for a few weeks, until you do find somewhere permanent to live."

"We'll see," Bennet said.

By late afternoon, Bennet had had enough. He'd been poked, prodded and handled in so many places so far removed, anatomically, from the afflicted joint that he began to wonder if he'd mistaken Dr Harald's romantic interest, given where the good doctor's hands had been as he'd elevated, twisted and manipulated Bennet's leg. Bennet had been scanned from the front, the side and from behind. He'd been scanned with his leg bent, with it straight, and if he hadn't protested, he was pretty sure he'd have been scanned with both legs waving in the air like flagpoles. He'd had a physical therapy tech demonstrate exercises for an hour, and had been made to do some himself. He'd hobbled around on crutches while they measured his mobility, been upgraded to walking canes to see how he managed with those (badly), and even taken a few steps without either, a medical orderly on each side of him to catch him when he fell. Two steps. That's what it took before the orderlies were called upon to do their duty.

In the end, they left him alone to rest for a couple of hours. "Before more physiotherapy," Harald said, tone bright and encouraging. He left, laughing at Bennet's response. The physical therapy tech went with him, looking hurt and unappreciated.

Bennet lay back on his pillows. The good thing about so much activity was it left no time to brood. The downside was that he had never felt so drained and tired. The room was quiet. No one nagged at him to do one more stretch or bend, no one poked at him to test his reactions and his knee had settled into a bearable, dull ache. The bed was surprisingly comfortable and warm, and the pillows soft... his eyes were just closing, when the door opened and a very large bunch of cream and yellow rosaceae walked in. Startled into wakefulness, he stared.

The bunch of rosaceae moved to the left to allow Flynn to peer from behind it. "Is it safe to come in? Is anyone lurking in your bathroom?"

Warmth spread through Bennet, like a sunrise. "We're all alone."

Flynn squinted over the top of the bunch. "Is this what it's like, infiltrating Maess bases?"

"No. Not really. I mean, usually they're shooting at me and I don't take them flowers."

"You have no idea about romance, have you?" Flynn sidled through the doorway and closed the door behind him. "What have they been doing to you? You look like you've been run over by a shuttle." He grinned. "Hey, by the way."

Bennet smiled and held out a hand. "Hey back at you. Why are you hiding behind the flowers?"

"Trying to avoid causing trouble," Flynn said and kissed him, his mouth curving up against Bennet's. "I'm sneaking."

"Is that what you call it?"

"Sure. I had my cover story all worked out. If anyone was in here, I was going to pretend I was the florist's delivery boy. Even the card here says it's from your unknown admirer. No names to give the game away."

"Very convincing." Bennet looked at the flowers Flynn had brought. "Rosaceae?"

"I promised you flowers. And underneath this scoundrelly exterior beats the heart of a complete romantic. What else but rosaceae?" Flynn dumped the flowers on a nearby nightstand. They gave off a heady perfume, rich and sweet. "The florist tried to tell me that roses are passé these days and the stylish lover offers his best beloved some misshapen orange things with green wings sprouting out of them. Honest, Bennet, they looked like something a nuke might create, caught halfway into mutating into something that would probably eat you. I'd rather be romantic than fashionable. Besides, the orange mutants cost too much. I'm romantic, but cheap."

Bennet grinned, and lay back on the pillows. "Romantic? You have changed."

"I did what you did. I grew up. I notice you don't query cheap." Flynn sat on the edge of the bed and took Bennet's hands. "So, how's the leg?"

"Fine. Better than fine! No more capsule and no more crappy medication. I can't even begin to tell you what that means, not to spend all my time feeling this nauseated all the time. I've started therapy and they said I should think about playing Tierce again. I'll get back to work if it kills me, and I can hardly wait!"

"Calm down! You'll excite yourself into a fever." Flynn frowned and tapped Bennet's knee with a gentle finger. "I'd hold off on the Tierce, if I were you. Crutches get in the way on the court."

"I've got a degree of fever, according to Doctor Harald. He said he'll give me something for it later. I reckon it could have something to do with them tormenting me for the last seven hours. Or it could be a trick on his part to keep me in here tonight so he can lust after my mother."

"Is that so? What does your mother say about that?"

"She's flattered. The man has a bad case of it. Terminal."

"Been there, done that, have it right this instant." Flynn tightened his hold on Bennet's hands. "Thank the gods you've lost the capsule, because I was up most of the night with a pen and paper, not to mention a setsquare and compass, trying to work out how the hell I was going to make love to you while you had that damn thing on your leg."

"Did you work it out?"

"Eventually. It took some three-dimensional geometry and triangulation and the loan of a computer with enough processing power to run the planet, but I did it. I was looking forward to demonstrating it to you."

Bennet laughed. "I can get them to put it back on, if you like."

"Naw. I'm adaptable and I'll improvise."

"I'll bet. Talking of which, what were you doing playing with geometry last night? I thought you were going to a casino."

"I went, but it wasn't that exciting. I was back in my monastic cell at the hostel by midnight." Flynn drew his mouth into a downward curve. "You're having a terrible effect on me. I just didn't enjoy myself. I thought about you all night instead."

"Didn't you enjoy that bit?"

Flynn smiled. "Oh yes. Every single time. And there were a lot of them."

Bennet laughed. The sun was warming him from the inside out. He was free and Flynn was home. He couldn't ask for more.

Flynn ran a finger down the side of Bennet's face. "So, what happened when you got home?"

The warmth and happiness vanished as if someone had thrown a switch. Bennet swallowed against the queasiness. "It's finished."

"Sorry. That must have been hard."

"It's not your fault," Bennet said. "He was waiting when I got back."

"You know, Bennet, I don't really think you should have come to meet me."

"No. I probably shouldn't have, not if I really wanted to stay with Joss. And like I said, I didn't intend to come until he said... he said something that made me change my mind about trying again with him. I realised I was wasting my time. You're right. I was out of line coming to meet you, but at least I didn't take you home and screw you senseless in our bed."

Flynn blinked. "He did that?"

"Some kid who couldn't have been twenty and who wanted to know if we wanted a threesome."

Flynn stared at him. "What the fuck? Hell, Bennet, that was... I don't even have a word for how fucked up that is. I'm one of the most inconsiderate bastards I know, and even I wouldn't do something like that. He must have been spoiling for one helluva fight."

"We didn't fight. He sent the kid on his way and we talked

most of the night." Bennet added, in a tone he was proud of for its detachment, "Joss was trying to make me mad, I think."

"And weren't you?"

"No." Bennet leaned into him. "No. I don't think I ever truly believed he'd never taken them home before. He always swore he didn't. But. I always called him from the spaceport. It didn't do just to turn up at home without giving him some warning. It just didn't do."

"I'd have killed him," Flynn said, pushing at it.

"A year ago, so would I. But now? Why bother? It's not like I didn't know there'd been dozens of others. The kid meant nothing in himself and if Joss enjoyed it..." Bennet shrugged. "I don't think he did. He was trying to rub my nose in it, I think, proving he can pull anyone he wants."

"Except you."

"Except me." Bennet's right hand clutched at Flynn's sleeve, the fingers clumsy. "Not anymore."

Flynn's slow smile lit up the room.

CHAPTER TWENTY-ONE

40 Quintus 7488: Military Hospital, Sais

"Left Joss?" Liam's voice rose, the instant their mother had finished speaking. "You've left Joss?"

Natalia's mouth opened, and she looked as shocked as if someone had jabbed her with a needle. Over by the window, Thea turned, but all she did was nod. She didn't look surprised at all.

"You mean like a divorce?" Liam's mouth was wide enough to trawl for flies.

Bennet doubted anyone had been able to shock Liam this much since his lamentably stormy adolescence and his consequent determination to be the one to do the shocking. It should have given Bennet more of a sense of achievement than it did.

Natalia's reaction was typical of her. She flushed pink and breathed out hard through her nose, her mouth tightening into a line so resembling their father in a temper, there was no doubting whose daughter she was. "That's dreadful!"

"It's overdue." Thea came to him, stooping to rest her face against his hair for a moment, putting her arms around him. "It's been hard, I know, little brother."

Bennet, who had almost had a heart attack with the arrival of his family not five minutes after Flynn's reluctant departure, put his head in his hands for a moment. He wasn't up to coping with this. What in hell's name had made his mother decide to tell the others now?

He must have said it out loud.

"Because Joss has been a part of our lives too." Meriel turned over Flynn's rosaceae, frowning, and sending another cloud of heavy perfume Bennet's way. "It's been hard to think of you without adding 'and Joss' in our minds, you know. I tried to welcome him as much as I could."

She had, too. Without her, Bennet would have been even farther away from the family than he was. She'd held it all together, and she'd done it by accepting Joss when it must have been damned hard for her, going against everything Caeden had said. Bennet had never thanked her for it, either. And he should. He looked up and managed a smile for her.

Natalia said something that sounded like "Hmmph!" and folded her arms over her chest.

Liam closed his jaw with a snap. "Why?"

"Evolution," Thea said with another of her little nods. "It's been coming for some time, I think."

"You never said anything!" Natalia scowled. She'd likely be picking over it all to see where it was an insult to her.

"I know Joss annoyed the hell out of you, fussing over you all the time," Liam said. "He wanted to make sure you never went back to Shield, didn't he? He liked you being an invalid."

"I was hardly going to leave him just because of that."

"No?" And Liam grinned. "Except he likes to run everything and so do you. The smash-up was inevitable."

"Well, I'm not sorry you're breaking up," Natalia said. "It was embarrassing, especially when that reporter picked up on you and Joss on AlbionNews after they found you on Telnos. People at the Academy didn't know what to say to me about it. You might have thought about the effect on other people's lives."

"Tallie!" Thea snapped, and Liam turned his back on Natalia, grimacing.

"That was uncharitable, Natalia," Meriel said, dispassionately. "And unattractive. You ought to try and curb your tendency to be sanctimonious."

Bennet could only stare. "Funnily enough, Tallie, whenever I had sex with Joss, I wasn't thinking of you at all."

Natalia, expression settling into misunderstood martyrdom at the rebuke from their mother, flushed scarlet with mortification.

Liam squeezed onto the end of the bed, sitting on Bennet's good foot. "Mind you, Tallie has a point. You are being selfish."

"Really."

"It's just not fair. I'll never be able to catch you up. You do all the big rebellious things in this family and all I'm left with are the little ones. It's depressing, being so far behind."

Bennet snorted. "So far as I can see, you make the most of your opportunities."

"Oh quantity! Of course when it comes to quantity I can beat you into the middle of next week—"

"As your poor father will bear witness," their mother said.

Liam turned to her. "But he does all the quality outrageous things, Mama. I mean, I can't be gay now, can I, because he's done that already and there's no shock value left in it. Dad'll be immune to that one. He's closed off me taking Shield instead of joining Fleet. And now he's beaten me in getting away with divorce."

"You'll just have to join the Infantry, dear. That would shock your father."

Liam recoiled. "I'm not that desperate!"

"Then I don't want to hear any more about it." Meriel patted Bennet's arm. "I'm sorry darling. I hope they won't bother you too much with questions." She added, with a breath-taking audacity, given she had just let felines out of bags all over the place, "The reasons are nobody's business but yours and Joss's. And I'm sorry

I had to tell everyone now, but they need to know before Joss arrives."

Bennet choked. "Joss is coming?"

"He called me earlier to say he would come to see how you got on today."

Bennet straightened up against his pillows. "And you said yes? Why?"

"I said that I didn't think it was a good idea. He didn't want to listen." Her tone sharpened. "I'm not your keeper, darling, much less his. He should be here any minute. The most I managed to get him to agree to was to signal me when he gets here and I'll get rid of the children. I can trust Thea—"

"I'm always civil," Thea said.

"But Tallie will moralise and Liam is almost certain to try and be clever and sophisticated, and that never ends well."

"I'll take them down to the coffee shop." Thea herded the other two towards the door, despite Natalia's sulks and Liam's protests. "We're all better off out of the way. Call me when you're ready to go, Mama."

They sat in silence for a moment or two after Thea closed the door. Meriel broke it. "I'm sorry about Natalia. I should have put my foot down when your father insisted on sending her to a school run by the temple. It pandered to all her worst characteristics. As a knee-jerk reaction to losing you to Joss, it hasn't done anyone any good. Especially her."

"She doesn't like me much."

"No. I don't think she does. But you know, Bennet, I'm not sure she likes any of us at the moment. She's definitely the cuckoo in the nest. She'll grow out of it, I'm sure. As for Liam..." Her mouth twitched. "I must be a very bad mother, Bennet, but listening to Liam feel outdone by you is so gratifying and soothing to the spirits. I've been his mother for eighteen years and I'm due some recompense, don't you think?" She twisted in her chair to touch the rosaceae again. "Did you tell Thea? She wasn't surprised."

"No, I didn't tell her. But she knew things were difficult."

"I wouldn't have been surprised if you'd told her, given how close you are. You know I'm sorry, Bennet, for what it's worth. I grew to like Joss. Not at first. You were just Liam's age, and that was hard to forgive, but Joss and I got on very well, in the end. Of course, he's far too old for you." Her gaze returned to the rosaceae. "Did Joss send you these? They're lovely but they need to be in water."

Bennet was saved by the low buzzing of her comlink.

"He's outside. Should I call him in, or send him home?"

Bennet hesitated. "I don't... Oh hell." He let his breath out on a long sigh. "Okay. I guess I need to keep it civil. All right. Stay, though. We may need a buffer."

"He said he wanted me here. He thought you'd be kinder, if I were here." Meriel echoed his sigh. "You know, darling, with the pair of you acting up to every stereotype there is, I feel as if I'm trapped inside one of the more dreary domestic dramas and I've forgotten my lines."

For all that, she pressed his hand and planted a kiss on his cheek before using the link to call Joss into the room. Doctor Harald came with him, bearing a hypo in a tray. Joss had a sheaf of orange and green flowers in his hands. Flynn was right. They did look like mutants.

"Hey," Joss faltered, looking as though he didn't know what to do.

Bennet nodded at him, trying to smile.

"Is everything all right, Doctor Harald?" his mother asked. "I hoped I'd be able to take Bennet home."

Harald glanced up from preparing the hypo. "A touch of the Telnos fever, Madame. It was too much to expect to get him through a procedure without it. This will help. It's something new we've developed from some material one of Telnos families brought out with them."

Oh thank the gods! A straw to clutch to delay another scene with Joss. "I'm not letting you near me with one of those bloody grubs!"

"Grubs?" The doctor looked astonished. "What grubs?"

"Leah brought out the grubs we used to control the fever."

"Oh yes, I remember seeing something about that in the research reports. You were getting your medicines second hand, Bennet. You really should have just used the leaves the grubs lived on." Harald pressed the hypo against Bennet's neck, making him wince. "Rest for an hour, then you can go home."

Bennet nodded. If Joss hadn't been there he thought he might have laughed at the thought of that horrible brew Ifan had forced down him for three days, but he couldn't laugh in front of Joss.

"Hello," he said, once the doctor had left. He winced at the inanity, but he couldn't think of anything else to say that wouldn't catapult them into disaster. "I wasn't expecting to see you."

"I wanted to come," Joss said. "Just to see how things went."

Joss looked terrible, uncertain and tentative, so unsure of his welcome that all Bennet's instincts made him forget everything, lift his arms and offer a comforting embrace. Joss dropped the lilies to cling to him. He shook and clutched, and shook some more.

"Don't go. Please don't go." Joss pressed his lips on Bennet's hair, mouthing kisses all over his face and brow. He kissed each of Bennet's eyes. "Oh please, love. Please stay. Please."

"Don't. Please don't, Joss."

His mother grimaced at him, looking torn between sympathy and a faint distaste. She was never keen on dramatics.

"I don't want you to go" Tears tracked down Joss's face to drip, unheeded, from his chin; a quieter, more muted way than he'd cried the night before when Bennet had decided it was beyond salvation.

The lump in Bennet's throat hurt. He had to swallow against it to speak properly. "Joss, please."

"I promise I won't ever bring one of them home again. I was mad to take him back with me. I shouldn't have done it and I'm sorry. I just wanted you to... I'm so sorry, love, I'm so sorry. I promise there won't ever be any more of them. Please, love."

Bennet shook his head. His mother's mouth half-opened and her eyes widened.

"He didn't matter. I know they don't matter," Bennet said. "I know they were just sex."

"Then why go? Why leave now, after all this time, if they don't matter to you? I promise, I promise I won't again. Ever."

"Because it's not the same." Bennet sought for something to explain it. "They don't matter to me anymore."

Joss pulled back, and stared at him. Maybe he filled in the words Bennet hadn't actually said, because the dull red staining his cheeks looked more like temper than anguish. "It's your fault. We could have worked it out. You shouldn't have gone to meet that pilot yesterday."

Meriel walked to the window and turned her back on them.

"No. No, I shouldn't, but I did and it's done and I can't undo it." Bennet touched Joss's hand. "I'm sorry for that, but don't blame him, Joss. He's a symptom, not the cause. It's been coming for a long time."

Joss shook his head, his mouth trembling. He dabbed at his eyes. "I'm going away for a while, I think. I can't bear that place when you're not there."

Bennet caught both Joss's hands and held them. Once, being touched by those hands had driven him mad with desire. Now all he felt was pity. "It's a good idea to have some time apart."

It was the wrong answer. It wasn't the answer Joss wanted. His mouth thinned down, and the blue eyes, eyes that had once looked at Bennet with love, flashed with anger and spite. He wrenched free, flinging Bennet's hands off him.

"Seven weeks of you being dead wasn't enough time apart for you, then? You know, Bennet, I'm beginning to wonder if it was enough for me, either."

"Joss's flowers will get crushed." Meriel stooped, picking them up from the floor. She put them onto the nightstand beside Flynn's rosaceae. Joss had tied a small package into the ribbon, and she teased it free.

Bennet couldn't speak. He'd said nothing to Joss after that vicious remark, said nothing through his mother's protests, Joss's apologies, the tears, the handwringing. He hadn't moved when Joss had gone at her urging, not reacting to the desperate kisses and caresses. Joss shouldn't have said that. He was desperate, maybe, but still. He really shouldn't have said that.

"I assume Flynn arrived home yesterday?" she said, when she'd disentangled the parcel. She tapped the rosaceae. "On leave?"

Denial was useless. Bennet nodded.

"I expect your father told you about that. I don't quite understand what he thinks he's doing, and I shall have to discuss it with him when I get the chance. I'm not very happy with him, Bennet, to tell you the truth. Or with you. You didn't tell me Flynn was coming to Albion."

She put the parcel, wrapped in soft linen, into his hands. His fingers curled around it on reflex. It was hard, heavy for its size. A rough oval wrapped in mummy cloth… he let his fingers map out its shape. He didn't need to open it to know what it was.

"You have every right to your private life, of course, but I don't have very much sympathy for either you or Joss. You're turning out to be rather secretive, even deceitful, and if I understood him correctly, Joss took some casual pick-up back to the apartment yesterday. It seems to me the pair of you are battling for the moral low ground, and I'm not prepared to take sides."

Bennet swallowed. No, she really didn't like dramatics.

She sat down on the side of the bed. They were silent for a few minutes until she said, quieter and calmer, "What's in the parcel?"

She put her hand over his. Bennet reacted to her touch, raising his hands and turning the parcel in them. She let her hand drop away. Bennet tugged at the cords holding the little package together and unfolded the cloth. It lay on his palm, bigger than life-size, the carving as fresh and deep as the day, thousands of years earlier, one of their ancestors had carved it on the long journey fleeing from a dying Earth.

The bloodstone heart scarab.

His mother tutted in what seemed to be faint disapproval. "Just the sort of thing you and Joss would give each other. It looks ancient."

"It is." He swallowed against the huge lump in his throat. "It's an exceptionally fine one. Museum quality. The Thebaid would love to add it to the collection there."

"It's a heart scarab, isn't it? I know all the amulets mean something, but I don't remember what that one signifies."

Bennet re-wrapped it, taking care to get it into the exact centre of the linen and folding the cloth just so. "I do. I know what it signifies."

I have brought for thee thy heart. Rejoice thou in it.

CHAPTER TWENTY-TWO

03 Sextus 7488: Sais

"Flynn? Listen. I'll be with you in about a quarter of an hour. Can you be packed and ready to go?"

From the quality of the transmission and the sound of a hovercar engine in the background, Bennet had to be on a mobile comlink and Flynn would have to shout to be heard.

"Go where?"

When the call had come at last, Flynn had been trying to eat an unappetising breakfast in the military hostel's dining room, pushing his food around the plate with a fork and quelling unwelcome attempts at conversation from the other residents. He'd watched the news on the wide screen with a lacklustre eye, only half listening to AlbionNews anchorman, Nathan, doing a breakfast special on the growing influence of the Phoenix League and the rumblings of discontent amongst the taxpaying citizenry about funding an expensive war. Nathan's interviewing technique with the PL's leader was enough to make a man want to throw his bacon at the screen—a faint complicit smile, an understanding nod, a simpering invitation to Seigneur Vines to lay out the impact his reform proposals would have on military funding, the delicate scoring of political points. Journalists were low. Just low. There was only so much grave discussion and political analysis Flynn could stomach on only a single coffee and he was fast approaching his limit. The call from Bennet was a welcome respite.

Flynn hadn't wanted to waste an instant going to his room to take this call, and he sure as hell didn't want to share his conversation with the rest of the losers living at the military hostel. He'd opted for the nearest private place, instead: the public vidbox in the hostel's main hallway. He slammed the door shut and keyed the screen into Bennet's call.

Bennet grinned at him. "I'm running away from home."

"Again? That's a bad habit you've got there."

"I thought you might like to run away with me and share my other bad habits."

Flynn smiled at the fuzzy and out-of-focus Bennet on the screen. "I might. Are we going someplace nice?"

"Bed," Bennet said, and smiled back.

Flynn let Bennet go with great reluctance, trying to content himself with the odd touch that reassured without demanding anything in return.

"I was worried when I didn't hear from you," he said, trying to keep it light.

It had been a lonely three days. Flynn hadn't wanted to go far from the hostel, afraid Bennet would come or call when he was out.

Bennet smiled at him in a way that had his heart doing some very peculiar things, as if it were trying to dance. It was probably more anatomically correct to put the blame for the weird feeling onto his stomach, which felt like it was turning somersaults, but that wasn't a terribly romantic thought and who cared about anatomy anyway? This drab, horrible little room at the hostel that had been his home for the last few days was suddenly brighter and better with Bennet, and that smile, in it.

He'd always loved that smile.

"I'm sorry," Bennet said. "I was groggy for a couple of days, and Mama carted me back to the house at Mendes. I'm a lot better without the damn drugs but I still slept a lot. Then I had to concentrate on placating her before I could run away again."

"Why?"

Bennet's expression was something between a grin and a grimace. "Let's just say her maternal instincts were blunted when she realised I wasn't an innocent, lily-white victim in all of this. She has an odd sense of morality, my Mama. Once she got used to the idea of me living in sin with Joss, she did a lot to turn Dad around on it. But she thinks of it as the equivalent of me being married and she's balking at me being unfaithful. A promise is a promise to Mama, however unofficial."

Flynn tried to control the sinking feeling his over-energetic stomach was indulging in now. It wasn't that he expected to meet any of Bennet's family while he was home, but he'd prefer Bennet's mother not to be actively hostile. Especially with her access to the commander. The prospect of Caeden getting stirred up didn't bear thinking about. Uneasy, he wondered how fairly Madame Meriel played.

Bennet looked at him, as if he was expected to say something, and he made himself concentrate on the conversation. He reviewed Bennet's last statement and came up with a suitable response. "That's not fair. Doesn't she know about him and his peccadilloes?"

"Oh yes. She's madder with him than she is with me. That's one comfort."

Flynn couldn't be certain, of course, having never experienced it for himself, but he rather imagined that a man would prefer his mother to leap to his defence along the lines of 'my son, right or wrong'. It had to be disconcerting to have a mother who was more clear-eyed about one's faults than that. A mother whose disconcerting gaze probably extended with disapproval to her son's new significant other, as well.

"It's all right, really," Bennet went on. "I got a fully-functional maternal kiss when I left this morning, but it brought home to both of us that you can't go back. I was a fish out of water back in my parents' house. I can't revert to being her innocent little boy, no matter how much I love her—and I do. I just can't live there."

"Sure?"

"Very sure. At least I've restored visiting rights, so that's something." Bennet grinned. "You won't believe this, but they hadn't changed my old room. It was quite touching."

"Nice," Flynn said, and meant it.

"Yes, it is. But I'm too old for posters of Hornets all over my bedroom walls. She's just about realising that too."

Flynn nodded. He'd had enough mother and son relations for the day. He didn't remember much about his own mother other than finding her hanging from a beam when he was eight. It wasn't much of a frame of reference for Bennet and Madame Meriel. He changed the subject. "So, where are we going?"

"I've got some agents looking for an apartment for me. Until they find something, I've booked into the Grande Hotel."

Flynn almost choked. He'd seen the Grande—from the outside. It was one of the biggest hotels in the city, overlooking the north end of the main central park. "Look, I know I've saved up for this leave, Ben, but I can't afford the Grande."

"Ben." Bennet gave him another of those bone-melting smiles. "You're the only one who calls me that."

"Do you mind?"

"I can put up with it. Don't worry about the Grande. I've moved out of Joss's apartment, but I can't live at my parents' house—"

"Because of the Hornet pictures on the wall?"

"That's a part of it. But mostly because it would be difficult to see you. Not impossible, but difficult. I'm homeless, really, and I need somewhere to live. I'd like it to be in the centre of town, so I'm moving into the Grande."

"You can afford that?"

"I'm nowhere near as rich as Joss, but yes, I can. For a few weeks, anyway. I'm inviting you to join me there for the rest of your furlough, just the way I would if I had an apartment of my own. That's all, Flynn. I'll be there anyway."

"Well…" Was it charity? It might be charity for the homeless orphan, and Flynn didn't like the thought of that. He didn't do charity.

"The thing is"—and Bennet patted the bed he sat on—"I don't think I want to be made love to on this."

Flynn, eyeing the narrow and uncomfortable couch the military authorities considered adequate for those of their sons and daughters who needed to take advantage of their hospitality, couldn't help but sympathise. Five nights of sleeping on the bed had him wincing at the thought of trying to make love on it— which was probably why the authorities provided that particular model in the first place. Authorities, by definition, tended to lack a sense of proportion about extra-curricular activities.

"Picky!" he said, trying to give himself time to think.

"Well, I picked you, didn't I?"

That wasn't fair! It was downright underhand, saying that and smiling at him. Flynn's defences crumbled, although he had enough self-respect left hidden somewhere in the core of all those melting bones creating the warm gooey feeling somewhere deep in his insides, to make a silent promise to himself to pay his own way. Somehow.

He picked up his kitbag, ready packed. "All right. Let's take you somewhere where you'll consent to be seduced."

Bennet struggled to his feet. "Do you think you'll have to work on it? Believe me, you won't. Where you're concerned, I'm a pushover."

Flynn followed him to the door, glowing inside as a few more bones melted into mush at this handsome tribute. Bennet moved without grace, clumsy on the crutches. He was too thin and his clothes looked too big, but the mere sight of him had Flynn's heart tripping the light fantastic again, all apprehension forgotten.

"Especially with those crutches," he said, more to fill the silence and to avoid having to say something more significant, than anything else.

Bennet stopped in the doorway and turned. Quite deliberately, he freed his hands from the crutches. "You won't even need to kick them out from under me."

Flynn dropped his kitbag, ready to leap forward. "Careful, you idiot! You'll fall over!"

"I don't think so. I think you'll catch me."

"Only if I get to keep you, once caught."

Bennet smiled at him, and laughed, and let the crutches fall away.

The Grande Hotel lived up to its name. The lobby was a marvel of marble and polished granite with columns holding up the ornate ceiling, bowing flunkeys who eyed Flynn askance, huge floral arrangements, and sofas so deep and cushioned they'd sleep five side by side with room to spare. Satinwood with a polished brass overlay embellished the elevator doors. Flynn had a hard time not getting fingerprints all over it. He grinned sheepishly at Bennet, when Bennet caught him trailing a fingertip over the scrolls and wreaths.

Bennet had hired a small suite. The sitting room, with a tiny kitchen off to one side, led through double doors into a bedroom with a huge bed. Thick rugs on the polished floors. Impossibly ornate curtains at the windows. And an open fire in the sitting room... that and the rugs had possibilities. Definite possibilities. The bathroom beyond had a shower big enough for two to play at whatever shenanigans Flynn's imagination could come up with.

Not to mention a tub so wide and deep, Bennet could do his physical therapy in it.

Mind you, Flynn only sort of noticed this stuff in passing. His focus was on a bed so big he could have landed the *Gyrfalcon* on it. He eyed the vast expanse of smooth linen. It wouldn't take long to get it seriously messy. He looked up to find Bennet smiling at him. Blood rushed to where it would do a man the most good.

Hell, no. It wouldn't take long at all.

He stared at Bennet, and just for a moment, everything froze. Flynn held his breath. Bennet leaned on his crutches, staring back, still and intent.

Flynn swallowed. He dropped his kitbag without looking to see where it landed, and shrugged out of his jacket. The jacket followed the kitbag. Under it, Flynn wore only a tee-shirt tucked into his pants. The aircon in the room must have been working overtime, because the hair on his arms rose and prickled. He swallowed again and hooked a finger into the neck of his tee, pulling it away from where his skin felt damp and sweaty.

Bennet eyes widened all of a sudden, and his thin face—too thin with those shard-sharp cheekbones and his eyes so big they swallowed light—flushed a faint pink. He was still beautiful. So beautiful, with his eyes wide and dark and the flush deepening, and the way the tip of his tongue flickered out to lick his lips.

Flynn took a step towards him, getting into reach, keeping eye contact so he could see Bennet's pupils contract and flare, see the heat rising in him. Bennet let one crutch fall away, and put his hand on Flynn's bare arm. Quick as a flash, Flynn brought his own hand up and put it over Bennet's, barely touching, careful of the healing wound on the back where the catheter had been. Bennet's hand was cool between the bare skin of his arm and his palm, fingers flexing against the muscle.

Flynn could have died happy under the kiss that followed. Bennet's mouth opened under his, widened as he thrust his tongue inside. He pressed in closer, knocking away the second crutch and not caring, sliding up against Bennet's body, becoming a living, breathing crutch to hold his lover up. When the kiss finished, a lifetime later, Flynn sighed and pressed his face to Bennet's.

It took him a couple of tries to get his lips to form words. They seemed more inclined to form more kisses. "Naked would be nice."

Bennet nodded. He ran his tongue over his lips again, and the surge of blood to Flynn's cock had his head spinning.

He pulled at Bennet's soft tee. "Lean on me," he said.

Bennet grinned and let him do whatever he wanted. When he'd freed the tee from Bennet's pants, he got one arm around Bennet's waist while Bennet raised his arms. The tee came off with only a few tugs, to an accompaniment of choked laughter and one muffled curse as Bennet's balance shifted. Flynn used both hands to steady him as they hobbled to the bed together, and he managed to get Bennet down without breaking anything.

Bennet lay back, still laughing. Flynn, solemn as if he were in church, slid his hand down Bennet's chest to rest on the soft skin of his abdomen. Splaying out his hand, he let it feel the warmth, let it feel the rise and fall as Bennet breathed.

Alive.

Bennet was alive.

There could be nothing better than this. Nothing.

He leaned down to nuzzle Bennet's neck. "Let me do all the work."

Bennet laughed softly and trailed a hand down Flynn's face. "I'm going to. Believe me, I'm going to."

Flynn, grinning, set to. He got Bennet naked without too much discomfort, and if Bennet's injuries meant it wasn't a sexy process, there was something more satisfying about being considerate and careful, something that reinforced everything he had always had with Bennet. This was about lovemaking, not sex. The passion didn't have to be wild and untamed to be deeply felt.

Although he wasn't sure what Bennet was well enough to

handle, even when the passion was slow and gentle, and as deep as a star-field, he knew what he wanted. During those long, miserable weeks when he'd thought that Bennet was gone and he'd never see him again—not that he'd ever expected to, but as long as he knew Bennet was alive somewhere in the world, then he'd had the vaguest of thoughts and dreams that if he was very lucky and the gods smiled on him, one day there may be a chance for them— well, when even this small hope seemed futile, the only comfort Flynn had had was in memories of the few nights they'd had together. He'd dreamed of this. Now he wanted nothing more than to lose himself in the well-remembered body, to convince himself there was life and breath and warmth where once he'd feared there was only cold and silence.

"You won't hurt me," Bennet said, mind reading.

"I'm scared," Flynn admitted, feeling like someone had handed him one of those thin, spun-glass globes people hung from the Yule tree; something so fragile he went in terror of breaking it, barely daring to breathe on it in case it shattered. He was so hollow he could be blown away by the lightest breath, and so over-solid that his insides were in intricate knots.

"Don't be. I won't break." Bennet squirmed under him to prove it, causing other physical sensations in Flynn far more pleasant than the hollow knots twisting inside him. And from the complacent expression on his face, Bennet had a very good idea of the effect.

Flynn nodded. Bennet was right. He got out of his own clothes and slid over Bennet, skin to skin, breath to breath. He took it slow, touching, feeling, letting his hands move over the body under his. His fingers faltered as they ghosted over the thin scars on Bennet's right shoulder.

Bennet, lying on his left side with his right leg drawn carefully up out the way and Flynn spooned up warm and close behind him, made encouraging noises that Flynn interpreted as instructions to stop worrying and get on with it. He chuckled, paused a second, then used his lips to follow the path his fingers had taken down the side of Bennet's neck, mouthing down the line of the scars as if to soothe them.

Bennet tilted his head back to meet Flynn's mouth with his, pushing up on his left elbow to twist his back enough to reach. For a second or two he nibbled at Flynn's lips, before running his tongue over them to cool them. Flynn's mouth opened for him, his tongue meeting Bennet's, questing and tasting.

"I dreamed of that," Flynn said, when at last Bennet broke free. "The kiss that would be banned in all but two of the nine provinces. Remember?"

"Uh-huh. Show me why it'll be banned."

Flynn didn't object to having his reminiscences cut off by another kiss. He kissed right back. He moved his hand down Bennet's right side, sliding it down to splay his fingers against Bennet's abdomen again, lying there lightly only for an instant before moving south and closing around Bennet's cock.

It leapt into life under Flynn's hand, and Flynn chuckled when Bennet's breath shifted into soft little gasps, matching the rhythm.

"I guess someone's feeling better." Flynn twisted to meet Bennet's mouth again, and again.

"I'd forgotten what it feels like with you," Bennet said, enclosing Flynn's hand in his.

Another breathy chuckle from Flynn. He kissed Bennet one more time before turning his attention to Bennet's left shoulder blade, using mouth and lips and tongue and teeth to work his way down to the base of Bennet's spine, pausing there to lick and kiss the little hollow above the swell of buttocks, making him complain about Flynn's teasing ways. With his injured leg drawn up, it made him vulnerable, opened him right up. It was a gift.

"You won't hurt me," he said again.

Flynn splayed his hand over the side of Bennet's chest, allowing it to rise and fall under his touch. Rise and fall. Breathe in. Breathe out. "I thought of this, of you and me, all the time after... well, after I saw the news lines."

"Don't think, Flynn. Just do."

Flynn laughed. That was one order he was very happy to follow.

And later, when the heat in his balls exploded like fireworks, the sparks painting the inside of his closed eyelids, he pressed in close and tight. Lightning ran in his veins instead of blood.

He tightened his arms around Bennet, the warmth in his chest surging and growing, closed his eyes and let himself drift away into sleep.

Keeping Bennet, now that he was caught.

CHAPTER TWENTY-THREE

03 Sextus – 19 Septimus 7488: Sais

"Come back to bed," Bennet said.

Flynn turned from the window. He'd got up to use the bathroom, careful not to wake Bennet, and had stood for a long time to watch the city take on its night-time garb of lights and shadows.

"Did I wake you? Sorry."

"I'm not sorry. But if you are, you can come back to bed and apologise nicely."

Flynn stayed where he was, where it was safer, where he was still Flynn, secure behind his boundaries. When he got too close to Bennet, the bounds melted away somehow, and he was less sure of himself than he was when they were apart. It was a worrying, intoxicating, marvellous, scary feeling.

"I was thinking," he said.

"Dangerous."

Flynn tried for humour. "Well, it is for me. I'm not used to it."

Bennet didn't answer. Flynn watched him struggle to sit up, his figure dim in the faint light coming in through the window.

"I wondered where this is taking us." He was glad he could be nothing other than a black shape against the window, that Bennet couldn't see his face. He thought he could control his voice or his expression, not both, and the gloom helped. "I mean—"

"I know what you mean."

"What will happen, do you think, about your leg?"

If Bennet was surprised by the question, his tone didn't show it. "I'll get back. It'll be months, the doctors said, but I will get back. But I don't think they'll let me back into Shield straight away. I think I'll be rotated out." He sighed. "Probably to Fleet, if I can swing it. I wouldn't want Infantry. I'd prefer to fly."

"Maybe," Flynn said, tentatively, "you could get the *Gyrfalcon*?"

"I hope the hell not!"

A kick in the gut by a Hornet on full throttle couldn't hurt worse. "Oh."

"If we're on the same ship, you'd probably be under my command. I'd go mad with you there and the fraternisation rules between us."

Another, different kick. "You'd let the rules keep us apart?"

"What choice is there?"

"Break the goddamn rules!"

"They've kept me from someone else in the past. That's why they're there. I can't help that."

"Break them."

After a short silence, Bennet said, quietly, "You know why the rules are there. You command a squad, Flynn. What would be the effect on them if you were having an affair with one of them?"

"The difference is that I don't fancy Carson or any other pilot in my squad."

Bennet sighed.

"I know. I do know. It's just that—" Flynn stopped. Bennet

knew, too, he thought.

"Yes."

Flynn turned back and stared out of the window. Fifteen floors down, the late evening traffic moved through the gathering dark, mere shapes and silent lights. "And if you don't get back?"

"Probably the Strategy Unit. Or I go back to the Thebaid, and unwrap a few mummies."

Where, Flynn suspected, Joss had always wanted him.

"Right," he said.

"And the fraternisation rules wouldn't apply."

Flynn swallowed hard. "Right," he said again, wondering what sort of job he could get if he resigned his commission and came home to live with a Research Fellow at the Thebaid Institute. What could a pilot do when the only thing he'd ever known was taken away from him? No, that wasn't fair. If he gave it up, of his own free will. Would it be compensation enough, learning to unwrap mummies too? Would it be compensation enough, loving Bennet?

He didn't know the answer, but he did grimace at the irony of Bennet becoming Joss and him taking on Bennet's mantle. The tension tore at him already, when this was only theoretical. What had kept Joss and Bennet together after Bennet had taken his commission in Shield? He'd have thought the stresses would be too great to be borne. Did Bennet love him enough to bear them, the way Bennet had borne them for Joss?

He sighed. It was all too theoretical. They were as they'd been before—together for a short time, no future, no ties. He turned back to face Bennet. "It isn't very long."

"We have more than five weeks." Bennet was mind reading again. "Longer by far than the five days we had on the *Gyrfalcon*."

True. Those five days had had to last him two years, and he'd once thought they'd have to last him a lifetime. They'd been beacons in the dark, but they hadn't been enough; just shadows of what he really wanted. Five weeks would cast a longer shadow, that was all.

"The thing is," Flynn said, apologetic and feeling foolish. "I'm getting out of my depth. I think I'm drowning, Ben."

Bennet laughed, a shaky, uncertain sort of laugh. In the dim light Flynn saw him lift the bedcovers.

"Come on in, Flynn. The water's lovely."

Well, what else could Flynn do but take a deep breath and plunge right in?

The biggest disadvantage of living in the hotel was that they couldn't stay in bed indefinitely. They might have liked to, but there were things like meals to worry about and the housekeeping staff had an annoying habit of wanting to come in and change the sheets.

"Although," said Flynn, surveying the wreckage that once had been a pristine bed, "I think we may owe them one helluva tip for their trouble."

Bennet's knee limited what they could do on foot, but he mapped out an entire itinerary of activities for those few hours of the day they weren't in bed fucking each other senseless. Flynn had confessed that his knowledge of Sais City was confined to bars, nightclubs and casinos. Its culture had passed him by.

"I don't really know the city that well. I'm Macedonian, remember," he said. "At least, I'm half Macedonian, on my mother's side. I don't know anything much about my father. Anyhow, I wasn't brought up here. I only came to Sais to go to the Academy."

Bennet, who had breakfast in one hand and a datapad in the other, plotting their day's route around the Old City streets south of the park, looked up frowning. "You were at the Academy for four years. You had ample time to do a bit of sightseeing."

"Oh, I saw a lot of sights. An awful lot of sights." Flynn grinned, all the better to convey just what sights he'd seen.

It had a remarkable effect on Bennet, that grin. Bennet stared, and even from a few feet away, Flynn saw his pupils dilate. Bennet tossed the remains of his breakfast and the datapad aside, and hauled Flynn back to make an even more thorough job of messing the bed. Not that Flynn put up much resistance and he didn't even spare a moment to consider the housekeeping staff.

The trouble was, Bennet couldn't be diverted from his itinerary for long. When they emerged from the hotel for the first time after two days' seclusion, blinking in the sun and (on Flynn's part, in any event) feeling both dazed and mellow, Bennet had that damn datapad clutched in his good hand.

"Do you plan everything in your life?" Flynn screwed up his eyes against the blinding bright sun. First stop would be somewhere to buy some sunglasses.

Bennet's expression was one of faint astonishment. "But of course."

Flynn sighed, agreed that yes, it would be good to explore the Old City and soak up some culture as long as Bennet's leg held out. It was true that until now his idea of culture had a been a good game of cards washed down with strong liquor and preferably followed by hot sex, but of course he was willing to have his horizons expanded. It would be educational. So long as Bennet didn't mean the opera. No? Oh good. Anything but singing. Or classical dance. He could live without classical dance, too. Art galleries? Fine, but anyone talking about the distinctive formal juxtapositions of the biomorphic forms and the reductive quality brought by the purity of line, would be risking grievous bodily harm. Even if it were Bennet who said it. Especially if it were Bennet who said it. Museums were fine too. But no, he quite saw that going to the Thebaid museum maybe wasn't a good idea in case Joss was around, and it *was* sad he would have to defer the pleasure of cooing over mummies and assorted grave goods. Yes, he did realise it was a sacrifice, but one he'd make for the sake of peace and quiet. And no, he didn't mind where else they went, provided there was lunch at the end of it, and at the end of *that* they could assume the housekeepers had wrought order out of chaos, and they could go back to the hotel and wreck their bed all over again.

Bennet's smile, when Flynn wound down, could have ignited rain. It was all Flynn could do not to spin him around and march him back into the hotel and be damned to the widening of his cultural horizons, but he got meekly into the cab called by the doorman and settled back to absorb Art and History.

The things a man did for love.

Two weeks after they started this whatever it was, this more than an affair, Bennet took Flynn out to the family home to meet his mother. Flynn had never given much thought to the house Bennet had grown up in and what that represented. Of course, the commander was one of the elite, a patrician who could trace his family line right back to Earth and one of the Ancestors who'd led the exodus when Earth went dark. And of course Flynn understood that meant power, influence and money. He simply hadn't realised just how much money.

The house itself was unimpressive seen from the road, just a long single story building set well back in extensive gardens. Only when he followed Bennet into a wide entry hall did Flynn see how deceptive that was. They came in on what was really the top storey, with the main part of the house clinging to the side of the cliffs below like a limpet to a rock. The whole of the seaward side of the house was nothing but glass, giving the impression it was open to sky and sea.

It was as luxurious as the Grande. More.

Flynn deliberately forced his mouth to close. It was uncouth to stand there with his jaw down at knee level somewhere. "Hell."

Bennet turned his head and grinned. "Worried?"

Flynn's heart leapt at that grin. Bennet was down to a single crutch now, which left him one hand free to hold Flynn's. Which was nice. *Comforting.* "Of course I am. I've never been taken home to meet anyone's mother before. I'm not usually thought of as take-home-to-mother material. And if I had been, it wouldn't have been to a house that's on the cover of *Mansion and Grand Estate*." He grinned. "*Hovel and Dirt Yard*, maybe. That's more my style."

Bennet's glance around appeared indifferent. Probably he was so used to it, it appeared normal. "It's all right, I guess. Come and meet Mama."

Madame Meriel's dark hair was smoother than her son's, but the wide-spaced grey eyes and those wonderful cheekbones... they were Bennet's inheritance, for sure. She was beautiful. She might be a grandmother, but she was beautiful.

She was affectionate, too. Bennet was 'darling-ed' and kissed, fussed into a chair and his hands held in hers. Mind you, she was polite enough to greet Flynn first, with an "I'm very pleased to meet you at last, Flynn," but her focus for the first few minutes was on her son. Flynn couldn't blame her. He could only imagine what the Telnos weeks had been like for her. He knew what they'd been like for him.

"I wanted to see you," Meriel said. "Just to be certain you're all right."

"I'm fine. My leg's a lot better."

"So I see. What about your hand?"

Bennet laughed, held out his right hand and made a ring with the tip of his thumb and the tip of his first finger. He did it with all four fingers, and grinned at her. "I've been a good boy and kept up with my exercises. And I'm eating a lot better and sleeping without drugs. Do I pass inspection?"

She nodded, apparently satisfied and turned to Flynn. By the time they left an hour later, he'd been thoroughly, but oh so kindly, interrogated in that gently-modulated tone. She'd extracted everything there was to know about him, from his political allegiance to his hat size. It hadn't even hurt. She was kind and interested and probably one of the military's secret weapons.

When Bennet said it was time to leave, she told him to go and see the housekeeper for five minutes and let her to have a private word with Flynn. "Hanna wants to see you, darling. It won't take five minutes and I promise I won't eat him."

Flynn blinked as he thought back on the conversation so far. "I think you already did."

Bennet protested, but she could out-stubborn him. He only left to pay his respects to the housekeeper when Flynn, curious, added his encouragement to Meriel's. Bennet limped off on his crutch, muttering.

Meriel's smile didn't waver as she looked at Flynn, holding him in her gaze. "I am not going to cause difficulties, Flynn. I wanted to ask you something private, and I doubt I'll get the chance to see either of you much while you're here on Albion. Bennet isn't good at sharing."

Flynn's face grew warm. "No. I guess we're a bit..." He stopped. Shrugged.

"Absorbed in each other. So I see. He asked me not to say anything to the rest of the family, you know. He said you were only here for a few weeks and wouldn't have time to socialise."

Flynn winced. "No. We don't have long. He said something about meeting Thea for lunch, but I don't know when."

"I wouldn't hold my breath, were I you. Bennet really doesn't share well. Thea will understand, of course, because it's just what she'd do herself." Meriel leaned forward and took one of Flynn's hands in hers. "Do you love Bennet?"

He looked his answer at her, astonished when her smile faded.

"Ah. I thought so. You have the same look about you that he does." She paused, her grip on his fingers tightening. "I know what I will be doing when you go back to your ship. What I wanted to ask you, what I want to be sure of... Flynn, is there someone you can count on there, back on the *Gyrfalcon*?"

Flynn could only stutter, bemused by the entire conversation. He managed a nod and Cruz's name, a stammered half explanation about her and how good a friend she was.

Meriel nodded. She stood up, using one hand to press on his

shoulder with his free hand, to keep him in his seat. "Good. Because if the way you look now is anything to go by, you're going to need her."

She stooped to kiss his cheek, and her eyes were wet.

Towards the end of the fourth week, the crew of the *Hyperion* came home.

The last home leave they'd had, nine weeks earlier, Bennet had still been in hospital and the entire crew of thirty or more—minus Shield Captain Tarrant, of course, who had apparently sensed he would not be welcome—had traipsed through Bennet's room to visit with their resurrected captain to see for themselves that he was alive and still kicking.

Rosie, Flynn learned, had visited often. Not quite every day, since she and Joss were cool towards each other, but as often as she could sneak into the hospital when Joss wasn't around. Thea, apparently, had helped with that particular infiltration job. And no, Rosie hadn't needed to pretend to be a delivery girl for the local florist. She never took him flowers, in fact.

Flynn wasn't surprised. She hadn't struck him as the romantic type.

This time, Rosie contented herself with a dinner date to check on Bennet's recovery: Bennet and Flynn, Rosie and an Infantry lieutenant she'd met on Telnos, who turned out to be relaxed and unfazeable. In fact, Grant was so laid back Flynn was concerned he was being out-cooled. It didn't help that they were late for dinner. Indeed, they almost didn't get to the restaurant at all. That had been Bennet's fault.

Flynn didn't have much in the way of clothes that weren't dark grey and regulated by the Quartermaster's service. He had no reason to wear civilian fashions back on the *Gyrfalcon*, so every trip he'd ever made home on furlough had involved some unenthusiastic shopping to vary his wardrobe. He'd made do so far with casual pants and shirts, only buying a more formal shirt for the visit to Meriel, but he'd had the feeling at Demeter that Rosie had her own reasons for holding him to a high standard. If he were going to dinner with the girl, he had to look his best. Hence, shopping. His new pants had Bennet smiling, but the green shirt proved Flynn's undoing. The instant Bennet had seen him in it, Bennet had him out of it again and, within a suitably sweaty and noisy interval, had him gasping and writhing in the one of the best orgasms of his life.

He met Rosie with a broad smile on his face. And he didn't let the smile falter even taking into account her propensity to take advantage of Bennet's visit to the bathroom to mutter things like "I hope you aren't messing this up, flyboy" and "I infiltrate Maess bases for a living—I sure as hell can get onto a Fleet ship if I need to." She gave up in the end, and delivered savage jabs at the steak on her plate, using her knife with impressive skill.

Flynn enjoyed his evening. It was always nice to have something someone else wanted. Even when the something was blithely oblivious.

And he really enjoyed the repeat performance with Bennet and the green shirt after they said their goodbyes to Rosie and Grant, and headed back to the hotel. Spectacular end to the evening, that was.

It happened every time he wore it. Over the next couple of weeks, Flynn took to wearing the shirt every day, even if only for a few teasing minutes. He was loud in his regrets about the necessity of laundering it. Luckily for him, Bennet's reactions weren't muted by either the shirt's dampness or its lamentably un-ironed state, as Flynn had taken care to prove by careful, scientific experimentation. Whenever he wore the shirt and no matter what its condition, they ended up naked and entangled in the sheets.

When pressed for an explanation, Bennet had been unable to account for the green shirt phenomenon, except for some broken and breathless words about the colour matching Flynn's eyes, but Flynn's tests and experiments proved by empirical measurement (he was always a man for keeping score) that the shirt was special.

Flynn gave serious consideration to having it framed and

preserved for posterity.

The last day... well. Flynn didn't want to think about the last day. Not about sitting in the hotel room, not speaking much, hands clasped in Bennet's. Not the ache that meant he pushed away every meal that day, untouched. Not the way he straddled Bennet that last night, leaning down to kiss him again. Flynn loved Bennet's long, slow kisses, taking every micro-ounce of significance from touch of lips or hands.

But this one tasted salty.

"Don't come with me to the spaceport tomorrow," he said, his mouth against Bennet's. "I couldn't bear it."

"Don't go—" Bennet stopped himself. He moaned as Flynn raised himself again, and sank again, enclosing Bennet, rubbing against him.

"Love you, Ben," Flynn said, rising again and falling again.

Bennet bowed his back to reach up for another despairing, salty kiss. "Love you, too," he said.

Flynn closed his eyes so he didn't have to see the expression on Bennet's face.

Cruz was waiting on the other side of the decontamination chambers on the *Gyrfalcon*'s cutter deck, offering an exuberant hug, slapping him on the back and squeezing the life out of him.

"Hey, was I missed or something?" Flynn pulled free.

"Something," Cruz said, her smile wide and happy. "I'm just excited about the present you've brought me."

"You get excited about a stick of candy with Sais City written all through it? Sad."

"It had better be better than that. Come on! Tell me all about it."

It was endearing, Cruz's eagerness. Flynn hugged her back and let her take the extra kit bag he had somehow acquired. He didn't normally come back from furlough with an extra bag stuffed full of civilian clothes, but when he'd come to pack he'd not been able to throw away that jacket because Bennet had bought it for him, or those pants because Bennet had been with him when he'd bought them and they'd brought a very predatory gleam to his lover's grey eyes that had been more than borne out when they had got back to the Grande. And most especially, he couldn't get rid of that green shirt.

"Well?" Cruz demanded, ushering him into the turbolift, breaking into his memories. "Tell me!"

"Well," Flynn said.

He might say, he supposed, he had been loved and cherished for almost six weeks. He might say this had been the first person in his life to show him what it was to love and be loved. Or this was the first person in his life with whom it had been more than just sex and physical gratification. He could say that, much as he'd loved those long pleasurable hours in bed, he treasured the gaps between lovemaking when they'd wandered the city, eaten in funny little cafés, talked for hours or just sat in companionable, contented silence.

Or maybe he might even say that parting from Bennet two days ago had near on broken him and he'd hidden for hours in the turbo-flush of the shuttle taking him to Demeter. And he might seek the understanding and comfort a good friend would offer by saying that knowing there was never going to be any future for them—unless Bennet remained crippled, and he couldn't wish that—meant he couldn't, just then, see any future for himself that wasn't bleak.

And he might say, with the gods' own truth, that there would never be any other man for him. Because the water had indeed been lovely, but as he'd feared, he'd drowned deep and now there was no one to throw him a lifeline.

"Well," he said again, and swallowed all of this, unsaid. Because in the end, there was no 'might'. He couldn't say it. "Pretty good."

"Pretty good? That's all you have to say?"

Flynn thought about it. "Yes."

Cruz groaned theatrically. "Come on, Flynn! Did you get to see him?"

"Oh yes."

"And?"

"And," Flynn said, reducing his life to its essentials, trying to tell Cruz everything and nothing, "no more men for me."

No more men. Not ever.

CHAPTER TWENTY-FOUR

5 Octavus 7488: Sais

"I like the apartment." Rosie paused in her efforts to drag boxes across a floor that would have to be re-polished when she'd finished. "But why didn't you wait until after you'd moved in to invite me over?"

"I needed the cheap labour." Bennet limped to the bookcase, balancing a box of books, the walking cane hooked over one arm. "And I had a deep desire to see you again, of course."

Rosie watched him settle the books into place. He was walking better and looking better, but she had never seen him so unhappy. The contrast to her last home leave a few weeks earlier was painful. When they'd met her and Grant for dinner, Bennet had been obviously, incandescently, happy. When he'd introduced Flynn, he might as well have said it with a flourish of trumpets. The flyboy had done that... well she supposed she was pleased, glancing into a nearby mirror and scowling at curls that were undeniably red, not the rich gold brown of Flynn's. She sighed.

"I guessed." She perched on the crate, watching as he moved around the living room. "The cheap labour, I mean. You're going to owe me lunch for a month."

"Not unless you earn it. On strike?"

"It's the inalienable right of the oppressed to withdraw their labour when they're dissatisfied with their working conditions." She jumped to her feet and went to him, slipping her arm around his waist when he turned too fast and had to clutch at the bookcase for support. "Come and talk to me. We can unpack later."

She pulled him over to a sofa, still in its wrappings from the shop, and swept all the bags and boxes on it down onto the floor. Bennet sighed but didn't object. He didn't object to her snuggling up to him either. She hoped he got some comfort out of it.

She dug a sharp finger into his ribs. "So, ever since I got here, you've carefully steered the conversation away from anything that really matters. This is me, remember? You're not allowed not to tell me. I had it written into the *Hype*'s operating rules."

Bennet made the most inelegant noise, a definite snort. "And does it work with that dickhead, Tarrant?"

"You know, it's almost a relief you were unconscious when we got you up to the *Hype*. I think you'd have killed him, just for having the temerity to have been given your ship."

"Some people deserve death."

She grinned. "I know. And only the Regulations stop you."

"That and being afraid of prison. Whoever designed the prison uniform definitely wasn't gay."

Rosie laughed. "That's rich, coming from you! It's not like you're the most fashionable man I know. With your dress sense, are you sure you're gay? Anyway, as soon as you're well enough to come back, tip me the word and we'll lose him out of an airlock."

"Don't hold your breath, love. I've seen the general three times now, and she never answers my questions about what they'll do with me. I don't think it'll be Shield. I think I'll have to take my rotation out, and I have a horrible feeling I'm going to get dumped on the Strategy Unit for a while."

"I'm surprised they haven't pulled you into that spider's web before now. You don't need two legs to think."

"Next week." Bennet looked rather gloomy, frowning, and his mouth turned down. "The medics said I'm fit enough for that. Three days a week."

"You should have bribed them better. But three days isn't too bad, is it?"

"No. I managed to negotiate myself a couple of days at the Academy as well. The strategy tutor there retires at the end of this semester, so I'll fill in for a while."

"You're going to try and teach your own brother and sister?"

"Only Liam. Natalia graduates next summer, you know. Liam's only just starting his second year."

"Poor Liam!"

Bennet grinned. "He was horrified, too, for some reason. He says he doesn't mind me being at the Academy but he seemed downcast by the subject. He claims strategic thinking was invented as some sort of punishment."

"It's not everyone's favourite subject." Rosie thought back to her own Academy days. "In fact, it's not anyone's favourite."

"I can't understand that."

"They don't understand it either. That's the problem."

"I, though, am pretty good at it." Bennet paused, and smiled. "And it will be one class Liam passes, if I have to work him into the ground. I owe Dad that much."

Poor Liam. She'd seen him at the Midnight Watch, of course—tall, taller than Bennet, and gangling, as if he'd grown too fast. His young face had been blank with bewilderment and grief. It would be helpful if Bennet understood how much the boy needed to prove himself, to get out from under their father's long shadow. After all, he'd had to make that same journey himself.

"You'll be a good tutor. Just don't get so good at it that they won't let you out later. And talking of tutors," she added, artfully, "you haven't mentioned Joss. How is he?"

"Getting along. I saw him a couple of days ago, just before he left. We got through dinner without a scene, so that's an advance."

"Left? Where's he gone?"

"There's some new star cruiser he heard about. He's gone on the maiden voyage. Lots of company, and every possible hedonistic luxury. He'll love it."

Rosie nodded, keeping to herself her opinion of Joss's folly. "He'll find plenty of rich playmates who don't think they need a job other than keeping him happy. How very Joss-ian. You know, Bennet, I think he'll get over you."

"I'm sure of it," Bennet said, dry as alum. "I hope so. At least he's talking to me now. I'm tired of communicating through his lawyer."

Rosie reached up and touched his mouth. "So it's not Joss dragging down the corners of this otherwise delectable facial feature. Now we come to the heart of it. You got in too deep, love."

"Drowned deep." Bennet sighed. "Pointless, too. There's no future in it."

"And that's important to you."

"Very. And I'm in Shield, and he's in Fleet. What chance we ever meet again?"

He'd looked almost frantic with it, she remembered. He hadn't been able to take his eyes off the flyboy all night. But fairness demanded she respond reasonably. "You did meet, though, when you weren't counting on it. You might again."

"Maybe."

"If they do rotate you out, you'll probably get Fleet." She planned on taking her own rotation in the Infantry, but then she was from an Army family, the way he was Fleet born and bred.

"I hope so. But that's at least a year off and even if it was the same ship, what could we do about it? I'd only want Fleet if I could get a flight command, and he'd be in one of the squadrons."

"You think too much of the fraternisation rules," she said,

frowning.

"There can't be any tie there, for either of us. He's free and I'm free." Bennet glanced at her and grimaced. "I don't like that. I don't like being on my own. I've never been on my own before, Rosie."

"There are other men in the universe, pet."

"Not for me." Bennet shook his head. "I need to love the person I'm with, you know. That's the way I'm wired."

She did indeed know. She sighed.

"So," he said, "I'm off men."

"What about girls, then? I mean, I know about your men, Bennet, but that didn't stop you taking the *Sagittera*'s navigator for a spin a few years ago. A very small spin, I grant you. Barely a twirl. But still... Are you off women, too?"

He shrugged. "I don't know."

Rosie glanced at him, then stared out of window. She pressed her lips together, trying to get back the sense-memory of a single kiss unlike any kiss he'd ever given her before. "I'm a woman, in case you hadn't noticed."

After a short silence, he said, "I'd noticed."

"What did the navigator have that I don't?"

"It was more what she didn't have. She didn't have my lieutenant's pips on her collar."

"I'm not your lieutenant any longer. You're not my commanding officer anymore. Was that it? The damn fraternisation rules? Well, they don't apply now, do they?" She waited, then added, "It fizzled out, with Grant, in case you're wondering."

He nodded. "I wondered why you hadn't mentioned him."

"And I know you, Bennet. I know you're mostly gay, but I don't think you're all the way over there, or why the navigator? And it doesn't bother me. It doesn't bother me at all."

He was still and quiet, and she clutched at her pendant like a talisman. The message he'd left with it was carefully preserved in her wallet, the scrap of paper loved and looked at often.

For the only girl who could have straightened me out

"I know you love Flynn. I know you have to love the one you're with. I can believe that. I know you. What you said when you left me this… Bennet, do you love me?"

"Very much," Bennet said.

"Could you love me, then? For real, I mean. A little bit? Because I don't like being on my own either."

She held his hands between both of hers in the silence.

He wouldn't look at her. "I don't know, Rosie. It's not fair on you…"

She shrugged. "That's for me to decide, isn't it? If I'm willing to take the risk, then it's down to me to decide if it's worth it." She tightened her grip on his hands. *Now or never.* "I think you're worth it. I've thought that for a long time. Years."

He looked at her then. "Rosie…"

Her chest tightened so much it was hard to breathe.

"It's not fair on you," he repeated, and if that was all the defence he had then maybe there was a chink of light and hope there for her to cling to. "I… I need some time. I don't know…"

No. He'd never known, the oblivious chump. First he'd been too dazzled by Joss, and then by the flyboy. But that chink of hope was there. It was there and it was hers. "I know. I know you need some time." She tightened her grip yet again, holding him so tight her fingers whitened. "Promise me something."

He nodded.

"Promise me that when you've had time to get used to it, you'll think of me first. That you'll give us a try. In three months, say. At Yule. I'm going to ask you again, and between now and then I want you to think about what you meant when you gave me this." She let go with one hand to reach up and touch her pendant. "And be sure you really meant it. Promise?"

It was the faintest of smiles he gave her then, but it was a real smile. The little lines at the corner of his eyes she'd seen and grieved over, smoothed out. He nodded. And from Bennet that little gesture was as binding as a vow.

She put her arms around his neck. His arms came around her, to hold her. He was warm and breathing and damn it, but it felt right, being held like this, to have him holding onto her like she was the straw saving him from drowning. And even though she knew that right then he sought the comfort she could give him, it was enough to start with. It was more than enough to start with.

She let out a long silent breath, rested her face against his neck. His head dipped to rest on hers. She smiled. She could wait. She'd waited so long, after all, what were another three months?

For the only girl who could have straightened me out

She'd hold him to that.

~end~

Continued in "Makepeace"

ABOUT THE *TAKING SHIELD* SERIES

Earth's a dead planet, dark for thousands of years; lost for so long no one even knows where the solar system is. Her last known colony, Albion, has grown to be regional galactic power in its own right. But its drive to expand and found colonies of its own has threatened an alien race, the Maess, against whom Albion is now fighting a last-ditch battle for survival in a war that's dragged on for generations.

Taking Shield charts the missions and adventures of Shield Captain Bennet, scion of a prominent military family. Bennet, also an analyst with the Military Strategy Unit, will uncover crucial data about the Maess to help with the war effort. Against the demands of his family's 'triple goddess' of Duty, Honour and Service, is set Bennet's relationships with lovers and family. When the series opens, Bennet is at odds with his long term partner, Joss, who wants him out of the military and back in an academic, archaeological career. He's estranged from his father, Caeden, who is the commander of Fleet's First Flotilla. Events of the first book, in which he is sent to his father's ship to carry out an infiltration mission behind Maess lines, improve his relationship with Caeden, but bring with them the catalyst that will destroy the one with Joss: one Fleet Lieutenant Flynn, who, over the course of the series, develops into Bennet's main love interest.

Over the *Taking Shield* arc, Bennet will see the extremes to which humanity's enemies, and his own people, will go to win the war. Some days he isn't able to tell friend from foe. Some days he doubts everything, including himself, as he strives to ensure Albion's victory. And some days he isn't sure, any longer, what victory looks like.

The Taking Shield books in order:

Gyrfalcon

Heart Scarab

Makepeace

The Chains of Their Sins

Day of Wrath

ABOUT THE AUTHOR

I love space opera, with spaceships and laser pistols and humanity fighting for its survival against unknowable, unfathomable aliens and, at the same time, against itself and humans' own worst traits. Yes, I'm hopelessly old fashioned!

I am currently working on two, quite different, series of books:

- The Taking Shield series is a classic space opera with handsome young men wielding lasers—a love story, but not a romance.

- The *Lancaster's Luck* series is a classic m/m romance, but with the added twist of a steampunk world where aeroships fill the skies of Victorian London and our hero uses pistols powered by luminferous aether and phlogiston.

To keep in touch with publication of new books in each series, you can follow my blog and sign up for my quarterly newsletter at my website www.annabutlerfiction.com.

Or email me at annabutlerfiction@gmail.com

GLASS HAT
PRESS

Made in the USA
Las Vegas, NV
10 January 2023

65386853R00179